Alice Little and the
Big Girl's Blouse

Alice Little and the Big Girl's Blouse

Maggie Gibson

VICTOR GOLLANCZ
LONDON

Acknowledgements

With thanks to Katy Egan, Christine Kidney,
George Capel and Damien Carley.

Copyright © 2000

All rights reserved

The right of Maggie Gibson to be identified as the author
of this work has been asserted by her in accordance with
the Copyright, Designs and Patents Act, 1988.

First published in Great Britain in 2000
by Victor Gollancz
An imprint of Orion Books Ltd
Orion House, 5 Upper St Martin's Lane,
London WC2H 9EA

A CIP catalogue record for this book
is available from the British Library

ISBN 0 575 067888

Typeset by Deltatype Ltd, Birkenhead, Merseyside
Printed and bound in Great Britain by
Clays Ltd, St Ives plc

For Mart and Katy

Chapter One

It wasn't the smartest thing she'd ever done, though with hindsight she could see that she'd been led by the nose. Roddy was a shrewd cookie, but worse than that he was small minded enough to bear a grudge, particularly when his inflated ego had been bruised.

If she could have turned the clock back, Alice would have kept her mouth shut, refused to be drawn in, but her temper got the better of her and she'd let fly. Home truths only added fuel to Roddy's fire. He'd gone brick red from the neck up, the little vein in his temple had started to pulsate and she realised, too late, that she had gone too far.

But it was a matter of principle. The strategy to attract a younger customer base had been her idea. A means by which to drag McAlester's Ladies' Wear into the twenty-first century. She'd worked long and hard and there he was claiming the credit.

'So what's new?' Conor had commented over a stiff g & t later that afternoon as they sat in Café en Seine. 'He always does it.'

The statement was valid enough. In the three years that Alice had worked for Roddy he had never once acknowledged her input. Things had deteriorated sharply after she had rebuffed his rather clumsy advances at the previous year's Christmas party, but she had been able to live with that to a degree. Up until the spring collection she had worked alongside him, he was the head of the team, but this was different. She had purchased the entire collection, shaped the sales strategy. It wasn't any wish on Roddy's part to let her shine, Utility Chic was a new concept that Alice felt sure would take off. She wanted to be ahead of the posse. He, on the other hand, was not as certain so, hedging his bets, had passed on the responsibility to his assistant. Now here he was after the event, after sales had rocketed, taking all the credit.

'Perhaps you shouldn't have gotten so personal,' Conor said, staring into the bottom of his glass. 'He *is* a tad sensitive about his height.'

Alice made a humphing sound. 'Short-arsed bastard. Sodding Hitler.' She paused to take a gulp of her drink. 'Spawn of the Devil.'

'True, but it was obvious where he was coming from. He was rising you, and you let him. You know he's wanted rid of you since you dissed him last Christmas, and what better way than to goad you into telling him to stuff his job?'

Alice sighed. She was painfully aware that Roddy had well and truly ambushed her and she didn't need Conor to rub it in. She lifted her glass to the light and studied the bubbles rising in the opalescent liquid. 'Actually my exact words were, "Stuff your fucking job, you oily, lecherous, mutant midget," but I didn't expect him to come back with, "Clear your desk by lunchtime." '

Conor gave her a wary look. ' "Mutant midget"? Don't you think that was just a teeny bit over the top?' He held his thumb and forefinger half an inch apart to illustrate the point.

Alice shrugged. 'You had to be there.'

Conor nodded and took a sip of his drink. After a pause he said, 'Maybe he was bluffing.'

Alice snorted, put down her glass and rooted in her bag, producing her P45. 'I don't think so. His parting words were, "You'll never work in this town again." If the implications weren't so serious, I'd have laughed in his face.'

Conor signalled to the barman for another round. 'Did you talk to McAlester?'

He was referring to Jock McAlester, arch misogynist and MD of McAlester's Ladies' Wear. Alice shrugged. 'I tried, but he didn't want to know. Roddy Sodding Blue-eyed-boy Groden got there first. He wouldn't even see me.'

'You could always go for unfair dismissal.'

'Yeah, right. That'd really do my job prospects a load of good. You know what a small community the rag trade is in Dublin. No one would touch me with a barge pole if I did that.'

Conor sniffed. 'It was just a thought.'

Alice was angry, but more than that she felt let down. It was not an unfamiliar emotion, not by a long way. All her life she'd been let down one way or another. By her father most particularly. Roland Little had been a great disappointment to Alice. An over-fondness of the drink and a lack of backbone had been his downfall.

Three years after Alice's mother Sandra had been killed in a road accident, Roland had married Patricia Partridge, a shrew of a woman, ten years his junior. He was a catch for Patricia. Although unmarried she already had a daughter, Melanie, the same age as Alice, and an accountant must have seemed like a good bet. He was totally smitten. Roland was never fond of children. Left to cope with Alice after Sandra's death, he'd abdicated all responsibility for her to a succession of house-keepers, none of whom had a motherly bone in their bodies.

At first when Patricia came on the scene, Alice had high hopes, but it soon became clear that she was to be a second-class citizen in the Little household and Melanie the princess. So besotted was Roland with Patricia that he humoured and catered for her every whim, hanging the expense. Patricia's habit of withdrawing connubial favours when in a sulk caused him teeth-rattling frustration and he usually took to the bottle on these occasions. Not good news for Alice. Drink rendered Roland both brave and truculent. Not brave enough to confront Patricia, but just brave enough to give his daughter a regular walloping.

Shortly after Alice's twelfth birthday, Roland took them all on an outing to Powerscourt gardens. It was a dismal affair. Patricia was sulking because she wanted to go to the races, Roland was in a foul hangover humour (due to Patricia's sex embargo) and Melanie had vomited every couple of miles for the duration of the journey. Only Alice was in good spirits. Days out were few and far between. Picnics unheard-of

3

occasions. It was an overcast damp day. Patricia sat in the car and refused to budge. Melanie, now green from carsickness, whinged incessantly, and Roland, unaccountably, insisted on taking Alice to the top of the waterfall.

Father and daughter climbed in silence. Conversation didn't come easily. All the same, Alice was happy. It was the one and only time she'd ever felt any closeness to her father. Roland huffed and puffed his way up. At the top, Alice sat on a rock and surveyed the view. Not a lot to see, due to the mist, but still she had a sense of achievement. She was about to say as much to Roland, when a movement behind her made her look round just in time to see him launch himself into infinity, over the edge of the waterfall. It was a perfect swallow dive. Sailing thruogh the air with his arms outstretched. He didn't make a sound. She watched open mouthed as he disappeared down through the mist.

It took Alice two hours to make her way down to the bottom of the waterfall again, by which time a passer-by, who had stumbled across Roland's mangled corpse (and is not the better of it yet) had called the Guards and an ambulance. Patricia had been located, Roland's body removed to Vincent's hospital morgue, and, excitement over, everyone had gone home. She sat in the car park numbed by the spectacle of her father's suicide, wondering what to do. Fortunately, after a few hours, Melanie remembered her, and told a nurse, who alerted the Gardai. Alice was found sitting in the car park seven hours after the event. A note Patricia later discovered on Roland's dressing table told the story. Roland was in over his head. To keep Patricia happy, he had embezzled cash from his clients' accounts and investments and was over two hundred thousand in the red. Instead of facing the music he chose to take the dive without the slightest thought for any of them.

In Alice's considered opinion, Roddy was as great a bully as Roland and equally spineless. She savagely poked at the lemon slice languishing in the bottom of her glass amongst the half-melted ice cubes. 'All I wanted was a bit of credit. I worked bloody hard on that collection.'

Conor nodded in agreement. He didn't know what to say.

He'd never liked Roddy Groden. Never quite trusted him. Granted his opinion was coloured by Groden's blatant homophobia, but it was more than that. He didn't like the way Roddy Groden treated people in general and he had been the butt of Groden's vicious sense of humour more than once. That the man had so completely shafted Alice came as no surprise to him. From the start it had been a situation waiting to happen. The truth was, Roddy Groden was crap at his job, and only maintained his position in the company because Jock McAlester was his godfather.

The barman slid their drinks across the bar and Conor handed him a tenner then squeezed Alice's hand. 'You'll get something else. Don't worry about it. You were wasted in that crummy operation anyway.'

Alice nodded, but Roddy's threat nagged at the back of her mind. She had no illusion about receiving a good reference. What if he scuppered her chances of a good job, any job, out of spite? She wouldn't put it past him. Under normal circumstances, negative thoughts like this were alien to Alice, but gin, taken in large enough quantities, always had that effect on her. She took another brain-debilitating sip. 'D'you think I should apologise?'

Conor inhaled his drink with shock at the concept, then spluttered and choked. Alice thumped him on the back. 'Apologise? To that creep? Are you out of your mind? After what he did to you?'

'Well, maybe I did go a little over the top.' The gin was now causing her to have major misgivings about her prospects. 'I mean he probably won't give me my job back, anyway I don't know if I'd want it, but he could be dangerous. He could put a serious spanner in the works for me.'

Conor was having none of it. 'Get a grip, Alice. The man's a lizard. Anyway what can he do? You've friends in the business. Talk to them. See what's about. Let them put in a word for you. You don't need the likes of that slime. You're better than that.' He put his arm around her shoulder and gave her a hug. 'Have courage. You can do it.'

Good old Conor. Suddenly she felt better. He was right. She

was better than Roddy. She swallowed the rest of her drink, and feeling slightly giddy, lowered herself off the bar stool. 'Absolutely! You're right. I'll go home now and get my CV together. And first thing tomorrow I'll ring around and see what's going.'

Conor grinned at her. 'Good woman yourself.'

Slightly unsteady on her feet, Alice tottered from the bar and headed for home.

Conor watched Alice as she made her way towards the door. He wished there was something he could do to help her. God knows she had never let him down, and despite his fighting talk, he too had no illusions about the lengths to which Roddy Groden, he of the inflated ego, would go to get even.

Alice Little was his best friend. She had come into his life six years before when she had moved into the bedsit next to his in a run-down rambling house in Rathmines. For the first couple of weeks they'd had only minimal contact, a nod in passing on the landing, then one evening, when Alice arrived home to find her room flooded and water pouring through the ceiling, she had knocked on his door for help to find him in a state of dramatic decline due to the *tragic* ending of a love affair. Nevertheless he girded his loins and together they had hunted down the source of the flood which turned out to be a burst pipe in the upstairs bathroom. The stopcock was closed, the landlord was located, and Alice had spent the night on Conor's sofa.

They had talked most of the night and discovered that they both shared a passion for old movies (anything with Bogart, *Casablanca* in particular), that they shared the same sense of humour, loved the same kind of music (old musicals, Judy Garland especially) and both had a talent for falling in love with totally unsuitable men. During this process, he forgot all about being so callously dumped and realised that he had found a real friend.

Conor Finn had always known he was different. Even as a child in the school playground he gravitated towards the girls' side. He hated the rough and tumble with the boys. Loathed football. Hated team games. Conor's mother called him sensitive. His father (*All Ireland Hurling finalist, 1956*), mortified by his son's lack of sporting prowess, called him a Big Girl's Blouse. The name stuck. The other kids in the village picked it up, and eventually, for convenience's sake, he became known as Blouse.

Conor's father, Mick Finn, found his son an embarrassment, but he was a kindly man and with the best of intentions set about toughening Conor up. He enrolled him in the local boxing club. Conor was useless. He was a slight lad for his age, so usually found himself fighting boys a couple of years his junior. This only added to his father's shame. Not only was his son beaten at every hand's turn, he was beaten by kids hardly out of nappies. Three broken noses and countless blackened eyes later, Mick Finn admitted defeat and acknowledged that Conor was not cut out for the fight game, or any manly pursuit come to that. He possessed no hand–eye co-ordination, so hurling was out of the question. He was nifty on his feet, so should have managed Gaelic football or soccer, but he ran in the opposite direction when the ball came near. Mick didn't even consider rugby as an option. He was despondent. What would become of Conor if he couldn't look after himself? Maura Finn couldn't see what the problem was. So what if her youngest son was hopeless at sport? Didn't Declan, the eldest, make up for it? Wasn't Declan in the county minor hurling team? She advised her husband to concentrate on Declan and leave Conor to her. Gratefully, Mick complied. Conor was just as relieved. He loved his father and longed for his approval, but if the only way to get it was to subject himself to having seven kinds of shit kicked out of him, then he decided he'd pass on that one.

What Conor would have loved best was to dance. His father was right about the nifty footwork, just not on the games pitch. Of course ballet was out of the question. Mick wouldn't have been able to show his face in the Gaelic Games Association club or Tommy Flannery's ever again if it got out that Mick Finn's son was taking the dancing lessons. Even though it was generally acknowledged that Conor was on the sensitive side, in the village of Tanagh, the notion that Conor

Finn was taking the ballet lessons would have confirmed the suspicion that he was a fairy.

Conor understood his father's problem and promised not to join, but that didn't stop him from sneaking round to the back of the Parochial Hall and watching through the window as the girls danced. Later at home he'd practise. First position. Second position. Port de bras and jeté in the privacy of his room. Sadly, he was only slightly better at ballet than he was at ball games, the only difference being the degree of his enthusiasm. After a year he admitted to himself that he'd never make a dancer and gave up the proxy lessons. Maura recognised his ability in the kitchen and taught him to cook. Mick could handle that. After all, weren't the best cooks in the world men?

As Conor reached a late puberty his confusion over his sexuality increased. He was expected to chase the girls. He went through the motions at the disco. Bragged along with his friends about how far he'd got. But it was all lies. Conor did like girls, but not in a sexual way. If he took a girl home he'd end up listening to her problems and empathising. For this reason he became popular with the local girls, and was rarely seen without one girl or another hanging round. Mick perked up at this development. The irony wasn't lost on Conor. What was frowned upon in junior school had suddenly become a virtue. Conor played along for the sake of peace but he wasn't a happy camper. He was struggling and confused. He didn't want to be different, but he strongly suspected that he was. Everything came to a head the summer he left school. He had secured a place at catering college starting in October, so he took a job in the kitchens of a hotel in Galway for the summer. It was the first time Conor had lived away from home. The first time he had spent any prolonged time away from village life and its attitudes.

That summer Conor lost his virginity to Helmut, a German tourist. Life would never be the same again. His confusion increased. He had enjoyed the experience with Helmut, but eighteen years of Catholic guilt kicked in, and he felt disgusted with himself. He sank into a deep depression. His saviour came in the unlikely form of Declan. Butch macho Declan, king of the hurling pitch. Master of the boxing ring. Towards the end of September, Declan went up to Galway to arrange digs for his final college year and bunked down on the sofa of Conor's bedsit. Conor was still in a decline, which Declan couldn't fail to notice.

'What's the matter with you?' he demanded. 'Is it a woman?'

Conor burst into tears and spilled the beans, expecting Declan to hit the roof. To kick the shit out of him. To howl with derision. Instead his brother sat on the bed next to him and put a comforting arm around his shoulder. This gesture made Conor cry even more bitterly. Declan just sat there, rocking him gently, saying nothing.

Eventually, when Conor could cry no more, Declan said, 'Look, Conor. You are what God made you. Why should you be ashamed?' Conor didn't reply. 'So you're gay. So what? It's not as if it's a surprise.'

'It is to me,' Conor said glumly.

'Then you're the only one. Get a life, Conor.'

'Easy for you to say.'

'Sure, it's easy for me to say,' replied Declan. 'But the way I see it, if you don't admit to yourself where your preferences lie, and do something about it, you're on to a loser. How can you possibly be happy?'

They talked on into the night. The pub was forgotten. Declan drew Conor out about his feelings and eventually got him to admit to himself that he had enjoyed the experience with Helmut. By the end of the night, Conor was in much better spirits. He was amazed by his brother's understanding. They had never had a conversation like that before. Never really had a conversation before. Declan and he had so little in common to talk about as kids. It was a bonding experience. After a while, emboldened by talk of coming out, Conor said, 'But what about Da?'

'What about him? What's different? This is about you. How you live your life. It's nothing to do with Da.'

Conor wasn't sure about that. 'But he'll hit the roof.'

Declan laughed. 'Only if you tell him, you eejitt.'

Conor was confused. 'But what have we been talking about for the past five hours? Weren't you just telling me I have to come to terms with being gay? I thought the whole gist of it was the fact that I have to come out of the closet?'

Declan looked horrified. 'Oh. I wouldn't go that far. Da wouldn't understand. It'd kill him . . . No, leave well enough alone in that department.'

'But . . .'

'One step at a time, eh?' Declan said patronisingly. 'One step at a time. Maybe in a while, but not right now, eh?'

They never mentioned Conor's gayness again, but at last Conor was free. If Declan approved, it had to be okay.

Conor's reverie was disturbed as he spied a familiar bulky figure approaching, and without warning his heart began to flutter. It was the Ukrainian, Hector something . . . The man stopped a short distance away and ordered a drink.

'Wodka. Beeg wodka.' He held up two fingers to the barman to indicate that he wanted a double.

Conor, realising that he was staring, cast his eyes down, but not before the older man had caught his eye. Conor felt himself blush.

'You drink with me?'

Conor looked up. The big Ukrainian was smiling and holding up his glass in invitation. 'Conor? Yes?'

Flustered and blushing madly, Conor said, 'Ummm, eh . . . yes. It's Conor. Ummm . . .'

The Ukrainian signalled to the barman again. 'And vot ever he has.'

The barman squinted at him for a moment before his brain kicked in and he unscrambled the order, then he went about preparing a g & t for Conor. Meanwhile the man slid his glass along the counter top and stood in close to Conor. He slapped his chest. 'I Hector. Hector Hanusiak. You ver at George, yes? Vith a small guy, vot his name?' He squeezed his eyes tight shut, trying to recall.

'Hugh.'

'Vot?' The man looked puzzled and slapped his huge hand against his chest again. 'Me?'

'No ... *Hugh*. That's his name. I was with *Hugh*.'

Hector threw back his head and boomed with laughter, simultaneously slapping Conor on the back, almost knocking the wind out of him. 'My English no so good, yes?'

Conor laughed with him. 'Your English fine, Hector.'

He was a bear of a man. Larger than life. Six feet four, barrel chested and hirsute. Conor had been introduced to him at the George the previous Sunday and had been immediately attracted. Therefore, as usual, he had been struck dumb. It wasn't that he had any doubts about Hector Hanusiak's persuasion the George was, after all, a gay pub, *the* gay pub in the city, but the fear of rejection and a total lack of self-esteem always rendered Conor either a babbling moron or speechless on such occasions.

'Do you, em ... er ... do you go to the George often?' Conor stuttered.

Hector grinned. 'I make you ...' He flapped his hand, searching for a word. 'I make you nervous, yes? Please. Not be afraid.' He paused meaningfully. 'I see you on Sunday, and I like vot I see. I vant to be friend. I vant to be *good* friend.'

Chapter Two

Alice stood before the full-length mirror, her head cocked to one side. She wasn't sure about the black. On anyone else the black trouser suit with the black silk T-shirt worn underneath would have looked too austere, but with Alice's shiny jaw-length copper bob, fair skin and tall slim figure it turned the corner from austere to elegant and businesslike. Still, she wasn't sure. She picked up the white shirt lying over the back of the chair and held it up to the jacket, squinting at her reflection. Already she had changed outfits four times. Despondently she slumped down into the chair.

What was the use anyway? In the past five weeks she'd had three interviews, and all had proved to be a disaster. Not that she hadn't interviewed well – she felt that she'd expressed herself perfectly – but she'd had the distinct impression that they hadn't been paying attention. It was as if they had just been going through the motions.

Of course it didn't take a genius to work it out. Roddy Groden had put his spoke in. Good old Roddy Groden. Wasn't he great crack. One of the lads, and why would he say Alice Little was Trouble if it wasn't true? Conor thought she was being paranoid, and she began to think that maybe he was right, until the third interview.

James Geldof had welcomed her with a firm handshake and offered her coffee. He was head of human resources for a small chain called Showoffs and she hadn't met him before. He had her CV open on his desk and things went pretty well until he asked her why she had left her last job. No one had asked her that before. (With hindsight she realised that this was because they'd already had Roddy Groden's version of events.) After further mumbling, breaking out in a sweat and averting her eyes, she ran out of steam.

Geldof had let the silence hang. He was leaning back in his chair with his fingers steepled. After what seemed like an age he nodded his head and exhaled. 'I see.'

There was a further protracted silence. He was now tapping his two index fingers together and staring at her. It was unnerving. Eventually he slid her CV back across the desk. 'You don't appear to have any reference from your previous employer, Miss Little.'

'Um, no. Eh . . . Well, you see . . . um . . . we didn't exactly part on good terms.'

Geldof nodded and stood up. 'So I understand from Mr Groden.'

Alice saw red. 'Don't believe what that bast— what Roddy Groden told you Mr Geldof. I did that *whole* collection, then he tried to take the credit. That's why I left.'

'The way I heard it, he sacked you for insubordination.'

Alice, who had opened her mouth to speak, suddenly had no idea what to say. If calling her boss a lecherous mutant midget amounted to insubordination, then she couldn't really argue the point. Anyway, he'd obviously made up his mind. Geldof handed her the CV.

'Well, thank you for coming in to see me, Miss Little'.

She took her cue, got up and fled to avoid further humiliation.

Even now her face burned at the memory.

'The poison dwarf's exacting his pound of flesh,' was Conor's thought on the subject.

Alice sighed and glanced at the clock. Two-thirty. Given a choice she would have loved to change into sweat pants and just veg out in front of the TV with a bar of Golden Crisp, but matters were getting desperate. She was running low on funds, was almost a month behind with the rent, and the dole wouldn't kick in for another week.

She heaved herself out of the chair and stood in front of the mirror again, holding the shirt up for comparison against the black T-shirt. Her mood dictated all black. She dropped the shirt and pulled her hair back behind her ears. Yes, that was the look. Elegant and businesslike. Time to be assertive.

In one way this interview was more hopeful. Unlike the other three, which had come about in response to her initial letter and CV, this one was as a result of an advertisement in *The Irish Times*. She was more confident in the knowledge that the company, Wearables, actually *had* a vacancy for a fashion buyer.

'Think positive,' she said to her reflection. 'He can't know *everyone* in the business.'

It was a bright, sunny, if chilly, day as she strode along the Quays and the brilliant weather lifted her spirits. It was almost Easter and since Paddy's Day, she'd noticed an increase in the number of buskers and street entertainers around. She stopped by the Halfpenny Bridge and listened to a young man playing a guitar and doing a not too shabby impersonation of John Lennon singing 'Imagine'. She dropped a fifty-pence piece in his guitar case and strolled on across the bridge. She was in plenty of time, no need to hurry.

Traffic streamed along the South Quays as she waited for a green man at the lights. She realised that every second car seemed to be a new BMW or other top-of-the-range foreign job. She reflected that Ireland certainly seemed to be enjoying the economic boom that the politicians were constantly bragging about. The Celtic Tiger economy. This thought cheered her. Booming economy equals jobs, right?

The traffic light changed to red and Alice trotted across the road and through Merchant's Arch. Since the early nineties, the Temple Bar area of the city had enjoyed a revival. It was sad but true that in some ways this was a double-edged sword. She had always loved this part of Dublin, full as it was of bohemian types and odd little cafés and arty shops. Now, sadly, some of the very people who had given the place its quirky atmosphere were being driven out by escalating rents.

At the corner of Crown Alley she encountered a rather pathetic mime artist wearing nothing more than a coat of silver paint and a posing pouch. She wasn't sure what he was supposed to be but felt sorry for him as she knew he must be frozen. He was truly terrible and his hat was empty bar a couple of coppers, so in a fit of magnanimity she groped in her purse and tossed him twenty pence.

It took a bit of manoeuvring to find the exact address on Dame Street. On the first attempt she walked right past and had to retrace her steps. The Trinity clock warned her that she was now in danger of being late. She quickened her pace and, thankfully, saw a number on one of the buildings which told her she was getting near to her destination. Four doors further on, she arrived. She checked her watch. Five minutes to spare. Before entering the lobby she glanced at her reflection in a shop window and fixed her hair. Butterflies were beginning to amass in the pit of her stomach. She closed her eyes and inhaled deeply, then exhaled slowly. Think positive. Be assertive.

Feeling once again calm, she opened her eyes and stepped towards the door. Suddenly she froze at the sight of a diminutive, all-too-familiar figure strolling towards her out of the lobby. There was no mistaking the blow-dried, 1980s highlighted hair, or the slouchy linen suit and built-up shoes. He reached the door and pushed it open. From six feet away she could smell his after-shave and felt nauseous. He stopped dead when he saw her.

Her blood boiled. Roddy sodding Groden. Her first instinct was to leap forward and scratch his eyes out, but she wouldn't give him the satisfaction so she restrained herself and instead attempted a bright and defiant smile. 'Hello, Roddy.'

He gave her an uneasy smile in return. 'Alice. How are you?' Alice was not aware of it, but the bright defiant smile had somehow transmuted into a vicious scowl, transforming her whole appearance from elegant and businesslike to threateningly fearsome. She frightened the life out of him.

'How am I? Never better, Roddy. And yourself?' She stepped forward. He looked startled for an instant, then, when he realised that she wasn't going to attack him, nodded. 'Well, must be going. Things to do . . .' And scuttled off.

Alice stood at the door watching his retreating figure. He gave a couple of anxious glances over his shoulder, before crossing the road.

For a moment Alice was amused. Smug in the knowledge that she had unnerved him to such a degree, the implications then dawned on her. What the hell was he doing there? How did he know? Surely he hadn't— Bastard! Of course he had. The network. He was laying his poison in the network again.

'Well, fuck the lot of you!' she exclaimed, startling a couple of passing nuns.

The anger rose up in her again. Seething, she stormed into the building. Just inside the lobby there was a curved mahogany desk with a security guard in attendance. 'Wearables. I'm looking for Wearables,' she barked. 'I have an appointment with Mr Hartigan.'

The security guard, a small, wizened man who looked totally unsuitable for the job, shrank back, took a sharp intake of breath and pointed at the lift.

'Third floor. Suite 310.'

Conor couldn't believe that his life could turn around so completely in the matter of only five weeks. Not only had he found love in the shape of Hector Hanusiak, but also a new job as head chef (well, *only* chef) in the Samovar, Hector's little bistro. He was happier than he had ever been.

In some small way, however, he felt slightly guilty to be so happy when things were going so badly for Alice. He also felt bad that, between one thing and another, he had seen so little of her over the past weeks, but the time had just flown. Between starting the new job and moving in with Hector he hadn't had a minute to himself. For that reason he had arranged to meet her, after her interview, in Café en Seine. He was sitting sipping a café espresso with a moronic grin on his face when he saw her walk in. Although he didn't realise it, whenever he thought of Hector the stupid grin appeared – he had no control over it. Alice looked around, then spotting him, strode over. She was all in black. A bad sign in Conor's estimation. Alice usually dressed according to her mood. 'Hi. So how did it go?'

Alice sat down on the bench seat and signalled to a waiter.

'Don't ask.' The waiter came over and Alice ordered four shots of tequila, then turned to Conor. 'What are you having?'

Conor, sensing that Alice needed a drinking partner, ordered a g & t, then sat back and waited for his friend to unburden herself.

She sat staring straight ahead for a couple of minutes. It was obvious that she was simmering with rage. Eventually, after the waiter had delivered the drinks and he had paid the tab, he plucked up the courage to ask. 'So what happened?'

'What happened?' She knocked back a tequila shot. 'I'll tell you what bloody happened.' She took another hit and slammed the shot glass on the table. 'I made a total prat of myself. That's what happened.'

Conor waited for her to elaborate in her own time.

Alice took another hit. 'A complete and utter prat of myself,' she repeated. She put her head in her hands. 'I was mortified. He'd no idea what I was ranting on about.' She looked up. 'He just sat there gaping at me. Of course I can't blame the poor man. He hadn't a clue. There was this mad woman storming into his office demanding to know why he was wasting her time when he had no intention of taking her on . . . And whatever happened to listening to both sides of the story before drawing conclusions. I can't believe I was so . . .'

Conor was at a loss. 'What are you talking about? What man . . . ? What mad woman?'

Alice looked exasperated. 'Me, of course. You're not paying attention.' She paused for breath, aware that she was running off at the mouth and making no sense. 'Okay. So I go to the interview, and as I get there I see Roddy Groden coming out of the building. Well, you can imagine, particularly on account of my recent experience, I put two and two together. I was fucking livid, so I stormed in and tore a strip off this poor guy, this Mr Hartigan. Anyway, it turns out the poor sod hadn't a clue what I was talking about. He's never even met Roddy Groden.' Alice picked up the fourth shot glass and took a sip from it, then lapsed into silence, staring at nothing.

After a pause Conor said, 'Soooo . . . apart from that, how d'you think the interview went?'

'I'm sorry, Alice, but I'm sure you understand. I've a mortgage to pay and, well . . .' Susan opened her hands in a helpless shrug.

Alice couldn't blame her. Susan hadn't pressed her for the rent, she'd been very understanding, in fact. But at the heel of the hunt it was an economic fact that she couldn't carry Alice any longer.

Alice was well aware that her landlady felt bad about it. They'd got on quite well since she had moved into the house, despite the fact that both Susan and her colleague Brenda, with whom she shared the house, were both teetotal, non-smoking, Christian evangelicals. As well as being Bible buddies, Susan and Brenda were both teachers and Alice had taken the place of a colleague of theirs who had moved out of the house when she got married. It was a fairly comfortable arrangement and Alice didn't see much of her housemates as when they weren't out evangelising they usually sat in the dining room marking students' work, or otherwise they went to bed early. She had the faintest feeling that they didn't altogether approve of her but, sensitive to the fact that the house belonged to Susan, Alice played by the unspoken rules and never came home wildly drunk or brought anyone back. Apart from Alex occasionally, and there was the one time shortly after she had moved in when she had invited Conor and his (at the time) boyfriend Ryan around for dinner. Not the most comfortable evening she had ever lived through. Ryan was unashamedly camp and prone to being outrageous whenever he sensed any hint of disapproval. In fairness, neither Susan nor Brenda had said anything after the event, apart from a couple of references to her unusual friends and promises to pray for them.

It was a new house on the north side of the city, small but convenient to town (walking distance at a push) and after a succession of grotty bedsits and unsatisfactory house shares, Alice enjoyed the comfort of having a place to live that she didn't dread going home to.

They were standing in the hall. Susan had obviously been waiting for her, and Alice was aware that Brenda was loitering behind the sitting room door listening. 'The thing is,' Susan continued, averting her eyes from Alice, 'a girl from our Bible group is looking for a place, and I . . . em . . . I sort of told her she could move in here.' She looked up at Alice again. 'I'm really sorry . . .'

'Move in? When?' Suddenly Alice didn't feel so understanding, particularly as it appeared that without notice she was about to be made homeless.

Susan looked down at the floor again and mumbled, 'Well, actually . . . um . . . at the . . . eh . . . the weekend.'

Alice stared at her. Just when she thought the day couldn't get any worse . . .

'I'm really, *really* sorry,' Susan whined, wringing her hands. 'If I could afford it I'd wait, but you know how it is . . .'

'Oh, that's great. I'm not only jobless, I'm homeless now. I've nowhere to go, Susan. What am I supposed to do? You could have given me a bit more notice.'

'It's not Susan's fault,' Brenda piped in, emerging from her hiding place. 'I think she's been pretty good under the circumstances.' She stood beside her friend, lending moral support. 'Susan's got a mortgage to pay. It's not her fault you got the push.'

Alice felt genuinely sorry for Susan, despite her predicament, but Brenda's attitude was pissing her off. 'Oh, that's very Christian, Brenda!' she snapped, causing Brenda to blush to the roots of her thin dishwater hair. 'Well, don't worry. I'll find myself a bin liner and a shop doorway. Don't worry about me.'

As Alice made for the stairs, Susan made a whimpering sound and touched her arm. 'Please don't be like that, Alice. If you're really stuck, you could always sleep on the sofa . . .'

Alice shrugged her off and stomped up the stairs to her room. As she closed the door she heard Brenda hiss, 'She's drunk! I could smell it on her breath. I *knew* she . . .' The closing of the sitting room door cut any knowledge of what Brenda *knew*.

Sitting on the end of her bed, Alice felt downhearted and empty. She hadn't felt that way since . . . she tried to remember. Since Patricia had informed her that she was being sent away to boarding school.

Boarding school conjured up thoughts of Mallory Towers and midnight feasts, so it was a shock to her system when *boarding school* in reality turned out to be a hostel run by nuns near Leeson Street bridge.

After Roland's suicide Patricia had gone into a short decline. It didn't last too long. There were practical matters to be attended to. Firstly she had been in danger of losing the house to Roland's creditors, and secondly, and more pressing, she had no visible means of support and two children to bring up. In the event, Patricia discovered that Roland had put the house in her name so at least she had an asset which no one could touch, a fact which delighted her, but not Roland's hapless investors. She immediately put the house on the market and bought a small, three-bedroomed semi. Alice was never privy to how Patricia managed to pay day-to-day expenses. She certainly didn't work, and always bought the best of everything. She also socialised a good deal, and it wasn't long before the three-bedroomed semi was up for sale and Patricia informed her that they were all moving to Blackrock to live with Maurice Broderick, her new fiancé.

She barely saw her stepmother's fiancé after they moved in as for most of the time, apart from when she was at school, she was confined to the top floor of Maurice's house. Patricia grandly called it the nursery wing. Alice wasn't sure if she was being sarcastic.

She had a large bedroom to herself. It could have done with a paint job, but it was clean and bright despite the shabbiness. The window afforded her a sea view as, apart from her homework and an ancient transistor radio, she had little else to do in the evenings after she had eaten her tea alone in the kitchen.

Melanie on the other hand had a large room on the first floor and her own private bathroom. She took her meals with Patricia and Maurice in the dining room. Alice was well pleased. She hated Patricia, couldn't stand the sight of Melanie, and had no wish to get any further acquainted with Maurice Broderick.

It was a month later when Alice came home from school that she found her bags packed in the hall. Patricia was moving her out.

Now history was repeating itself. At the age of twenty-six here she was being thrown out again. The only difference was that this time she had nowhere to go.

Chapter Three

Although Conor was thrilled to be in a relationship again – and he was mad about Hector – after five weeks he was beginning to notice those small itty-bitty things that irritate. For instance, since he had started work at the Samovar it had become clear that Hector wasn't fond of work and was taken to disappearing from time to time on unspecified business. He also had a rather cavalier attitude towards hygiene. Not his personal hygiene, mind you, in that respect he was meticulous, taking at least an hour every morning in the bathroom, but Conor couldn't fail to notice that the Samovar could do with a good clean. It was fortunate that the lighting was restricted to a couple of dimmed wall lights and candles stuffed into the necks of empty wine bottles because in the cold light of day the shabbiness of the establishment was all too evident.

Another problem was Ciara the waitress. In the three weeks since Conor had worked in the Samovar's kitchen, Ciara had turned up for work either late, or not at all. Hector grudgingly took over the task on these occasions, but it wasn't a perfect solution. Hector was not created to deal with the public at large. Firstly his limited knowledge of the language and his thick accent led to a number of misunderstandings with the orders. He had a short fuse, and when the punters complained, his first response was to throw them out on to the street after a tirade delivered in Ukrainian. This didn't enhance the bistro's reputation.

After one such incident Tony, the comis-chef, had confided in Conor that Hector had thrown out the food critics of both *The Irish Times* and *The Sunday Tribune* when the Bistro had first opened.

Not surprising then that the Samovar's normal evening clientele was restricted to rowdy stag parties or the very drunk, and the bistro's busy time was well after when the pubs closed. There was, however, a reasonably brisk lunchtime trade for soup, sandwiches and pasta dishes due to the proximity of a number of large offices, but none of the lunchtime customers ever darkened the door after five p.m.

Conor realised that if the Samovar was to survive, changes had to be made. He further realised that a certain amount of diplomacy was called for. Prioritising, he decided that Ciara had to go and a decent waitress employed. He rationalised that this would kill two birds with one stone. Firstly it would, as he so diplomatically put it, free Hector up to do what he did best, namely greeting the punters, and secondly, preserve the custom of any new punters who came unwittingly through the door. Hector was agreeable to this suggestion for obvious reasons. After all, waiting on tables required effort.

When he talked about employing a cleaner, however, the only response from Hector was, 'Vee can't afford it.' He rubbed his thumb against his fingers to add weight to the point. 'Hector not rich man.'

Conor, not wanting to upset his new lover, put that suggestion on the back burner and set about finding a new waitress. It was only as he picked up the phone to call *The Evening Herald* that he had a flash of inspiration.

'But you could do it until you get something else,' Conor said. 'You need a job and the Samovar needs a waitress.'

Alice wasn't sure. It felt to her like defeat to take a waitressing job when she was looking for something in fashion. The fact that the prospects of any job in the rag trade were diminishing fast due to the Poison Dwarf's intervention, she'd pushed to the back of her mind.

'Please, Alice, you'd be doing me a favour,' Conor pleaded. This was an overstatement, but he knew how Alice's mind worked. 'And there's a flat.'

At the mention of the word 'flat', Alice's ears pricked up. 'A flat?'

Conor rocked his head from side to side. 'Um ... well, a bedsit anyway.' Here he felt the need to improvise and, as the room (the second bedroom of his and Hector's flat) was empty anyway, where was the harm? He'd fix up the details with Hector later. 'It's rent free. It goes with the job.'

'A bedsit.' Alice betrayed a note of disappointment.

Conor didn't give her any opportunity for negative thoughts. 'It's really cosy. You'd love it. And the job's lunch times and then the evening shift, so you'd have plenty of time to look around for something permanent. Come on ... What d'you say?'

'But what about Hector? What'll he say?'

'Hector's fine about it. In fact when I told him how you were fixed right now, he thought it was a great idea. And we really do need a waitress.'

'But I never waited on tables in my life.'

Conor glanced over his shoulder towards the kitchen and lowered his voice. 'Don't mention that, okay? I told Hector you'd lots of experience.'

Alice opened her mouth to protest, but Conor cut across her. 'How hard can it be? Come on, Alice. You'll solve your accommodation problem, earn a few bob at the same time, and it'll give you a bit of breathing space to find the job you want.'

She had to admit he had a point. How hard could it be? And on the accommodation front things were now desperate as Susan's and Brenda's Bible buddy was moving into her old room the following day. She dithered for a moment, then gave a half-hearted nod. 'Okay. I'll give it a shot.'

'Good woman yourself.'

Alice looked around. The Samovar Café was not very inviting. It was dim, dowdy and had an air of faded ... something. The only colour in it was the checked red and white tablecloths with candles stuck into empty wine bottles. Its only saving grace was the delicious aromas wafting from the kitchen. A couple of old biddies with wheelie shopping bags were sitting at a table drinking tea, but apart from that the place was empty. Alice couldn't see why they'd need help but, in her present straits, wasn't about to stare this particular gift horse in the mouth. 'So how much are you paying?'

Conor cringed then mumbled, 'Ninety quid and tips.' He couldn't look her in the eye. 'B-but there's the flat,' he stuttered, 'and all meals are included.'

Alice, stunned that anyone would do a week's work for £90 just gulped.

'And there'll be tips,' Conor added with an air of desperation, 'plenty of tips.'

The flat was a lot brighter than the café. Flat was an exaggeration, it was definitely a bedsit, but in proportion to the dimensions of the walls, the window was quite large and it flooded the room with light. Eyeing the scuffed paint and nicotine-stained ceiling, Alice made a mental note to buy a couple of tins of white emulsion and to refrain from swinging the cat.

As Conor helped her to lug her stuff up the three flights, he indicated the doors on the second landing. 'Madame Maxine has those rooms, but she shouldn't disturb you. She's only there at night.' He didn't elaborate further and Alice was left wondering if this Madame Maxine was some kind of gypsy fortune teller or, taking Hector into account, some ex-patriot Ukrainian aristocrat down on her luck.

After thoroughly scrubbing both the bedsit and what was laughingly called the bathroom, she elicited a promise from Conor that he would help her to paint the place the following weekend.

Although she had obviously heard of Hector, he being Conor's current squeeze, she had never actually met him, so she was somewhat taken aback by the sheer bulk of the man, and how immediately his personality filled the room. He swept her into a bone-crushing hug.

'Velcome, velcome. You are velcome to our little bestro, my angel.' He held her away at arm's length and stared at her, then whooshed her into another hug. 'Lovely, lovely,' he murmured, then looked at Conor. 'Your friend, is she not lovely?'

He was a sight to behold, wearing leather trousers (for which, Alice estimated, at least three cows must have given their lives) together with a starched white collarless shirt and heliotrope, deep blue and gold brocade waistcoat. The sleeves of the shirt were rolled up to the elbow revealing the hairiest arms she had ever seen. On his feet he wore patent leather slip-on shoes with no socks.

Despite herself, Alice couldn't help but be charmed by him. No sooner had the introduction been made than he grabbed his coat and a canvas cash bag and said that he had to go to the bank.

She started work the next day, Saturday. She was to work a split shift, lunchtime and evening. A dozen or so punters came and went at lunchtime, and couple of dozen more for take-aways. She couldn't blame them, in fact she was surprised that anyone would risk eating anything that had passed through the café on the way from the kitchen. But the fact remained that Conor's food was wonderful.

Hector returned just as the last lunchtime customers were leaving, and Alice patted herself on the back for managing so well after being thrown in at the deep end, so to speak. Conor, however, unwittingly burst her bubble by commenting that Saturdays were always quiet.

After resetting the tables for the evening trade, she sat and ate a very pleasant lunch with Conor and Hector. The special of the day was a mouth-watering lasagne and Hector insisted on opening a bottle of champagne to celebrate her arrival. She was quite touched that he would do such a thing. After coffee, somewhat squiffy from the mid-afternoon drinking, she retired to her room to unpack some of her things.

Despite its smallness (bordering on poky) the room had potential. There was a tiny fireplace fitted with a gas fire, and a quite comfortable sofa bed (granted it was a musty shade of brown Draylon). There was an old badly painted pine sideboard and an armchair, and in the alcoves on either side of the fireplace there were cupboards. One with a hanging rail, the other contained a small sink, though when she looked for somewhere to plug in her portable TV she discovered the flaw in the plan. The room boasted only one electric socket. She made a mental note to buy a three-way adapter and plugged in her lamp instead. She abhorred overhead lighting. There were no cooking facilities of any kind, but she was as well pleased. Cooking smells would seep into everything, the room was so small. Anyway, she reflected, remembering Conor's promise of all meals being provided, there was the electric kettle for tea, and she could eat in the bistro after hours.

By the time she had put away her clothes and found places to stow her other bits and pieces, it was time for the evening shift. It was quiet enough to start with, no one came in at all until gone ten, but by eleven-thirty all hell had broken loose. Her confidence plummeted after suffering verbal abuse from a couple of punters the worse for wear, who insisted that she had brought the wrong order, and she found that she had to be pretty nimble on her feet to avoid being not so subtly groped. Hector put in an appearance not long after midnight and, witnessing her discomfort, threw the offending pair out, to applause from the other diners who, although merry, were not yet at the obnoxious stage.

At one-thirty a stocky, tough-looking punter came in. At first Alice thought he had just called in to see the rather weedy man who was sitting alone at table six noisily quaffing a plate of spag bol. The man stood there for a few seconds, staring, then he mumbled something. The diner shook his head and she heard him say, 'But I'm eating. I'm in the middle of my dinner.'

Without warning the larger man grabbed a handful of the diner's hair and smashed his face into his plate. Alice was dumbfounded. The move had been so violent and so sudden. She looked around for Hector but he had vanished. The six other patrons were studiously ignoring the incident, eyes glued to their plates. Her sense of natural justice urged Alice to intervene, but her sense of self-preservation and the shock of the incident held her back. By this time the hapless diner was wiping the spaghetti sauce from his face. The thug picked up the diner's plate and placed it on an empty table, then slid out a chair, inviting the diner to sit. The man opened his mouth, Alice supposed, to protest, but the larger man mumbled again, and he shut it abruptly, struggled from his seat, then shuffled over to the proffered chair. The tough guy sat down at the vacated table and, noticing the silence, cast a glance around the room at the half dozen or so pairs of covertly staring, worried eyes and said, 'My seat. I always sit here. He was in my seat.'

The chatter nervously resumed, as if that explained everything. Alice hurried behind the bar, ran a clean tea towel under the tap and took it over to the diner, who was still endeavouring to remove splodges of the meat and tomato sauce from his face with the completely inadequate paper serviette which was now saturated and on the point of dissolving.

'Are you okay? Can I get you anything?' Puerile question.

The man looked up at her. There was a chunk of red pepper clinging to his eyebrow. 'Erm . . . just the bill, please.' She could see his hands were shaking.

'There's no charge, really,' Alice babbled, stabbing at a couple of congealed bits of mince that had collected in his shirt collar. 'Honestly, no charge.'

'Miss . . . Miss.' She felt a poke in her back. 'Gimme a menu.'

Alice hesitated, still dabbing with the tea towel. The diner gave her a weak smile. 'It's okay. You go and serve him.'

Alice took over a menu, then retreated to the bar. 'What was *that* about?' she asked Conor who had suddenly materialised.

'That's Joxer Boxer. He's a regular. Always has the steak au poivre, medium rare. Always sits at table six. Likes to be near the window.'

'But what was that *about*? He attacked that man. Where's Hector? Why didn't Hector do something?' Alice was appalled that Hector appeared to have fled without making any kind of objection. He was a good bit bigger than the thug. 'I can't believe Hector just let that happen.'

Conor gave her a cautionary look. 'Leave it, Alice. Look on it as damage limitation. The last time yer man kicked off and Hector tackled him it cost us a new plate glass window and he broke two of Hector's ribs.'

'So why didn't you call the cops?'

'Hector wouldn't let me.'

'Why not?'

Conor shrugged.

'Then why do you let him in here?' Alice hissed.

Conor cringed. 'He likes the food. We can't stop him.' He paused. 'Oh, and, em . . . he never pays.'

'You're not serious?'

Her friend gave an embarrassed shrug.

'Well, I wouldn't let anyone get away that. I'd make him pay, or I'd refuse to serve him.'

'Yeah. Right.'

As Conor had predicted, the man called Joxer ordered steak au poivre, medium rare. She was a tad dubious about dealing with him but, after the initial poke in the back, he surprised her by being the epitome of politeness. When she returned from the kitchen the spag bol man had gone, and when Joxer Boxer had finished his meal, as predicted by Conor, he left without paying.

As her first evening shift dwindled to an end at three a.m., exhausted from being on her feet for so long and brain-dead from dealing with the numerous obnoxious drunks and one psycho, she kicked off her shoes, sat down at a table and poured herself a coffee. Conor and Hector, who was wolfing down the last of the goulash, were sitting at the bar.

'My feet are killing me,' she groaned.

Conor looked round. 'We're not always that busy. I think it's because of the football.'

Tired and grumpy, Alice miserably studied the dregs in the bottom of her coffee cup. What a come-down. From fashion buyer to greasy-spoon waitress in the space of six weeks. It had to be some sort of downwardly mobile record. And worse, she couldn't see any immediate way out of her predicament. Distasteful as it was, she needed this job, not only for the paltry wages, but also for the room. She didn't fancy the thought of sleeping in a doorway.

As these thoughts were going through her mind she heard the door open. A tall woman of indeterminate age tottered in on impossibly high-heeled shiny PVC boots. She was heavily made up with pale foundation. Her eyes were aggressively lined in black and the eyebrows heavily accentuated. She had two slashes of blusher emphasising her cheekbones. Her lips were deep burgundy. The whole effect was Gothic to say the least. All this was topped off by close-cropped blue-black hair. She wore a faux leopardskin coat (at least Alice assumed it was faux having never seen a blue and black spotted leopard) and she strutted over and sat down at Alice's table.

'Give us a cuppa coffee, there's a pet,' she said in a husky voice to Conor. 'I'm fuckin' shagged.'

As she sat, her coat fell open revealing a leather basque, out of which her ample breasts were making a valiant attempt to escape, and – as far as Alice could make out – a studded leather G-string. The black PVC boots were thigh length, above which peeked fishnet tights. Alice was struck dumb.

The woman rummaged in her bag, produced a pack of cigarettes then looked at Alice. 'D'yeh mind?'

Alice shook her head. Even if she had objected, she'd have been too afraid to say. On closer inspection she noted that although the woman's face was white as porcelain, every other visible part of her (of which there was an abundance) was quite deeply tanned.

The older woman gave Alice a smile and shot her hand across the table. 'How'ya. Madame Maxine. Dominatrix. All credit cards welcome.' Alice gulped. Madame Maxine looked up at the ceiling. 'Me an' me assistant trainee, Celeste, work upstairs.' She paused. 'Call me Max.' She looked over at Conor and Hector. 'They do.'

Alice shook her hand. 'Um . . . Hi. I'm, um . . .' (her mind went blank).

Conor, sensing her confusion, cut in, 'This is Alice. Our new waitress. She's taken the empty room in our flat.'

So much for the Ukrainian artiso and fortune teller. Alice, who still hadn't recovered use of her vocal cords, took a sip of coffee.

'Good t' meet yeh, Alice. I hope we won't be disturbin' yeh.' She glanced over towards the bar. 'How'ya, Hector?'

Hector, too intent on quaffing his goulash, raised his huge hand in acknowledgement.

Conor brought over the coffee pot and a clean cup and set it down on the table. 'How was the holiday?'

Madame Maxine, who was in the process of lighting a cigarette, inhaled deeply, then turned her head and blew the smoke away from the table. 'Grand. Nice an' quiet.'

Conor nodded. 'Busy night?'

The woman took another drag on the cigarette and nodded

her head. 'It's with me bein' away. It's always busy when I get back. Yeh know yerself.'

Alice found herself nodding inanely. 'Yes.'

The dominatrix poured herself a cup of coffee and then took a sip. Conor was back at his seat by the bar with Hector, who was wiping his plate with what was left of the garlic bread.

'Trainers,' Madame Max said out of the blue.

'Trainers?'

The woman pointed at Alice's red swollen feet. 'Yeh need the trainers. Standin' kills yeh. I only wish I could get away with them meself.' She threw her head back and roared with laughter. A vision of the dominatrix in her ensemble teamed up with Nikes flashed across Alice's mind and she too laughed.

'Thanks. I'll bear that in mind.'

Hector, who had now cleaned his plate, yawned, then stretching his massive arms above his head said, 'Hew haff game of chess viss me, Madame Max, no?'

'Sure, why not?'

Hector went behind the bar and rummaged for a minute, then produced a chess set. Alice took the opportunity to excuse herself and trundled exhausted up to bed where she slept the sleep of the dead.

The Samovar was closed on Sundays and Mondays. Although in Alice's opinion this was not a good business move, she wasn't complaining, glad to have a couple of days in which to give her feet a chance to recover. She got up late, showered then fixed herself some breakfast. Conor came in shortly after she sat down, with the Sunday papers.

'How did you sleep?'

'Like a log, but my feet are killing me.' She reached for *The Sunday Tribune* and immediately turned to the Appointments page.

'You should take Madame Max's advice about the trainers,' he said as he reached for the tea pot.

Alice skimmed the fashion vacancies, but saw nothing of interest other than a vacancy for an assistant buyer at McAlester's.

'Hector said I can take the car if you want to pick up the rest of your stuff today,' he said. 'And we could stop off at Woodies and get some paint too.'

Alice knew he was only trying to cheer her up but in her present state of mind she didn't want to be cheered up. Her feet were sore, she was living in a shoe box, her job prospects were nil and her earning power reduced to a pittance waiting on tables. She had a right to be miserable. She looked over the top of her paper and scowled at him.

Conor shut up. He knew where she was coming from. He'd been there. Not for the same reasons, but usually as a result of being dumped. He tried a different tack. 'You know, there are other things you can do just as well. You don't have to stick to fashion.'

Alice said, sulkily, 'Such as?'

Conor shrugged. 'Anything. You have to admit you've an instinct for business.'

That was true, and she had the qualifications. She had studied business management at night and had the diploma to prove it. Still, fashion was her first love, and she wasn't ready to give up on it yet.

'I don't know,' she said. 'It sticks in my throat to let the Mutant Midget drive me out of something I like doing, and that I'm good at.'

The thought of Roddy Groden had risen angrily in her again along with the urge to show him that she was better than him. But she couldn't fail to notice the potential of the Samovar. It was a gut reaction and Conor's suggestion that she didn't have to stick to fashion got her thinking. As he had pointed out, she was a natural when it came to business. Also her temperament dictated that whatever she did, it had to be to the best of her ability. So she was a waitress right now, but she still gave it her best shot. It was plain that Conor's food was wasted on the current clientele, but the state of the place precluded all but the very drunk, or those who had nowhere else to go and didn't care about the cheerless surroundings. But what could she do? She was only the hired help. She filed these thoughts to the back of her mind and quietly fantasised about Roddy in the hands of Madame Maxine and her able trainee assistant, Celeste.

Chapter Four

Late on Sunday afternoon, Conor drove Alice over to Susan's to collect the last of her stuff. The front door was open when they arrived. A VW Golf van was in the driveway, the back full of boxes and cartons and what appeared to be a rocking chair. They parked by the grass verge and walked up the path. Susan met her at the door.

'Alice! Hi.' She cast a glance over her shoulder. 'I hope you don't mind, but I put the rest of your things in the dining room.' She sounded anxious, as if afraid that Alice would make a scene or something.

Alice shrugged. 'Fine.' What was the point in being bolshie? Susan's buddy moving in was a done deal. Anyway, as things stood, she couldn't afford the rent, let alone the arrears, so it was time to be gracious.

Susan stood back to let Alice and Conor pass. A girl of about twenty or so walked down the stairs. Alice vaguely recognised her as a friend of Susan's. 'You remember Paula Holland?' Susan's voice was bordering on manic now.

Alice nodded and smiled. Paula smiled back. Susan relaxed a little.

'Thanks for letting me have the room,' Paula said, as if Alice had had a choice. They all stood in the hall. It was awkward with no one having the courage to move.

Conor took the initiative. 'Well, best get on.' He headed down the hall to the dining room and Alice followed. There wasn't a lot to move. Just a carton of books, a box of CDs, her electric kettle and three bags of clothes. Seeing it stacked up, though, it suddenly struck Alice that she'd be hard pressed to find anywhere to put it.

She picked up the box of books and made her way out to the car. Paula was just coming in the front door with a suitcase and they did the sort of jig you do, Alice moving one way to let her past and Paula moving in the same direction. After two false starts Alice managed to successfully navigate her way out of the door.

On her way back to collect a bag of clothes she had to stop by the door as a tall man of about thirty was trying to manoeuvre the pine rocking chair through the storm-door. He was having a problem with the rockers, which, whatever way he tried, were stoutly refusing to go through the gap left by the double-glazed sliding door. Conor came through the hall and tried to help.

'Maybe if you turned it on its side.' He dropped the bag of clothes he was carrying onto the floor and stood surveying the problem.

'I tried that,' the man said. 'But the arms still get in the way. The door's too narrow.'

The chair was now jammed in the opening and wouldn't budge in either direction.

Alice sat down on a concrete flower urn. 'Maybe you should saw the legs off,' she said in a jaded voice.

The man turned round and grinned at her. 'Might have to,' he said. 'Do you have a saw?'

Alice grinned back.

Susan and Paula appeared at this point. 'Can't you turn it on its side, Sean?' Paula offered.

'Already tried that,' Sean replied. 'It seems to be stuck.' He looked over at Conor. 'Can you give it a shove, and I'll pull at the same time?'

Conor braced himself and gave the chair a hearty shove. Nothing happened. Then, aided by Paula and Susan, he tried again.

There was a splintering sound and the next moment the chair shot backwards out of the door, knocking Sean off his feet. The backwards momentum of Sean, the chair, Conor, Paula and Susan was only halted as they careered into Alice sitting like a gnome on her concrete urn. She in turn was catapulted backwards onto the lawn and ended up tangled in a flower bed, with Sean on top of her and Conor, Paula and Susan in a similar heap amid the splintered remains of Paula's rocking chair.

They lay winded for a moment, then Sean rolled over on to the grass and started to laugh. Alice too started to giggle. He picked himself up and held out his hand to help Alice up. 'Hi. I'm Sean, Paula's brother. You must be Alice.'

Alice grabbed his hand and he heaved her up. 'Hi.'

Conor and the two girls were just getting to their feet. The chair was in pieces. Susan was more interested in the storm-door and hurried back to inspect it. 'Pity about the chair,' Alice said, picking up a stray leg. 'But you've got all the pieces, maybe you could glue it together.' She had to fight to kill the snigger twitching at the corner of her mouth.

Paula poked at an unrecognisable piece of splintered wood with her toe. She had an anguished look on her face. 'Hardly. It's destroyed.'

Alice caught Conor's eye and they drifted back into the house to collect the remaining bags of clothes from the dining room along with the box of CDs, leaving the others surveying the pile of firewood.

No one was in sight as they were leaving except for Susan who was out in the front garden examining the urn which was lying where it had landed on the lawn. Alice went over to her. 'I'll let you have the rent I owe you as soon as I'm straight.'

Susan gave her an awkward hug. 'Don't worry about it. No hard feelings. You know if I—'

Alice cut her off. 'No hard feelings. Really.'

Susan looked relieved. 'I'll say a prayer for you.' She paused and looked over Alice's shoulder at Conor. 'For both of you.'

'Lucky me,' said Conor as they were driving away.

'Hey, don't knock it. I don't know about you but I need all the divine intervention I can get right now.'

At the end of her first week Hector handed her her first full pay packet. Along with the ninety quid, she estimated she'd made about a tenner in tips for the whole week. It was a lesson learned. The criminally rat-arsed are lousy tippers. Somewhere between throwing up in the gents and crawling outside to the taxi, they lose all appreciation for the quality of service rendered.

In celebration of her new found wealth and in great need of strong drink, she decided she needed a break. It was a while since she'd had a good night out. This was untypical of Alice. She had always enjoyed a decent social life, that is until the pressure of getting the spring collection ready for McAlester's had left her exhausted every evening, and since Roddy had sacked her, it was a case of having neither the inclination nor the money. She phoned Annie, only to be told that she had gone home to Mayo for the weekend. Then she tried Claire, an old drinking chum from McAlester's, to discover that she had gone off to Tenerife for two weeks. Katy, a friend since school, was delighted to hear from her, though. 'But where have you been?' she demanded. 'You just disappeared off the face of the earth.'

'It's a long story,' Alice said. 'So how are you?'

'Great. You know I got engaged?'

Alice hadn't heard. 'To who? Since when?'

Katy filled her in on the details. His name was Mikey and she'd known him three months and they planned to get married the following January. They'd got engaged five weeks before. Alice was pleased for her but a little miffed that this was the first she'd heard of it.

'Do you fancy a girls' night out?' she asked.

'Oh . . . well, the thing is we're going away for a few days to see his folks. Maybe another time.'

Three further calls didn't bring a result and by this time Alice was becoming paranoid. 'What's wrong with me? Why doesn't anyone want to go out with me?'

Conor, who was sitting at the bar reading the paper, looked up. 'What?'

'Why can't I find anyone to have a night out with?'

Conor shrugged. 'I don't think it's personal,' he said. 'You haven't been in touch with any of your friends for ages. Not since . . .' he looked up at the ceiling and screwed up his eyes as he tried to remember '. . . since well before you left McAlester's.'

Alice thought about it. He was right.

'Why don't you come out with Hector and me? We're going to that new club, TransV.'

Alice hadn't heard of it. 'TransV? . . . As in transvestite?'

Conor grinned. 'Loosely speaking. Come on. It'll be fun.'

What the hell. 'Okay.'

Hector had excelled himself. Over the dead cow trousers he was wearing a black silk ruffle-necked shirt and long frock coat in fuchsia and silver brocade. This he teamed up with fuchsia patent Doc Martens. By comparison Conor looked pedestrian in dark green moleskin trousers and a mustard-yellow shirt.

Alice hadn't a clue what to wear, it was so long since she had dressed up for a night out. In the end she decided on the all-black approach. Black leather pants (the half-cow version), a Karen Millen black silk jersey halter-necked top she'd picked up in the Brown Thomas sale, teamed up with high-heeled suede ankle boots. her hair had grown an inch (due to lack of the finances for a decent cut) and it suited her. She stood on the toilet seat to get a proper view of the bottom half of herself in the bathroom mirror. She thought she looked very cool.

Hector and Conor were sitting at the bar when she came down.

'Alice. Alice, you look vonderful,' Hector enthused, taking her hands and swinging her around. 'I think ve have good time, yes? Maybe ve find you a man.'

'That isn't the object of the exercise, Hector. I'm out to bop till I drop and get completely twisted. Men aren't on the agenda.'

Conor winked at her. 'I don't know, you might pick up someone in a natty off-the-shoulder evening number and size elevens.'

TransV was situated in a disused warehouse on the south docks, and just a stone's throw across the river basin from the new Custom House development, a further paw print of the ubiquitous Celtic Tiger. The taxi dropped them off nearby, though if they had been in any doubt of the club's exact whereabouts, the sight of a number of six-foot drag queens tottering ahead of them was a dead give-away. Alice remembered the club in a former incarnation as the Watershed. It was a large Victorian brick building four stories high. On the ground floor there were bars and a dance area. On the next level was a gallery with tables overlooking the dance floor, on the next, food was served and on the top floor there was the VIP room which was closed to ordinary mortals. Alice didn't care much for VIP rooms. In her experience they were usually full of wannabe celebs, models and visiting English footballers.

The club was pleasantly full. Room to move around comfortably, yet enough people to create an atmosphere. The new owners hadn't gone overboard on the revamp, their efforts confined to painting the previously bare brickwork deep red or black. They were obviously relying on the clientele to add that certain je ne sais quoi. Apart from the drag queens, there were a few timid TVs, a few less so and a good number of people of the straight persuasion (commonly known by Conor and his friends as tourists) whom she didn't recognise.

Since being friends with Conor, Alice had become accustomed to hanging out in gay bars from time to time, and was on good terms with a lot of his friends. For the most part they were a nice bunch and good fun to be with, though she found it difficult to keep up with their frenetic love lives.

Hector pushed his way through to the bar and Alice and Conor followed in his wake. 'Vot you drink, Alice?'

She ordered a tequila and grapefruit. Hector ordered himself a vodka and a gin and tonic for Conor. The DJ, a short fat guy called Spike, with tattoos and a penchant for body piercing, was terrific and as soon as she'd finished her first drink she dragged both Conor and Hector on to the dance floor. Conor was a good dancer but Hector, despite his size, was outrageous and soon Alice forgot all her troubles. She danced for a good twenty minutes without a break before leaving Conor and Hector to it. She found an empty table and quickly claimed it.

Then she grabbed a passing waiter and ordered a round of drinks.

Looking down at the dance floor she picked out Conor and Hector dancing together and felt a pang of jealousy. It was ages since she had felt that close to anyone. Not since Alex, but the less said about him the better. Another in a long line of terrible choices who had dumped her for a man called Richard whom he had met at Conor's birthday bash the year before. Of course he hadn't had the decency to come out and tell her, or indeed to come out of the closet, though she should have read the signs. He led her on for two months until she caught the two of them in bed together.

'I can explain,' he had bleated.

'I think I get the picture, thanks,' she replied before storming out. Susan and Brenda had really liked Alex and she had taken a certain perverse pleasure in regaling them with the gory details.

The waiter returned with the drinks at the moment she saw Hector's bulky figure reaching the top of the stairs. He looked around and she stood and waved to attract their attention. As she did so she caught sight of Roddy Groden. He was in the company of a young leggy blonde. It was his usual MO. He'd spin them a spiel about how he could get them into modelling. He looked the worse for wear. If Alice had had a couple more drinks she would probably have attempted to wind him up. After all, she had nothing to lose, he'd already spoilt her prospects for the foreseeable future, or at least until the dust settled and he got tired of that game. But she didn't feel like it. She wanted to have a good time and forget about all that. Why did he have to show up?

Conor caught her eye and waved, so she sat down again and took a gulp of her drink, hoping that the brave Roddy wouldn't notice her.

Hugh and Sonny, pals of Conor's, joined them a short time later along with Jojo, Hugh's younger sister. Jojo was petite and pretty and was with a scary-looking woman called Gilda who, it turned out, was her current partner. She had cropped yellow blond hair and was dressed from head to toe in black.

More drink was ordered and Alice forgot all about Roddy. Mason arrived then. He was also a friend of Conor's. An Irish-American actor over from New York looking for work. He had just started as a barman in TransV and it was from him that Conor had obtained their free passes. He was breathtakingly gorgeous, a Diet Coke man. It only went to reinforce the universal theory that all the best men were either married or gay. The music was loud, the atmosphere was good, the craic was mighty and Alice was fast getting to the giddy stage. As she was laughing at the punch line of one of Conor's less funny jokes, a joke that had she been in any other mood wouldn't have raised even a titter from her, she felt a hand on her shoulder. She looked around to see Joxer Boxer, standing over her, grinning. It took her a moment to place him. It was something to do with him being so out of context.

''Scuse me, miss. Wanna dance?'

'Um . . .' Not wishing to cause him offence, she groped in her drink-enfeebled brain for a suitable response. The DJ had put on a tango and a couple of drag queens were gliding across the dance floor below, dancing bust to bust.

'Um, I . . . um . . . Sorry, I can't do the, um . . . Latin dance . . . thingy.'

He hoisted her to her feet. 'No problemo, miss. I'll lead.'

'But—' She looked at her friends helplessly, but they were all engrossed in some scandalous bit of gossip that Gilda was imparting. A moment later she had been yanked down the stairs and on to the dance floor.

'Please, Joxer . . . I really can't . . .'

His face went stony. 'You refusin' me? I'd be very upset if you was refusin' me.'

'Um . . . er, no.'

One of Joker's meaty hands lightly rested in the small of her back, the other held her arm stiffly out to the side. The drag queens made another sweep across the floor, sequins flashing in their wake. Joxer, remarkably light on his feet, propelled her forwards across the floor, stopping and turned abruptly with the music. His movements were dramatic and jerky, but he was an expert dancer and led her impeccably. She had never attempted any ballroom dancing before, but suddenly she found she was actually dancing the tango passably well. After what seemed like a lifetime, the final chords of the tango came to a staccato end and Joxer finished with a flourish, swinging her round and bending her backwards over his hip. The drag queens, determined to upstage him, did an extra couple of twirls and dips.

'Fuckin' freaks,' he growled as he snapped Alice back into a standing position, almost causing her whiplash with the suddenness of the move. 'Can't stand fuckin' queers.'

'So what are you doing here? Alice asked, immediately regretting that she had opened her mouth.

'Doin' a bit'a business,' Joxer said. 'Then I heard the music. Never get proper music these days, never get proper dancin'.'

He left her at the foot of the stairs and headed for the exit, muttering to himself. It had been a surreal experience, to say the least. Tangoing across the dance floor with the man whom she never in her wildest dreams would have imagined would list Latin American dancing on his list of hobbies and pastimes. GBH, drinking and looking menacing, maybe, but certainly not ballroom dancing.

'Where were you?' Conor asked, as she returned to her seat.

'Tangoing with Joxer Boxer.'

Conor laughed. 'Yeah. Sure.'

She didn't bother to argue.

Much later, as Alice was bopping away on the dance floor with Hugh, Sonny and, to her surprise, Gilda (who danced like a *Thunderbird* puppet), she felt a tap on her shoulder. She looked around to find Roddy. He was red faced, sweating and wore a lop-sided sneer on his blubbery lips.

'Any luck on the job front?'

Alice tried to ignore him and moved away to dance in front of Gilda, but Roddy was having none of it. He poked her in the back and when that move elicited no response he barged in front of her. 'This the new girlfriend?' he asked smugly. His belief that Alice must have been a lesbian to have turned him down was now confirmed.

Gilda elbowed him out of the way. Alice winced. She had

got him just below the breast bone and it looked sore. Emboldened by the drink, Roddy asserted himself. 'Now look here, you muff muncher . . .'

Gilda cast a withering glance in his direction and nudged him out of the way with her hip.

'Fuck off, tourist!' she snarled.

Roddy tottered backwards but kept his balance. That was when he lost it and made a run at Alice, grabbing her by the shoulders and shaking her, his face puce, the little vein doing a rhumba. 'I knew you were a fucking dyke. I knew it!'

Alice was so stunned by the ferocity of his onslaught that she froze. Roddy ranted on, his face only inches from hers. She could feel little globs of spit hitting her cheek. 'If you think you'll ever get a job in this town again, you lesbo . . .' (probably not the most prudent reference given their surroundings). He gave her a shove and she staggered backwards and bumped into a group of dancers before losing her balance and stumbling to her knees. At the same time Gilda grabbed Roddy from behind and frog-marched him from the floor towards the exit to a round of applause, his protests drowned out by the throbbing techno beat. The leggy blonde, mortified, had melted into the crowd.

'Are you okay?'

Alice immediately recognised Sean Holland, Paula's brother, as he helped her up. Embarrassed by the incident, she mumbled, 'I'm fine . . . thanks.'

'That guy needs certifying.' Like she needed to be told. 'We seem to be making a habit of bumping into one another,' he added lamely then gave her a grin. 'Can I buy you a drink?'

Alice just wanted to get away. As she rubbed her elbow, which had begun to sting, she saw Gilda returning. 'Thanks, but I'm with friends,' she said and hurried off towards the stairs.

Conor and Hector, who had witnessed the incident from the balcony, were outraged. Hector was all for *going after zat gobeshite* (he had picked up a few local expressions) and *giving him lesson he von't forget*. Conor, who was opposed to violence of any kind, was just outraged. They all congratulated Gilda for her timely intervention.

'Can't stand fucking tourists,' she muttered, then shot a coy look at Alice, 'present company excepted.'

The eveing was spoiled for Alice and the shock of the incident had sobered her considerably, but she didn't want to spoil it for everyone else by breaking the party up, so she set about a quest for oblivion and started on the tequila shots.

Hector, assisted by Conor, poured her into a cab just after three, and they all went home.

Chapter Five

In the early hours of the following Saturday morning, at the end of a particularly gruesome shift (three stag parties and a hen night) Alice suddenly said out of the blue, 'You know, Conor, this place could do with a good clean. Your food's great, but if the place was clean and we gave it a couple of coats of paint . . .'

Hector lifted his head from the trough. 'You say my place dirty?' He sounded indignant.

Conor hadn't been aware that he was listening. Neither had Alice. She wondered that he heard her at all, what with the noise he made while he was eating. It surprised her that his table manners were so awful. She wondered if it was a Ukrainian thing.

'How dare you say this!' Chomp, chomp. Slurp, slurp.

'Are you trying to tell me it's clean?' Alice retaliated.

Conor, although pleased that Alice had brought the subject up, winced. Hector gnawed on the garlic bread and glared at her. After a moment's thought he decided not to rise to the challenge. 'No money for cleaning person.' Slurp, slurp. 'The cleaning person she cost much money.'

Conor flashed Alice a warning look so she let it drop and joined Madame Max and Celeste (a younger version of Madame Max in identical gear) who were sitting at a table enjoying a late-night snack of cheese on toast which Conor had made for them.

Maxine looked exhausted. She was wearing her work ensemble covered only by a shiny black PVC mac. It was perfectly co-ordinated with the black PVC stiletto thigh boots.

'You look as shattered as I feel,' Alice said as she slumped down at the table. 'There should be a law against stag parties.'

'Yeah. Crowd of shites, aren't they?' Madame Max said, obviously referring to the last three punters who had just lurched out of the door, dressed in seventies flared suits and Afro wigs. They'd been giving grief ever since they'd staggered in two hours previously. Maxine lit a cigarette and offered the packet to Alice. Alice had quit the previous year but took one anyway. She needed it.

'Yes. Crowd of shites,' Alice agreed. 'And they're *always* like that.'

'Yeah,' Maxine said. 'For the most part. Pay a few bob and they think they can treat yeh like dirt.'

Conor, who overheard the comment, thought it an astute observation. He had always been of the opinion, having briefly flirted with bar work, that dealing with drunks when sober is a danger to your mental health. He could see why Alice was pissed off and was glad that his job confined him to the kitchen.

'Now our crowd . . .' Maxine was warming to the subject. 'Our crowd know their place. Don't they, Celeste?'

Celeste nodded. 'Yeah, they know their place all righ'.'

Madame Max took a good slug from her wineglass then continued. 'Fifty quid an' I get the room cleaned. An' I mean *cleaned*. Yeh could eat off the bleedin' floor.'

'You pay them to clean your room?' Alice looked aghast. Conor sniggered.

'Not me, yeh eejitt. Them. They pay me fifty quid an' I let the bastards clean me room, then if they're very good boys, I beat the shite out a' them.'

'That's nice,' Alice said feebly, at a loss for what else to say. 'It must be easy money.'

'Easy? Are yeh kiddin' me? Did yer hear that, Celeste?'

Celeste nodded, her mouth full of food.

'After a nigh' batterin' TDs' an' judges' arses I'm feckin' shagged.' Madame Max roared with laughter. 'Well, *I'm* not shagged, but yeh know what I mean. That's why Celeste an' me take it in turns. Yeh couldn't manage to do them all every bleedin' day. It'd feckin' wear yeh out.'

'So these guys pay you and they do your cleaning?' Alice said.

Maxine nodded. 'Well, yeah. Among other things. That's only a small part of it. It's the humiliation they want. Turns 'em on. Then there's the beatin's. A lot a' them just want the beatin's. I think it's a throwback from the Christian Brothers meself. It makes 'em feel secure.'

'But about the cleaning? Some of them do cleaning, you said.' Alice glanced meaningfully at Conor.

''S'righ'. That's the humiliation thing. I batther them if it's not up t' standard.'

'So what if you were to get some of your clients to clean up down here?'

'Wha'?'

'Clean up down here. The place is full of grease and grime. You could probably charge them extra. What do you think, Conor?'

Conor was more than interested, but played it cool for the benefit of Hector. 'What do you think, Hector?'

Hector hadn't been listening this time, too intent on shovelling in what remained of his supper. He smacked his lips and wiped the back of his hand across his mouth. 'Think off vot?' he asked.

'Getting the place cleaned up,' Conor said.

'Vy? It clean.' He turned to Alice. 'You say my place not clean? Vare not clean?' He looked thoroughly affronted. His voice was rising.

Conor held his breath. Alice stood up. Hector stood up. Alice only came up to his shoulder but she stood her ground. Conor was anxious. He'd never seen anyone stand up (literally) to Hector before.

Alice planted her feet apart and pointed to the grubby floor. 'There. It's filthy.' She stabbed her finger towards the grimy walls. 'And there. It's disgusting.' She walked behind the bar and ran her hand along the glass shelf, leaving a path in the dust. 'The whole place is a disgrace. It's filthy.'

Hector took umbrage. His bottom lip quivered and he sat back down. 'My place clean! My place it got atmosphere. How dare you say this.'

There was a strained silence.

Conor said, 'It's for free, Hector. It won't cost a penny.'

Hector's expression changed from indignation to curiosity in a flash. He narrowed his beady eyes. 'No cost? How no cost?'

'Madame Maxine's clients will do it for free.' Conor waited for that to sink in. 'It wouldn't do any harm, Hector.' Then, tentatively, 'The place could do with a coat of paint too while we're at it.'

'Oh, I don't think my punters paint,' Maxine said. 'But the cleanin's another thing. In fact, Hector baby, ye'd be doin' me a favour.'

Maxine's diplomacy eased the situation. Hector agreed that Maxine could bring punters down between the hours of three and six when the café was closed. After Maxine had gone and Hector went up to bed, Conor locked up and poured two large brandies.

'What's that for?' Alice asked.

'By way of thanks.' Conor raised his glass in salute. 'I've been at him since I got here about doing something to the place. You were great.'

'You should have insisted before this.'

Conor felt himself redden. He stared at his shoes. 'I'm not good at confrontation. I hate arguments.'

'You don't need to argue with him, just be a bit more assertive,' she said. 'Don't be such a wimp.'

They sat in silence sipping their brandy.

Alice broke the silence. 'You know, this place has real potential.'

'You really think so?'

Alice looked round the empty café. 'Yes. Your food's divine, but it's not enough. Even after the place has been cleaned up, we have to think of a plan.'

'A plan?' Conor perked up.

'You've got to get through to Hector somehow.'

Conor sagged. 'The flaw in the plan.'

It took a good three weeks to get the Samovar into any sort of shape. Hector thawed out long before then and seemed pleased with every little bit of progress. From time to time Alice and Conor thought they recognised a face or two scampering into the café through the back door, clad in pinnie, rubber gloves and little else. Maxine was a hard task mistress, but then that's what she was being paid for. Towards the end of the third week, Alice, having forgotten her bag at the end of the lunch-time shift, popped into the café to pick it up. Maxine was sitting on the bar, legs crossed. She was a fearsome sight in her black leather studded basque, leather G-string, fishnets and PVC thigh boots, brandishing a leather bull whip. The punter was on his hands and knees scrubbing the floor. Occasionally Madame Maxine gave his bum a clatter with the whip, at which point he stopped what he was doing, kissed the toe of her proffered boot and said, 'Thank you, mistress.' Before resuming with the scrubbing brush, Maxine gave her a wave and Alice quickly left.

It was as she was watching the *Six-One News* that she recognised Maxine's punter, now sporting clerical collar and bishop's purple instead of pinnie and Marigolds, holding forth in front of Leinster House about the decline of family values.

The sit-down lunchtime business increased in direct relation to the progress of the renovations. Early evening business also increased by leaps and bounds. Regular bona fide diners out for a civilised evening. By the end of Alice's second month at the Samovar, trade had trebled. She was now taking in twice as much in tips as she was in wages, though not without effort.

Things were looking up for Conor too. Even Hector, who was in brilliant humour due to the bigger turnover, took more of an interest and was in attendance far more often. He was even seen to clear a table from time to time when they were very busy. Even he had to admit that Alice's suggestions were very effective. Hector let Conor hire another waitress, Jean, and a washer-up, and they closed at two a.m.

I want a piece of this, Alice thought. How or when, however, were two questions to which she had no answers.

Chapter Six

Conor had a plan. It had come to him out of the blue as he sat watching Alice and Hector discussing the problem. At least Alice was trying to discuss the problem. Hector was in a state of complete negativity and wallowing in the drama of it all.

The situation had arisen without warning. Conor had had no inkling that there was even the remotest chance of such a thing happening so, when the letter arrived, he had been completely shattered. The thought of having Hector snatched away from him when things were going so well appalled him. 'Why didn't you *tell* me?' he had pleaded. 'I might have been able to help.'

'How you help? No one can help me. I am doomed.' Stoic until that point, he dissolved into tears.

Conor couldn't handle Hector crying. He'd never seen his lover fall apart before. His usual response to a crisis was dramatic, theatrical maybe, but there hadn't been tears. It was unsettling, it made Conor think that perhaps there was no way out. He stood helplessly with his arm around Hector trying to calm him down, and that was the way that Alice had found them. Hector approaching apoplexy and Conor on the weepy side.

'What's up? What the hell's happened?' she asked a snivelling Conor.

'It's Hector,' was all he had managed to say, before melting into tears.

'What about Hector? Is he sick? He doesn't *look* sick.'

'I go. Immigration say I go back to Ukraine.'

'Why? Why do you have to go?'

He handed Alice the crumpled letter, the gist of which was

that Hector was summoned to attend a meeting at the Department of Foreign Affairs to discuss 'visa irregularities' at the end of the week.

'Where does it say you're to be deported?' Alice had asked, aggressively. 'It just says here they want to see you.'

'But I don't have papers,' Hector had wailed. 'They send me back. I know they send me back.'

Conor, who had recovered his equilibrium, explained. 'Hector's an illegal. He's been here five years and he only had a six months' visitor's visa.'

'You're kidding.'

Conor shook his head. 'I didn't know till now either.' He was still close to tears but didn't want to break down again. He was desolate at the thought of losing Hector. And what would Hector do? If what Hector had said of his former life was anything to go by, he'd never survive the privations of the Ukraine after living in Dublin for so long. It had struck him briefly that he could always go too, but he hadn't been too keen on that possibility. Far better to find some way of keeping Hector in Dublin, or at least in Ireland.

Alice meanwhile had been trying to calm Hector down. He was threatening any minute to erupt into hysterical gnashing of teeth and possibly tearing of hair. 'Surely they can't just throw you out like that? Can't you claim political asylum?'

'This I tried,' he'd wailed. 'They refuse. They don't believe how I suffer in old country.'

'My God! Were you persecuted?'

Hector wiped his eyes with the heels of his hairy hands. 'Sure I persecuted. They vant to put me in prison.'

'But surely that counts as persecution? Didn't you tell them that? Didn't you say your government wanted to throw you in the slammer?'

'No!' Hector said, slapping the bar in frustration. 'Your people. Your people vant to put me in prison.'

'Oh.'

Alice couldn't see any way around the problem. But it did explain Hector's reluctance to report Joxer Boxer to the cops. If they had started to ask awkward questions Hector could have found himself on the next plane back to the Ukraine. It was well known that the Irish government were getting quite squiffy about illegals lately.

'Then I'm afraid it looks as if you've had it,' she said.

That was when Conor came up with his brainwave. 'Not if he was married to an Irish national.'

'Yeah, right,' Alice scoffed. 'Somehow I can't see the Department of Foreign Affairs recognising a gay marriage, can you?'

'I wasn't thinking of a gay marriage. I was thinking more along the lines of a regular man–woman thing.'

'Voman! How I marry voman?' Hector sounded disgusted.

Conor took Hector by the shoulder and led him into the kitchen. 'Excuse us for a minute.'

After making sure that the door was firmly shut he said, 'Look, Hector. If you marry Alice, you'll get an Irish passport. You'll be able to stay. We can be together.'

'But I not love Alice. I love you.'

Conor's heart lurched in his ribcage. He hugged Hector. 'I know, Hector, and you know I want to be with you too, but the way I see it, Alice is our only chance. And it'd be in name only. Just so you can get a passport.'

'But vill she do this? Vy she do this?'

From the restaurant Alice heard Hector scream, then she heard Conor mumbling. What was Hector's problem? If he married an Irishwoman he'd get this passport. She did wonder, however, what class of eejitt would agree to such a marriage. She'd heard of women being paid to marry non-nationals, perhaps that was what Conor had in mind. Maybe Madame Maxine would know how to go about it.

After another minute of muffled mumbling from the kitchen, the door opened and Conor and Hector emerged looking sheepish. There was an awkward silence, then Hector nudged Conor in the ribs. 'You say,' he urged his lover.

Conor took a deep breath. 'Okay. Here's the deal. You marry Hector and you get twenty-five per cent of the Samovar.'

Alice was horrified. 'Me? Marry him? Jesus, what the hell do you think I am?'

Hector looked crestfallen for a moment, forgetting his objections, only minutes before, about marrying a *voman*. He pulled himself together. 'For visa I marry you, yes?'

Conor, sensing that Alice wasn't wholly receptive to the idea of having Hector Hanusiak as a husband, played the friendship card. 'Please, Alice. Please. Help us. I don't want Hector to go. I love him. We love each other.' He put a protective arm round Hector's (approximate) waist.

Hector kissed the top of Conor's head and stifled a sob. They looked pathetic. Like a couple of fawns (at least Conor looked like a fawn. Hector was more like a grizzly bear).

Alice, still in shock at the notion, shook her head. 'Look, guys. I'd help if I could, but the Immigration people would never buy it.'

Conor sighed pathetically. 'You don't know that. Anyway, what have you got to lose? If you marry Hector, you get a quarter of the Samovar. You know you want it. And if not, well, look at it this way. The Samovar closes and you're out of a job.'

'Right. Like I couldn't walk out of here right now and get another job?' Alice snapped defensively.

Conor didn't dignify her jibe with a reply.

Alice, backed into a corner, examined the options. It occurred to her that maybe this was a window of opportunity. *The* window of opportunity, the break she'd been hoping for. And where was the harm? It wasn't as if she had any marriage plans of her own. And the way her luck with men was going, it wasn't even a remote possibility for the foreseeable future.

'Okay,' she said after a while. 'Fifty per cent, and I'll do it.'

'Fifty! That half!' Hector spluttered.

'Well spotted. That's the deal. Take it or leave it.'

Alice thought Hector was going to explode. His face had turned bright puce. Conor gave his shoulder a squeeze. 'Go on, Hector. It's the only way.'

Hector was still uncertain. Alice was about to adjust the figure downwards, when he gave in. 'Hokay. Ve haf deal.' He spat on the palm of his hand and thrust it out towards her. She hesitated, then patted him on the shoulder instead.

'Deal,' she agreed, then added, 'I'll need it in writing, of course. We'll need to draw up a proper contact.'

Without giving Hector a chance to protest, Conor jumped in, 'Of course. No problem. No problem.'

The lunchtime customers drifted in at this point so further discussion on the practicalities of the plan had to be postponed until after three o'clock. They passed Celeste on the way out through the back door. She had a short bespectacled man in tow on the end of a dog leash. Conor drew Madame Maxine's trainee assistant to one side. 'Would you get him to have a proper go at the ovens today, Celeste?'

'No problem, love.' She booted her punter in the rear to hurry him along.

As Alice headed up the fire escape to Hector's and Conor's flat, she heard the punter babbling, 'Thank you, mistress. Thank you.' The complexities of the male psyche would never cease to amaze her.

There were plans to be made. Apart from the wedding, Alice had no intention of going ahead with anything until a proper legal contract had been drawn up, passing over fifty per cent ownership of the Samovar to her, as from the time the ink dried on the marriage certificate. Then Conor brought up the matter of the marital home. Alice didn't particularly want to share living space with anyone at that point of her life, let alone a couple. 'Is that necessary?'

''Fraid so,' Conor said. 'Like you said yourself, Immigration will assume that it's just a marriage of convenience. We have to prove otherwise.'

'Why? Why do we have to prove it? Surely it's up to them to prove *their* case?'

'Didn't you see *Green Card*?' he asked in a jaded voice. Alice looked blankly at him. '*Green Card*, the movie?' he persisted.

'The one with the French guy with the big nose?' Alice had a vague recollection.

Conor continued. 'Well, yer man ... the guy with the big nose, he and yer woman ... you know? the one who was in

Four Weddings and a Funeral? Well, they had the same problem. They took photos of the wedding and the honeymoon and everything, so it would look kosher . . . Those guys are like fucking pit bulls once they sniff anything even remotely iffy so we can't afford to give them any excuse.'

'Honeymoon!' Alice didn't like the sound of that.

'It's cool . . . It's cool. You won't be going on an *actual* honeymoon. The point I'm making is, we have to make it look as real and authentic as possible if Immigration are to believe it.' He was really getting into the spirit of the thing now.

Alice eventually gave in, mainly at the thought of having a half share in the Samovar, but partly, if she admitted it to herself, because Conor was her friend and she felt sorry for him. On further discussion it was decided that they would all share a two-bedroom apartment. Alice would scatter some of her belongings strategically round Hector's and Conor's room in the event of a visit from the Foreign Affairs hit-squad.

Conor was getting quite excited about the wedding. Between them, he and Hector decided to make it a double celebration. A gay vicar friend would perform a marriage ceremony, joining the two of them in holy gay matrimony as soon as they all returned from the more conventional doings at the registry office. 'If we're going to all this trouble, we may as well. Shame to waste the outfits,' Conor said. 'Anyway, we want to make the commitment.'

As it was no skin off Alice's nose, she agreed to the plan, even offering to be a witness.

Hector managed to evade the Department of Foreign Affairs, citing illness. He produced a sick note. A further appointment was scheduled for six weeks' time.

The day before the big event, Conor, still full of enthusiasm, brought up the matter of bridesmaids. Alice was by this time getting fed up with the whole business. She couldn't understand why Conor had to make such a big deal out of it. It wasn't as if it was for real.

'What *about* bridesmaids?' she asked with gritted teeth.

'You'll *need* a bridesmaid. Who ever heard of a bride without a bridesmaid? Who'll you throw the bouquet to?'

'What bloody bouquet?'

Conor shook his head in despair. 'You're really not taking this seriously, Alice. Marriage is a serious business, not to be entered into lightly.'

'What the hell are you ravelling on about?' she snapped. 'You and I know why we're going through this charade. You want to keep your boyfriend in the country and I want a slice of the Samovar. End of story.' As soon as the words were out of her mouth she was sorry. Conor looked thoroughly dejected. It dawned on her that he was so excited because, for him, it *was* to be a real wedding. He and Hector were making a commitment to one another. Her sham wedding day was his actual wedding day.

'Sorry,' se said. 'I didn't mean that.'

Conor shrugged. 'I wouldn't blame you if you did. Why would you put yourself out for me?'

Now she felt thoroughly ashamed. 'Because you're my best friend?' She walked over to where he was sitting and gave him a hug.

Conor hugged her in return then released her. 'Now, about the bridesmaids?' he said.

Alice gave in. But this did pose a problem. And she had no intention of telling anyone about her forthcoming nuptials, she was particularly deficient in the bridesmaid department. Once again Conor came up with the solution. 'How about Madame Maxine?'

'Why not?' said Alice wearily, now resigned to the fact that Conor wasn't going to let it go. 'No better woman.'

Chapter Seven

Alice Little married Hector Hanusiak on a bright sunny mid-June afternoon. The bride wore black. The groom wore an understated cream Nehru-style coat with a plain white collarless shirt underneath and matching cream trousers. He chose embroidered silk slippers for his feet. Before leaving for the registry office, Conor had presented Hector with a pale pink and cream orchid corsage and there had been tears and much hugging. The ensemble was very understated for Hector, but he looked almost handsome.

Conor, in his role as both best man and soon-to-be groom, wore a charcoal grey three-piece suit with a pale blue shirt and the Versace tie that Alice had bought him the previous Christmas. She was touched and pleased that he had chosen to wear it on his big day. To Alice's surprise and relief, Madame Maxine was wearing an elegant, duck-egg blue Armani suit. It put Alice to thinking that maybe she had made the wrong new career choice, wondering, albeit briefly, if Madame Max might have a vacancy for another trainee.

The service passed without incident. Both Alice and Hector said their *I do*s and *I will*s (or in Hector's case, *I vill*), and at the end, everyone applauded as they were pronounced husband and wife.

The bride tossed her bouquet from the door of the registry office to an excited Celeste and, after the all-important photographs, the wedding party made their way back to the Samovar.

It was a gay affair in every sense. About two dozen or so of Conor's and Hector's friends turned up, including Hugh, Sonny, a very excited Jojo and Gilda, who was clad in tight yellow trousers and a loose yellow top (which, when combined with her yellow-blond hair, made Alice think of Big Bird) and a broody-looking Mason who had equally broody-looking boyfriend in tow. The clerical acquaintance performed the alternative ceremony. Alice gave Conor away, and found it hard not to shed a tear when the happy couple made their vows. In fact there wasn't a dry eye in the house. The wedding party soon was in full swing. Conor had prepared a magnificent buffet and there was plenty of drink. Alice relaxed and enjoyed herself. She and Madame Maxine (*call me Max, love*) were danced off their feet.

It was a while since she had enjoyed herself so much. Working nights in the Samovar meant she'd lost touch with most of her friends. If she was honest she would have to admit that maybe she was avoiding them due to a certain embarrassment about her present career. It didn't take Einstein to imagine Roddy's smug reaction if he discovered that she now earned a crust waiting on tables.

She had a long chat with Madame Maxine. She discovered that the dominatrix had fallen into her present line of work by accident. Abused by a succession of her alcoholic mother's live-in boyfriends, Maxine was a very disturbed and disruptive child. She was taken into care at the age of thirteen. At fifteen she ran away and lived on the streets where the necessity to survive drew her into prostitution. She hated the life. Hated how worthless it made her feel. She was one of the luckier girls as she didn't have a drug habit to support, so at least her lifestyle wasn't as sordid as some of the others. One night a punter got rough. He was a small weedy man, so Maxine retaliated by giving him a hefty wallop across the face, then continued battering him with her shoe. The car door was locked so she couldn't escape. She was in a panic, certain that she was going to die, until she realised he wasn't hitting her any more. He was lying across the seat with a smile on his lips as she rained blows down on him. When she stopped he begged her to carry on. Offered her double the going rate for sex if she'd spank his bare bum.

Alice was fascinated. It was a whole new world to her.

Madame Maxine went on to explain how the encounter turned her life around.

'It was like therapy, yeh see. I took out all me latent anger on me punters. Of course, I've had counsellin' since, but that was the start of it. I got rid a' me hatred for men,' she said. 'An' the bastards paid me for the bleedin' privilege!'

'But don't you ever get afraid, dealing with weirdos?'

'Oh, they're not all weirdos. They just got hang ups. Some folk go to a shrink. Others comes t' me. I'm even fond of some a' them. They're all regulars. They tell me about their wives, grandchildren, the lot.'

Gilda and Jojo joined them at that point and dragged them both back on to the dance floor. Spike was in top form and the music was terrific. Hector was having a ball being as outrageous as ever.

Just after ten, hot and breathless after dancing non-stop, Alice escaped to the sanctuary of the fire escape to cool down. Conor joined her a short time later. 'Is there room for a little one?' he asked, handing her a fresh bottle of beer. Alice moved over and he sat down next to her. 'Did you enjoy your wedding?' he asked.

'Did you?'

He put his arm round her shoulder and gave her a squeeze. 'Yes, thanks. Lots.'

He was bursting with happiness. It had been a perfect day. He rotated the wedding ring on his finger. It was identical to the one he had put on Hector's finger only five hours before. Alice had insisted on something cheap and understated for herself.

They sat in silence, aware of the party noises from inside the Samovar and the traffic sounds on the street. 'You know you're in danger of becoming a gay icon?' Conor qualified the statement, 'In a very small, local way.'

'Should I be pleased about that?' Alice was amused.

'Absolutely. You're in good company.'

'Oh?'

'Yeah. You and Judy Garland. You know yourself. You've

been going around with queens long enough to know the score.'

Alice grinned at him, secretly quite pleased.

He felt a sudden surge of warmth towards her. After a few minutes he said, 'Alice, we're friends, aren't we?'

'Yes. Of course. Didn't I give you away at your wedding?'

Conor decided it was time to be assertive. 'Well, would you do something for me?'

Considering his last major request, Alice was suddenly a wee bit wary. 'I don't know. What is it?'

'Would you come down home with me next Sunday?'

'Em . . . I suppose so . . . Why?'

'I want to tell my folks. I want them to know about Hector and me.'

Alice, who had just taken a long swallow from her bottle of Miller, choked. Beer gushed down her nose and Conor had to wallop her on the back before she recovered enough breath to say, 'Jesus, Conor! They don't even know you're gay. Don't you think that's just a tad too much information in one go?'

'Declan knows,' he said defensively.

'Is that so? Well, if he's so approving, how come he isn't here?'

'Because he's away in New York.'

'But you told him about Hector?'

'Not exactly,' Conor hedged.

'How, not exactly?'

'Okay, so he doesn't know about Hector,' Conor admitted. 'But he was the one who convinced me to come clean with myself and admit I'm gay. He was the one who said I should be true to my feelings.'

'But presumably not to the point of telling your folks.'

'Well, now you come to mention it.'

'So why now?'

'Why do you think? If you got married . . . I mean *really* . . . wouldn't you want your folks to meet your partner, the person you love more than anyone?'

'Bit difficult. They're both dead.'

'Now you're splitting hairs,' Conor sulked. 'You're just like Declan. What *is* your problem?'

Alice sighed. 'Hey, at the end of the day, it's nothing to do with me, Conor. If you want to tell your folks, tell them. All I'm saying is, go a bit easy on them. One thing at a time, eh?'

'But what about Hector?'

Alice put her arm around his shoulder. 'Like I said, one thing at a time. Let them get used to the idea that you're gay before you hit them with Hector.'

'You think?'

Alice nodded. 'Absolutely.'

He frowned, considering her advice for a moment, then nodded. 'And you'll come with me?'

Mellowed by seven bottles of Miller and warmed by affectionate friendship and her newly elevated gay-icon status, Alice agreed.

Chapter Eight

As neither of them owned a car, Conor and Alice took the train to Tanagh. It was a complicated business necessitating a change of trains at Port Arlington and a one-hour-and-forty-minute bus journey from Killmuchross to Tanagh. It took half the day as none of the connections were synchronised. They set themselves up for the odyssey by indulging in a huge fry-up in the train's buffet car.

Conor was sick with anxiety. Half of him was excited at the thought of coming out to his parents, of ending the lies. The other half was terrified that they would hate him. Unknown to Alice, he hadn't only invited her along to Tanagh for moral support, he was banking on her presence preventing a scene should things go against him. He knew his parents were far too polite and hospitable to have a row in front of a guest, and a stranger to boot.

Despite Declan's assertion that he should keep his parents ignorant, he'd tried many times to pluck up the courage to tell them, but had always chickened out at the last minute. He knew exactly what he wanted to say, rehearsed it word for word, but when the time came, the words wouldn't come out of his mouth, his throat constricted and he ended up waffling on about anything bar what he really wanted to say. This time it would be different. This time he was determined.

The bus finally pulled up outside Tanagh Parochial Hall at four-fifteen. 'I can't believe it took us seven hours to get here,' Alice griped. 'We'd be in New York sooner.'

'There's Da.' Conor gave a wave in the general direction of a group of men who were standing at the corner of the church, talking. A large stocky man detached himself from the group and ambled over.

'Is it yerself, son?' he said, clapping Conor on the back. 'And who's this?'

'This is Alice.'

'Yer welcome, Alice.' Mick pumped her arm nearly out of its socket. He nudged Conor and gave him an exaggerated wink. 'Any friend of Con's is welcome in our house.'

Conor recognised the inference, but let it go.

Mick took Alice's overnight bag and strode off towards the Land Rover. Conor and Alice followed. As soon as they were installed in the front seat Mick set off like a bat out of hell. Alice, sitting in the middle of the bench seat, hung on to Conor who, in turn, hung on to the passenger door. The journey to chez Finn proved not to be by the direct route. After two minutes of a white-knuckle ride, with G forces in excess of those on the space shuttle, Mick screeched to a halt outside Tommy Flannery's Select Lounge & Bar.

'Are we not going straight home?' Conor asked.

Mick opened the door and hopped out. 'I've a surprise for yeh. Come on in to Tommy's, the two a' ye.' He marched over to the pub and disappeared inside.

'Now's your chance,' Alice said. 'He'll be more relaxed after a pint.'

Conor hesitated. 'I think I'll wait till I've got him and Mam together.' Now that the act of coming out was no longer theoretical, now that he was home, he was getting cold feet. He helped Alice down and they followed Mick into the pub. It took a moment for their eyes to become accustomed to the dimness. Nothing had changed since his last visit. Tommy Flannery's was a fairly typical rural pub. Middle-aged farmers in their Sunday suits leaning against the bar giving out about the Common Agricultural Policy and farm subsidies over pints of the black stuff.

Mick was over in the corner. He beckoned. Suddenly Conor saw a familiar face. 'Bloody hell. I don't believe it.' He bounded over to where Mick was standing with a tall, dark, good-looking man. 'Jesus! Declan! I thought you were in the Big Apple?'

Declan thumped him on the back then they hugged each other. 'I'm back since this morning,' he said.

'He's got a big job up in Cork,' Mick said proudly. 'Sure he couldn't stay away.'

'Yeh look like a bloody Yank!' Conor walloped his brother on the shoulder. 'The state a' yeh.' Suddenly Conor's accent had reverted to its roots. He was delighted. He hadn't seen big brother for a good eighteen months.

Alice was standing, feeling awkward, a little apart from the group. Declan caught her eye. 'Who's this?'

Conor introduced Alice, this time qualifying the introduction by saying, 'We're old friends.'

Declan shook her hand and smiled. 'Pleased to meet you, Alice.'

His handshake was firm and he looked her straight in the eye. He wasn't at all what she had expected. He was no babe, but nice-looking all the same. In fact, he bore more than a passing resemblance to Mick – tall, though a much younger, leaner, fitter version. Alice estimated he was about twenty-nine or thirty.

Conor went to the bar to get the drinks in. His stomach was still churning in anticipation. He ordered two pints of Guinness for himself and his da, a gin and tonic for Alice, a pint of Smithwicks for Declan as well as a shot of Bushmills which he knocked back to try and calm the butterflies. He wondered, as he waited for the Guinness to settle, if this would be his last visit home. Would Mick go off the deep end? He was losing his nerve fast. He looked over at Alice. She was chatting away to Mick and Declan. She looked over at him and smiled.

'Home for the big reunion, are ye?' the barman asked as he handed the pints across the bar.

'Right enough,' Conor replied.

He carried the drinks over to the table and sat beside Alice. Sensing his nervousness, she squeezed his hand. An action that didn't go unnoticed by Mick. Conor and Declan slagged each other off for about fifteen minutes. Mick looked on, proud as punch to have both his sons home (and Conor with a woman). After a while Mick went off to phone Maura to check on what time the dinner would be ready and Conor went up to the bar to get one for the road. Declan and Alice were left alone.

'So what's the story?' a now earnest Declan asked, as soon as they were out of earshot.

Alice didn't know what to say. She wasn't certain it was her place to tell Declan of Conor's plan to confess all to his parents.

'Come on. I know something's up,' he persisted. 'Conor never brings anyone home, especially a woman.'

To hell with it, Alice thought. 'He's involved with someone. He has a partner. He wants to come out to your parents. That's all.'

Declan was appalled. 'You're not serious!'

'Serious about what? Conor having a partner, or about him telling your parents he's gay?' Declan's attitude was pissing her off.

'You know what I mean,' Declan growled. 'He can't tell Mam and Da! Da'll go ballistic and it'll kill Mam.'

'Don't take that tone with me!' Alice hissed. 'I just came to give him moral support.'

'Why? What business is it of yours?'

'He's my friend,' Alice snapped. 'That's what friends do.' Mick and Conor were on their way back from the bar.

Declan leaned towards her and grabbed her arm. 'You've got to stop him! Get him to leave well alone.'

'So what's with all the serious talk?' Mick asked as he set the glasses down on the table. 'We'll have none a' that serious talk here t'day.'

They sat down and Mick asked Conor how he thought the Dubs would do this year and if he thought Kerry had a chance. They discussed the matter in some detail. Neither of them noticed the looks that Declan was shooting Conor's way. Mick was clearly relishing the fact that he was discussing manly things for once with his younger son.

Eventually Mick looked at his watch and drained his glass.

'Well, lads, the dinner should be on the table any minute now. We'd better make tracks or yer mother'll skin us alive.'

Declan insisted that Conor ride with him in the back of the Land Rover on the way home. Alice had no doubts about why. On the journey, with Mick achieving speeds in excess of warp-drive seven along the narrow lanes leading to the Finn farm, Declan pleaded with Conor to change his mind. But to no avail. Conor was adamant.

'It's a time to end the lies, Declan. You said it yourself, I am what God made me.' His courage was increasing in direct proportion the amount of alcohol being absorbed into his bloodstream.

'Aw, come on, man! You can't. The old man'll go mad, and what about Mam? It'll kill her. She'll be mortified. This is Tanagh we're talking about, not Dublin, for God's sake. They won't understand.' He paused, clinging to the side of the Land Rover as Mick tore along the lanes. 'They'll think it's their fault.' Here Declan clutched at a straw. 'And what about Da's heart? You know his heart's not the best.'

Conor sat saying nothing. He hadn't banked on Declan being home, and much as he was glad to see him, he wondered why he had to choose this weekend above all others. They were approaching the farm gate now and Mick slammed on the brakes, lurching the two men up against the cab. Declan moved towards the back to get out and open the gate. 'Please, Conor. Don't do it,' he said, then he opened the tail-gate and jumped out.

Despite Declan's plea, Conor was still resolute. He felt he owed it to Hector, to himself. He started to hum 'I am what I am' just to boost his courage. The Land Rover took off again and Conor saw his brother close the gate and walk up the drive after them. He was sorry that he wasn't going to get any support from Declan, but so be it. He'd made up his mind.

On arrival at the farm Conor introduced Alice to his mother. 'Ma, this is my friend Alice. We work together.'

Conor's mother, Maura, looked over Alice's shoulder and winked at Mick, then unexpectedly hugged her. 'An' sure you're *welcome*, Alice. Welcome, welcome, welcome.' The hugging continued for some time.

Slightly overwhelmed by the effusive, but obviously genuine welcome, Alice felt herself blushing. 'Um . . . thanks. It's lovely to be here,' she mumbled. 'Conor's told me so much about you.' This wasn't strictly true. In fact, in the six years that Alice had known Conor he'd rarely spoken about his family. They heard the front door open and Declan walked in. He shot a thunderous look at Conor and Alice but neither Maura nor Mick seemed to notice, too intent on staring at Alice. She began to feel distinctly uncomfortable.

Maura nodded and smiled. 'Now ye must be only starvin'. Get into the dining room with ye. The dinner's ready.'

Both parents were so deliriously happy to have both their sons sitting at the table that they still failed to notice the brittle atmosphere that had so very suddenly developed between them. They all sat down around the table.

Maura asked Alice all the polite questions about her family and so forth, and showed appropriate sympathy when Alice told her that both her parents were dead and, no, she didn't have brothers or sisters.

As Maura was clearing away the remains of the roast beef, and Mick was spooning out the sherry trifle into the glass dessert dishes he and Maura had been given thirty-two years before as a wedding present, Conor decided that this was the time. His father was nicely mellow after a good meal and a few drinks. His mother was in excellent humour and, despite Declan's show of non-support, he felt sure that Alice would back him up.

He looked over at Declan and Alice. Alice, figuring that this was it, smiled encouragement. Declan stiffened and a sweat broke out on his forehead and his upper lip. Undeterred, Conor took the bull by the horns. 'Mam, Da, there's something I want to tell you.'

Declan put his head in his hands. Maura gave Mick a knowing look and smiled. Mick handed round the bowls of trifle. 'D' yeh think we don't know, son?' he said, giving his wife a wink.

'You know?' Conor was stunned. 'How?'

Declan sat bolt upright and all the colour drained from his face.

'Sure, why wouldn't we?' Maura said. 'Didn't yeh say ye'd something important t'tell us, then yer father phoned me from the pub?'

'But how?' said Conor. 'How did you guess? How could you know? The wedding was only last Monday.'

Maura walked round the table and stood beside Alice's chair. As she spoke she picked up Alice's left hand. 'Sure, didn't yer father spot the ring the minute ye got off the bus.'

Conor, Alice and Declan sat, mouths agape for a full five seconds, before Maura kissed Alice on the cheek. 'Welcome to the family, Alice.'

Conor was still in a state of paralysis.

Alice's heart began to thud and her face burned scarlet. She had completely forgotten about the wedding ring, probably because it meant so little to her.

Her brain refused to engage think mode. 'Conor?' she squeaked. 'Conor, I think you'd better put your parents right.'

Conor tried to speak but no sound came out of his mouth.

'Put us right about what?' Mick looked at Conor.

Declan jumped to his feet. 'She means she wants Conor to tell you why you weren't asked to the wedding. But it was all because of Alice being an orphan. There was only the two of them and a couple of witnesses . . .' He was babbling.

'Conor?' Alice repeated with an air of desperation.

'Don't worry, son,' Mick said. He was too relieved to see his son married to worry about the fact that he and his wife hadn't been asked to the wedding. It was something he'd suspected he'd never see. Maura was of the same opinion.

It was at this point that Conor bottled out. 'Thanks, Mam. I knew ye'd understand.'

Declan sagged with relief. Alice was speechless and Maura and Conor hugged each other. Mick took out a bottle of brandy. Alice gratefully knocked back a large measure. 'Worried about meeting the in-laws, eh?' Mick winked and poured her another.

At nine, the Finn family plus one drove back down to the pub. Maura was anxious to show off her new daughter-in-law and Mick dying to tell as many people as possible about Conor's recent nuptials. Alice was mortified, but without any means of escape, had no choice but to play along.

As they walked into the pub there was a cheer. Mick, unable to contain himself, had phoned a couple of friends to share the good news. As they made their way to a table there were shouts of 'Well, Blouse, I didn't think yeh had it in yeh,' and 'Good on yeh, Blouse. Good luck, boy.'

'Why do they call you Blouse?' Alice muttered as they squeezed together on the red plush banquette.

'It's short for Big Girl's Blouse.'

'Oh.'

The following three hours were awful, the air thick with innuendo and the odd comment to the effect that they never thought they'd see the day etc. 'Probably grateful to get him,' Alice heard one girl say.

Things went from bad to worse when they got back to the farm. Maura had hastily moved Declan's things out of his room into the smaller back bedroom so Conor and Alice could have the double bed.

Alice was seething with Conor for dragging her away on a fool's errand. Even without the epic journey she'd have been annoyed.

In the early hours Conor lay awake looking at the ceiling. He heard Alice sigh in her sleep from time to time. He was disgusted with himself. But even if he could pluck up the courage, how could he tell them now? He knew he'd missed his opportunity to come clean. They thought he was married. They thought he was . . . normal. And what about Alice? What if she spilled the beans?

Alice too had a restless night, tossing and turning. She always found it hard to sleep in a strange bed. She awoke, still annoyed with Conor. Still angry about the way that he and Declan had clutched at the straw that Maura had thrust in their direction. He was the one who had been so determined to come out to his parents. He'd even wanted to tell them about

Hector, for God's sake. She could hear him gently snoring beside her. She turned on to her side and stared at his back. She wanted to hit him. But at the same time, grudgingly, she felt sorry for him. She could see his dilemma. It couldn't have been easy growing up gay in a rural community with all his father's macho expectations. Even she had noticed the pride in his parents' faces at the thought of him having a wife. A proper wife.

Conor stirred, opened his eyes, then groaned. 'Oh, God! I was hoping it was just a bad dream.'

'No such luck,' Alice said, then gave him a kick on the leg. 'The least you could do is go downstairs and make your wife a cup of tea.' She was trying to make light of it. Trying to ease his guilt and disappointment.

'You must think I'm a total spa,' he said.

'Not a *total* spa.'

He sighed. 'Oh, God. I've really blown it, haven't I? What am I going to do now? How can I tell them now?'

Alice didn't have an answer for him. It wasn't really her problem. It was only as Maura and Mick hugged her at the bus stop with promises to drop in on them next time they were up in Dublin that it occurred to her that it was very much her problem. In the space of twenty-four hours she had suddenly acquired a set of in-laws. A set of over-the-moon-that-they-had-a-daughter-in-law, hoping-for-a-grandchild kind of in-laws. She leaned her head back against the headrest. As if my life isn't complicated enough, she thought as she closed her eyes and tried to sleep.

Chapter Nine

The following week they moved into the apartment which was a pleasant change from the bedsit. It was on the second floor of a new block on Winetavern Street, though at first sight the exterior gave no hint of its recent construction, so cleverly designed was the façade. It blended in seamlessly with the adjoining Georgian buildings in the Wood Quay area, where the Vikings had first settled. Alice had a good-sized bedroom and sole use of the main bathroom, as Conor's and Hector's larger bedroom had its own en suite. There was a big living-cum-dining room with a balcony overlooking Christchurch Cathedral, and a reasonably sized, well-equipped kitchen. The décor was on the muted side for Alice's taste, mostly cream and magnolia, but it was warm, clean and comfortable.

Business was booming, partly due (unaccountably after his previous experience at the hands of Hector) to a good write-up by *The Irish Times* food critic, and partly to rapidly spreading word-of-mouth recommendation by their patrons. Because of this welcome development, Conor employed a comis-chef called Colin and another waitress, Mandy, and a washer-up called Joe. Between them, Conor and Alice revamped the menu, adding a couple of different specials every night. Another food critic, who incidentally also gave them a glowing review, described the food as *fusion cuisine*. Conor was much amused by this description.

Hector, assisted by Alice and Conor, wrote to the Department of Foreign Affairs, informing them of his recent marriage and enclosed a copy of the marriage certificate. Conor was happier than he had ever been and the only thing that could have made his happiness more complete was if he could have shared it with his parents. But he knew he'd missed his chance. It would be difficult enough to break the news to them on the basis of him being gay and with a partner, but he knew their disappointment now would be all the greater as they were so thrilled to have a daughter-in-law and the possibility of grandchildren. He put it to the back of his mind.

Alice, meanwhile, had been studying the accounts, or more accurately the pile of tattered receipts and bills that Hector kept in the shoebox under the bar. She had a good idea of the bistro's turnover so, correlating the cash receipts and the outgoings, she couldn't understand why there was so little money in the bank. It occurred to her that maybe Hector, he of the big personality but short arms as far as money was concerned (except when spending it on himself), might have deposited it in some kind of high interest savings account. She decided it was time for a meeting. She needed to know the situation. She had plans for the Samovar.

Hector, not yet accustomed to having a partner, didn't understand the concept. 'Meeting? Vy meeting? Ve see you every day.'

'We need to talk about the Samovar. I have plans,' Alice said.

Hector didn't look happy. 'You have the plans, for *my* Samovar?' He drew himself up to his full height and puffed out his chest.

'It's not *your* Samovar now, Hector. It's *our* Samovar, remember?'

Conor, noticing Hector reddening from the neck up, made the save. 'Alice only wants what's best for the Samovar, Hector. Listen to her. It can't do any harm.' When that didn't appear to appease him, he added, 'You'll make more money.'

Talk of money did the trick. 'More money? That different.' He sat down and gave Alice his undivided attention.

Alice put the shoebox on the bar along with the till receipts.

'There doesn't seem to be any of your tax stuff here,' she said.

'Vot tax?'

Alice's heart sank. 'Income tax. Tax on your profits. Don't tell me you're not registered.'

'Vot this registered? Hector no pay tax.' He folded his arms across his chest in defiance to add weight to the point.

Alice shot a dismayed look in Conor's direction. He was studying the toe of his left boot. Alice looked at the sheet of paper on which she had scribbled some salient points and made a note. *Not registered with the Revenue.* 'Okaaay. We'll deal with that later. Now.' She smiled at Hector to try and lighten the atmosphere. 'I was thinking, with what you must have put by, we could extend the restaurant. Of course we'll probably have to borrow from the bank, but the way things are going . . .'

Hector cut in, 'Vot money put by? Hector have no money put by. I not rich man.'

Frustrated, Alice picked up the till receipts and waved them at him. 'But where is it, then? It doesn't add up. What did you do with it?'

Hector hiked his shoulders and threw out his hands. 'It gone. I spend it.'

It was a simple enough answer. Alice had been expecting some sort of complicated story so he took the wind right out of her sails. 'You *spent* it?'

'Sure. I spend it.' He fingered the lapel of his jacket. 'This jacket, it raw silk. Not come cheap, the raw silk.'

'So you've no money in a building society or anything?'

Hector shook his head.

'And you probably owe thousands in tax?'

Hector shook his head again and Alice felt a twinge of hope, until he slapped his hand aggressively on the bar, rattling the stacked espresso cups. 'I no pay taxes. Taxes bad. Hector not pay.'

'But, Hector. They'll catch up with you. With us. They always do.'

Alice's plans were crumbling before her eyes. It hadn't occurred to her that Hector wouldn't have kept proper accounts or that the Revenue would have left him alone for so long. She had a strong wish to panic. 'Get a grip, get a grip,' she whispered to herself. Then aloud, 'Okay. We can sort this out. I'm sure we can sort this out.'

'I no pay taxes,' he whinged and looked over at Conor for some positive affirmation.

Conor looked on helplessly.

Hector was getting right up Alice's nose now, and Conor wasn't much better sitting there all mealy-mouthed. The Samovar was her future and she wasn't about to let an over-the-top Ukrainian mess it all up. The situation had to be salvaged.

'Shut up, Hector, and pay attention!' she snarled. Conor was startled. Hector shut up in mid-whinge. 'This can't go on. We have to do something positive. We have to increase the turnover, keep proper accounts. And you,' she looked directly into Hector's eyes, 'you have to stop treating the till as if it's your own private money box.'

Hector, surprisingly, said nothing, just assumed a hang-dog expression. Conor was still staring at the toe of his left boot.

'Right,' Alice said. 'First thing tomorrow we go to see the bank manager to try to fix up a loan and there might be some way we can do a deal with the Revenue.'

'I told you. I no pay! . . . I von't . . .'

Alice gave him a look that would strip paint and the sentence petered out. 'It's not up to you now, Hector. We're partners and equally liable. And I for one have no intention of letting this business go to the wall on account of your dubious principles.'

The rant helped to subside the panic that had risen in her chest. Hector was now also examining the toe of Conor's left boot and the room was completely silent.

It was a Zen moment.

Madame Maxine broke the spell as she bustled in the back door.

'Give us a cuppa, Conor, there's a love.'

She was dressed in her day clothes and looked very business-like and smart, carrying an expensive-looking leather briefcase. 'Just been t' the bleedin' accountants,' she said as she sat

73

herself down at a table. 'I'll have some of yer lasagne too, love, with the garlic bread if it's on today.'

Conor stood up and reached for the coffee pot.

'Is he good?' Alice asked.

Madame Max gave her a quizzical look.

'Your accountant? Is he any good with, say, tax problems?'

The dominatrix nodded her head enthusiastically. 'The best.' She leaned forward conspirationally. 'He just sorted out me last five years' accounts an' I ended up paying half what I thought I'd hafta. There's this tax amnesty on at the minute.'

Alice hadn't heard of any tax amnesty.

Seeing her surprise Madame Max continued. 'Not many people know about it. The government's kept it quiet. Richard, that's me accountant, reckons they only brought it in t' stop one a' them government scandals over TDs an' their tax affairs, what with the bleedin' election comin' up. Yeh know yerself.' She tapped the side of her nose to make the point. Nudge nudge, wink wink.

Alice shot a look at Conor. 'And d'you think he'd do our accounts?'

Madame Max took a gulp of her coffee. 'Sure, why not? Isn't that what he's in business for?' She delved into the briefcase and handed Alice a business card.

Since the one incident with the spag bol man, Joxer Boxer had been well behaved, mainly because Alice hadn't given him any excuse to kick off. She made up a reserved sign and placed it on table six every night just before midnight, just in case. He came in most nights around twelve-thirty and ordered, as ever, the steak au poivre. He was polite when ordering, but always left without paying. Alice supposed he must work nights, probably as a bouncer or something. Neither Conor nor Hector seemed to know anything about him other than that he was not to be messed with. The situation annoyed Alice but, ever the pragmatist, she realised that five or six steaks a week was a small price to pay for keeping the peace.

That evening, as she went through the usual charade of giving him the menu, allowing him time to peruse it, then returning to the table to take his usual order, Joxer departed from the normal routine by saying, 'Place has changed, wha'?'

Alice looked at him blankly. Joxer swept his paw around in an arc to indicate that he was referring to the Samovar.

'Oh . . . yes. We . . . um . . . we decorated. Cleaned the place up a bit.' She gave a nervous laugh.

Joxer nodded. 'Must be doin' a lot better these days then? Hope the big fairy give you a rise.' He grinned.

'We're partners,' Alice said proudly. 'Hector's my partner now . . . business partner, that is.'

Joxer gave a guffaw. 'Hardly yer fella, wha'?'

Alice cleared her throat. 'Um . . . the steak au poivre, is it?'

Joxer ignored the question. 'So I suppose yer makin' money now, wha' with all the changes?'

Not sure where this was leading, Alice gave a shrug. 'Well, not that much. It'll take time to build the business up, but we've got plans.'

Joxer nodded. 'Good. I like t' see a place makin' money . . . I'll have the usual.'

Wondering what that was all about, Alice took his order to the kitchen. She hoped Joxer didn't fancy her. She hoped his attempts at conversation weren't a prelude to him making any further advances. She shuddered at the thought. How would she handle that? Still, she had other more important things on her mind. The tax man for one.

Hector was subdued. It wasn't that he disapproved of borrowing money, he just wasn't that keen on spending it refurbishing and extending the Samovar. There were far better things, to his mind, on which to spend money. Clothes, perhaps, champagne, vodka, the odd snort of recreational drugs.

Alice had laid out her plans to him and to Conor the night before and Hector had been impressed to a point. Knocking through to the back room to enlarge the bistro made sense as there'd be room for twice as many punters so they should make more money. But what was the point when she was determined to give it to the Revenue? Then there were her plans for the basement. A private drinking club for the well-off thirty-something beneficiaries of the fruits of the Celtic Tiger?

'They've money to burn,' she'd said enthusiastically. 'We can give them somewhere exclusive and classy to go to after work.'

'But it cost money,' he'd protested predictably.

'You have to speculate to accumulate, Hector. I know what I'm talking about. Trust me.'

The door opened and a thin, balding, bespectacled man in a pin-striped suit stuck his head out. 'Mr and Mrs Hanusiak?' he enquired. 'Sorry for the delay.'

Mr Henderson was dwarfed by his huge dark wood desk, the top of which was scrupulously tidy. 'Please take a seat,' he invited, straightening a biro into perfect alignment with the top of his blotter. 'I understand you are seeking a loan, am I right?'

Alice thought his tone rather condescending. It was a bad start. Beside the blotter was a neatly folded computer printout. Alice took a surreptitious squint and saw Hector's name. Obviously his bank records. She felt some assertiveness was called for. Positive action.

'Absolutely right, Mr Henderson.'

Henderson gave her a gracious nod.

'We have plans to extent the bistro.' She opened her bag, took out her business plan and slid it across the desk. Henderson took it and she saw him scanning the first page. 'As you can see, with the extra seating capacity, the projected turnover is greatly increased, as at the moment we don't have the space to meet current demand at our peak hours. In short, Mr Henderson, we're turning customers away. And I'm confident that if we extend, refurbish and refit, we can not only cater for those people but also for many more new customers.' She paused for a moment to give him a chance to read down the page. 'If you turn to the next page you'll see my estimate of the cost involved and the projected profits.'

Henderson nodded his head then cast his eyes down again and turned the page. Alice looked over at Hector and smiled. After a while Henderson looked up. 'This is a very good plan, Mrs Hanusiak. I can see you've thought this through from every aspect, but I'm afraid there's still the matter of the outstanding loan.'

Alice was confused. 'The outstanding loan? There must be some mistake.' She looked over at Hector again. He was smiling and nodding like an eejitt.

Henderson said, 'The term loan. The loan for three thousand pounds taken out by you, Mr Hanusiak.' He looked over at Hector. 'Last year?'

'Da, da. The money for the car. I get money for car.'

'That's right, Mr Hanusiak. But I'm afraid you're in arrears.'

'Vot?'

Alice cut in. 'How much exactly is the amount outstanding?' A hollow feeling was invading her gut.

Henderson glanced down at the printout. 'As of the end of business yesterday, two thousand eight hundred and ninety-four pounds.'

She wanted to be sick. She had a frozen smile on her face. 'Okay. Then I suppose the best way to handle this is for us to pay off the outstanding amount out of the new loan.' It was her best shot.

The bank manager straightened the biro again. It was at least one hundredth of a millimetre out of alignment with the top of the blotter. 'Um, I'm afraid it's not as simple as that, Mrs Hanusiak. You see, your creditworthiness is in question here. I'm afraid, all things considered, we can't offer you finance at this time.' He pushed the business plan back across the desk towards Alice. 'However, if over the next, say, twelve months, matters improve and you can prove to be a better risk, we can look at your proposal again in a more favourable light.'

'But the bistro's under new management now. Couldn't I take out the loan? Couldn't you lend the money to *me*?' She knew she sounded desperate.

Henderson shook his head and stood up to signify that the meeting was at an end. 'I'm sorry.'

Alice left the office, mortified. Hector looked as if he didn't give a damn. 'Why the hell didn't you tell me about the car loan?' she raged as soon as they were on the street.

Hector lifted his shoulders in an exaggerated shrug. 'Vot it matter? Ve okay as ve are.'

'No, we're not okay as we bloody are, Hector. I had plans.' She was standing on the pavement with her hands on her hips, caring nothing for the glances of the passing pedestrians. 'I had big plans.'

Hector curled his lip. 'You had plans,' he said disdainfully. 'Alvays it vot you vant.'

That hit a nerve. At once on the defensive Alice stood her ground. 'We had a deal, Hector. If it wasn't for me you'd be back in the bloody Ukraine. Your feet wouldn't have touched the floor before the immigration bods would've dumped you on an Aeroflot jet down in Shannon.'

'If it vasn't for you? I don't need you.' His lip curled as he said the words. 'If Immigration come for me, I go to London. I go somevare, but I not go back to Ukraine.'

Alice couldn't have been more stunned if he had hit her in the face. 'But what about the Samovar? What about Conor?'

Hector hiked his shoulders again.

'But I thought you married me to stay here? To stay with Conor?'

'I did. I did. But this before you are bitch, spending all my money.'

In one way, even though she was almost incandescent with rage, Alice could see his point of view. The new regime in the Samovar must have been a bit of a culture shock to him. The prospect of losing the privilege to take money (money he considered to be his) at will must have been daunting for the likes of Hector, whose lifestyle was, as their current difficulties proved, way above his means.

'Look, Hector. I know this is difficult for you. And I appreciate how you feel.'

Hector's eyes narrowed and he pursed his lips. 'You paronise me now.'

'No. No, really, Hector. I'm not trying to patronise you, but the point is, if we don't do something, and something fast, there won't be any Samovar. It's for your good as well as mine.

In the end you'll be better off. You'll have a lot more money. Real money. Money the tax people can't take away from you.'

As usual talk of more money calmed Hector down. Alice saw his expression soften at the mention of it. She pressed the advantage home. 'In time, maybe, you'll have a chain of bistros. Who knows?'

That all this was impossible without the bank loan, for which they had just been turned down, was beside the point. She was trying to calm him down. Trying to get him to see that staying was a better option than running. That pulling in his horns was a better option than the Samovar going bust. The last thing Alice wanted was for Hector to bolt. Not that she cared that much about him on a personal level. He was okay, but the charming over-the-top persona was wearing a bit thin on her now, particularly in the light of his revelation that he was prepared to up sticks and hop it without a thought for Conor, even in the knowledge of how much Conor loved him. She'd never forgive herself if Hector bolted on account of her. Conor would be devastated.

She softened her tone and, playfully punching him on the arm, cajoled, 'Come on, Hector. Let's go back to the Samovar and have a drink. I'm sure we can come up with some plan that'll suit you.'

Fat chance.

Because she thought the circumstances a bit suspicious, Carmel McGuire passed on the papers to Sean Holland. 'I'm not sure if it's legit,' she said, handing him the photocopied documents. 'The timing's a little coincidental, don't you think?'

He took the papers from her hand. 'How long have we been looking for him?' he asked.

'We haven't actively been looking for him at all,' she said, referring to an A4 sheet of paper still on her desk. 'His appeal against deportation just floated to the top of the pile. You know what the backlog's been like these last few months.'

She didn't need to tell him. The department was horren-dously short staffed, what with the moratorium on recruitment and the increasing case load. 'So what are his grounds for appeal?'

'Says he's a political, but there's no proof of that. I sent out the stock letter asking him to come in and see me.' She handled Holland a further scrap of paper. 'But he sent in this sick note, then a couple of weeks later he writes in and sends those.' She indicated the photocopied certificates in his hand. 'Now I suppose we'll have to start again on account of the marriage. What do you think?'

Sean Holland studied the marriage certificate and the accompanying birth certificate. He shrugged. 'I suppose we'd better do a home visit and check it out,' he said. 'The last thing we need right now is another fiasco like the Mulligan case.'

He was referring to a case some months before when a Nigerian national married to an Irish woman had been deported on the grounds that his was a marriage of convenience. He'd been frog-marched from his home at six one morning and put on a plane. Then, tipped off by the Mulligan family, the press had got hold of the story and unearthed documents not previously produced, proving that if the man returned to Nigeria there was every chance that he would be executed as a dissident. Apparently his family were heavily involved in some anti-government group. Then Angela Mulligan, clutching her new-born baby son, held a press conference and claimed that the Department of Foreign Affairs had been well aware of her husband's probable fate, a fact they strenuously denied. Holland knew that the most likely explanation (not for public consumption) was that the documents had probably been either misfiled or, worse, mislaid. Fortunately, as soon as Holland became aware of the developing situation, he'd managed to have the man taken off the connecting flight for Nigeria at Heathrow, with only minutes to spare, and returned to Dublin. The ensuing media furore had made the department look like heartless thugs. And in one of the tabloids it was obliquely suggested that their motives were racist.

'What's he like, this . . .' he glanced at the paper, '. . . this Hector Hanusiak?'

'I haven't met him, it was one of James Godley's cases.' She crossed herself. 'God rest him.'

Holland nodded. 'Okay. I'll do a home visit in the morning then. How are you fixed?'

Alice and Hector returned to the Samovar just as the lunchtime rush was drawing to a close. Conor was still finishing up in the kitchen so Alice set about sorting out the lunchtime dockets. Mandy and Joan were resetting the tables for the evening trade. Hector went behind the bar and poured himself a large brandy, then sat quietly sulking. Although Alice had managed to calm him down, he was still smarting from their altercation.

Alice had decided to ignore Hector, who was in the grip of a huge sulk.

Just as Mandy and Joan were finishing up, Madame Maxine strolled in through the back door, poured herself a cup of coffee and sat up at the bar with Hector. She gave Alice a wave which Alice returned.

A minute later Conor came out of the kitchen. 'You're back.' He sounded surprised. He couldn't fail to read Hector's grumpy expression or notice that Alice wasn't particularly jumping for joy. 'How did you get on?'

Alice shook her head. 'No luck.' She shot a look over at Hector who was carefully setting up the chess board to continue an unfinished game with Madame Max. 'Henderson won't give us the money on account of the little matter of a previous unpaid loan.'

'What?'

Alice filled him in, trying desperately not to sound judgemental in case she set Hector off again.

Madame Maxine moved a piece on the chess board. 'Checkmate,' she said and Hector slapped his hand to his head and groaned.

'So what do we do now?' Conor said.

Alice sighed and sat down at a table. 'I don't know. I suppose we could try somewhere else, but the question is, where?'

Chapter Ten

Alice arrived back at the apartment just before two-thirty a.m. after the evening shift, alone. Conor and Hector had gone out on the town. She wasn't in the mood and anyway she was angry with Hector for screwing up the best opportunity she'd had in a long time. She was depressed. Why was it, she pondered miserably, that just as things were looking promising on the career front, they were falling apart again?

She ran the bath, lit candles, and opened a bottle of wine then lay back in the bubbles and reviewed the situation. Roddy had completely scuppered her chances in the rag trade, in Dublin at any rate. That was cruel. But what was more so was that the perfect opportunity in the shape of the Samovar had presented itself briefly, only to be snatched away again just as she reached out to take it.

Fact one: life is cruel.

Fact two: life is fucking cruel.

She took another slug of wine and her thoughts turned to Patricia. It was a long time since she'd thought of her stepmother. Perhaps it was the notion of life being cruel that brought her to mind. Memories of the hostel on Leeson Street came flooding back. In some ways it hadn't been that bad, and it was certainly better than being confined to a garret out in Blackrock, the poor relation. And school was okay too. She'd enjoyed school and, being quite bright, was looking forward to perhaps going on to college, so it was a complete bombshell when Patricia had turned up on her sixteenth birthday to announce that she was starting work the following Monday at Dunning's department store in the ladies' wear department. Patricia had fixed it up through a friend of hers. It was a bolt out of the blue, Alice was devastated. She had protested, cried, argued that she wanted to go on to college, to make something of herself, but Patricia was having none of it.

'You think I can afford to keep you indefinitely?' she said. 'I think I've done enough. It's time for you to earn your own living. I'll pay your keep here for another month, then you must make your own arrangements.' And that was that. The wicked stepmother was adamant that not another penny would be spent. On her behalf, one of Alice's teachers made enquiries about grants, but to no avail. As Patricia was of sufficient means, and still Alice's legal guardian, there was nothing to be done. Alice had to bite the bullet and accept the situation. She hadn't laid an eye on her stepmother since and had no wish to.

Alice poured the last dregs of the wine into her glass. The water was cooling off so she topped it up and lay back wallowing in hot water and self-pity, a lethal combination. Fortunately the bath was neither deep enough nor long enough to put her in any danger of drowning, because she awoke at four-thirty, frozen stiff, wrinkled like a prune and with the hangover from hell.

Conor came in around eight with a mug of coffee and a piece of toast on a plate. He pulled the curtains back and sat on the end of her bed. 'Had a great night last night,' he said enthusiastically. 'Went to Raynards. Hector was in much better form after it.'

Alice struggled into a sitting position, screwing up her eyes against the light, and reached out for the coffee. 'Well, bully for Hector.'

Conor was anxious. He was worried by Hector's obvious antagonism towards Alice that he had displayed the night before over the first couple of drinks until the alcohol had lightened his mood. He wanted them to get on. After his parents they were the two most important people in his life. He tried the conciliatory route. 'He'll get used to the idea, you know, Alice. Having a partner's a new deal to him. He's not used to it. You'll have to make allowances for him for the time being.' Alice gave him a withering look and reached for the coffee mug. 'Anyway,' Conor said, getting up and heading for the door, 'why don't you stay there for a while? You look like you could do with a lie-in and we'll manage up until lunchtime.'

'Well, if you're sure,' she said. She knew Conor was only humouring her, but never one to look a gift horse in the mouth, she snuggled under the duvet. Let Hector do a bit of work for a change. It would do him good.

She awoke again at ten-thirty and had a long shower and washed her hair. She felt better. Not so grumpy at any rate. As she finished dressing the intercom buzzer buzzed. She pressed the button. 'Hello?'

'Is that you, Alice?' Immediately she recognised Maura Finn's voice. She thought about denying all knowledge of Alice Little, aka Alice Finn to those who took a drink in Tommy Flannery's pub, but realised it was futile. 'Hello, Maura.'

She let Maura into the building and went out to wait for her by the lift. Maura appeared a minute later, laden with shopping bags and full of enthusiasm. 'Em ... Conor's not here, Maura.' A look of abject disappointment crossed Maura's face. 'When did you come up?' Alice asked, leading the way back into the apartment. And more worryingly, 'Where are you staying?'

'I came up this morning,' she said, adding conspiratorially, 'I shouldn't really be here. I'm supposed to be at an Irish County Women's meeting, but I thought, how can I be in Dublin and not visit my son and his new wife?'

'How indeed?'

Maura plonked herself down on the sofa and kicked off her shoes. 'So, how are you getting on? How does married life suit you?'

'Fine,' Alice said feebly. 'Em ... would you like a cup of tea ... ? Em ... the thing is, Conor's gone straight to the Samovar. He won't be back here at all before lunch ...'

Maura shrugged. 'Never mind. I'll pop along there later. In fact, I booked myself in there for dinner with five of my friends, but don't say a word to Conor. It's to be a surprise.'

'Oh, it'll be that all right,' Alice said. 'I'll make the tea. Where did you say you were staying?'

Maura followed her into the kitchen. 'We're all going back tonight. We hired a bus. We do it every year.'

Alice made the tea and rooted out an unopened packet of Jaffa Cakes. Maura was good at talking. In fact, if there was a donkey in the vicinity, it would have been well advised to get as far away as possible to avoid having the hind leg talked off it. She hardly paused for breath. This suited Alice. There was no way she would be rude to Conor's mother. After all, the woman meant well, and she was under the impression that Alice was now her daughter-in-law. Maura talked on. Alice took a drink of her tea just as Maura nudged her in the ribs and said, 'An'thin' stirrin'?'

Alice choked. 'What? Um . . .'

Maura was having none of it. 'Aw, come on . . . Yeh can tell me, sure I won't say it to a soul.'

'No, really, Maura. Really. I'm not pregnant.' She felt a cold sweat break out on her forehead.

Her newly adopted mother-in-law's face dropped, then she recovered. 'Well, early days yet.' She patted Alice's hand. 'The clock's tickin', though. Yeh wouldn't want t' be leavin' it too long, now.'

'No. No, of course not.'

The door buzzed again. Alice was grateful for a reason to escape the talk of babies. She excused herself and fled into the hall. As she hit the intercom someone tapped on the door of the apartment. She opened the door.

Sean Holland was taken aback when he recognised Alice. 'Oh . . . hello . . . um . . . Alice, isn't it? I'm sorry, I must have the wrong address. I was looking for Hector Hanusiak.'

'What?' Alice was confused. Why would Paula Holland's brother be looking for Hector?

'Sorry.' He looked at a document in his hand and checked the number in the apartment door. The two tallied. 'Does Hector Hanusiak live here?'

Alice glanced over her shoulder conscious of Maura in the

sitting room. She lowered her voice. 'Eh, yes. But he's out. What did you want him for?'

Holland's face registered surprise. What was she doing here? Then the name registered. Hector Hanusiak was married to an Alice Little. 'Are you his wife?' Surprised.

Alice was now very anxious to get rid of him. 'Yes, as a matter of fact. What business is it of yours?'

Holland, still rather nonplussed, took out his ID. 'Um, I'm with the Department of Foreign Affairs,' he said. 'Eh, I suppose you're aware that Mr Hanusiak is claiming residency?'

Alice was paralysed. From the sitting room, she heard Maura. 'Who's that? Is that Conor?'

'No, Maura . . . It's okay,' she muttered. Sean Holland was staring at her, obviously waiting to be asked inside. 'Eh . . . yes, of course I know, but my husband's not here. He's at the restaurant getting ready to open up for lunch.' Her voice was two octaves higher than normal. 'Do you want to leave a message for him?'

'The restaurant?'

'The Samovar, in Leeson Street,' Alice said, quietly cringing, as to her knowledge residency applicants were not supposed to work.

The civil servant appeared to let that pass. He looked over her shoulder into the hall. 'I really wanted to interview the two of you together . . . You and your husband.'

Alice cringed again. 'Em . . . er . . . the thing is, my stepmother's just dropped by, and . . . em . . . er, well, the thing is . . .' Alice looked furtively over her shoulder.

'Are you all right? You don't look well.'

'I'm fine,' Alice said, her voice almost falsetto by this time. 'It's just . . . well, my . . .' She lowered her voice and leaned towards him. 'My stepmother and I don't get on. We were in the middle of a row . . .'

'Alice?' The door of the sitting room opened and Maura came out into the hall. 'Oh, who's this?'

'Eh . . . So I'll get my husband to . . . em . . . to call you to arrange another time, shall I?' Alice said, bypassing Maura's question. Tension was oozing out of her every pore.

Sean Holland looked at Maura and then back at Alice. He handed her a card. 'The visits are supposed to be unscheduled, you underst—'

'Oh, right,' Alice cut across him. She was bordering on manic now. 'No worries. But my husband . . . We're usually at the restaurant between ten and three, and then between six and whenever . . . Just so you know . . .'

He was staring at her. Alice wasn't surprised. She must have sounded like a mad woman. Later it occurred to her that that was probably a good thing. I mean, who but a mad woman would marry Hector Hanusiak?

The bemused civil servant was left staring at the door as it closed in his face. He was still not over the surprise of finding Alice there. If truth be told he was also a little disappointed. He'd been quite attracted to her on the couple of occasions that they had literally bumped into each other. There was something about her. But then, when she had careered into him at TransV, and he'd seen her in the company of the large scary-looking blonde woman, he had wondered if she was perhaps gay. If that was the case what was she doing married to the Ukranian? Unless, of course, it was a marriage of convenience. He headed back to the office to discuss the matter with Carmel McGuire.

'Who was that, dear?' Maura quizzed.

'Oh, just someone looking for Hec— for Conor. Nothing important.' She could feel perspiration breaking out on her forehead. 'More tea?'

By the time Maura's cab arrived, Alice was stressed out. Maura kissed her on the cheek. 'I'll see you later, Alice. Now not a word to Conor. I want to see the look on his face when I walk in tonight.'

Alice promised to keep 'their little secret'. As soon the lift doors closed, however, she rushed back inside the apartment and phoned the Samovar to warn Hector and Conor about Sean Holland.

'He won't come here,' Conor assured her. 'It's supposed to

be a home visit. You know? A visit at *home*. To make sure you're living together?'

'You don't get it, do you?' she raged. 'It was Sean Holland. The sister of the guy who Susan gave my room to. Remember?'

'So?'

'So . . . I don't know. What if he talks to Susan about me? She knows I wasn't even going out with anyone when I was living there.'

Conor didn't get the point. 'So?'

'So he's from the Immigration hit-squad, you eejitt. It's probably in his job description to be suspicious. Even looking at it in a charitable light, Hector and I getting married's a bit on the whirlwind side, don't you think? The story was that we were supposed to have known each other ages, or had you forgotten?'

The implications still hadn't hit Conor. He made light of it. 'So it was love at first sight. It's not so far-fetched. That's how it happened to me. You know Hector. He's irresistible.'

'Don't get snotty with *me*, Conor, not after the couple of hours I've just had.' She went on to tell him about Maura's visit. Why should she be the only one on stress overload? For some reason, known only to himself, Conor thought it was funny. Alice was incensed. 'Okay, sunshine! You think it's so funny. Maybe I'll tell her the truth when she and her five buddies come in for dinner tonight!'

'My mother's coming to the Samovar?' He didn't sound so amused now.

'That's right. Her and five of her ICA sisters.'

'Oh, shit!' There was silence the other end of the line for a full minute. Then she heard Conor clear his throat. 'Please, Alice. I'm sorry. Please don't say anything to her.'

'What happened to all the *I can't live a lie* crap?'

'So I'm not good at confrontation,' Conor whined. 'Please, Alice.'

Alice relented. 'Oh, all right. But you'd better get Hector ready for this home visit. Tell him what to say and make sure he'll behave himself, or they'll sling him out of the country and probably sling me in jail.'

Too angry and irritated to do the lunchtime shift, Alice stayed home and watched daytime TV, and only put in an appearance at the Samovar in time for the evening shift. Happily by the end of the night the atmosphere between Hector and herself had thawed somewhat, mainly because he had become so carried away by his Mister Nice Guy image when Maura and her friends arrived that he forgot that he was peeved with her. For her part, as she hated a bad atmosphere, she went along with it. Conor affected utter surprise and there was much hugging when he was called out of the kitchen by Hector. Alice introduced Hector as an old and valued friend and the ladies of Tanagh were utterly charmed.

As it was a relatively quiet night, they closed the doors at one-thirty, but not before Madame Maxine came down for her nightcap.

'Listen t' me,' she started. 'I couldn't help overhearin' yeh talkin' the other day about yer loan an' how ye were turned down.'

She had both Alice's and Conor's full attention, but Hector was too busy rooting out the chess board, still smarting from the metaphorical beating the dominatrix had given not two days before.

'So, anyways, what's yeer bank?'

Conor told her, then added the 'Baggot Street branch'.

'Thought so,' Madame Max said smugly. 'This Henderson. He's a small thin baldy fella with glasses, right?'

'Right,' Alice said. 'D'you know him?'

Madame Max hiked herself up on to the bar stool and picked up one of the pawns between her finger and thumb, placing it on the board in reply to Hector's opening move. 'Oh, I know 'im all right.' She grinned. 'Yeh should go an' see 'im again. Just mention my name. That'll do the trick.'

Chapter Eleven

Carmel McGuire was convinced that Hector Hanusiak's marriage was suspect, particularly when Holland mentioned his suspicion that Alice might be gay.

'Well, there you are,' she'd said triumphantly. 'That proves it.'

Suddenly Holland wasn't quite so sure. 'I said *might* be gay. I'm not certain about it,' he prevaricated. It was for this reason that he was making his way across town to visit Paula and to ask Susan and Brenda a couple of casual questions. He didn't want to go in all guns blazing to find out that he was mistaken and the marriage was perfectly above board. The Department was fair game for another media-bashing since the Mulligan fiasco.

Paula was pleased, if not a little surprised, to see him but explained that she and her friends were going out shortly to a prayer meeting. Brenda cut in and told her not to be silly and insisted that there was plenty of time for tea. When he broached the subject of their former housemate, Brenda left him in no doubt of her opinion. The words *drink* and *weird* and *strange* came up a lot. At the same time he felt vaguely uncomfortable as she kept giggling coyly and making eyes at him, taking every opportunity to grab his arm to make a point. Susan was less nasty about her former tenant. In fact, she wasn't openly derogatory at all, but she did mention that Alice had some very strange friends, and that a previous boyfriend, whom they (she and Brenda) had really liked, had turned out to be a homosexual. In the end he was none the wiser as to where Alice's preferences lay. He decided to wait until he had done the home visit to draw any firm conclusions.

*

Alice called Mr Henderson's secretary to make the appointment and as luck would have it he had a 'window' in his diary the following afternoon. He was naturally surprised to see them back so soon.

'What can I do for you?' he asked, clasping his hands together on the desk top. Alice noted that he was careful to place his hands on the blotter, no doubt to avoid leaving any finger marks on the glossy veneered desk top.

'It's about the loan, Mr Henderson,' Alice started off. 'I was wondering if you might reconsider?'

'Reconsider?'

'Well, yes.' She looked at Hector. 'A mutual friend suggested we talk to you again. She said she couldn't understand why you turned down our application.'

Henderson shook his head. 'I'm sorry. I thought I made that clear. Your creditworthiness . . .'

Alice cut in, looking across at Hector again. 'What was it Madame Maxine said about Mr Henderson?' She glanced back at the bank manager. He was still sitting in the same position but all the colour had drained from his face.

'She say he good man. She say maybe he can vip up loan for us.'

'What?' Henderson was straining to understand Hector's fractured English. Alice couldn't even imagine what was going on in his head. She almost felt sorry for him. Well, she did feel sorry for him but that didn't affect her determination to get the loan by whatever means. 'He said Madame Maxine, oh, and her assistant Celeste, they both thought you could probably whip up a loan for us if you looked at it again.' She put particular stress on the word *whip*.

Henderson shifted in his chair. His face was tinged with grey now and Alice noticed a film of perspiration clinging to his upper lip. He cleared his throat. 'I think you're mistaken. I don't know any Madame Maxine.' He attempted to smile, but it didn't come off. Alice wasn't sure what to do next. She balked at actively threatening him. Fortunately Henderson continued, 'However, as it happens I was re-reading your proposal last night.' He coughed nervously. 'And, um . . . I think I may have been a touch hasty, particularly in view of . . . em, in view of the, um . . . the fact . . .'

Alice handed him the straw he was frantically trying to clutch. 'In view of the fact that the bistro's under new management?'

Henderson nodded, frantically mopping his brow with a handkerchief which he'd fished from his pocket. 'Precisely. New management.'

'And as I have perfectly sound creditworthiness . . .'

'Exactly.'

Even Hector, who hadn't been particularly enthusiastic about Alice's plans, was delighted that they had managed to swing (figuratively speaking) the loan. Once they were outside he picked her up and swung her around. 'Vonderful. Vonderful. Ve must celebrate. Ve need champagne. Ve drink champagne. Ve celebrate.'

Mindful of the need for fiscal rectitude, Alice was about to suggest that a quiet toast with a glass of house red might be more appropriate, but Hector's enthusiasm, when he displayed it, was infectious. They returned to the Samovar and toasted the future with an equally delighted Conor.

Later that afternoon, Alice rang a couple of builders to get estimates for the renovations.

Although they had overcome that hurdle, Conor was still concerned that the Department of Foreign Affairs could still deport Hector if they saw fit. Therefore it was more imperative than ever to get it right with their Immigration hit-squad, namely Sean Holland, when he called for the home visit. He was also on edge, fearing that the more pressing threat of deportation might cause Hector to panic. Consequently he insisted that they all sit down and thrash out a consistent story. He hired a copy of *Green Card* from the video shop and made Hector watch it several times, to get it clear in his mind the sort of questions the Immigration hit-squad would ask. He even went so far as to make them rehearse. The concocted story went as follows:

Hector and Alice had met twelve months before in Hogan's on Great George's Street. They became friends. After losing her job she went to work for him in the Samovar, and then, realising that they were deeply in love, they got married. This got over the problem of Alice having never mentioned Hector to Susan and Brenda, should Holland make enquiries about her. Hector managed to retain that much, but got confused when Conor complicated matters by asking him where he proposed to Alice, where they went on honeymoon, what first attracted him to her, etc. Alice, for her part, was becoming increasingly irritated with Conor's nit-picking of the tiny details. She recognised it as one of his less attractive traits. He retaliated by making her watch *Green Card* for the umpteenth time, just to illustrate how devious Immigration people can be. While Alice and Hector were watching the video and making notes, Conor sifted through the wedding photos and sundry other manufactured occasions, slipped the best into frames and dotted them about the room. There was a colour shot of Hector and Alice outside the registry office, smiling into the camera lens, one at the reception dancing together cheek to chest, and a third, taken on a sunny day in Dalky. They were sitting on a wall in shorts and T-shirts, squinting against the sun and smiling like lunatics. Leaving nothing to chance, he then insisted that Alice move all of her clothes out of her wardrobe and put them in his, just as a precautionary measure. 'It would be awful if they found my clothes in Hector's room,' he said, when Alice accused him of being paranoid. 'How would you explain it?'

'They'll hardly root through the wardrobes,' she'd protested, to which Conor fast forwarded through *Green Card* again and she shut up.

Despite all the preparation, however, the visit, when it happened, was a disaster. It started off well enough. Sean Holland had arrived at nine one morning with Carmel McGuire. Alice immediately took a totally irrational dislike to her. It was something about the pale blue embroidered twin-set, the knee-length pleated skirt and the rather prissy glasses she wore that turned her off. She couldn't have been more than thirty but her clothes and general appearance were so dowdy she looked as if she was hurtling at speed towards middle age.

Carmel in turn wasn't particularly enamoured of Alice, having a preconceived notion that she was (to her mind) a pervert and might make a pass at her or something equally objectionable.

When the intercom had buzzed and it became clear who the caller was, Conor had made good his escape by the back stairs and had headed off to the bistro, but not before making Alice promise to phone him the *minute* that the hit-squad left.

Alice introduced her *husband* and Hector shook Holland's hand, then, clicking his heels, drew Carmel McGuire's hand up to his lips and kissed it. 'Pleasure to meet you,' he purred.

Carmel's cheeks burned and she stammered a rather hesitant, 'How do you do?' in return.

Introductions over, Alice offered them coffee and, as she returned with the tray, noticed the *Green Card* video lying by the sofa close to Carmel McGuire's foot. Her efforts to conceal the offending material involved squeezing herself on to the seat beside Carmel and back-heeling the carton under the sofa. Carmel reacted by crossing her arms and her legs and edging herself into the farthest corner of the rather small two seater.

Holland opened proceedings. 'Now, Mr Hanusiak, it seems that since your appeal your circumstances have changed.'

Hector reached over and grabbed Alice's hand. 'Da. This is so. I married my Alice. My wonderful Alice.' He dragged her hand to his lips and kissed it. Alice gave an uneasy smile.

'Congratulations.'

Alice looked over at Holland. 'Thank you.'

As he spoke Holland opened his briefcase and took out a folder, then leafed through it. 'It says here you were married on June the seventeenth last – would that be correct?'

Alice nodded, retrieving her hand from Hector's vice-like grip. 'That's right. We didn't want to wait. We wanted to get married as soon as possible, isn't that right, darling?'

Hector reached for her hand again and crushed it between his own. 'This true. Ve are in lov.'

Carmel McGuire nodded. 'Um . . . so how did you two meet?'

Alice and Hector replied simultaneously. 'At Hogan's,' said Alice. 'At the Samovar,' said Hector.

'Um . . . well we *met* at the Samovar, but our first date was at Hogan's, wasn't it, darling?' Heavy emphasis on the *darling*.

'Vot? Oh, yes. Yes. Hogan's. That's how it vos,' Hector said. 'I lov her so much, I forget these little things.' He kissed her hand again and smiled at her like a lovesick puppy.

Carmel McGuire's 'I see,' was loaded. 'And when was that exactly?'

'A year ago,' Alice said, then, as she was about to go into their prepared statement, Hector launched into a speech of his own. It was only as he was about three minutes in, and had Holland and McGuire in rapt attention, that Alice realised that he was reciting word for word a particular scene from *Green Card* in which Gerard Depardieu is explaining details of his life with his new wife, and how much he loves her, to the US immigration officials. He had even adopted an approximate and somewhat irrelevant French accent.

In a panic, Alice leapt up and, sitting on the arm of Hector's chair, threw her arms around him and placed her head on his shoulder. 'And we're *soo* happy,' she cut in.

Hector stuttered in mid-sentence. Fearing that he was gong to launch into the scene again, Alice kissed him firmly on the lips to shut him up. 'More coffee?' she enquired as she came up for air. Fortunately Hector's shock at being kissed passionately on the lips by Alice was such that he was stunned into silence.

Carmel McGuire got to her feet. 'Eh . . . Could I have a look around the apartment? Do you mind?' she asked rather apologetically. She'd was very taken with Hector now since his speech, thought he was charming, very romantic and, though it made her blush to think about it, rather sexy. And although she thought Alice a bit strange, she was beginning to doubt that she was a lesbian. I mean, Hector Hanusiak was so obviously a full-blooded (dare she say it) heterosexual man, he'd hardly marry a lesbian. Pity he'd chosen to fall in love with a woman so obviously unworthy of him.

Alice jumped to her feet, relieved that Conor's paranoia had caused her to move her clothes into the big bedroom. 'No problem. Look around all you like. We've nothing to hide.'

Cringe. She hoped Holland and McGuire missed that little guilty slip of the tongue.

She led the way to the bedroom and Carmel McGuire had a perfunctory look around. 'Who sleeps in here?' she asked as she looked into the smaller (Alice's) room.

'Um ... Conor Finn. He's a friend. He's the chef at the Samovar. He and I are old friends from way back. It was through him I met Hector.' Aware that she was running off at the mouth, she shut up. They returned to the sitting room to find Sean Holland and Hector deep in conversation. Holland was totally bemused by the mad Ukrainian, but on the face of it could see no reason to doubt that the marriage was for real. He seemed to be completely besotted with Alice, and she, though he couldn't for the life of him figure out why, with her husband. Later, on the drive back to the office, Carmel had listed the reasons why any woman would be mad about Hector. He was so charming, so romantic etc., etc.

Unaware of this, however, Alice was in a mild state of panic. Hector couldn't see what her problem was. He thought things had gone off okay, until she pointed out that he had recited half of *Green Card*. 'Why the fuck didn't you stick to the story? You were supposed to stick to our story.'

'My story better. I vatch *Green Card*. I do vot man do on *Green Card*.'

'That's just the fucking point,' she agreed. 'You're Hector Hanusiak, a Ukrainian, you're not a bloody Frog actor.'

In a huff, Hector stomped off to the restaurant without her.

As usual, after a couple of hours both Alice's and Hector's irritation with each other wore off, but not before Alice had had a moan to Conor about how Hector had probably messed things up. But for now at least, despite her fears about Sean Holland and his henchwoman, Alice was looking forward to implementing her plans for the Samovar.

Chapter Twelve

As it was impossible to carry out the building work, that is the knocking down of the partition wall and the plastering and wiring, while they were open for business, it was inevitable that they would have to close the Samovar for about two weeks. Alice informed all their regular customers and Conor printed up a notice on his computer which they stuck on the window.

The builders set to work on the Tuesday following the August bank holiday. And because the Immigration section hadn't stormed the apartment with the cops to drag Hector off into exile within the first few days after Holland's and McGuire's visit, things seemed to be going well.

Conor was still uneasy and although he was putting on a brave face for Hector, reassuring him at every opportunity, constantly bringing the subject up only served to unsettle his lover. As usual he had completely swept the problem aside, but Conor's constant reminders only made him jittery.

Towards the start of the second week it became clear that the work would take longer than the builders had anticipated. It being an old building they hit a couple of snags, but they weren't unduly worried. The delay would be worth it in the end.

Strangely, as soon as the bistro closed, Hector seemed to lose interest. Every time Alice tried to get him to discuss the progress of the renovations or décor ideas, he changed the subject, or he'd flap his hands and say, 'I no good at this. You and Conor, you do this. I no good.'

'But you are, Hector. You've got a terrific sence of style,' she'd protested, but Hector abdicated all responsibility. Alice thought he was just being petulant on account of his disapproval of spending good money on anything other than on himself, but in Conor's opinion it was just a sign that his partner was worried about the deportation and urged Alice to make allowances.

By the middle of the third week the first stage of the building work was drawing to a close and the painters came in. Stage two was to be the renovation of the basement for the club, but that was put on hold for the time being as Mr Henderson wasn't so intimidated as to be reckless enough to lend them more than he felt they could reasonably afford to repay, and in the meantime Alice, in discussion with Conor (it was pointless talking to Hector), had refined the concept, resulting in the cost being increased considerably. Together they agreed that they would be better served to wait six months or so until, having proved their creditworthiness to Mr Henderson, they could borrow enough to do the thing properly, thus doing away with the need to imply any further threats to the poor man.

Conor in the meantime with the help of the two comis-chefs, Tony and Colin, set about scrubbing the kitchen from top to bottom. Sadly a refit of the kitchen was out of the question as the budget wouldn't run to it. It was a pity, especially as the cooking range was speeding towards obsolescence and only Conor's TLC was keeping the thing going, but there was enough to replace the elderly espresso machine and buy a dishwasher, as well as a small second-hand Ford Escort.

One morning, as Alice sat reading *The Irish Times* waiting for the delivery of the new tables and chairs, and Conor was out with Tony picking up the new linen and some glassware, Hector strolled in. He looked remarkably chirpy for one who had been in the depths of gloom not three hours before. 'Alice, Alice. I have good news.'

Delighted to see him enthusiastic for a change, Alice put down the paper. 'What it is it? What's happened?' Her first thought was that he had been granted permission to stay.

'I find cooking range. Good friend from old country, he give me special deal. It cheap.'

Slightly disappointed, but nonetheless interested, she said, 'How much is cheap?'

Hector shrugged his shoulders in his usual fashion. 'I not know exactly. But it cheap?'

Alice was at once suspicious. 'What's wrong with it?'

Hector threw his hands in the air in exasperation. 'Nothing! Nothing wrong vit it! Vot you think I am? You think Hector fool!'

Taken aback, and feeling slightly guilty, Alice tried to placate him. 'No, Hector. No. Of course I don't think that. I'm sorry. It's just . . .' She shrugged. 'I don't know . . . It just seems too good to be true.'

Hector stared at her through narrowed eyes. 'You not trust Hector? You think Hector fool?' He folded his arms across his chest and managed to look both affronted and dejected.

Conor walked in at that point with a box full of linen, followed by Tony carrying the boxes of glassware. He was in fine form, grinning from ear to ear. 'Then linen's only gorgeous,' he enthused. 'And you should see the glasses. I got a great deal on the glasses. Show them the glasses, Tony.' He was oblivious of the strained atmosphere.

Tony, however, picked it up immediately and, having witnessed Hector in full sulk mode, which always preceded a scene of some sort, didn't want to be around when the fuse blew. He put the boxes down on the floor. 'Um . . . eh . . . well, I think I'll just go and, umm . . .' He scurried into the kitchen.

'Alice, she think I fool,' Hector started. 'I get good deal on cooking range and she say I fool.'

'I said no such thing.'

'You did.'

'Didn't.'

'Did.'

'Didn't.'

'Stop it,' Conor cut in. 'What's this about a new cooking range?' He directed the question at Hector and Hector told him about the cooker and how it was cheap, and how it was offer *ve can't refuse*. Conor thought about it. After a moment he turned to Alice, who was now the one in sulk mode.

'What's the problem? We could really do with it, and if it's as cheap as Hector says . . .'

There followed a rather futile discussion regarding the provenance of the cooking range, which according to Hector was all above board. Alice couldn't see how it could be, but Conor's plea of 'So what if it is a bit dodgy, we really need it?', particularly as he was backed up by Hector, won the day. She was out-voted. Hector plonked the cheque book down on the table for her to sign.

'But there's no amount here,' she protested.

Hector looked insulted again and whined to Conor, 'I don't know exact amount. I tell her this. Vy she say these things?'

Conor put his arm around Hector and shot a withering look in Alice's direction. 'Give him a break, Alice. He knows what he's doing. Sign the cheque. He'll fill it in when he finds out how much the thing's going to cost.'

Alice was dubious. 'Have you seen this cooker? Shouldn't you go with him, Conor, to make sure it's okay?'

Hector, in a dramatic gesture, dropped his head to Conor's shoulder and wailed, 'There! She think Hector fool. I told you! I try to help, and this vot she do.'

Conor gave his lover a comforting hug and glared at Alice. 'Come on, Alice. You're always complaining that Hector doesn't pull his weight. Give him a break. You're supposed to be partners, for God's sake.'

Alice sighed. In some ways, by complaining about how little Hector usually contributed, she'd painted herself into a corner. Despite her misgivings, she slid the cheque book across the table and signed her name under the spidery scrawl that constituted Hector's signature. 'Well, okay. But don't hand over the cheque until you've seen the cooker.'

Hector stuffed the cheque into his inside pocket then, curling his lip, sneered, 'Has if.'

She watched as Conor walked with him to the door and stood outside chatting for a few minutes before Hector patted him on the back and strode off towards Stephen's Green.

Because the Samovar was closed for business Alice decided to make the most of a rare midweek night off by going to see a movie. Conor wasn't up for it as he and Hector had plans of their own so in the end, after a fruitless search for company, she went by herself, only to bump into Jojo and Gilda outside the Virgin multiplex. After the movie, which Alice and Gilda really enjoyed, but Jojo thought overhyped, they all went along to the Elephant and Castle for a bite to eat, after which they moved on to The Palace. The pub was fairly dull and, in the crush, Alice bumped into Claire and a couple of her old work mates from McAlester's. She spent what remained of the evening getting quietly smashed while they all slagged off Roddy Groden. Clare and her friends, who had initially seemed a tad wary of Gilda (she of the cropped yellow hair and bulging biceps), revised their opinion somewhat when Alice regaled them with the story of how she had unceremoniously frog-marched the Mutant Midget from TransV. They all hooted and clapped in approval. More drink was bought and everyone was having a good time. Gilda and Jojo, and Claire and the girls were all for going on to a club but Alice called it a night as she was tired, though in brilliant humour. After saying her goodbyes, she left them all standing in Fleet Street, outside the pub, discussing which club they'd all go to, and jumped into a cab and headed home.

The sitting room light was on and the dining table set. Two candles had burned down to stubs. Conor was lolling on the sofa dozing. He stirred and opened his eyes when she walked in.

'Sorry.' She sniggered, put her finger to her lips and staggered slightly. 'Shhhh. Didn't mean to wake you. Sorry.'

Conor looked past her towards the hall. 'Is Hector with you?' he asked half hopefully, but his voice betrayed a tinge of annoyance.

'Hector? No. I thought you were cooking for him.' She looked over towards the undisturbed dining table.

Conor sat up and rubbed his eyes. His brow was furrowed into a worried frown. 'He hasn't been back.'

It took a moment for the words to register. 'What d'you mean? Since when?'

'Since he went off to get the cooker.' Concern crept into his voice now. 'You don't think he's had an accident, do you?'

Alice was equally concerned now, but rationalised that surely if he'd had an accident the cops would have been in touch. It wasn't as if he'd no identification on him. 'Did you call the hospitals?'

Conor nodded. 'Tried that. No joy. Where d'you think he could be?'

'Did he say nothing about this friend from the old country? The one he's getting the dodgy cooker from?'

'What d'you mean, the old country?'

Impatiently Alice snapped, 'The bloody Ukraine. The guy with the cooker's from the Ukraine. Where d'you think?'

Conor's hand shot up to his mouth. 'My God! You don't think he's been done over, do you?'

'Oh, don't be so melodramatic,' Alice said, but on further reflection it was a possibility. Tentatively she asked, 'Have you, eh . . . have you met this guy? D'you know where he lives?'

Conor threw his arms up in frustration. 'What guy? I don't know who you're talking about.'

'The guy he's getting the iffy cooker from, who the hell d'you think? Didn't Hector tell you when you were outside the Samovar before he went off?'

Conor shook his head. 'No. He just said he'd be home in time for dinner. He didn't say anything about the old country. If he had I'd have never let him go through with it.' He stared at the floor, remembering the conversation. Suddenly he leapt up from the sofa and grabbed Alice by the shoulders. 'Jesus! What if something's happened to him? What if this guy's from the Russian Mafia or something? What if they took the money and then shot him? You should never've encouraged him. You should never have let him go.'

'Me!' Alice was outraged. 'You were the one who said I should cut him some slack. You were the one who insisted I sign the bloody cheque. Don't lay this on me. Anyway, don't you think you're jumping the gun a bit talking about the fecking Mafia, if you'll pardon the pun? There's probably a perfectly good explanation. He'll probably walk through that door any time now. He probably went for a celebration drink or something. You know what he's like.'

In truth Alice wasn't as cool as she sounded about the situation. She was having a few misgivings herself, but she didn't need Conor kicking off before she'd had time to think through all the possibilities. That a) as she had said to Conor, he could have just forgotten the time and was out celebrating the purchase of the new cooker with his old buddy, b) he might have had to collect the cooker from some distant location and maybe had a breakdown, but in that case why hadn't he phoned? or c) what if he *had* been duped by the Russian or Ukrainian or whatever Mafia and was lying in a ditch somewhere, his throat cut?

As if reading her thoughts, Conor grabbed hold of her shoulders again and started shaking her vigorously. 'My God! He's dead. He's dead. I know he's dead.' He was working himself up to a state and the more hysterical he got the harder he shook. Alice's brain was rattling around inside her skull. To prevent further brain damage she employed a move, lingering in the distant recesses of her memory, that she had learned years before on a self-defence course (on the one session she had attended) and shot her two arms up through Conor's, flinging them outwards and breaking the pincer-like grip he had of her upper arms. At the same time she yelled, 'SHUT UP, CONOR! YOU'RE FUCKING HYSTERICAL!' and slapped him hard across the face.

That did the trick. Stunned and half-deafened, Conor gaped at her open-mouthed, his eyes as huge as saucers, and touched his hot, reddening cheek. Alice put an arm around his shoulder and gently led him towards the sofa. 'I'm sorry. Look. Sit yourself down. Sit here. I'm sorry.' Meaningless prattle, her voice soft and comforting, in an attempt to calm her friend down. Hysteria would get them nowhere.

Conor meekly sat. 'I lost it,' he muttered, still fingering the angry welt on his face. 'I'm sorry.' Even though the apartment was warm, he was shivering now.

'Sit there. I'll get you a sweater,' she said, and trotted off to his bedroom.

The note, lying on the dressing table under the box of tissues, merely said, 'Gone with Colin. Sorry.'

Gone where?

She returned to the sitting room holding the note, with the box of tissues in the other hand. 'Did Hector say anything about going somewhere with Colin?' she asked.

'Colin? No. Why?' Alice handed him the note. Conor stared at it. Alice stood by waiting for him to say something. Then without warning she saw the tears streaming down his face. They were positively spurting from his eyes.

'What's up? What's the matter?'

Unable to speak, Conor flapped his hands and shook his head. Alice hadn't a clue what the problem was. Sure Hector was late home, but now there was a perfectly good explanation. Hector had gone off somewhere with the comis-chef. Why was Conor making such a big deal out of it? It wasn't as if . . . Oh, shit! 'Is Colin gay?'

Conor made a few gasping sounds, mouthing words before he regained the use of his vocal chords. 'Evidently,' he croaked, then dissolved into rigorous sobbing.

Alice didn't buy it. 'Oh, come on! Why would Hector stand you up for Colin?' It was too ridiculous for words.

Conor shook his head in irritation. He was still sobbing as he stumbled from the sofa into the bedroom. Alice followed. 'Conor. Calm down.' But he wasn't listening. When she caught up with him he was standing by the wardrobe door staring into the empty space within.

'Heeb god abay,' he wailed through his sobs. 'Heeb god bid Codin.'

Alice gaped at the empty wardrobe. Only a couple of metal hangers were left on the rail. Gone obviously meant just that. Gone with a capital G. But why?

Conor's crying had run the major part of its course for the moment. He slumped down on the end of the bed giving the occasional hiccup. He should have seen it coming, what with Hector's fear of deportation. He'd had his suspicions about Colin too, and Hector had been paying him quite a lot of attention. He looked up at Alice. 'He was afraid that the

Immigration crowd were going to arrest him and dump him on a plane home, but I never thought he'd do this. I didn't think he was *that* worried.'

'But why, Colin? If he was going to hump off, why didn't he take you?'

Conor gave a cross between a snort and a cough. 'It's obvious. He's turned me in for a younger model.' He started to weep again. Alice sat down on the bed next to him and put a comforting arm around his shoulder. 'The bastard! The rotten bastard.'

The cop in the Garda station was less than sympathetic. 'So let's get this straight.' He was trying unsuccessfully to hide a snigger. 'This fella, yer husband, cashed a cheque that *you* signed and *you* gave him?'

'Yes,' Alice said. 'But the money was for a new cooker . . .'

'Eight thousand pounds seems a lot of money to pay for a cooker.' The cop leaned his elbows on the counter top. 'Wouldn't yeh say?'

'Eight thousand and fifty-three pounds,' Alice qualified. 'But all the money wasn't for the cooker. I left the cheque blank. He filled it in for the amount that was left in the account.'

'Yeh left the cheque blank?' the cop said in a weary, *why are you wasting my time?* voice. 'So what are yeh complainin' about? The way I see it yer husband cashed a cheque *you* gave him from yer *joint* account. What's wrong with that?'

Conor took her elbow. 'Come on, Alice, it's pointless talking to him.'

'But the bastard cleaned us out! We can't just lie down and take it. What'll we do? We can't afford to finish the work and pay all the bills. What about the ten-grand loan?'

Alice turned back to the cop. He had lost interest in her and was filling in some sort of form. Alice noted that his lips moved as he read it. 'What are you going to do?' she asked belligerently. 'I'm here reporting a serious fraud and it seems to me you're doing feck all about it.'

The cop looked up and carefully put down his biro. 'First of all,' he said, 'what yeh say is a fraud is no such thing. Yeh gave yer husband this cheque, so how can it be fraud if he took the money out of his own account?'

'Our joint account,' Alice stressed.

'Okay. Yeer *joint* account,' the cop said in a patronising voice. 'Did he force yeh to sign the cheque?' Alice shook her head. 'Did he threaten violence?'

'Well . . . no.'

'Then there's no crime. If yeh want yer money back ye'll have t' pursue it through the civil courts.' He went back to filling out the form. His attitude pointedly, and wordlessly, said *Domestic*.

It had been a rough morning one way and another. Alice had eventually managed to calm Conor down, mainly by getting him angry with Hector. She felt that good old-fashioned anger was a lot more healthy and productive than Conor's choice of snivelling self-pity. She'd been down this road before on a number of occasions. Conor's ability to fall in love, apparently at the drop of a hat, meant that most times he was on a hiding to nothing, and she was left to help him pick up the pieces.

They got back to the apartment at eleven. Alice checked the letter box and found half a dozen bills adding up to a couple of thousand pounds. On top of that the builders would soon be pressing for their final payment. She dropped the brown envelopes on the dining table. 'What the hell are we going to do now?' Conor didn't reply. He was sitting with his back to her on the sofa. 'Conor? I think we need to talk about this. From where I'm standing it looks as if the business is about to go down the tubes.'

Conor still didn't say anything. He put his head in his hands and wept, silently at first, then bitter, drawn-out, coughing sobs. His feeling of rejection was overwhelming, all-consuming, a physical ache that transcended the anger. He loved Hector. Hector loved him. He'd said so. How could he do this? Alice was still wittering on about the money, but he wasn't listening. He felt as if his head would burst. He wanted to die. He wanted to scream. He wanted Hector.

Suddenly Alice shut up. In all the confusion and excitement

the momentum of her anger had caused it to slip her mind that as well as losing everything they had worked for over the past few months, Conor had also lost the love of his life, at least this particular love of his life. Even though the thought of *anyone* loving Hector was alien to her right now, the fact remained that Conor loved him deeply. Suddenly she felt ashamed. She sat next to him on the sofa, cradling him in her arms like he was a child, and let him cry it out. It took some time.

Eventually, when Conor could cry no more, Alice said, 'I'm sorry, Conor. I didn't think, but we have to move on now.' She paused for a moment then added, 'Stay angry. It's easier.'

Chapter Thirteen

Hogan's wasn't particularly crowded for the time of night which rather defeated the object of the exercise. There was little atmosphere; in fact, the place was downright sombre, or maybe it was just the humour they were in.

Alice had been thinking about trying to coax Conor into a night out to forget about their troubles for a while, to drown their sorrows. Sitting in the apartment brooding wasn't helping either of them. She'd imagined that she would have to nag him into it, so it was a surprise when he'd suggested the excursion himself.

He'd been a bit wobbly all day. His grief and anger came and went in alternate waves. Alice, who was making do with incandescent rage, found his moods hard to keep up with. Her own anger finally waned at around four p.m. It would have been easier if she'd been able to get out of the apartment, but she was afraid to leave Conor on his own and he was determined to wait in by the phone in case Hector called (as if). She'd never seen him this low before. Then he dozed off on the sofa mid-afternoon and had woken up with the suggestion, quite out of the blue, that they should go out on the town. Without waiting for her opinion he'd jumped up and disappeared into his room to get ready.

Conor hadn't really been sleeping, he'd just been lying there with his eyes closed, thinking. Alice was right, anger was far easier. Apart from the fact that Hector had stolen all the cash, leaving them to carry the can, what made the whole business worse was that he hadn't had the courage to confide in him about his plan to flee. Maybe if he had they could have worked out some sort of scheme whereby he could have just gone into hiding or something until it all blew over. There had been no call to follow the path he had ultimately chosen. And then there was Colin. Why Colin? What the hell did Colin have that he hadn't?

Hector for one thing.

It surprised him that that thought didn't kick-start the urge to cry again. Maybe it was the anger. Yes, it definitely was the anger. He thought of Hector again just to test the theory, but still not a tear. Maybe that was the problem with all his previous failed relationships. Perhaps if they'd stolen from him too he'd have found them easier to get over. But then it crept up on him again and a tear leaked out of the corner of his eye. Yes, he felt betrayed, but the problem was, he still wanted Hector.

Alice on the other hand was standing in front of her mirror having a conversation with herself. 'So what now? What the hell are you going to do now?' She thought through their options. 'Well, you could always go back to that nice Mr Henderson.' She dismissed that idea. She hadn't the stomach for it. She'd felt bad enough about it the first time. Well, not at the time, but afterwards. 'Okay. What about one of those unsecured loan companies then?' She'd seen them advertised in the papers. *Loans! Loans! Loans! Unsecured loans up to fifteen thousand pounds. Arranged over the phone.* Again she wasn't keen. The advertisements had a ring of 'Loan Sharks Я Us' about them. But what other options did they have? They needed the cash now. No, they needed the cash yesterday. Alice ran the brush through her hair and stared at her reflection in the mirror. 'Fat lot of good you are,' she said aloud.

They were sitting together at a table solemnly staring into their drinks. Conor was on the g & t's but Alice, mindful of the depressive effect that gin had on her, was sipping from a tall glass of tequila and grapefruit. Conor's conversation was hardly sparkling, confined as it was to the odd *hmm* or *yeah*. In desperation, she was just about to suggest that they move on somewhere else, somewhere livelier, when the door opened and Hugh, Jojo, Gilda and Mason walked in together. Alice gave them a frantic wave and they came over. She moved her bag out of the way and there was the general moving along and grabbing of spare chairs. Mason went up to the bar to get a round of drinks in and Hugh plonked himself down next to Conor. His first words were, 'So, where's Hector?'

Conor didn't bat an eyelid. 'He fucked off with Colin our comis-chef.' That kind of stopped everyone in their tracks. At first they weren't sure if he was joking, but when neither he nor Alice broke a smile they realised that he wasn't.

'You're not serious!' Hugh said. 'So who's this Colin?'

Jojo gave him a dig in the ribs. 'Hugh!'

Hugh returned the withering glance and said, 'Well, I was only asking. I've never heard of this Colin bloke. Didn't you know Hector was carrying on then?'

Conor gave an heroic sigh. 'They say the partner's always the last to know.'

Jojo, who was training as a counsellor, grabbed both of Conor's hands in hers. 'Never mind him, Conor. So how do you *feel*?' she asked sympathetically.

Alice was with Hugh. She knew that Jojo's approach, kindly as it was, would only pander to Conor's self-pity as opposed to his rage, which she found far easier to deal with seeing as she was still livid beyond reason with Hector. She cut in before Conor could think about how he felt. 'And the bastard emptied the bank account. Took every penny.'

'You're not serious?' Hugh repeated, throwing up both his hands and his eyes. 'How much?'

'The lot. Over eight grand, the money we borrowed for the renovations.'

There was a collective gasp. 'So what are you going to do?' Gilda asked.

Alice shrugged. 'Don't know. Try and get another loan from somewhere, I suppose. I doubt the bank'll give us any more.'

Mason came back with the drinks at this point. Hugh grabbed his arm and he put down a pint of Guinness. 'You'll never guess what. Hector's buggered off with Colin.'

'Who's Colin?' Mason asked, and cast a sympathetic look at Conor.

'The comis-chef,' Conor said, this time with an angry but brave edge to his voice. 'So now, apart from everything else, we'll have to find someone else to work in the fecking kitchen, and I was just getting used to Colin.'

Alice didn't like to point out that the way things were shaping up there wouldn't *be* a kitchen unless they could find another eight grand. There was a further uncomfortable pause before everyone spoke at once. Hugh started off telling a humorous getting-dumped story. Alice cringed until Conor laughed, and then every one started to top one another's stories. They all had a story of some sort to tell, some funnier than others. More drink was bought and consumed. Alice observed that Conor's mood was lightening up and was relieved to see it.

After a while Gilda leaned in to Alice and said, 'So how are you going to raise the money you need now?'

Alice shrugged. 'I suppose we'll have to go to one of those companies advertised in the papers, you know, unsecured loans over the phone.'

Gilda shook her head. 'You can't do that, they'll skin you alive on the interest.'

'I can't see we've any other choice. Our creditworthiness, thanks to Hector, isn't the best.'

'Well,' Gilda said conspiratorially, 'a few years ago I used to work for one of those advertising free sheets, you know the ones? they come through the door.' Alice nodded, wondering where this was leading. 'Anyway, one time there was this ad, *Earn three hundred pounds a week from your own home, send sae and £5 for details.* Well, being as I was skint, I was only earning peanuts at the time as a sort of cub reporter, I sent off my fiver.' She paused grinning at the memory.

'And?' Alice encouraged.

Gilda laughed. 'I got back this little scrap of paper. And d'you want to know what it said?'

Alice nodded, waiting for some sort of punch line.

'It said, do this.'

'What?'

Gilda grinned. 'Do this. Like the ad . . . get it? . . . do this.'

She convulsed into paroxysms of mirth. Alice stared at her, mouth agape.

'What's so funny?' Conor asked.

It was an audacious scam but with the amount of alcohol that they had now imbibed it seemed like a hilarious idea. Gilda had to repeat the story half a dozen times and everyone laughed all the harder with each telling.

'But is it legal?' Conor asked.

'Of course it's legal ... at least it's not illegal,' Gilda said. '... as far as I know.'

Gilda had a way with storytelling. This surprised Alice because her first impressions had been that Gilda was a morose, aggressive sort of individual, but then she had only really been in her company a few times, and on one of those occasions she had all but beaten up Roddy Groden.

They fell out of the pub long after closing time and, after standing around outside the pub saying protracted farewells, walked home, their problems temporarily forgotten.

The following morning at about six, Alice staggered out of bed and did the Solpadine and water thing, before falling back under the duvet until a more reasonable hour. Conor came in with a mug of coffee at around eight-thirty and sat on the end of her bed.

'How d'you feel?'

Alice heaved herself up and leaned her head against the top of the bed. She blinked a couple of times. 'Okay, I think. How about you?'

Conor shrugged. 'Not bad in myself, but what the hell are we going to do about the money?'

Alice sighed. 'I don't know. But we'll have to do something pretty sharpish. The painters'll be finished tomorrow and expect their money. Then there's the furniture to pay for, and as far as the builders go, well, we'll just have to keep a low profile till we can figure something out.'

'What about Gilda's thing? You know, the scam? According to her it isn't illegal.'

'As far as she knows,' Alice said. She was doubtful, but her fears were not so much about the legality or otherwise of the scheme. In the cold light of day, and in a state of total sobriety, her conscience pricked her. It went against the grain to cheat ordinary decent folk out of their hard-earned cash. But also there was the question of whether they would be able to raise enough cash as quickly as they needed it.

'I can't see any alternative other than going to a loan shark, can you?' Conor said.

'But we'd hardly raise eight grand from one ad in a free sheet.'

Conor nodded. 'I know, I know. But I was thinking about that. What if we were to place ads in local papers all around the country? Lots of ads. Surely statistically we'd be bound to get lots of replies?'

He had a point. 'But . . . I don't know, it doesn't seem right. It's like stealing.'

Conor shrugged. 'Not really. We could always keep the names and addresses and send it back once we're straight.' He could see that Alice still wasn't convinced. 'It need only be a loan, Alice. Really. We can pay them all back eventually.'

Even though the hapless punters wouldn't be aware of that fact, and with the threat of penury once again looming, Alice was eventually persuaded. At the heel of the hunt she hadn't a lot of confidence in the scheme anyway. Despite Conor's talk of statistics, they'd hardly raise enough in fivers to solve their financial problems, so where was the harm? 'Okay,' she said reluctantly. 'But only on condition that if there isn't enough to get us out of this hole, we pay it all back straight away. And if we do raise enough (ha, ha) we'll pay every penny back once we're able.'

Conor, who had far more confidence in the plan, readily agreed. Now all they had to work out was a plan of operation. Conor pointed out that it was important to have as many of the ads as possible to appear in the one week, in case anyone kicked up a fuss and went to the national papers about the scam or, worse, the radio.

This presented certain logistical problems. They would have to place the ads in person, to avoid giving the paper a postal address, by which they could be traced in the event of the excrement hitting the fan. For similar reasons they would also have to pay for the ads with cash. Fortunately, Alice had about four hundred pounds in her own account which was supposed to cover her share of the rent, so weighing up the pros and cons they decided to postpone paying the rent on the apartment and to use the cash to pay for the ads. Next there was the problem of transport. The Escort they'd bought had broken down and hiring would deplete their cash reserves. In the end, on the pretext that they needed to get away for a few days to unwind, Hugh agreed to lend them his trusty VW Polo. Despite Conor's confidence in the plan, he too was a tad embarrassed to tell Hugh that they actually intended to go through with Gilda's scam.

Next, they went to the public library and checked the lists of all local papers in the country and made a note of the ones with the largest circulations. Back at the apartment Conor dug out a road map and they worked out a route around the country. Starting in Dublin, west along the N4 taking in Lucan, Maynooth (because of the large student population), Mullingar, Longford, then they cut across country to Athlone and Roscommon, down to Ballinasloe and across to Galway. They figured out that that portion of the journey, taking into account stopping and placing the ads, would take the best part of a day. They planned to stay in Galway overnight then turn south and head for Limerick, Cork, across to Waterford, then turn north again towards Wexford, Carlow, Wicklow, Bray and back to Dublin. Starting early they hoped to cover that part of the journey on the second day.

The planning took the whole of the afternoon, but before getting started they'd called round to the restaurant to check on the painters' progress. Thankfully the painter in chief was on his own, and full of apologies that the work was delayed because two of his men were off sick. Alice suspected that he'd moved them on to another job, but didn't make a fuss as the delay suited them. Conor caught sight of the builder pulling up across the road. He nudged Alice to get her attention, then they fled the painter in mid-excuse and made their escape through the back to avoid the builder and any demands for payment.

After picking up Hugh's Polo at the crack of dawn, they set off. Conor drove like a madman. 'I bet your father taught you to drive,' Alice said as she closed her eyes and clung onto the dashboard.

'How did you know?'

'Lucky guess.'

After a white-knuckle twenty minutes, Conor pulled up across the street from their first port of call. As it was still only eight a.m. the office was not yet open and they had to sit in the car for an hour killing time. After the terrifying ride and sixty interminable minutes in which to imagine all the things that could go wrong and Conor dozing in the driver's seat, apparently unconcerned, Alice got out of the car. Her legs were a bit wobbly, she had broken out into a sweat and her hands started to shake. She felt like a criminal. Her body language probably made her look like a criminal, or at least like someone up to no good.

Conor's cheery 'good luck' didn't help, it only reinforced the idea in her mind that any minute now the cops would screech up, sirens whooping, to arrest them both. Outside the bank she noticed a CCTV camera. As she passed she ducked her head away and imagined herself on the video file segment of *Crimeline* with Marian Finucane passing comment to David Harvey about what a mean and cowardly person it was who would cheat old ladies out of their pension money. She stopped for a moment and told herself to get a grip. Who was to say who'd invest? Invest. That was a more comforting, conscience-assuaging way to look at it. They were investors and would all get their money back in the end, right? But what if the paper refused to take the ad, or started asking awkward questions? The flight response, she decided. She'd just make some caustic comment and leave.

The girl in the office was on the phone when she went in. Another girl was typing at a computer. Alice stood waiting by the counter. After a couple of seconds the girl on the phone looked up smiled and mouthed, 'Won't be long.' Alice attempted to smile back but her facial muscles wouldn't cooperate and the smile died somewhere between a twitch and a sneer. She was sweating profusely now and her heart was thumping to beat the band. The girl finished her call and hung up. 'Sorry about that,' she said. 'What can I do for you?'

Alice had now lost the use of her vocal chords and croaked, 'Umm . . . eh . . .' and pushed the sheet of paper, on which she had written out the ad, across the counter, her hand leaving a sweaty trail.

The girl picked up the paper and looked at it. 'WANT TO PLACE AN AD, DO WE?' The tone and volume of her voice suggested that she thought Alice mentally retarded, which was understandable.

Alice nodded. 'Uh . . . yes.' She could feel a hot red blush creeping up her neck.

The girl smiled at her again then looked down at the page and her finger traced the words, counting. 'Fine,' she said after a moment, then repeated, 'FINE . . . UNDER BUSINESS OPPORTUNITIES, OKAY?' Alice nodded like an eejitt again, wishing she had a remote control to turn down the volume. The girl scribbled a notation. 'YOU WANT A BOX NUMBER?'

More nodding from Alice. Then she remember that she had to ask the girl to forward the replies to their PO box in Dublin. Here she turned into Homer Simpson. 'Replies. PO box . . . send on?' She reached over and stabbed the note near the bottom of the page where the Dublin PO box number was written, her sweaty fingertip causing the outline of the number to become somewhat fuzzy.

The girl patted her hand and nodded, then totted up the cost. 'THAT'LL BE NINE POUNDS EIGHTY INCLUD-ING VAT, LOVE!' she yelled. 'NINE EIGHTY, OKAY?' She held up nine fingers, then looked down helplessly at her hands wondering how to sign the eighty pence. After a moment she gave up and Alice shoved a ten pound note over the counter. The girl handed her a twenty pence piece in change. As she got to the door she heard the girl say to her friend, 'Isn't she great?'

Apparently the mentally handicapped are also deaf.

One down, however many to go.

They underestimated the traffic, the fact that newspaper offices closed for lunch and that they couldn't place any ads after six when all the offices closed for the day, so the task in the end took three days. This meant that not all of the ads would apper in the same week as some of the papers went to press on different days. They travelled on, placing the advertisements and hoping for the best. By the time they reached Cork Alice had become desensitised to the terrors Conor's driving induced. Though, considering what she was doing, anything was relaxing by comparison.

Conor was in good spirits most of the time, his confidence in the plan far higher than Alice's. And he was slowly convincing himself that Hector was a bastard, mainly due to the knock-on effect his desertion had had on Alice. She was co-responsible for the bank loan, so in effect he'd stolen the money from her. So intent on this train of thought was he that he hardly noticed Alice's agitated state.

They arrived home weary and travel-sore at seven on the Wednesday evening. All that remained was to wait and see what would happen. As the restaurant was all but finished, there was little for them to do except evade the various people looking for money, so they confined themselves to the apartment during daylight hours. Time hung heavily. They were both jumpy, and Conor went away and had the occasional weep from time to time as the hurt of Hector overcame his resolve to hate him.

On Sunday evening they sat in watching television, even though there wasn't much worth watching after *Coronation Street*. Conor retold her the story of his coming out of the closet and how surprised he had been by Declan's supportive attitude. Alice listened again, but pointed out that Declan had been less supportive about his attempt to come out to his parents. Conor said that, in the end, Declan was probably right. It wasn't something his parents needed to know, and it would probably break their hearts anyway. He further pointed out how thrilled they were when they thought that he was a regular married man. More proud than they were of Declan, and him with his economics degree and the big job in Cork.

Family closeness like that was beyond Alice's experience, but she did wonder about his parents. Surely if they loved him they'd accept him for what he was? She commented thus, but Conor just repeated the argument about his parents being brought up in rural Ireland. And how they wouldn't understand. And how he didn't want to disappoint them. He'd missed the point, but Alice didn't labour it.

For convenience and security, Alice had organised the Dublin PO box in order that the papers could forward the replies. With hindsight she saw it as a blessing as she would have been unable to stand another whiz around the country at breakneck speed, or indeed be able to face the staff of the various offices again.

Two days afer the first publications were due on the news stands, she checked the PO box. She looked shifty to say the least in her dark glasses with a fleecy hat pulled down over her hair. It was a wonder that she didn't put the wind up the counter assistant, or that she wasn't carted off by the cops, but fortunately it was busy at the time and no one seemed to notice. Conor counted a rather disappointing forty-five replies. Undaunted, they shoved the inserts in the self-addressed stamped envelopes. 'Early days yet,' Conor said to his partner in crime. Alice had to remind him to make a note of the names and addresses of the investors.

The following day there was a better response. Alice brought home 307 envelopes posted in various parts of the country. It was at that stage that she experienced pangs of guilt again, but they were only slight, and the sight of all those money orders soon made her forget. She went to the bank and cashed them straight away, paying the money into the Samovar account.

Her jagged nerves weren't helped any when, on her return from the post office, she saw Sean Holland coming out of her apartment building. She ducked into a doorway until he drove off. When she had agreed to the bogus marriage to Hector, the promise of a partnership in the Samovar had blinded her to the implications should they be found out. The sight of Holland brought it home to her that she'd be in serious trouble if

Hector couldn't be produced on demand. She resolved to get together with Conor and cook up some sort of story.

Day three brought 425 replies and Alice forgot all about Sean Holland. Day four a disappointing 203. Conor put this down to the varying days that the papers hit the streets.

The next day was Sunday, so Alice did some book work and paid off several pressing bills.

On Monday Conor brought home an all-time high of 517. That made a total to date of £14,979.

Tuesday morning dawned. Alice lay in the bath listening to Marion Finucane on the radio and felt very smug. All their financial troubles were over. The very next moment she heard Bridie from Birr complaining about '*Some con man put an advertize-ment in the local paper about earnin' money from your own ho-am.*'

She sat bolt upright in the bath.

'*They said to sind a fiver,*' she complained, '*an' I sint me fiver, but all I got back was a bitta paper sayin' do this. Can yeh believe that?*'

Marian thought it rather funny and explained that although immoral, the money-making scheme didn't appear to be illegal. After all, judging by the number of calls coming into the programme, she reckoned a person could earn a lot more than the sum promised, and in a way it was no worse than a chain letter. Several callers phoned in disagreeing with her and saying that the country was going to the dogs. Others phoned in to say that it was all down to people's greed and they'd only got what they deserved.

Alice was momentarily tempted to phone in anonymously to say that they'd pay back the money in time, but regained her sanity. Conor thought it was great craic and laughed all morning about it. Alice found this rather disconcerting. Apart from the stress of the past couple of weeks, she'd been walking on egg shells, trying to keep him on an even keel. One minute he was weeping in his room over Hector, the next he was high as a kite, slagging his ex-lover off, and positive to the nth degree.

At that point, though, they decided to call it a day. They had exceeded their target and, anyway, due to the media exposure, it was unlikely that any more replies would follow. Conor sheepishly checked the PO box for the last time and found a paltry 21 replies.

The new Samovar opened with a flourish three and a half weeks late in the middle of September. Conor managed to get a replacement comis-chef, a quiet young man called Louis, and a kitchen helper. Mandy and Jean came back to work along with Mason, who was currently *resting* and needed the job, also Joe the washer-up, who was much impressed with the new dishwashing machine.

They were booked to capacity for the opening night. At the end of a very busy shift Alice slumped down at a table with a double espresso. Madame Maxine wandered in, her working clothes covered by a long black trench coat in deference to the last straggle of diners lingering over their coffee and liqueurs. Earlier in the day a huge good-luck bouquet and a magnum of Dom Perignon had arrived from her and Celeste, and Conor brought it out suitably chilled. He opened it with much ceremony and all the staff toasted the future of the Samovar.

Much later Alice lay in bed exhausted but too wound up to sleep. She could hardly believe that things could turn around so dramatically in so short a time when not more than a month ago they'd been facing ruin. She also couldn't fail to notice over the previous few days how Conor, aided by the support of Mason, seemed to be making a speedier than usual recovery from his betrayal by Hector. The weeping periods had all but ended and he was in a more stable frame of mind all round. As she turned on her side, it briefly crossed her mind that maybe things were going *too* well.

Chapter Fourteen

Joxer Boxer was not happy. All this talk of sales targets and percentage increases was baffling. Why not call a spade a spade? he wondered. But then, that apart, he *was* enjoying his new status. Sales Manager. The middle-range Beemer, the bespoke suit, the briefcase. Joxer was a small man by the standards of his profession, only five eight, but what he lacked in height he more than made up for in muscle. He was stocky and well made, worked out most days. The meeting had unsettled him, though. The boss was agitated, had bawled him out in front of the others. He felt he'd lost face and that angered him. Brought back memories of his childhood when he was thin and scrawny and the bigger kids used to pick on him and regularly beat him up. It wasn't so much the beatings, it was the humiliation he couldn't stand. But he'd shown them. He grinned in satisfaction at the memory of Leemy Duggan's face just before he'd fallen. He'd been hanging on to the ledge on the top of the old Sheriff Street flats by his fingertips, which was ironic. It was the very ledge that Leemy and JP had shoved him over, holding him by the ankles. He'd shat his pants before they pulled him up. Even now his face reddened when he thought of it.

'Pleeease, Joxer. Fuckin' lemme me up, will yeh?' his old tormentor had pleaded. 'I never done nottin'. On me ma's life. I never done nottin'.' But Joxer just smiled at him, then swung the baseball bat and gave his fingers a clatter. He'd disappeared from view with an extended yell of 'Nooooo!' receding ino the distance. It was like something from a cartoon.

'Noooooo,' Joxer repeated quietly, mimicking the receding Doppler effect as he peeked over the edge. Leemy was lying splattered on the concrete with a small crowd gathering around him. Maurice and Jimmy were frozen to the spot, gobs hanging open. 'That'll teach the fucker not to mess with me,' he'd muttered to himself, but loudly enough for the other two to get the message.

Not that Leemy *had* been messing with him, but he'd been messing with the boss, skimming cash off the top, and that wasn't on. The boss had been impressed. He'd told him as much. Told him in front of the others. Held him up as an example. Joxer's chest swelled in pride as he recalled the incident. He reached into his pocket and took out a packet of mints, flicking one off the top with his thumb and popping it into his mouth. Beside him Billie sat dozing. He glanced at the clock on the dashboard.

Across the street he could see that the place was empty now. Only herself behind the bar counting the takings. Pity in some ways, but he couldn't let the opportunity pass. Not now the boss was on his back. He gave Billie a dig in the ribs.

'C'mon. Time to do the business.'

It was late. Alice was on her own enjoying a nightcap. Conor had gone out earlier to the opening night of some club with Mason. It was she who had encouraged it. He needed to get out, to get on with his life. It was only six weeks since Hector had gone and, although Conor appeared to be getting over it, she thought he needed a diversion to keep up the momentum of his recovery.

She looked around the empty restaurant and sighed in satisfaction. The place looked great. It was booked solid most nights, even at the beginning of the week. They'd introduced an early-bird menu to attract punters after work or before the cinema and it was proving to be a huge success. At this rate, she calculated, they'd be able to pay back the *investors* by Easter, even approach poor Henderson again (legitimately this time) to top up the loan so that they could make a start on the their plans for the club. She drained her glass and, standing up, stretched her back. Time for bed. Just then the door swung open and Joxer walked in with another man.

'I'm sorry, Joxer, I'm afraid we're closed,' she said, smiling, 'And, um . . . the chef's gone, otherwise. . . .'

Joxer ran his hand along the bar swiping half a dozen glasses to the floor. 'Is that so?'

The smile froze on Alice's lips and an unpleasant feeling gripped her stomach. 'Hey, there's no need for that. What are you doing?' She looked towards the kitchen, hoping that Joe might still be finishing up, but she heard no movement.

Joxer turned to his associate and said, 'She wants t' know what we're doin', Billy.'

'Is that righ', Joxer?' Billy picked up a bottle of wine in each hand and hurled them to the floor. The bottles exploded, splattering the contents everywhere.

Alice screamed. 'Okay, okay. I'll cook you a steak. I'll put one on now, no problem. Just please, don't do that.'

Joxer placed his briefcase on the bar and snapped the locks open. 'We havent come to eat. Billy is just illustratin' what a dangerous place Dublin can be without the proper sort of insurance,' he said.

Halfway between angry and terrified, Alice spluttered, 'But we've got insurance.'

Billy elbowed a pyramid of espresso cups off the bar. They bounced across the tiled floor. 'Not the right insurance,' Joxer said, leering at her. 'Yeh never know when a fire'd break out in a place like this . . . like in the early hours when yeh'd be tucked up in yer bed.'

Alice was beginning to get the picture. 'What do you want?' She tried her best to sound tough.

'We're offerin' yeh the opportunity t' purchase insurance from us . . . Isn't that so, Billy?'

Billy took his cue and convulsed with laughter. 'Yeah, Joxer, yeah . . . purchase insurance.' He was helpless, leaning his hand on the bar and doubling over in a paroxysm of mirth.

Alice had graduated from anger to a state of abject terror. She knew she was at the mercy of the two apes. Billy, recovered from his attack of hysteria, was glaring at her menacingly. Joxer was examining his fingernails. 'We want two fifty a week,' he said matter-of-factly. 'We'll collect this night, every week.'

'Two pounds fifty?' Alice was confused.

'No, yeh stupid bitch ... Two *hundred* an' fifty!' Joxer yelled. Alice flinched away. 'We'll take the first instalment now, seein' as we're here.'

'Two hundred and fifty pounds? Are you out of your mind?' Alice was incensed. Terror was now replaced by fury.

'No missus, bu' you are, if yeh don't feckin' pay up,' Billy roared.

'Maybe I'll just just call the cops,' Alice reached for the phone. Joxer melodramatically ripped the phone cable from the wall. 'That wouldn't be smart,' he said. 'We know where yez live.' He looked around the restaurant and smiled. 'I knew this place had potential. I knew yeh wouldn't let me down. You and your fairy friends.' He looked at Billy. 'See, Billy, queers know about this sort of thing. About style. You've got to hand it to them. They know all about style.'

Alice was afraid again. Her hands were shaking and her legs had turned to jelly. Joxer, tired of hanging around, grabbed her by the hair and dragged her towards the till. 'Open the friggin' thing,' he ordered.

Alice opened the empty till. 'The money's gone to the night safe at the bank,' she managed to say. 'My partner took it there. He's due back here soon, though ... him and his friends.' Her feeble attempt at intimidation fell on deaf ears.

'Yeh think we're worried about yer man an' his fairy friends?' Billy jeered.

Joxer let go of her hair. 'We'll be back t'morra at me usual time. Have me steak and yer payment ready, or it's no more Mister Nice Guy ... wha'?'

Billy once again laughed like a drain. To reinforce his point, Joxer demolished a large vase of lilies on his way out.

Alice stood by the till shaking uncontrollably. The place was a shambles. Red wine splattered across the floor and up the walls. Broken shards of crockery and glassware littered the floor. She bent down and picked up a battered lily from the debris, then jumped sky high as she heard the kitchen door open. Joe was standing in the doorway. 'Are they gone?'

'Well, thanks a bunch for your help!' she snarled.

'Gimme a break. Them fellas're animals. I didn't want me nose broke.'

'Well, the straw's finally broken the camel's back. He's gone too far. I'm going to do what Hector should have done in the first place. I'm calling the cops.' She knelt down and plugged the phone into the wall socket. 'Stupid prat, like I can't plug the bloody phone in again.'

'I really wouldn't do that, Alice.' Joe put his hand on her arm. 'They know where yeh live.'

Alice hesitated.

Joe said, 'He works for Jesse James. He's his right-hand man. If it was me, I'd give 'em the money. You wouldn't want t' mess with the likes of Jesse James.'

The name sounded familiar, then Alice realised why. 'Jesse James? Who the hell's Jesse James?' Despite the terror she couldn't help but smirk. 'Is he for real?'

'Too bleedin' right, he's for real. An' he don't take no hostages. Yeh think Joxer's a psycho. He's only trottin' after James. I'd pay up and be glad he don't want more.'

It was enough to stop her in her tracks. She sat down on the floor with her back against the wall. Joe handed her a large glass of brandy. 'Here, drink this,' he said, and sat down next to her. 'So what are yeh goin' to do?'

They heard the door open. 'Christ! What the hell happened here?' Conor's voice. Mason was with him.

She heaved herself up from the floor. Suddenly she was weary. 'Someone else recognised the potential of the Samovar.'

'What are you talking about?' He was at a loss to understand. He looked around at the mess.

'Our friend and valued customer Joxer Boxer came in looking for protection money, but he called it insurance.'

'What! You can be serious. That stuff only happens on TV. Did you call the cops?'

'In yer dreams,' Joe snorted. 'Call the cops and they'll burn yeh out.'

'Who's they?' Mason asked, refilling Alice's glass with amber liquid. 'Here, drink this, you're shaking.'

Alice picked up an overturned chair and sat down. 'Some guy called, would you believe, Jesse James. Apparently the brave Joxer works for him, and he was sent in to redecorate.' She looked around at the wine-stained floor and the broken glasses and cups and sighed a heavy sigh. 'How are you back so soon? I thought you were going on to a club?'

'The club was crap, but pity we were out at all,' Conor said, sounding dazed. 'Not that I'd fancy my chances against Joxer.'

'How much were they looking for?' Mason asked.

'Two fifty a week.'

'Two pounds fifty?' Mason and Conor chorused.

Joxer dropped Billy off at the corner of Meath Street and then headed for home. His luxury Sandymount apartment was a long way from the Sheriff Street flats he grew up in. It had been a satisfactory evening's work. Yer woman'd pay up, no problem. Her and her fairy friends. Between her and the Asian all-night convenience store he was well in excess of this month's sales target. He'd told his neighbour, Mrs Heart, an elderly widow who had taken quite a shine to him, that he was Sales Manager for an insurance firm. She'd been suitably impressed, even asked his opinion about her own policy. Yes, Joxer liked his new life. He smiled to himself as he parked the car. His car. His BMW, in front of the low-rise development with sea views and thought, Yeah. A long way from Sheriff Street flats, wha'?

After the shock had worn off, they cleared up the mess and, as they were dong it, discussed their options. Mason was still in favour of calling the cops. Conor, who was crouching down picking through the broken shards of crockery, trying to find any undamaged espresso cups, stopped what he was doing and looked up. 'All right for you to say. They don't have your address.'

'Anyway,' Alice added. 'What if the cops find out about me

and Hector? I could be prosecuted. I could be carted off to jail. No. We can't risk the cops. We'll have to take our chances.'

'But if we don't pay, this Jesse James character could get physical. Like Joe said, he could burn us out.'

It was a dilemma. Pay up and avoid arson and at best grievous bodily harm, or go to the cops and risk both the former scenario and Alice being slung in the slammer.

At the end of the day, unpalatable as it was, they realised that they had no other immediate option but to pay up until they could think of a better solution for keeping both themselves and the Samovar in one piece.

The following night at closing time, Joxer Boxer turned up with Billy. They both enjoyed the usual dinner on the house before relieving the Samovar of the tidy sum of two hundred and fifty pounds. It was to be the first payment of many.

Chapter Fifteen

Two weeks before Christmas, Declan turned up on the doorstep. After their last meeting, and the part he'd played in convincing Mick and Maura Finn of Conor's supposed marriage, Alice was not particularly pleased to see him. For Conor's sake she hid her animosity, though not very well, apparently, because Declan's first words to her were, 'I suppose I'm the last person you wanted to see.'

She stood back to invite him in. 'I wouldn't put it quite like that, but what brings you here anyway?' Any explanations had to wait a while as Conor, on hearing his brother's voice, rushed out of the kitchen and there was the usual banter for five minutes or so.

Alice left them to it and went about washing her hair. When she returned to the sitting room half an hour later the two brothers were deep in conversation, which ceased abruptly as she entered the room. After a few seconds Conor said, 'Isn't it great? Declan's moved to Dublin.'

'Oh? What happened to the big job in Cork?' Alice replied, failing miserably to keep the sarcastic edge from her voice.

If Declan noticed, he ignored it. 'Got a new job. I thought I should be up here where all the action is.'

'He's working for an investment bank,' Conor said proudly. 'He was head-hunted.'

'Bully for Declan.' Alice flopped down on the sofa and picked up a magazine. Conor and Declan continued to talk together. Alice wasn't listening. She wasn't interested in anything Declan had to say, but the sound of their voices was intrusive and she couldn't help but overhear. Conor asked Declan about the job, and it transpired that Declan was to be head of some high-powered International Futures division. He told Conor about his new apartment. How handy it was for the office, situated as it as in the new Custom House development.

After a while there was a lull in the conversation. Then Conor said, 'Alice. What are you doing about Christmas?'

Alice looked up from her magazine. 'What do you mean, what am I doing about it?'

Conor shrugged. 'Well, have you any plans?'

'Not especially.'

'Great! The thing is . . . How would you feel about coming down to Tanagh with Declan and me?'

'I'd rather put my hand in the liquidiser.'

Declan, Conor and Alice set off for Tanagh at the crack of dawn on Christmas morning. Even by the time they were halfway there, she still hadn't figured out how they had talked her into it, though in reality the reasons were not especially complicated. After all the stresses of the last couple of months associated with Hector and the Immigration hit-squad and then their financial problems Alice needed a break. She needed time away when she wouldn't have to think about the likes of Joxer Boxer and Jesse James. She needed to have at least two days when she didn't feel the need to look over her shoulder for fear of bumping into Sean Holland.

Conor, on the other hand, seemed to be taking it all in his stride. She had long ago come to the conclusion that he was quite straightforward emotionally. When good things happen, enjoy. When bad things happen, be desolate for a while then go on to the next experience. Maybe it was all the practice he'd had, falling madly in love one moment only to be dumped for one reason or another the next. Like her, Conor had a penchant for thoroughly unsuitable men.

Mercifully, in Declan's brand spanking new top-of-the-range Mercedes, the journey only took four hours, though if Conor had been driving it would probably have been short-ened by a further hour. Alice dozed for most of the way. They arrived at ten a.m. and, after an enthusiatic welcome from both Mick and Maura, they were whisked off to Mass. It was the first time in years that Alice had darkened the door of a church. She felt like a child again.

Halfway through the service she realised that she was enjoying it. The choir singing carols, the smell of the incense, and the bells jingling at the consecration. She had to take her cue from Maura as far as the kneeling, sitting and standing thing went. All the rules seemed to have changed since her last visit, which was the day she had left the nuns at the hostel and got her own bedsit.

It seemed a bit picky not to take communion, so when all the family filed out of the pew to take the sacrament she joined in with the spirit of the thing. Carried away, she enthusiastically shook hands with all in the pew behind and in front, when the priest asked the congregation to show the sign of peace, and sang her heart out along with the choir when the organ played 'Silent Night'. By the end of the service she had completely forgotten about the potential horrors that would inevitably follow over the next day and a half.

After Mass was over, Maura had a showing-off-my-daughter-in-law fest outside the church. Alice's good humour was tested when she noticed Declan smirking. 'I suppose you think this is funny,' she snarled under her breath.

'In the extreme,' he sniggered. 'Mr Monroe. Have you met my sister-in-law?'

Mr Monroe, it transpired, was both Declan's and Conor's primary school teacher. He pumped her hand, then thumped Conor (who had just wandered over) on the back. 'Well done, lad,' he said a touch too jubilantly. The subtext of the remark being, And I always thought you were a queer.

When they got home, gifts were exchanged. Conor had shopped for the two of them. To Maura he gave a chunky red cardigan. Maura was thrilled. Alice later found out that Conor gave her a chunky cardigan every year, albeit in a different colour, and his mother now possessed a wardrobe full. For Mick he bought a bottle of fifteen-year-old single malt. (She heartily approved of that one.) For Declan a Newcastle football jersey (Alice was dubious about this gift until she saw

Declan's positive reaction). And for her, he and Mason (whom she now considered as Conor's new significant other) had bought the tiny Canon APS camera she had expressed a liking for in passing. She was quite touched by the thought Conor had put into her gift.

She bought Conor the Versace shirt she knew he had been drooling over for some weeks.

Next, Maura handed out her gifts. To Conor, she gave a maroon shirt and tie set. To Declan, an olive-green, thick-knit, zip-fronted cardigan with suede pockets and suede patches at the elbows.

Maura proved to be big into cardigans and Alice was struck dumb as she handed over an oversized chunky hand-knit creation in varying shades of beige and brown which Declan, sensing her discomfort, malevolently insisted that she put on. She, in turn, insisted that both Conor and Declan do likewise with their gifts.

When it was Declan's turn, he handed his mother an envelope. 'It's a joint present for you and Da,' he said. Maura excitedly opened the envelope and almost expired with pleasure. It contained tickets for an all-expenses-paid trip to America, in order that Maura and Mick could visit with Maura's brother, Paddy, the priest who lived in Philadelphia.

Bloody show-off, Alice thought.

He gave Conor a mobile phone, then handed Alice a gift-wrapped box. When she opened it she found a large atomiser of her favourite Issey Miyake perfume. She thanked him graciously, but it didn't soften her opinion of him.

Maura was a hearty cook. Christmas dinner was a gargantuan affair. There seemed to be enough food to feed an army, with a turkey the size of a small goat. Alice offered to help, but was discouraged. Mick pointed out that it never works out to have two women in a kitchen. The table was laden to the point of collapse and decorated with crackers and holly-printed paper serviettes. Alice, who had never been allowed to enjoy even the remotest semblance of a family life, found it rather overpowering at first. Life had made her cynical about such things. But after a couple of glasses of wine, she began to relax and appreciate being treated as part of an extended family, however erroneously. After the Christmas pudding, with both custard and brandy sauce, she sat back and watched the interaction between the others at the table. Maura was bringing her sons up to date on the doings of their contemporaries and from time to time Mick would butt in with some comment or other. Heavy-handed references were made to so-and-so who'd just had a baby, and them only married a year. Or *that one*, having twins and them only five minutes married.

Alice, through her comfortably drunken haze, thought it was like watching a soap on TV.

Mick went out to the kitchen to make Gaelic coffee (a Christmas ritual, apparently) and Maura opened a tub of Roses chocolate.

Alice thought she was going to explode. She would have liked to have gone for a long walk to work off part of her dinner, but it was raining heavily so that put paid to that. Instead, she fell asleep in front of the television with the rest of them for the rest of the day.

She awoke at around seven with a pounding hangover and a mouth like the bottom of a bird cage. For a moment she thought she might have a temperature until she realised she was still wearing Maura's present. Maura, chirpy as ever, wheeled in a trolley piled high with turkey sandwiches, Christmas cake, mince pieces and tea. Conor was still asleep and Declan had gone off somewhere. Mick roused himself and rubbed his hands when he saw the supper.

Maura said, 'I thought we'd have the supper early, then have the sing-song.'

The sight of all that food made Alice nauseous. The only way she would have been able to manage another morsel was if Maura had liquidised it and fed her through an intravenous line. Furthermore, as she had never been what one would call a *joining-in* person, the prospect of the community singing was not especially attractive either. She mumbled an excuse and fled to her room, where she sat on the window seat in the dark. In fairness to Maura and Mick, they had made her very welcome and assimilated her into their family, but she was beginning to feel smothered. What with Maura's heavy hints about babies, mischievously encouraged by Declan, she was sorry she had allowed herself to be talked into the trip. After the Christmas rush at the restaurant, maybe what she really needed was some time to herself.

Declan was having a ball at her expense. He thought her predicament hilarious. She couldn't figure out why he was being so obnoxious. (She thought it was pretty damn good of her to play along with the bogus marriage story in the first place.) Maura, on the other hand, seemed determined to administer death by food.

A car drove up to the front door and a middle-aged couple jumped out. Light spilled on to the porch as the front door opened, and she heard Maura and Mick welcoming the newcomers. A couple of minutes later she heard Mick calling her. She tried to feign deafness, then seriously considered feigning death when, a minute or so later, Maura shouted, 'Come on down, Alice, or you'll miss the sing-song.'

The evening descended beyond the gruesome. What appeared to be hordes of the Finns' neighbours and friends came to join in with the entertainment. One woman even brought her harp.

Mick kept refilling Alice's glass with whatever bottle he had to hand. He was bordering on tipsy, but handling it well. For the amount of alcohol he had consumed throughout the day, Alice decided that he must have hollow legs. She gratefully knocked back whatever he poured into her glass, as oblivion seemed the best option on offer.

At one point, after a particularly embarrassing duet between Maura and her best friend Winnie (they chose 'The Wind Beneath My Wings', with close, off-key harmonies), Declan said, 'Won't you give us a song, Alice?'

'I don't sing,' Alice said curtly. The drink was making her feel fierce.

'Well, what about a pome?' Maura suggested. 'You must have a party piece?'

The whole company was looking expectantly in her direction. There were a few muttered encouragements like, 'Go on,

Alice', and 'Good on yeh, girlie'. Alice looked over in Conor's direction. He was studiously examining his fingernails. Declan was smiling innocently. 'I don't know any poetry, or have a party piece,' Alice said stiffly. 'In fact, I think if you don't mind I'll go and have a lie down.'

As she made her way unsteadily from the room she heard Maura whisper to Winnie, 'She's a bit depressed. *Women's trouble*, you know. An' she's only dyin' to get pregnant. Declan told me.' Alice let out an involuntary whimper.

With difficulty, she removed some of her outer clothes and fell into bed. She didn't hear Conor when he came into the bedroom and slept like a corpse until just after dawn the next morning.

Her head was still thumping when she opened her eyes and she had to run to the bathroom to be sick. She tried to be quiet, not wanting to build up Maura's hopes, then went downstairs to the kitchen to hunt for some Solpadine.

Declan was sitting at the kitchen table tucking into fried eggs and bacon. He looked disgustingly fit and well. Maybe he'd inherited Mick's legs. The need for a hangover cure was more pressing than her with to avoid him so she curtly said, 'Do you have painkillers?'

He hadn't heard her come into the room as she was barefoot. He looked up from his breakfast. 'Feeling a little queasy, or would it be morning sickness?' He couldn't resist the temptation to wind her up.

In her present fragile state she wasn't able for him and couldn't come up with anything more original than, 'Piss off.'

Declan grinned and reached up to a high cupboard and handed her a box of Panadol, then got a glass from the cupboard and filled it from the tap. 'Here you are.'

She threw three tablets into her mouth and took a long drink of water. Declan sat back down at the table and watched her. Even though she was still crumpled from sleep and the worse for wear after the night before, it occurred to him that she was a fine-looking woman. He had never really noticed before so the notion surprised him. Pity she was such a prickly customer. 'Fancy a fry?'

'Get a life!' she snapped and flounced out, back up to bed. Declan went bck to his rasher and eggs.

Conor turned over and opened his eyes as she slid under the covers. 'You owe me, big time, for this,' she snarled as she pulled the duvet over her head and wished for death.

Conor was at a loss. He didn't know what he was supposed to have done. As far as he was concerned she'd had a good time. Wasn't she drinking to beat the band the night before?

In the end he put her foul humour down to the drink, and made a mental note to warn her about mixing the grape and the grain in future.

Chapter Sixteen

When Joxer and Billy turned up at the end of the week for the protection payment, they demanded a seasonal increment to the order of another two hundred and fifty pounds. Alice was outraged.

'But that's double.'

Joxer looked at Billy and made a show of counting on his fingers. 'Yeah, yer righ'. That's double. It's customary at Christmas for yeh t' give us a bonus. Kinda like a Christmas box, wha'?' There was no such protocol but mindful of his sales targets and percentage increases, Joxer was anxious to be ahead of the game. Also, as an additional incentive, James had said he would give his right-hand man a bonus if he exceeded those targets.

Billy took his cue and laughed uproariously. 'Yeah, Joxer. Ho ho ho. The Christmas bonus. Heh heh heh.'

'What are you? Some sort of double act?' Alice snapped. 'Five hundred's too much.'

'Suit yerself,' Joxer said. Alice waited for Billy to fall about laughing again, but it seemed Joxer's last remark was not supposed to he humorous. Joxer looked around the restaurant and rubbed his chin. 'Yeh've a good business here. It'd be a pity t' throw it away for the sake of a couple a' hundred quid.'

Alice knew they'd have to pay up in the end, but it went against the grain. They'd worked hard for what they'd got. She couldn't see why a bully-boy like this Jesse James character should just be able to walk in and skim off their profits. Grudgingly she handed over the cash.

When they had gone, she went to find Conor in the kitchen.

He was doing some preparation for the following day's lunch menu. 'I suppose the slime balls came for their cut,' he said.

Alice leaned on the counter and watched him preparing the dough for the bread rolls. 'They doubled the ante this week, what with it being Christmas and all.' Her tone was as sour as the dough.

Conor stopped kneading abruptly. 'Five hundred quid?' He was as outraged as Alice. 'That's ridiculous. What are they trying to do? Put us out of business?'

'Oh, apparently, it's only a seasonal thing. A sort of Christmas box. Billy thought it was hilarious. Those two are a regular Laurel and Hardy.'

'This can't go on.' Conor folded his arms across his chest. 'We've got to do something about it.'

'Like what? Cut out the middle man and torch the place ourselves?'

'Maybe if we reasoned with James? Pointed out that he's in danger of ruining us?'

It sounded too easy to Alice. She said as much to Conor. He shrugged and went back to kneading his dough, this time with increased vigour. He thought Alice was being unnecessarily negative. The way he saw it, James was killing them. Were they supposed to just lie down and die? He'd discussed the matter with Mason who was still of the opinion that they should have gone to the cops in the first instance. He was inclined to agree with the logic, but Alice's fears couldn't be discounted. After all, although she had acquired half of the restaurant as payment for marrying Hector, hadn't she also done it for him, as his friend? It didn't seem fair to put her in jeopardy of prosecution should the cops start digging around. Personally he couldn't see any reason why they should. However, Alice was of a different opinion. And she'd proved her friendship by insisting, after the renovations had been completed, on drawing up another contract making them equal partners. But at the end of the day, Jesse James was in serious danger of draining the business dry. Something had to be done. 'Well, I think we should talk to him. Try to negotiate.' He gave the dough a bash with his fist. 'Maybe we'll catch him on the hop. Maybe no one ever tried to reason with him before.'

Alice was the one caught on the hop by Conor's sudden attack of assertiveness, and she doubtfully agreed to the plan.

They found out from Joe the next day that Jesse James ran what he called a finance house from offices on Mercer Street. When Joe mentioned the name, Quick Call Finance, Alice remembered seeing posters for the company. The wording was along the lines of, 'Trouble-free unsecured loans. The no-hassle way to get the things you want without the wait.' There was also a free-phone number. There would be no hassle as long as the punter paid up the exorbitant repayments on the nail, otherwise the very big men with ugly dogs, or was it the ugly men with very big dogs, came round.

After they closed the following afternoon, Alice and Conor got a cab round to Mercer Street. The offices of Quick Call Finance were situated above an off-licence. The logo painted on the glass door had a perky cartoon telephone with a smiley face. It all looked very welcoming. Conor shoved the door open and they went in. A bored-looking bottle blonde, with over-permed hair and a sunbed tan, sat at a word processor, painting her nails. Another girl, who could have been a clone, leaned over the counter reading the *Irish Mirror*. She begrudgingly looked up, but only after Alice and Conor had been standing there for about half a minute. 'Can I help you?' she asked, unenthusiastically.

'We're here to see Jesse James,' Alice said.

'D'you have an appointment?'

'No, but he'll see us.' Alice looked at a door that led to an inner office. 'In there, is it?'

She didn't wait for a reply, but barged over and opened the door. The girl made some protest but by that time they were standing in the lion's den. Jesse James was sitting behind a large desk reading *The Irish Independent*. He was younger than Alice had expected, late thirties or early forties, she estimated. He was good-looking in an unrefined sort of way and had the appearance of someone who probably worked out but not excessively.

'Who the hell are you?' he asked.

'Alice Little and this is my partner Conor Finn. We have the Samovar.'

The girl from reception hurried in. 'I'm sorry, Mr James. I couldn't stop 'em.'

Jesse James waved her away. 'It's okay, Deirdre,' then to Alice and Conor, 'To what do I owe the pleasure?'

'It's about the protection money,' Alice said.

'You mean the insurance payment?'

'Insurance payment, protection money, what's the difference? Whatever you call it, it's too much. We can't afford it. It's driving us out of business.'

'Well, it's up to you. I mean if you're finding it a problem you can always stop paying.' James' tone was even and reasonable. He looked relaxed and calm.

Alice, who had been expecting a psychopath, was taken aback. She had no notion that it would be that easy. 'Oh . . . Really? Well that's fine, then.' She looked at Conor and smiled. 'That's fine, isn't it, Conor?'

Conor couldn't believe Alive could be so gullible. 'Get real, Alice. You don't think he means it, do you?'

'But he said . . .'

'I said, you can stop paying if it's a problem.' James was cleaning his fingernails with the tip of a letter-opener. 'Of course, if you want to risk something happening to your business, that's up to you.' Then he laughed.

Alice felt like a prat. Conor, ever the diplomat, tried reason. 'Look, Mr James. You're crippling us. How about you reduce the payments? Surely it's in your interests for us to stay in business? It's January. It's our quietest time of year.' He thought he had made a reasonable point. He waited for James to respond.

James stretched and gave an exaggerated sigh. 'What am I going to do with you?' he said patronisingly. They waited. Standing there in front of his desk, Alice felt like a schoolgirl waiting for the Mother Superior to read the riot act. Conor shared similar feelings, though his concerned Brother Martin and a hefty leather strap.

'Okay,' James said after a while. Alice looked hopefully at Conor. 'Okay,' he repeated. 'I'll cut the payments . . .' Alice gave a sigh of relief, which soon turned to a gasp as he finished the sentence. '. . . for the months of January and February, then I'll up the payments to three-fifty a week for the rest of the year.'

'You can't do that,' Alice exploded. 'That's criminal!'

Jesse James laughed again. 'Criminal? It's that, all right.'

The last remark caused Alice to totally lose it. 'You bastard,' she screamed, 'you fucking bastard!'

James stopped laughing. In a flash he jumped out from behind the desk and belted Alice hard across the face. 'Don't you fucking swear at me, you slag!' he yelled.

'There's no need for that!' Conor tried to move between Alice and James. James swatted Conor out of the way, whacking him in the solar plexus with his elbow, and sending him flying across the room. Conor, winded, landed in a crumpled heap by the door. He was gasping for breath. He was afraid, but he was also very angry.

James grabbed the front of Alice's coat. He was only a couple of inches taller than her, but there all similarity ended, because he was as strong as an ox. He all but lifted her feet off the ground. His face was only inches from hers. 'Don't you ever even *think* of calling me a bastard again, you slag, do you hear me?'

His breath smelled of mint. His eyes were wild and scary, the pupils tiny dots of black. Terrified, she revised her original opinion of his psychopath status. Conor, still fighting for breath, struggled to get to his feet. He had never felt so inadequate in his life.

James's outburst was nothing personal, it was solely a reaction to Alice calling him a bastard. Jesse James despised being called a bastard. It was a throwback from his childhood when a particularly evil teacher, one Brenden Braden (a spoiled priest, by all accounts) took a set against him and regularly humiliated him in front of the entire class because he had no father. He would cast up to him how worthless he was, and repeat the word *bastard* like a mantra, with every slash of the strap as he leathered the boy's backside.

Conor, who was using the door for support, was still gasping for breath and staggered to his feet. He wanted to be sick.

'You don't think I believe this crap about you going out of business, do you? What kind of eejitt do you think I am? Don't you think I do research? This is a business I'm running here. Just like you, all I'm trying to do is run a business. I can't have the likes of you coming in here, giving me fucking sob stories. I've an image to maintain.' He lowered Alice to the floor.

Conor, rubbing his midriff, was at last upright and breathing again. His heart was pounding in his chest. He could hear it in his head. Ker thump, ker thump, ker thump. He clung on to the door frame.

Like Conor, Alice was stunned speechless. She had never witnessed a display like it. It was so sudden. Jesse James was like two different people. As suddenly as the episode had started, it ceased and he was Mister Reasonable again. 'Right, then,' James said. 'One-fifty for January and February, then I'll expect three-fifty thereafter. Okay?'

The *okay* sounded like a genuine 'Is that all right? Does that suit you?' sort of okay, but they were no longer under any illusion that Jesse James was anything other than psychotic. But James hadn't finished. As he brushed an imaginary piece of lint of the lapel of his very well-cut suit and sat back behind his desk, he smiled at Alice. 'And then, of course, there's the small matter of your husband.'

'What?' Alice's guts did a jig. 'What are you talking about?'

James picked up the letter-opener again and took up where he'd left off, cleaning his already pristine nails. 'I told you. I run a business here. I do my research and a little bird told me that you married a woofter Russian so she could stay in the country with her boyfriend here.' He gave his head a chuck in Conor's direction.

Alice shot a look at Conor. 'I don't know what you're talking about,' she croaked.

It wasn't as a result of active research on James's part that he'd found out about Alice and Hector and the dodgy marriage but by accident. Joxer collected from TransV and had overheard people talking. He'd filed the information away in case it might be useful at a later date.

That was part of Joxer's value, he kept his eyes and ears open. At the time, despite the fact that he regularly ate there, he hadn't thought the Samovar a worthwhile gig. Thought it was blood out of a stone. He'd recognised that there was potential, particularly after the young fella went to cook there, and had said as much to James but decided that it was better to wait a while. To give them the chance to build up the turnover. Good call.

James had always believed in the market economy and that was the beauty of offering incentives to his most trusted man. Joxer couldn't afford to let any opportunity slip by. Just as when it became obvious that the Samovar was now a paying proposition he'd been right in there. Joxer was glad to be able to fill the boss in on the background, it being useful information should they get iffy about the payments. Both he and Jesse James liked to keep something in reserve to save any unnecessary violence. Not because they had a distaste for violence, in fact from time to time Joxer got twitchy if he hadn't worked someone over, but James was smart. Unnecessary violence only gave the cops an excuse, and there was no point in inviting that inconvenience if it could be avoided. They were only looking for an excuse.

He put down the paper knife and slid open a desk drawer, removing a hard-backed A4 diary. He opened it and flipped through the pages. 'Let me *seeee* . . .' He settled on a page and his finger skimmed down words line by line. 'Here we are.' He read the notation. 'Hector Han . . .' He looked up. 'How do you pronounce that?'

Without thinking, Conor said, 'Hanusiak.'

'Right. Hanusiak.' He smiled again and tut-tutted. 'Serious business, marriages of convenience. I wonder what the cops'd make of that.'

'Well, that went well,' Conor said, once they were back outside on the street. 'We should've kept our mouths shut.'

'You don't mean that. We had to try.' Alice gingerly patted the side of her face and felt it hot. 'Lambs to the slaughter or not.'

Chapter Seventeen

Melanie Broderick would have known Alice Little anywhere even though it was over fourteen years since she had laid an eye on her. It was a surprise to see her working in the restaurant – as far as she'd been aware, Alice was a shop assistant. At least that's what her mother had told her. When she'd walked in with Declan and recognised her stepsister her first inclination had been to turn and flee. Not because she disliked Alice but, considering the way her mother had treated her, she was embarrassed and a little wary about facing her again. What if she made a scene? Melanie couldn't stand scenes. That was down to her mother too. Patricia, if the silent treatment failed, always managed to get her own way in the end by causing an unholy scene.

'Hello, Alice, good to see you,' Declan said pleasantly. Caught on the hop, Alice didn't have any smart remark ready, so she smiled back at him in a professional manner and picked up a couple of menus.

'Hello, Declan. Table for two?' Then she caught sight of his dinner companion. 'Good grief, Melanie!'

'Hello, Alice!' It was obvious that Melanie was equally surprised.

'Do you two know each other?' Declan asked.

'You could say that,' Alice replied. 'Melanie used to be my stepsister.' The *used to be* wasn't lost on Melanie.

'How are you?' Melanie gushed. 'It's been ages.' She lunged forward and kissed Alice on the cheek.

Alice fought the urge to cringe away. 'Yes, eh . . . ages.'

'You look wonderful. What are you doing working here? I thought you were in fashion?'

'Oh . . . em . . . I gave that up. I work here now.' Alice bit her tongue. She knew this was neither the time nor the place to have a slanging match with her former stepsibling.

'She's in partnership with my brother Conor,' Declan said.

'A partner!' Melanie said breathlessly. 'With your brother? How wonderful.' She beamed at Alice. 'We must do lunch some day to catch up on things.'

'Eh . . . Yes. Yes, we must, er, em . . . *do* lunch.' Alice felt that she would sooner stand in a tub of boiling lard. 'Shall I show you to your table?'

Melanie had been a sickly, whiny child whose life had seemed to be filled with prolonged bouts of either whinging or vomiting. She did both on a regular basis, the latter in copious amounts. After a while Alice became immune to moaning. It became just a background noise, like the radio, but the vomiting was a different matter. Sometimes, caught unawares, Melanie's vomit was truly projectile, and Alice always made sure to sit out of range. She was relieved that, after the move to Maurice Broderick's house in Blackrock, she ate alone in the kitchen, rather than being present in the dining room for the spectacle.

Fortunately, by the time Melanie was twelve, just before Alice was banished to the care of the nuns, a new and efficient GP, whose sister had the disease, diagnosed Melanie as a coeliac. Her diet was radically altered. Both the vomiting and the whinging ceased, and Melanie, subsequently, blossomed. Alice hadn't been around to witness the blossoming.

All through the evening Alice found herself staring at Melanie. She was the image of Patricia, except for the fact that she was blonde. Unlike her mother who, Alice recalled, always favoured the more flashy designer wear such as Moschino and Versace, Melanie was soberly dressed in a black business suit. It was well cut and smart, but to Alice's professional eye, it was obviously chain-store. Also, unlike Patricia, who was into big hair in a huge way, Melanie had hers well cut, short and straight. Alice wondered what had become of Patricia and if she was still married to Maurice Broderick.

Later, whilst in the kitchn collecting a fresh pot of coffee, she mentioned to Conor that Declan was in the dining room. 'And you'll never guess who he's with.'

'Who?' Conor asked, as he artistically drizzled a ribbon of sauce round a particularly scrumptious piece of rare fillet.

'Melanie.'

He stopped in mid-drizzle. 'Melanie? Your stepsister? She of the projectile puke?'

'The very same.'

When things quietened down, Conor came out of the kitchen and joined his brother and Melanie at their table. From time to time, Alice caught them looking over in her direction as if they were talking about her. Mason, noticing her sombre humour, sidled over and put his arm around her. 'What's up?'

'Oh, nothing,' Alice muttered grumpily. 'Just your boyfriend fraternising with the enemy.'

'Declan's not the enemy . . . is he?'

'No . . . Melanie . . . My awful stepsister. And they're talking about me.'

Mason gave her a squeeze. 'Chill out, Alice. That sounds dangerously like paranoia to me.' He kissed the top of her head and joined the others at the table. There was a round of introductions and much laughter. By the time the final straggle of customers were leaving Alice was seething inside. How bloody dare they talk about me! she raged to herself. Conor walked over and filled five brandy goblets. 'Come on, Alice. Lighten up. She's okay. Really. Come and join in.'

With the restaurant empty of customers, Alice felt it was safe to sit with Melanie. She was ready for an argument if Melanie saw fit, fired up for one, in fact. She poured herself a coffee and sat down next to Mason. 'Sooooo, Melanie,' she said for openers, 'and how's my wicked stepmommy?'

'I don't know.' Melanie looked down at the tablecloth. 'We had a falling out a few years ago and she threw me out.'

Alice felt suddenly deflated. Melanie wasn't following her script. She wasn't prepared for this. 'Oh,' she wavered. 'I'm . . . em . . . I'm sorry.'

Melanie reached across the table and placed her hand on top

of Alice's. 'Why should *you* be sorry? My mother treated you appallingly.'

'I know, but she's your flesh and blood.' Alice felt genuinely sorry for Melanie.

Mason nudged her elbow. 'See,' he muttered. 'Paranoia.'

Melanie picked up her glass and raised it in the air. 'I think we should drink a toast to survivors.' She looked over at Alice. 'And to the fact that, thank God, you can choose your friends if not your relatives.'

'I'll drink to that.' Alice lifted her glass, pointedly shooting a look in Declan's direction, before she remembered that he wasn't a relative at all.

It was as they were making the toast that Melanie noticed the ring. 'You're married!' she squealed, grabbing hold of Alice's left hand and peering at the ring. 'Oh, I'm dying to meet him. Does he work here?'

Alice shot an anguished look in Conor's direction. 'Ummm. Well . . . My, eh, my husband . . .'

'He left,' Conor said. 'Alice's husband left a little while ago, I'm afraid.'

'Left?' There was a pause, before Melanie's hand shot to her mouth. 'Oh . . . *left*, as in . . . eh . . . left.' She gripped Alice's hand all the harder. 'I'm so sorry. How awful.' She was mortified to have mentioned it.

Alice gave a heroic smile and then a little shrug. 'Those are the breaks,' she said. 'You put your trust in someone and they let you down. You know how it is.'

Melanie nodded in agreement then gave her hand an extra squeeze before releasing it. Alice was dying to get the gory details of Melanie's and Patricia's falling out. Three brandies later she threw caution to the wind. 'So what happened? What did you and Patricia fall out about?'

'I told my mother a few home truths too many, Alice, and she took exception.'

'What home truths?'

Melanie wasn't so forthcoming on the details. All she would say was, 'Well, about the way she treated you for one. There she is sitting on charity committees for homeless children and famines, and whatever ladies who lunch do. I just couldn't take the hypocrisy of it any more . . . And then there was,' she faltered. '. . . there was other stuff.'

'What other stuff?'

Melanie shook her head. 'Em . . . just stuff. You know Mother.' She smiled brightly again but the smile didn't reach her eyes this time, they were deep and sad.

Alice opened her mouth to ask for more, but Mason kicked her in the shin. 'Leave it there, Alice,' he whispered. 'Leave it there.'

Despite herself, Alice enjoyed what remained of the evening. Melanie, it transpired, was a bond trader and worked for the same bank as Declan, though not in the same department. Alice commented that she always thought the stock market was like a glorified bookies.

'Absolutely,' Declan agreed. 'It's the buzz of gambling with someone else's money and winning.'

'It must be very stressful,' Mason remarked.

'Only if you lose, and your position is down a few million,' Melanie said. 'Of course in a bad week that could happen a couple of times, but if you're lucky you recoup it by the close of business.'

When she went off to the ladies, Declan told them that she was considered a bit of a whiz kid in the bond trading field with a killer instinct for it. It all sounded very high powered and high pressure to Alice.

She idly wondered if Declan and Melanie were an item. She was surprised and a little alarmed when she realised that this prospect gave her a sudden pang of jealousy. She dismissed it as ridiculous. Why should she be jealous of Melanie and Declan? What was that about? Later, she rationalised that it wasn't the fact that *they* might be an item. It was the fact that she didn't have anyone. It brought it home to her, seeing Conor with Mason, and Declan with Melanie, how alone she was. Nevertheless, she decided to grill Conor later on the subject.

The conversation was jovial for the remainder of the evening and she even found herself enjoying what Declan had to say.

They called it a night at three a.m., with Alice and Melanie exchanging phone numbers and promising to meet for lunch some time.

'I misjudged Melanie,' she said to Conor and Mason when they got back to the apartment. 'She's so totally different.'

'People change,' Mason said. 'What was she like as a kid?'

Alice thought about it. 'Now I come to think of it, I don't really know. I never saw that much of her. I haven't seen her since I was twelve. I just took it for granted that I should hate her as much as I hate Patricia.'

'Well, I think it's nice you have someone you can call an almost relative,' Conor said, adding as an afterthought, 'apart from Mam, Da, Declan and me, of course.'

'Of course,' Alice said dryly.

Chapter Eighteen

A couple of days later, as the last lunchtime punters were leaving and Alice was totting up the dockets, Mason went into the kitchen to see Conor. 'Did you mention it?' he asked. 'Did you mention I'd be moving in?'

Conor shook his head. 'I thought we could tell her together.' The fact was, Conor needed some moral support. He wasn't sure what Alice's reaction would be to Mason moving in. Not that she had any right to veto his plans, but after the trauma of Hector he was uneasy. In some ways he wasn't sure if he was ready for Mason to move in. Mason moving in put a label on their relationship. It said, we're an item. But on the other hand he was afraid of losing him. He thought he might be in love with Mason, but he wasn't sure. Was it really the L word or was he merely infatuated? He was never able to tell the difference until he was either dumped, abandoned or cheated on, and then it was only the speed of his recovery that gave him any hint.

'Whatever,' Mason replied, shrugging his shoulders. 'D'you think there could be a problem?'

'No. No. Why would there be?' Conor said. 'We'll tell her when she's finished doing the cash.'

Mason had no such doubts about his feelings. He knew he was in love with Conor. In fact, he'd wanted Conor from the first day he had met him, but at that time, of course, he was with Hector. He'd never trusted Hector. He'd seen his predatory type before. Seen the way Hector eyed up any new young talent that came on the scene. Was Conor blind? Why didn't he see it too? He was surprised that Conor had been so shocked when Hector had run off with Colin, he'd sensed it was coming from way back. In some ways, he reflected, it was all for the best, and he was there to help Conor to pick up the pieces. Now he wanted to commit and, more importantly, he needed Conor to make some small commitment too. Despite his confident and charming appearance, Mason was prone to bouts of serious insecurity and self-doubt. He put his arms around Conor and kissed him. 'C'mon,' he said. 'Let's go tell Alice the good news.'

Alice was hardly surprised. In fact, she was amazed that the way things were going, and taking into account Conor's usual haste in such matters, that Mason hadn't moved in sooner. On that point she was actually pleased. She wasn't sure she could face any further drama of the like she'd lived through after Hector had hopped it, but looking at it rationally, Mason was a good sort and seemed to be genuinely fond of her friend. 'What took you so long?' she quipped before opening a bottle of bubbly to celebrate the milestone.

Conor was delighted. If Alice thought it was okay, it must be so. Later, after he'd had a hasty check around to make sure no sign of Hector remained, he helped Mason to move his stuff into the apartment. It took only the one trip. As they slammed the door on his old place, Mason slapped him on the back. 'Now all we have to do is tell your folks.'

Conor froze. 'Em . . . well . . . that's, eh . . . that's something we need to talk about.'

Chapter Nineteen

January meandered on into February, February into March. Alice and Conor were starting to feel the pinch of the increased protection payments to Jesse James. Not that they were badly off, it was just that the extra outgoing of three hundred and fifty a week made it feel as if they were running only to stand still.

Their club was to be different, not like the usual Leeson Street dive, but something a bit more classy, to cater for well-off thirty-somethings. A real members-only club, where the patrons might go after work or after dinner. Not just a late-night joint serving cheap plonk to after-hours drinkers where middle-aged married men come on the prowl for a bit of illicit available totty. As things stood they knew there was no way that they would be able to get the necessary capital together for such a venture, and a further foray into newspaper ads and postal orders, or intimidation of kinky bank managers was out of the question.

Conor, Mason and Alice sat in the apartment one night after work discussing the matter. Mason hadn't been working at the Samovar since the beginning of February as he had had a part in a revival of Wilde's *An Ideal Husband* at the Peacock. 'It just makes me sick that we can't do anything about it,' Alice groaned. 'You'd think yer man would have the sense to know that he's sucking us dry.'

'He knows, all right,' Mason said. 'He just doesn't give a damn.'

'Well, we have to do something or we'll never get enough together to open the club.' Conor, stating the obvious.

'Ain't that the truth,' agreed Alice. Then a thought struck her. 'This guy, Jesse James. He's a businessman, right?'

Conor nodded. 'If you want to call it that. What are you getting at?'

'Well, what if we were to go to him with a proposition? What if we were to ask him to invest in the club?'

'I don't think he'd buy that,' Mason said sceptically. 'He's more into extortion than investment.'

'Not necessarily. At the end of the day, he's a businessman and interested in the bottom line, right? If we can persuade him that his bottom line would be healthier if we can earn more, he might cough up for the club.'

'But that means we'll be paying him more money,' whinged Conor.

'Sure,' Alice said. 'But we'd still be better off personally. I know it's a pain in the bum handing over cash to the low life, but at the moment, until we can think of some other way around it, it's the only way we can increase our profits. We'll just have to look at it as a business expense.'

Conor was doubtful. He tried to put Alice off. 'I don't know. I hate the thought of giving the likes of him more of our money. I can't see him going for it anyway.'

'Do you think I like paying that jerk? And what have we got to lose by trying?'

Mason looked at Conor. 'She has a point.'

Conor couldn't argue with that, but he hadn't forgotten how useless James had made him feel on their last mission. He was afraid that they'd be on a hiding for nothing. His bowels suddenly turned to water.

Despite his misgivings, however, and on his part in an effort to impress Mason, he and Alice made the trip to the Mercer Street offices of Quick Call Finance, but only after he had imbibed a hefty, and clandestine, double brandy. The same two clones were manning the office with equal enthusiasm. Alice didn't bother to talk to them, just repeated her barging-in strategy of the previous visit. This action dragged a startled gasp from the clones.

Jesse James was sitting at his desk eating a Big Mac. He

looked up when they burst in, pausing only for a moment, before he took another bite out of his burger. Getting straight to the point before his nerve left him, Conor said, 'It's about the Samovar. We have a proposition for you.'

James swallowed. 'Please, have a seat.'

All very civilised so far. James picked a small piece of food from his tooth. Conor looked at Alice, and they sat down on a leather sofa which was placed at right angles to the desk. The previous night they had discussed how they should deal with Jesse James. It was decided that it was best approached in a non-confrontational way, much to Conor's relief, by stressing the benefits to Jesse James, rather than trying to haggle about the protection money. That approach had failed so spectacularly before and they didn't want to risk antagonising James into upping the ante again.

Alice outlined their plans for the club. Jesse James listened attentively. When she had finished with the bumph, she said, 'And we thought we'd give you the opportunity to invest.'

'Invest?' James said it as if it was an alien word he didn't know the meaning of. 'How do you mean, *invest*?'

'Put money into it.' Alice ignored the inferred sarcasm. 'It's a golden opportunity.'

Jesse James threw back his head and guffawed. 'I'll say this about you. You've got balls. Why the hell should I *invest*, as you put it?'

Alice was ready for this. 'Look. At the moment you're bleeding us dry. If it goes on the way it is, you'll lose the money we're giving you, because we'll be out of business. However, if we can open the club and increase our profits we'll *all* be better off. And you'll own part of a business rather than just getting a payment every week. What have you got to lose?'

Jesse James leaned back in his chair. He had a half-smile on his lips. After a pause he said. 'What's to stop me opening a club anywhere? I don't need you if I want to open a club.'

Conor, emboldened by the drink, stated, 'Sure. That's true. But the difference is, we can make it work. We know what we're about. Anyway, do you really want all the extra work of running a club?'

James thought about that. 'Okay. I'll grant you it sounds like a good idea. Have you any costs and projections?'

Before the words were out of his mouth, Alice got up and handed him a sheet of paper, on which she and Conor, assisted by Declan, had done the sums. Despite himself, James looked impressed. He scanned the list. 'Down to the last ashtray, I see. Looks good. Looks very good.'

Alice sneaked a look at Conor. Things were going well. Maybe Jesse James wasn't such a hard man after all. Maybe the psychotic behaviour was all for show. He could obviously see the virtue of sound investment.

'Okay.' James stood up and started to pace. He had his hands clasped behind his back and he stared at the carpet as he laid out his terms. 'Here's what I'll do. I'll lend you the capital sum and—'

Alice cut across him. 'But wouldn't you rather be a partner?' They had settled on that tactic, the logic of it being that if he was a partner it would make more sense for there to be big profits and a healthy business rather short-terms gains.

James, still pacing, talked her down. 'I'll lend you the capital sum, and you can sign over half of the profits of the club to me.'

'What! . . . Over my dead body,' Alice snarled. 'Do you think we're some class of eejitts?'

Jesse James came to an abrupt halt and turned to face them. 'Take it or leave it. But the way I see it, you need my money or you can't afford to expand. It's a simple fact. Your outgoings are too high for you to get a bank loan. If you want to open the club, I'm your only option.'

'But the outgoings are only too high because you're ripping us off,' Conor spluttered.

Jesse James looked affronted. 'Ripping you off?' He looked outraged. 'The cheek of you. I supply you with a legitimate insurance and security service. No one forced you to join our scheme.'

'Bullshit!' Alice raged. 'That's bullshit. Your heavies broke the place up, and threatened to burn us out.'

James's eyes were laughing at them. He was enjoying

himself. Lambs to the slaughter again, Alice thought. We're way out of our league here. James walked behind his desk and sat down. His eyes had stopped laughing. 'Let's cut the crap, shall we? I'll advance the capital at one point below my normal rate.'

'That's big of you,' Alice muttered.

'Very big of me,' James said. 'I'll get the paperwork sorted and you can sign over half the profits to me as soon as it's up and running. Okay?'

Conor stood up. 'We'll need to think about it.' He just wanted to get out of there. The situation was shaping up to be even uglier than the last time. He unconsciously rubbed his midriff. 'Come on, Alice.'

Alice slithered sideways along the sofa and stood up, trying to salvage what was left of her dignity. 'We'll get back to you.'

As the office door closed behind them, they heard Jesse James laughing.

'Well, that went even better than the last time.' Conor didn't hold back on the sarcasm. 'We should have just kept our heads down.'

Alice cringed. Things had definitely not gone accordng to plan. Jesse James had eaten them up and then spat them out again. 'Don't be such a defeatist,' she snapped. Okay, it had been her idea to ask Jesse James to invest. It had seemed like the perfect plan at the time. She just hadn't reckoned on him being such a greedy bastard. 'I think we should go ahead.'

'Are you serious?' Conor was flabbergasted.

'Of course. We'll use his money to open the club and, in the meantime, think of another way to get him off our backs.'

'Just like that?'

'No, not *just like that*!' Alice replied. 'The way I see it, the only way we can get rid of that scumbag is to put him in the same position we are.'

'I'm not with you.'

'We'll have to get some dirt on him. The kind of scum he is, he has to have an Achilles heel.'

'I follow your logic,' Conor said. 'But how exactly are we going to do that?'

'I haven't a clue.' Alice said, then a thought struck her. 'But I know a woman who might.'

Conor hailed a cab and they drove out to Dalky to see Madame Maxine. They had never been to Madame Maxine's Dalky home before and it was something of an eye-opener. Max looked like a typical corporate wife. A lady who lunched. Conor wondered if her neighbours knew how she earned a crust. Though on further thought it occurred to him that some of her more august neighbours could well be clients.

Alice would have been surprised by the place had she not been aware to some degree of Madame Maxine's real circumstances. Through shrewd investment on advice from various in-the-know clients, the dominatrix had built up a healthy portfolio of investments including a large number of rental properties, not to mention their building on Leeson Street. When this had come up in conversation once, Alice had asked her why she bothered to continue working. Madame Max had explained that both she and Celeste looked on their profession as a humanitarian service, as a sort of sex-therapy clinic. 'Anyways, love,' she'd said, 'I'd miss the sad old fuckers if I gave up.'

As it was a lovely sunny day, she brought them through to her conservatory, which overlooked a beautifully kept garden and had a stunning sea view. A housekeeper brought in a tray of tea and cakes and placed them on a small table. Not wanting to appear rude, they chatted for a while, catching up on this and that, then Madame Max cut to the chase. 'So what's the problem, Alice?'

'Have you heard of a man called Jesse James? And I mean the local gangster, not the cowboy.'

Madame Max smiled. 'I know who yeh mean. An' if I was you, I wouldn't have nothin' t' do with him. He's a mean bastard.'

'We haven't a lot of choice, he's ripping us off for three hundred and fifty quid a week.'

Madame Max gave a low whistle. 'That's a lotta bread.'

'It's killing us.' Madame Max nodded, understanding. Alice

went on, 'The thing is . . . If we wanted to get some dirt on him, how would we go about it?'

Madame Max sighed. 'Hard t' know.' Then, as if inspired, 'I suppose yeh could get one a' them private eyes. Get him follied. It'd cost money, though. It wouldn't come cheap.'

'In the long run it would have to be cheaper than paying that scumbag for years.'

'Well, that's true,' Madame Max agreed. 'I always say yeh have t' speculate, t' accumulate. What were yeh thinkin' of doin' if yeh get somethin' on him?'

Alice hadn't thought that far ahead. She shrugged. 'I don't know. Go to the cops, I suppose.'

Madame Max shook her head violently. 'Yeh could, I suppose, but unless it was pretty serious shit, like murder or somethin', he'd be out in no time, then where'll you be?'

Alice's heart sank. 'So what do you suggest we do?'

Madame Max got up and walked over to the window. She was silent for a while. Alice hoped she was thinking of a plan. Finally she said, 'Yeh need somethin' that'll frighten the shite outta him.' Conor couldn't imagine Jesse James being frightened by anything. Madame Maxine continued. 'Yeh need somethin' that yeh can blackmail him with, personally. Somethin' he wouldn't want anyone else t' know abou'.'

'Like what?'

'Who knows, darlin'?' she said, breaking her heart laughing. 'But it doesn't harm to keep yer eyes an' ears open in this life.' She tapped the side of her nose. 'In my line a'work, I learned the hard way t' take out me own insurance. I've a sorta endowment policy, if yeh get me drift.' They didn't. Maxine winked at them. 'Apart from me houses, me clients are me endowment policy, if ye'll pardon the pun. I keep a file on all a' them.'

Madame Maxine was speaking from bitter experience. Early on in her career she experienced consistent harassment from the forces of law and order, to the extent that she was paying as much in fines as she was earning. She learned it pays to have the Polaroid handy at all times, particularly when in the process of flogging, beating and generally humiliating the

Great and the Good. She explained to them that her set-up was more sophisticated these days and involved hidden video cameras and listening devices. Alice was mesmerised. When it was time for them to leave she said, 'Thanks for the advice, Max. D'you know any private eyes?'

'Not offhand,' her friend said, as she stood in her million-pound driveway. 'Let yer fingers do the walkin', wha'?'

When they got back to the restaurant, they took their fingers for a walk in the golden pages and made a couple of calls. Eventually they came up with a Mr Parsons of AAA Investigations. They phoned for an appointment. His secretary told them that he was out of town on a case that week but made an appointment for them for Friday of the following week.

'He must be good if he's that busy,' Conor commented.

'Let's hope so,' Alice replied. 'Our future's riding on it.'

Chapter Twenty

Maura phoned that evening. Conor took the call and was on the phone for ages. Alice was in the bath at the time, so later on, after the restaurant closed for the night, he filled her in on their conversation.

He told her that Maura, Mick and half of Tanagh were heading up to Dublin that weekend as Maura had reached the national final of Country Wife of the Year.

'What's that?' Alice asked.

'Haven't you ever heard of it?' Conor was surprised. 'It's huge. On TV, the lot. Joe Kenny's the compère. Mam's more excited about meeting him than she is about the competition.'

'Oh.' Alice picked up the nights dockets and sorted them into some sort of order. 'That's nice. I must ring her to wish her luck.'

'The thing is,' Conor said, 'she sort of wants us to go along to the Point to support her.' Alice gave him a weary look. 'It's on a Sunday, so we'll be closed.'

He knew his mother would be disappointed if Alice wasn't there to support her, so he put on his wheedling voice. 'She'd love you to be there too.'

Alice wasn't keen. The thought of spending her night off sitting in the Point Depot watching a group of middle-aged women strutting their stuff, and doing whatever Country Wives of the Year were expected to do, didn't fill her with enthusiasm. But Conor was well aware that, although she could flatly refuse him, she wouldn't be able to think of a suitable excuse for Maura. This fact was his secret weapon. She caved in.

Mick and Maura were being put up at the Westbury by the

organisers, which eased matters somewhat, as it saved Mason having to find somewhere else to stay. They were arriving on the Sunday afternoon accompanied by a busload of supporters from Tanagh, then heading straight for the Point Depot to meet the judges, so Alice, Conor and Declan weren't going to get to see them until the live TV show that evening.

By the Sunday evening, Conor was depressed. Mason was on the sulky side. He didn't approve of the sham marriage and, since he had moved in, he'd been nagging Conor about coming out to his parents. Since the play at the Peacock had closed and he had failed a couple of subsequent auditions he felt were a sure thing, his insecurity was kicking in again. He said he felt *diminished* that Conor would deny him. It was a side of Mason Conor hadn't seen before. It made Mason anxious and, worse, needy.

Mason started again in the cab on the way to the Point. Alice thought he was being a drama queen and told him so, to which he responded, 'Well, my folks didn't have any problem with it.'

'Mason, your folks live in Greenwich Village, not Tanagh,' Alice said, astounded that he would even compare the two situations. 'And as I remember it, you said that your father was bisexual in any case.'

Mason didn't make further comment. Conor, anxious to avoid a row, tried to change the subject, but Alice wouldn't let it go. 'And another thing, as far as Conor's parents are concerned, we're married. Got it? Married. You knew that when you moved in, so it's not really fair to start whinging about the situation now.'

The atmosphere in the car dropped a further couple of degrees. Conor was in bits. He tried to pacify Mason, but to no effect. The more he tried, the more stubbornly silent Mason became. It was shaping up to be a grim evening.

They bumped into Declan, who had brought Melanie along. Melanie was delighted to see her and Alice was just as pleased to see her. They greeted each other like long-lost buddies. Inside the auditorium Alice caught sight of the Tanagh supporters' club, who were sporting big banners with legends such as UP TANAGH, GOOD ON YEH MAURA, and GO MAURA GO. Mick was with them. He waved and they went over and took the five seats that he had saved for them.

Conor introduced Mason, making matters worse between them, by saying he was a friend of Declan's, though Mason, ever the actor, was charm itself to Mick. He then introduced Melanie as Alice's long lost stepsister. Mick was thrilled to bits with Melanie. He gave her a bear hug and exclaimed to the half of Tanagh that was present, 'Isn't this only great? Alice found her long-lost stepsister. And her thinkin' she was alone in the world.'

Melanie looked on bemused. Alice winked at her.

There were six finalists. Maura was on third. When Joe Kenny announced her name, she came onto the stage at a trot, sporting one of her own hand-knit chunky cardigans, with her hair neatly washed and set. She waved over at the Tanagh crowd, who cheered wildly.

'Now, Maura,' Joe said. 'And you're from Tanagh.'

'Yes, Joe,' Maura said coyly, 'that's right.'

'A beautiful part of the country, I know it well. And you're a farmer's wife. Tell me about yourself. What kind of things are you involved in down there in Tanagh?'

'Well, Joe. As you said, we have the farm. Me and my husband Mick. We've two sons, Declan and Conor. Declan works in the bank . . .' Alice sniggered. '. . . and my younger son Conor has his own restaurant in partnership with his wife Alice.' Declan sniggered.

Maura waved over at them.

Joe said, 'Let's see the family. Stand up the Finn family.' Alice and Declan stopped sniggering. Mick stood up and held his sons' arms aloft, dragging them to their feet. With his free hand, Declan's vice-like grip on Alice's wrist hoisted her out of her seat, and the four of them stood in a row with their arms in the air. The Tanagh supporters' club gave a cheer. Briefly Alice felt they should be swaying from side to side with lit cigarette lighters in their hands. Mason glowered from his seat. The spotlight swept on to them. Alice felt like a prat, but no more so than Conor and Declan.

Thankfully Joe got quickly back down to business, and they sat down again. Maura told him how she had been a member of the Irish County Women's Association for nearly thirty years. How she was involved in the running of the farm, meals on wheels, Gaelic football with the GAA, the Special Olympics, the local drama group, the church choir and, of course, in her spare time she liked to knit. Joe gallantly admired her cardigan and Maura blushed.

Next it came to the optional part of the competition where the contestants, if they so chose, could do their party pieces. Of the two previous contestants, only one had performed. She chose to sing and annihilated 'She Moved Through the Fair'. Nevertheless, her supporters cheered and stamped their feet in approval.

Alice was hoping and praying that Maura wouldn't follow suit and perform. 'And you have a little poem for us, I believe, Maura,' Joe said. Alice sank down in her seat.

'That's right, Joe,' Maura simpered. 'It's a pome written by Oscar Wilde when he was only thirteen, lamenting the death of his little sister Iosla. It means a lot t' me because I lost a sister when I was that age, and when I read this pome for the first time, it comforted me to know that there was someone who had put into words the way I was feeling.'

The lights dimmed and Maura stood alone in the centre of the stage. She cleared her throat. '*Requiescat*, by Oscar Wilde.

> 'Tread lightly, she is near
>   Under the snow,
> Speak gently, she can hear
>   The daisies grow.
>
> 'All her bright golden hair
>   Tarnished with rust,
> She that was young and fair
>   Fallen to dust.
>
> 'Lily-like, white as snow,
>   She hardly knew
> She was a woman, so
>   Sweetly she grew.

'Coffin-board, heavy stone,
    Lie on her breast,
I vex my heart alone,
    She is at rest.

'Peace, peace, she cannot hear
    Lyre or sonnet,
All my life's buried here,
    Heap earth upon it.'

Alice was astounded. Maura had recited the poem with perfect feeling, diction and clarity. Her voice was crystal-clear and perfectly modulated. The hall was hushed for a full five seconds after she had finished, then erupted into applause. The lights came up and Joe shook her hand. 'Well done, Maura. Well done. Good girl.'

Maura floated off stage on cloud nine.

Alice looked round at Declan. 'She was wonderful. Amazing.'

Declan said, 'That's my mother. A woman of many talents.'

The three other contestants followed Maura. One, Bronagh Holland, from somewhere in County Offaly, did a spot of Irish dancing. Her interests included fishing and macramé. She was also on the Tidy Towns committee.

Another Maura, this time from Mayo, enjoyed swimming and reading, hill-walking with the blind, as well as cooking and looking after her husband and family. She played the fiddle passably well. Alice found it hard to concentrate on what Nora, the last contestant, had to say as, by this time, she was on saccharine overload.

When the contestant part was over, there was a musical interval while the judges made their final decision. Alice escaped to the bar on the pretext of going for a pee. She bumped into Declan and Melanie on the stairs, who'd obviously had the same idea. 'Enjoying the show?' he asked, a half-smile on his lips.

'Almost as much as you are,' Alice replied.

'I think it's great,' Melanie enthused as they made their way up to the bar. 'And Mrs Finn was marvellous. I'm sure she's going to win.'

'I hope so,' Declan replied, then turned to Alice, 'What's up with Mason?'

'He and Conor had a tiff,' she said. 'He wants Conor to tell your parents he's gay.'

'You mean they don't know?' Melanie sounded amazed. She blushed. 'Sorry. It's none of my business.'

Declan put his hand on her arm. 'It's okay. It's a family thing. They eh . . . they think he's married to Alice.'

'You're not serious?'

Embarrassed by the stupidity of it, Alice cringed. 'Yes. I'm afraid he's serious. But it's a long story.'

'And I suppose you're on Mason's side?' Declan said.

Alice was incensed. 'Well, actually, you arrogant smart-arse, I was the one who told Mason to stop being such a bloody prima donna.'

Now it was Declan's turn to be astonished. 'Oh, sorry. I just assumed—'

'I know,' Alice snapped. 'You assumed.'

'I'm sorry, Alice. Really.' He sounded it too.

'Well, you should be. Conor couldn't keep the fairytale going if it wasn't for my cooperation.'

'I know and I'm sorry. But as a matter of interest, why are you?'

Alice shrugged. 'Why shouldn't I? It's no skin off my nose, and anyway I like your parents. They've been good to me. I don't want to see them hurt . . . but that doesn't mean to say that I don't believe it would have been better all round if he'd come clean in the beginning. It's just too late now. The whole thing's too complicated to unwind.'

'I know. Oh what a tangled web we weave, and all that,' Declan said. He caught the barman's eye and ordered drinks.

For an instant, in the bar mirror, Alice caught sight of a familiar face. She looked again, but it was gone. Melanie was talking but she wasn't paying attention, searching the reflected images.

'What's the matter?' Declan asked, handing her a glass of

Budweiser. Whatever Melanie had been saying must have required an answer, and it was obvious that Alice hadn't been listening.

'Sorry, what?'

'What's the matter? You look as if you've seen a ghost.'

'It's nothing. I thought I saw someone I knew, that's all. I was mistaken.' She smiled at Melanie. 'Sorry, Mel, what was it you were saying?'

On the way back to the auditorium Melanie went to the ladies and they stood by the top of the stairs waiting for her. They were uneasy in one another's company, avoiding eye contact and conversation, too accustomed to sniping. After an uncomfortable half-minute, Declan said, 'Look, Alice. Can't we call a truce? I'm sorry if I automatically jumped to the wrong conclusions about you. I know you've been a good friend to Conor.'

Alice shrugged. 'I suppose so.'

Declan gave a wry smile. 'Well, don't get carried away with enthusiasm.'

She laughed, the tension broken. Maybe he wasn't that bad after all. 'So,' she said after a further silence, 'are you and Mel an item, then?'

Declan gave a half-shrug. 'I wish.'

'You wish?'

Immediately he felt uncomfortable. It was an unintentional admission. He stared at the floor for a couple of seconds feeling himself redden, then felt obliged to fill the silence. 'She has a few problems ... She's not ready to be involved with anyone right now. It's complicated.'

'Problems? Like what?'

'Oh, personal stuff I can't go into. You understand?'

Alice nodded. 'Sure. But you're hanging in there anyway, right?'

He gave a nod and a half-smile. 'Something like that.'

He looked vulnerable at that moment and it surprised Alice. She never imagined that he'd be in any way vulnerable. Tough, clever, got-it-all Declan. She felt quite sorry for him. Melanie came out of the ladies then and they all returned to the auditorium just as the musical interval drew to a close.

They resumed their seats. Mason had switched places and was now sitting in Melanie's seat at the opposite end of the row from Conor. 'I see Mason's still got the hump,' Alice whispered to Conor, as the lights went down.

'I know,' Conor said miserably.

'Maybe you shouldn't have introduced him to your father as Declan's friend,' she hissed.

Joe returned to the stage and called out all the contestants, one at a time and, to remind the viewers who they were, gave the audience a brief résumé of each candidate's talents. They stood in a straggly row at the back of the stage, looking uneasy but expectant.

Joe handed over to the managing director of the firm sponsoring the event and he thanked everyone in the universe, it seemed individually, for their support. Eventually he got down to it.

'And now . . .' He paused to increase the tension. 'And now it falls to me to announce the winner – and sadly there can be only one winner. But that doesn't mean to say that those who didn't win are losers.'

He slowly ripped open the gold envelope. The previous year's recipient stood by with a huge bouquet of flowers and a sash at the ready.

'And the winner of Country Wife of the Year is . . . (a long pause and then a drum roll sounded) Maura Finn!'

There were whoops of delight from the massed ranks of the Tanagh supporters' club. Alice found herself on her feet cheering wildly as were Mick, Conor and Declan and Melanie.

Maura looked stunned. She was still standing at the back of the stage staring out into the auditorium. The other contestants converged on her and she disappeared from view as they congratulated her.

Joe marched over and the women parted and let him lead Maura to the front of the stage. 'Come on up here, Mick,' he said into the mike. Mick didn't need to be asked twice. He bounded down the aisle and up on to the stage, where he hugged his wife. He was beaming with pride. The previous year's winner looped the sash over Maura's head and plonked the flowers into her arms, then the managing director of the sponsors handed her an envelope with the winner's cheque and vouchers for a weekend's stay for two at Drumoland Castle.

Joe looked out into the audience again. 'Let's have the whole family up here. Come on.'

The spotlight swung round again and blinded Alice. Conor grabbed her by the hand and dragged her after him towards the stage. Declan followed. Before she knew it, Alice was up on the stage at the Point Depot while a couple of photographers snapped away at the new Country Wife of the Year. The new Country Wife of the Year and her husband. The new Country Wife of the Year and her sons and daughter-in-law, then the group shot.

After the mayhem there was a reception at the Westbury Hotel. Mick and Maura were in fine form and insisted that they all go along. Maura and Mick were driven by limo, and Alice, Melanie, Mason – who had thawed out somewhat – and Conor followed in Declan's car.

As they arrived, Alice suddenly saw Sean Holland. He was getting out of a cab in the company of Paula. She grabbed Conor's arm and dragged him up the steps, in the door and behind a large palm plant. 'Quick. It's Sean Holland.'

'Who's Sean Holland?' Conor thought perhaps he was a movie star or something.

'The guy from the Immigration hit-squad, you eejitt,' she hissed. 'The guy who was grilling us to find out if my marriage to Hector was one of convenience. Remember now?'

Just then, Sean Holland, along with Bronagh from county Offaly, his sister, Paula, and a man who, judging by his features, was Holland's father, walked through the lobby and climbed the steps to reception. Declan, with Melanie and Mason in tow, was hard on their heels, with a bemused look on his face. He was scanning the lobby, wondering where Alice and Conor had disappeared to so suddenly. He spotted them peeking out from behind the palm plant and they all walked over. 'What the hell are you doing?' he asked. 'Why did you rush off like that?'

'No reason,' Alice snapped. 'Come on, Conor, I'm really tired. Let's go home.' She made for the door.

'You can't go. Mam and Da are expecting you at the party.'

Conor said, 'I'm not feeling great either, Declan. We're tired. Tell Mam we'll see them here tomorrow for breakfast.' He glanced sheepishly at Mason. 'Are you coming?' He received a curt nod in reply. Alice gave Melanie a hasty hug and before Declan could offer any further argument, Conor and Mason followed her as she fled outside and jumped into a cab.

'I'm sure I saw him at the Point,' Alice said once the cab was under way. 'The woman from Offaly must be his mother.'

'Maybe he didn't see us.'

'Right! Very likely, especially with us up on the bloody stage for ten minutes under ten-zillion-watt spotlights.'

'He might not've recognised us. Your hair's different now.'

'Not that different, Conor.'

'Well, so what? There's no law against you going to the Point Depot.'

'I know that, you eejitt. But the law might be a tad iffy about me being supposedly married to you when as far as they're concerned I'm supposed to be married to a fucking Ukrainian.'

'You're overreacting,' Conor said.

'We'll see.'

Chapter Twenty-One

'I told them you were tired and not feeling too well.'

Alice and Conor met Declan the following morning at eight outside the Westbury, on his way in to breakfast with Maura and Mick.

'God! I hope your mother doesn't think I'm pregnant,' Alice whinged as they made their way up to the dining room. 'I couldn't handle that today.'

Conor laughed. He was in deadly form. High as a kite. He and Mason had had a long talk after Alice had gone to bed and Mason had explained his insecurity and fear that Conor was still hankering after Hector. That prompted Conor to say the L word to Mason for the first time. He explained his reasons for not coming out to his parents. How, apart from their disappointment, he was afraid that they would turn their backs on him. Mason listened but, after seeing how close Conor was to his parents, and how much they obviously loved him, it was beyond his comprehension that they would do such a thing. However, ecstatic that Conor had said the L word, he'd let it go.

Declan was blissfully unaware of Alice's worries concerning Sean Holland. He also had no idea that she was, in reality, married to an abscondee Ukrainian homosexual. He grinned. 'Don't worry. What with your *women's trouble* being the talk of Tanagh ICA, I doubt she thinks that.'

Alice wasn't altogether sure she was glad about her gynaecological bits and pieces being the talk of Tanagh ICA but, on balance, she realised that it was better than having Maura waiting with baited breath for her to produce a grandchild.

'We'd better go in,' Conor said.

They spotted Maura, sitting alone at a table in the restaurant eating her breakfast. She had a copy of *The Irish Times* on the table. Her face lit up when she saw them. 'Is it yerselves!' she exclaimed at the top of her voice, jumping to her feet. Alice cringed and looked furtively around, hoping that Sean Holland wasn't sharing breakfast with his mother. He wasn't. Just as well. Her body language screamed, *Look at me. I've got something to hide. I'm a mad, bigamous, axe murderer with seventeen kilos of smack concealed about my person.*

'Where's Da?' Conor asked.

'Feeling a bit under the weather,' Maura said. 'Drank a drop too much last night. Wasn't Joe Kenny only wonderful?'

'Wonderful,' Alice agreed. Then her eye caught the front page photo on *The Irish Times*. It was the family group-shot in living colour. Maura with her arm around Conor, Conor with his arm around Alice, Declan and Mick standing behind with Joe, all beaming into the camera lens. The caption listed their names, referring to Alice as daughter-in-law: Alice Finn and her husband, restaurateur Conor Finn.

Maura was chatting away to her sons. Alice nudged Conor and shoved the paper over to him.

'Great photo,' he said, missing the point.

'Isn't it only wonderful,' Maura enthused. 'Who'd have thought we'd ever be on the front page of *The Irish Times*. And with Joe Kenny himself.'

Conor still thought she was overreacting. Alice glared at him until he gave in, muttering. 'Okay, so I'm sorry. But I still think the immigration guy'll have forgotten all about us. He's other things to worry about now, what with all the Albanian refugees.'

'Don't be so naive, Conor,' Alice hissed under her breath. 'His kind are like fucking pit bulls. Once they get their teeth into flesh they never let go. You were the one who made us watch *Green Card* a dozen times, remember? Have you forgotten what they're like already?'

Even though Sean Holland hadn't shown up by the time she and Conor had said their goodbyes to Maura, Alice was still anxious. And although she could have done with a holiday, the thought of six months in Mountjoy didn't appeal.

Lunchtime at the Samovar was reasonably quiet. At one point, when she and Mason were standing together by the bar, she said, 'I'm glad to see you and Conor made up. I'm glad you cleared up your differences.'

Mason sighed. 'Not exactly cleared up,' he said. 'More, put on hold. I can't see what his problem is. I don't buy this stuff about his folks hating him if they found out. What do you think?'

Her first instinct was to tell him to feck off, that he didn't know what he was talking about, that circumstances had made coming out far easier for him, but in a way she could see his point. She explained how she had gone home with Conor when he'd had every intention of coming out to his parents, and about the resulting misunderstanding. 'So you see, he did try, he just lost courage. You met them. They're lovely people, but they live in a small village in rural Ireland. Now that everyone thinks Conor's a straight married guy, from their point of view, imagine what it would be like for them if it came out in Tanagh.'

'So you think he was right?'

Alice shrugged. 'No. I think he should have told them back then, but I don't see how he can now. I think he's missed his opportunity.' She paused. 'I think if he had his time over, he'd have bitten the bullet and told them, but how can he do it now? It'd break Mick's heart.'

Mason sighed. 'I guess you're right. I guess I Just needed to know how he really felt about me.'

And that was that. Subject closed.

Maura and Mick put in an appearance as the last lunchtime diners were leaving. Alice gave them a great welcome and sat down at a table with them. Mason brought them all coffee and went into the kitchen to tell Conor that they were in the restaurant before hurrying off to an audition. Maura was still up on cloud nine and Mick had made a miraculous recovery due, no doubt, to the Finn hollow-legs gene. They declined lunch, having eaten earlier.

Conor came out of the kitchen to join them. Maura was all agog about the competition. She outlined her duties for the year. It involved opening events of a rural nature, livestock shows, flower shows and the like. She was excited at the prospect, but worried that it might cause her to neglect Mick. He reassured her that, sure, couldn't he cook a good fry-up, and bacon, spuds and cabbage with the best of them. Observing their closeness, Alice felt a twinge of jealousy.

At twenty to four Maura and Mick got up to leave. They were to meet the hired bus from Tanagh at four o'clock near the Stephen's Green Centre. Alice hugged her ersatz in-laws and promised to visit soon. Mick mooted the next bank holiday, but Alice put him off, citing pressure of work. They all settled on August and, as it was far enough away, Alice agreed.

She heard the door open behind her and was about to explain to whoever that lunch was over, and that they were due to re-open for dinner at seven-thirty, when she recognised Sean Holland. Her heart did a double somersault. He was accompanied by two burly cops.

'Mrs Hanusiak,' he said. Alice was dumbstruck. His use of the formal Mrs made the situation sound dangerously official. Conor gulped. Mick and Maura looked around the room for Mrs Hanusiak.

'Erm . . .' Alice stumbled. 'I can explain.'

'It's not what it looks like,' Conor said.

The cops were standing blocking the door, obviously under the impression that Alice was a desperate criminal and might make a break for it. Sean Holland said, 'I think an explanation would be in order, Alice. So what's the story?'

'What are yeh talkin' about?' Mick said, jovially. 'Sure, isn't this Alice? Our daughter-in-law. Alice Finn.'

'Well, erm . . . I'm afraid he's right, Mick. I am actually . . . well, erm . . . *legally* Mrs Hector Hanusiak.'

Maura's lower jaw dropped as far as her chest. She was shaking her head and looking from Conor to Alice and back to Conor again. 'Wha . . . But you're married to my Conor . . .'

Sean Holland cleared his throat. 'Is that true, Alice? Did you marry this man?'

Later, when she thought it through, Alice realised that if she had been searching for the perfect opportunity to set the record straight and end the charade, then this was it. She looked over at Mick. He was staring at Conor, a bewildered expression on his face. Maura was equally gob-smacked, but along with the confusion, she also looked devastated. Her whole being drooped like a half-deflated balloon. Alice drew breath. 'Well . . . not exactly.'

A strangled whimper escaped from Maura's throat. Conor was paralysed, his face the colour of uncooked pastry.

'Not *legally* married. But he *is* my common-law husband.' Alice grabbed Conor's hand and as she hugged it to her chest she heard him exhale. 'Hector ran off and left me,' she continued. 'He emptied the bank account. He left me penniless. Conor and I just, eh . . . we just fell in love. Didn't we, darling?'

Conor stared at her. She nudged him in the ribs with her elbow. 'Eh . . . yes. We, erm . . . we just fell in love.' He gave a nervous giggle. He looked over at his mother. 'I'm sorry, Mam. We didn't know how to tell you.'

'So you didn't go through a bigamous marriage with Mr Finn here?' Holland said.

'No, Mr Holland . . . Sean.' Alice was surer of her ground now. 'I know we're not married in the eyes of the state or the church, but that's only because I'm still legally married to Hector.'

Holland stood his ground, but he didn't look too happy. Pre-empting his next logical suggestion, Alice said, 'And despite what you think, my marriage to Hector wasn't a marriage of convenience. I thought he truly . . .' She paused here for a moment, biting her lip. 'I thought he truly loved me. Though I can see now that he just used me. Used me to get a passport.' She buried her head in Conor's shoulder and gave way to an approximation of silent sobbing. Conor put his arms around her and murmured comforting words.

'And have you any idea where he is now?' Holland asked.

Alice shook her head and dabbed at her eyes with the paper table napkin that Maura had thrust into her hand. 'No.'

'So he doesn't know that he's no longer an illegal?' Holland had the hint of a smile on his lips.

'What?'

'We sent him a letter some time ago informing him that his application for residency had been accepted. Didn't you know?'

Conor blushed. Weeks previously he had found a letter addressed to Hector in the mail box and in a fit of temper had torn it into shreds and chucked it in the bin unopened.

Alice shook her head. 'No, I'd no idea.'

The civil servant nodded. 'Right. And you're positive you've no idea where he could be contacted?'

Alice shook her head. 'No, and if we had you'd have to drag me off him before you got your turn,' she said. 'We'd be after him for the money he stole from us, wouldn't we, Conor?'

'You can say that again,' Conor affirmed.

Sean Holland nodded again. He'd had his suspicions about Hector Hanusiak. He'd had the impression that the man might be gay, he wasn't sure why, but he'd let himself be swayed by Carmel McGuire's opinion. Not that he was a homophobe, but in the context of Hector Hanusiak's visa application and his appeal on the grounds of his marriage to an Irish national, it was relevant. What surprised him even more though was that Alice now appeared to be in love with Conor Finn who was, as far as he was concerned, very obviously of the gay persuasion. Pity. She was a fine-looking woman. Still, there was no accounting for taste. Feeling vindicated, he mentally tore up Hector's visa. 'Well, if you do catch up with him, leave enough of him intact for us to kick out of the country, will you?'

'Absolutely,' Conor and Alice chorused.

As they were leaving the two cops looked disappointed. They'd been hoping for a bit of action. Alice and Conor jointly heaved a sigh of relief, Alice because Holland hadn't pursued the marriage of convenience and bigamy business, and Conor because Alice hadn't spilled the beans to his parents.

Maura and Mick were still standing motionless, staring at Alice, waiting for her to say something more. Unfortunately

Alice didn't know what else to say. After the silence grew to an uncomfortable length, she bit the bullet. 'I'm sorry. We didn't know how to tell you.'

Maura snapped out of it first. She hugged first her son, and then Alice. 'You poor dear.' She almost squeezed the life out of her. 'First you lose your parents, then you're abandoned again. You poor wee soul. As far as Mick and I are concerned, you're our daughter-in-law, and part of our family. Isn't that right, Mick?'

Alice felt distinctly uncomfortable, but at the same time a surge of warmth towards Maura. She hated deceiving the Finns, they'd been so kind to her, but she was between the proverbial rock and the hard place. What was the alternative? Devastate them even further and tell them Conor was gay? And he was no help, standing there, leaving it all to her.

Mick cleared his throat. 'What your mother says ... well, erm ... that goes for me too, son.' He sounded less enthusiastic about the situation than his wife, but under the circumstances it was understandable. Self-consciously, he patted Conor on the shoulder. Alice made a shrewd guess that, weighing up the pros and cons, Mick would rather have his son married, however unconventionally, than to be worrying about him being a queer. And anyway, who was to know that they were really living over the brush?

Thankfully the awkward situation was brought swiftly to a close as the Finns had to rush off to meet the bus. Conor offered to drive them, but they declined, wishing to have the opportunity to talk before meeting up with their friends for the return journey to Tanagh.

'Eh ... Thanks, Alice,' Conor said after they left. 'Thanks for ... well ... you know.'

Suddenly Alice was weary. The stress of the whole business, first with Holland, then cobbling together a story for Maura and Mick, had finally drained her of energy. She flopped down on a chair and closed her eyes. Her neck was as stiff as a ram-rod. Slowly she rotated her head, first to the left, then to the right. Conor was standing staring at her, one arm as long as the other. 'Alice? Are you okay?'

'Not really, Conor. I'm shagged. And for the record, I didn't do it for you, I did it for your parents.' With her eyes still closed, she heard Conor walk over to the bar, a squeak of a cork and a gurgle of liquid filling a couple of glasses.

'I'm a spineless eejitt, aren't I?' He carefully placed the brandy goblet in her hands.

'That about covers it.' Alice knocked back the brandy. It hit the spot. She gave a heavy sigh and looked up at him. 'But we're stuck with each other, aren't we?'

Conor's expression told her that it wasn't the right answer, at least not the answer he wanted. What he really wanted was for Alice to tell him it wasn't his fault. That he was great. That they were friends again. Alice took pity and let him off the hook. 'Anyway,' she added, taking the harm out of it, 'I suppose as big girl's blouses go, you're not that bad.'

In spite of everything, she was relieved. At least the spectre of Hector, of Sean Holland and the Department of Foreign affairs was out of the way. 'I think this calls for a celebration,' she said.

'What?'

'A celebration. With all the guff about Hector cleared up as far as the Department of Foreign affairs is concerned, that's one less thing Jesse James can hold over us. All we need to do now is get something on him.'

'*All* we need to do?'

Chapter Twenty-Two

'Well, bugs come in all shapes and sizes. And then again, it depends on the location.'

'Well, just say, hypothetically speaking, that someone wanted to plant a listening device in a room that could record conversations.' Conor said.

'Over a long period of time?'

'Perhaps.'

'And would ye want a transmitter or just a hidden recording device?'

'Is that important?'

He gave them a withering look. 'Of course it's friggin' important. If ye ... sorry, if the *hypothetical* person had easy access to the room then a recorder'd do. But if access isn't that easy then a transmitter'd be yer only man. And a voice-activated one at that.'

Conor shot a look at Alice. 'So where could a hypothetical person get one of these transmitters?'

'A hypothetical person couldn't,' Leggo Parsons said flatly. 'That's where my technical expertise comes in. Now, where did ye say ye wanted it planted?'

'We didn't,' said Conor.

How Leggo Parsons had acquired his nickname no one knew for sure, and even he had all but forgotten his given name. Some speculated that Leggo was short for Legover and referred to his boasts of sexual conquests. But others knew that if he hadn't been tagged Leggo, Fibber would have been just as appropriate. They were further aware that the nickname had been with him since childhood and probably referred to his screams of 'leggo, leggo,' when the bigger boys set about him.

His office should have warned them. It was on a floor above a butcher's shop on Thomas Street, and it was distinctly seedy-looking. Alice was sceptical about even going in but Conor, who had spoken to him on the phone, thought he sounded very efficient, and had gone along with high hopes.

A stout woman in her fifties with yellow-blonde hair and dark roots was sitting behind a scuffed desk in the outer office typing away on an ancient-looking electric typewriter. She had a cigarette in her mouth and her left eye was screwed shut against the spiralling smoke. The typewriter made a dull metallic thub thub thub sound. It was years since Alice had seen one in operation. She vaguely remembered that Roland used to have one in his upstairs study. The woman eventually stopped typing and removed the cigarette from between her lips. It sported a long worm of ash which disintegrated, scattering the pale grey powder down the front of her maroon jumper. She brushed it away absentmindedly, then looked at them over her glasses. 'You'll be Mr Parson's three-fifteen,' she said, and without waiting for a reply, yelled, 'Leggo! It's yer appointment.'

He bore such an uncanny resemblance to the woman in the outer office that both Conor and Alice independently assumed that they must be brother and sister. Both were (to be kind) chunky, and it was a hard call to decide which of them had the heavier set of jowls. The woman had a sizeable bosom and Parsons a protruding belly straining against the belt of his low-slung trousers. But where the woman had black roots and yellow hair, Leggo Parsons had only a thin band of unnaturally dark hair clinging to the periphery of his head. A few waxy-looking strands meandered across the top but they were fighting a losing battle to his encroaching baldness. What made him look all the more strange was the fact that he had the bushiest eyebrows either of them had ever seen, which met across the bridge of his nose like a giant caterpillar crawling across his face. Losing concentration briefly Alice wondered why he didn't just comb his eyebrows back across the baldy patch. He too had a cigarette between his lips and the front of his jacket bore the powdery grey tracks of many others. He was in his mid-fifties and looked the worse for wear.

Conor was having a few misgivings now. As if sensing this, Parsons ushered them into his office denying them any chance of escape and, after removing a stack of files from the pair of chairs in front of his desk, invited them to sit.

The office was small, containing only Parsons's desk and chair with a couple of chairs for clients in front. A four-drawer metal filing cabinet stood next to a set of shelves crammed with telephone directories (some foreign) on top of which sat a suitcase. Next to the window there was a TV set with a bunny-ear aerial on top. Other than that there was no other furniture. A number of buff-coloured files stuffed with papers were stacked next to the desk. It was obvious that Mr Parsons had no time for computer technology. It was a rather worrying thought. Prominently positioned on the wall behind his desk hung a black and white photo of a cop in uniform shaking hands with Charlie Haughey. Both the cop and the politician looked about fifteen years younger. The eyebrows gave it away. The cop in question was Parsons. Beside it, and hanging slightly askew, was another photo. It was of Leggo Parsons shaking hands with a former Minister of Justice. They both had frozen smiles on their faces for the camera and Parsons was holding up a small open case containing a medal.

He straightened the picture. 'That's me and Padraig Flynn when he gave me the medal for bravery,' Parsons said. 'Nineteen eighty-eight, it was. I poleaxed a gunman, and me unarmed.' He pointed to the other photo. 'And that's me and Charlie, when he was Taoiseach.' He stared wistfully at the photo for a moment then, reputation enhanced, or so he hoped, he sat down. 'Now what can I do for ye?'

Not wishing to be specific at this stage Alice had set the ball rolling. She told him that they needed to have someone followed.

'For why?' Parsons asked. 'For a divorce, is it?'

'No,' Conor replied. 'Nothing like that. We just need to find out ... er ... well ... *stuff* about someone.'

Parsons leaned back on his chair and gave them a what-the-feck-are-ye-on-about look. 'Stuff?'

'Yes,' Alice said, taking the bull by the horns. 'We need to get some dirt on someone.'

Parsons shook his head. 'I don't do blackmail,' he said. 'I wouldn't touch anythin' like that.'

'It's not for blackmail purposes,' Alice cut in hastily, 'at least not in the way you mean. This character's causing us a lot of hassle, and all we want to do is have something over him so he'll stop.'

'He's blackmailing *ye* then?'

'Not exactly.' Conor shifted uneasily in his seat. 'He's, I suppose you'd call it, extorting money out of us. Protection money.'

Parsons looked interested now. He scuffled with a soft pack of Camels and lit one up from the embers of the last. 'So what d'ye expect ye'll find out by follyin' this fella?'

Alice shrugged. They still hadn't thought that far ahead. 'We've no idea. But we have to do something. He's bleeding us dry.'

'I take it there's some reason why ye're not going to the Guards?' Parsons said, a wry smirk on his lips.

'We're afraid he'll burn us out.'

Parsons nodded, taking a long drag on the cigarette. He pulled the smoke deep down into his lungs then exhaled through his nose. After a further pause he said, 'From personal experience, I've always found that the most efficient method of gettin' dirt on a subject is by means of listening devices. Bugs.' He paused to take another long drag on his cigarette, then, after he had exhaled, he continued. 'For one thing it's more cost effective and for another it means ye've evidence in the tape recordings.'

Despite her initial misgivings, Alice was impressed. 'What kind of bugs?' she had asked and that was when Parsons had launched into the *hypothetical* situation. When he had finished Conor asked, 'So what if it wasn't possible to actually get a transmitter inside a room?' Leggo shrugged and pulled at his bottom lip. 'Then ye'd need yer parabolic job.'

'What's that?'

A further drag on the fag was followed by a bout of coughing. 'It's a remote device.' He leaned down and rooted in the bottom drawer of his desk. 'See this?' He held up what looked like a mini cross-bow and bolt with a suction cup fixed to the end. 'Well, this is yer transmitter. Ye fire it at the glass of the window of the room ye want to bug, and then sit outside in yeer car and pick up the signal on yer directional parabolic receiver. But I don't have one a' them here at the minute.'

Conor didn't fancy that. It seemed a bit hit and miss, so to speak. 'Okay. Scratch that. What if we *could* get into the room then? How easy is it to plant the transmitter and what are the chances of it being found by accident?'

'So we're not bein' *hypothetical* any more, then?' Leggo paused, waiting for one of them to comment. Neither spoke. 'Suit yeerselves. How easy would it be to plant? Well, ye'd need a professional to do it right. My rates are reasonable, and ye want it done properly, don't ye?'

Conor looked at Alice who shrugged in reply. 'Okay,' he conceded. 'If you say so. When could you do it?'

'Whenever,' Leggo said. 'When did ye want it done?'

'As soon as possible,' replied Conor.

Leggo Parsons opened his notebook. 'Okay, who's the subject of the surveillance?'

Conor cast an eye in his partner's direction. Alice nodded. 'A man called Jesse James. 'He's a loan shark.'

Parsons snapped his note book shut. 'Are the two a' ye some sorta eejitts? D'ye know what that bastard'd do t' me if he caught me?'

'What do you mean, *if he caught you*? I thought you were supposed to be a bloody professional.' Alice pointedly cast a glance over his shoulder towards the photo of him with Padraig Flynn getting his medal. 'So much for your bloody bravery award.'

That hit a nerve. 'Ye don't know what ye're talkin' about,' he snapped. 'This is different. James knows me well. I wouldn't have a pig's chance of gettin' near him. If ye want to plant bugs ye'll have to do it yeerselves. Ye'll have a better chance than me.'

'Us?' Conor was horrified.

Parsons nodded then opened a drawer and rummaged inside for a moment before producing a thirteen-amp three-way adapter. 'This'll be yer only man for the job.'

Conor and Alice stared at the white plastic appliance. 'That?'

Parsons picked it up. 'This little jobby has a miniature voice-activated transmitter concealed inside.' He heaved himself out of his chair. 'It's cutting-edge technology. State of the art.'

'Are you serious?' Alice imagined that a state-of-the-art bug would be something the size of a rice crispy. 'Isn't it a bit . . . well . . .' she searched for the right word, '. . . isn't it a bit big?'

The private eye heaved himself out of his chair and lumbered around the desk to the set of shelves where he proceeded to lift down the suitcase from the top shelf. He lugged it back to the desk and, hoisting it on top, reached for the bug. He picked it up lovingly. 'The trannie inside here's the size of a pea. The beauty of this fecker is that as it's plugged into a wall, as well as bein' a transmitter, it also works like a normal adapter and has an unlimited power source. Yer subject, even if he was the kind who'd look for a bug, wouldn't suspect a thing.'

Conor said, 'Wow.' Alice was heard to mutter, 'So much for the need of the technical services of a dedicated professional.'

Parsons ignored the remark. 'I told ye. Cutting-edge technology.'

'Okay. So how do we get it back to hear the tape?' Alice asked.

'Ye don't *need* to get it back,' he said scathingly. 'It's a feckin' transmitter.' He snapped the locks and lifted the lid of the suitcase. 'And this is yeer receiver.'

Chapter Twenty-Three

Back at the apartment, Conor and Alice held a council of war. It was going to be down to them now. However they tried to persuade him, Parsons wouldn't hear of doing the job himself but agreed to supply them with the necessary equipment. Fortunately, however, because the sudden addition of half a dozen three-way adapters might cause some suspicion on Jesse James's part, as well as the transmitter concealed in the adapter, he gave them also four teeny tiny bugs to conceal under table-tops or shelves or the like. He explained that these had a limited life span due to the fact that they were battery powered, so advised them if possible to use the adapter transmitter where they thought their subject spent most time.

Because it was highly unlikely that once they had planted said pieces of equipment they'd get the chance to go back in to retrieve them again (neither of them being suicidal) they had to actually *buy* the bugs, but he let them hire the receiver at a reasonable rate, at least reasonable in relation to its size. On further discussion Parsons advised them that although the Quick Call finance office was by far the easier option in which to place the bugs, in his experience, if they were looking for dirt, something personal that James wouldn't want anyone to know about, then they'd have a better chance if they planted the bugs in his home.

Naturally, Alice wasn't too keen on that idea for obvious reasons, neither was Conor, but Parsons put it to them, 'Look. If ye want the *real* dirt, in my experience ye'll only find it where the subject's off his guard.'

'We could call him up and tell him we want to take up his offer for the club,' Conor suggested.

'It's as good an excuse as any to get in there, but what if he wants us to go to the office?'

Conor thought about that. 'We could always call him late afternoon when he's about to go home. Say we want to see him that night and offer to go out to his house.'

It was worth a try. At five-twenty Alice dialled the number. One of the bimbo clones answered and grudgingly put her through. It was surprisingly easy. James was in a very affable mood. Must have ripped someone's toenails out after lunch, Alice thought in passing, then regretted that she had reminded herself what kind of animal they were dealing with.

Jesse James lived just off the coast road in Sutton. The bungalow looked fairly ordinary from the outside and, except for the electronic gates, it bore no resemblance to the image of a typical gangster's abode. Conor had expected at least a Gothic folly and Alice a Georgian mansion. 'Is this it?' He sounded disappointed. 'By the looks of it, he must still live with the mammy.'

Alice snorted. 'James couldn't possibly *have* a mother.'

Their appointment was for eight p.m. sharp. As the gates swung open and they drove up the driveway to the front door, two very large Rottweilers bounded round the corner of the house and started salivating and pawing at the car windows. Alice and Conor sat tight and waited. The driver's side window was slimy with doggy drool by the time the front door opened and a grinning Jesse James sauntered out. He clicked his fingers and the two beasts, in proper Pavlov mode, trotted over and sat meekly by the flower bed.

'Come in, folks. Don't worry about the dogs.' He was still grinning broadly, enjoying their discomfort. It was evident that no expense had been spared on the décor of Chez James. Marble floors alternated with deep-pile Wilton, and there was an abundance of chrome and wrought iron. It was all in the worst possible taste. The lounge led off the end of the hall. It was immense, at least thirty-five feet long. Black and gold embossed wallpaper, capable of inflicting GBH on the eyeballs, covered the walls. Two extra long, custom-built, zebra-striped leather sofas sat on either side of the huge slate fireplace. Long-haired goatskin rugs lapped against the hearth, covering the black-and-grey-striped carpet.

Three crystal chandeliers were spaced at intervals down the centre of the ceiling. The coffee-table base was in the form of a life-sized bronze female figure on her hands and knees wearing nothing but a pair of stiletto-heeled shoes. The smoked-glass top rested on her shoulder blades and buttocks. A giant-screened television and a profusion of video and hi-fi equipment occupied most of the wall to the left of the fire and rows of leather-bound video cassette cases and CDs filled a bookcase beneath. Halfway down the room there was a second glass-topped table, but this time the nude was supine with her hands and splayed knees supporting the glass. The end wall was also of glass, leading on to a floodlit patio and probably a swimming pool, though it was not visible due to a vine-covered pergola.

'What d'you think?' asked their host, sweeping his arm around the room to indicate that he was referring to the decor.

Alice was speechless.

Conor spluttered, 'Awesome.'

That seemed to satisfy him and he beamed with pride. 'Would you like a drink?'

Alice nodded. She felt as if a stiff brandy would bolster her up for the task in hand. 'Thanks. I'll have a brandy.'

James picked up a remot-control device and pointed it at the wall. It slowly revolved to reveal a drinks bar with thatched roof and cut-stone front. The backlit shelves were crammed with bottles of every conceivable drink and an ice bucket with Playboy Bunny ears adorned the end of the smoked-glass bar-top. It was Conor's idea of lifestyle hell. He was amazed that there were no fairy lights along the top of the bar's thatch, but lacked the courage to say so. James was clearly living in a late seventies/early eighties, *Sun*-buying, *Playboy*-reading time warp.

'Now, to business.' James slumped down on the sofa. 'What can I do for you?'

That's rich, Conor thought. You could just leave us alone.

Aloud he said, 'We'd like to take you up on your offer. We'd like you to give us a loan so we can open the club.'

James nodded and a broad grin spread across his face. 'I knew you'd see sense. I'll have the papers drawn up by next week.' He got to his feet. 'Is that it?'

Alice spluttered. 'Um . . . well, no. Um . . . We were wondering if you had any . . . em . . .' she frantically trawled her brain for a reason to stay longer '. . . um . . . any ideas about the, em . . . the décor, that kind of thing.'

Conor shot her an astonished look.

James hiked his eyebrows to his hairline too, but he looked quite pleased. 'Oh,' he said. 'I hadn't really thought about it, but now you come to mention it, a Spanish hacienda look would be nice.'

'Spanish hacienda,' Conor repeated. He couldn't keep the disgust out of his voice.

James lost his Mister Happy face. 'What's wrong with Spanish hacienda?' he growled.

Alice kicked Conor in the shin. 'Nothing at all. Spanish hacienda's . . . lovely,' she burbled. 'Really, em . . . Spanish. But don't you think it could be maybe . . . that is to say . . . eh . . . It could be . . . em . . .' She looked to Conor for help. James's expression was darkening by the millisecond.

'Could I have a drink of water?' Conor croaked.

James looked from one to the other, not sure what to make of them. 'What?'

'Water. May I have a drink of water?' Conor repeated.

James was confused. He shook his head, not sure whether to be bemused, or angry at the affront of the fairy to even think of criticising his idea. And after *them* asking for an opinion.

'Water,' he repeated, choosing bemused. 'Fine.' And he walked out of the room. They heard him muttering, 'Fucking cheek. Fucking head-cases,' to himself as he disappeared along the hall to the kitchen.

Conor ran to the door. 'Quick. Stick the thingy somewhere. I'll keep watch.'

Alice paced round the room in panic. Quickly she took the adapter from her handbag and plugged it into a socket behind the sofa. For good measure she then stuck one of the small jobbies on the belly of the kneeling bronze woman/coffee table. She had a little difficulty here, as the sticky pad wouldn't properly adhere to the slightly rough bronze surface. Footsteps in the hall heralded James's return so, in haste, she gave it a thump with her fist and scurried back to the sofa. James handed Conor a Waterford crystal glass.

Conor gave him a strained smile. 'Thanks.'

James sat down again and patted the seat beside him, smiling at Alice. She swallowed hard and moved up the sofa. 'About this club?' he said. 'If you don't like the idea of a Spanish hacienda motif, what did *you* have in mind?'

Alice dived in at the deep end. 'Well. We were thinking along the lines of a fairly minimalist approach.'

James looked uncertain. 'Minimalist?' All the evidence around them suggested it was a concept he was unfamiliar with. 'What? Like bare walls?'

'To a degree,' Alice replied, carefully choosing her words. 'But we'd put in big squashy sofas and chairs, to encourage the punters to stay longer and . . .'

'Just a couple of sofas and chairs?' James curled his lip. 'What kind of a crap idea is that?'

Conor said, 'It's a concept for the new millennium. It has class.' James took that as a criticism and he glowered at Conor. Conor held his nerve and continued. 'It'll attract the right sort of member. The kind who are tired of ordinary run-of-the-mill clubs, the kind of punter with lots of disposable income, who'll spend lots of money.'

James stood up and paced the room. His expression gave nothing away. Suddenly Alice glanced down and saw that the transmitter was lying on the goatskin rug under the coffee table. Conor saw it at the same instant and quickly reached down and grabbed it before James started his return journey up the room.

'Could I use your bathroom?' Alice spluttered.

'What?'

'Could I use your bathroom, please?' she repeated.

James frowned, not pleased with the interruption to his train of thought. 'Okay, okay,' he said impatiently. 'It's left at the top of the steps and second on the right along the passage.'

'Sorry?' She adopted a helpless expression.

He walked to the door and directed her along the corridor. Conor meanwhile re-planted the bug under the rim of the mantelpiece.

The integrity of the general ambience of house was not in the least bit compromised by the bathroom décor. The sunken bath was green onyx, as were the toilet, bidet and twin hand-basin. All of the taps were gold plated, as were the soap trays, loo-roll holder and loo brush. Green, probably hand-knotted at great expense, swirled carpet covered the floor, and the walls and ceiling were mirrored. The whole effect bordered on bilious.

She stuck the bug under the rim of the bidet, figuring no one ever used bidets anyway so it would be least likely to be disturbed there. She sneaked out and along the corridor trying the doors as she passed.

Jesse James's bedroom was positively restrained compared to the rest of the house. A queen-sized four-poster bed with mirrored canopy, mahogany night tables and glass-doored wardrobes were the only furnishings. The colour scheme was Laura Ashley-inspired. Alice idly wondered if Jesse James's mammy had chosen the wallpaper. (Maybe gangsters do have mammies.) The bed was covered with a matching floral duvet set, and the carpet was pale blue. She crept over and planted a bug under the bedside table just as the phone rang, making her jump sky-high.

On her way back to the living room she sidled into the kitchen. It was all country cottagey pine with frilly floral knicker blinds. It was spotlessly clean and looked as if it had never been used.

'Lost our way, have we?' James's voice behind her.

She spun around. 'I was just looking for a drink of water,' she quavered. She could feel perspiration running down the small of her back.

'Are the two of you hungover or what?' James was looking at her quizzically.

'What?'

'Dehydration . . . a sign of a hangover.' He picked a glass out of a cupboard, filling it from the tap.

Grabbing the opportunity, Alice stuck the final bug under the breakfast bar.

'Here you are,' he said. 'Now can we get back down to business please?' They returned to the living room.

'So what d'you think?' Alice asked.

James shrugged. 'I'm not sure about this minimalist crap. Are you sure that's what the punters go for these days?'

'The twenty-five to thirty-five upwardly mobile types do,' Conor said, 'and they're the ones with the money.'

Jesse James didn't get where he was by being stupid. On matters where he knew he was ignorant, he always paid for the best advice, seeing it as a worthwhile investment. Astutely, he decided that Alice and her faggot partner knew what they were talking about. Queers and fag hags knew about that sort of thing.

'Okay. If that's what you think.' He added ominously, 'Don't disappoint me.'

Alice and Conor assured him that they wouldn't and took that as a cue to go, leaving James wondering just what the hell the visit had been about. As they drove out of the gate, a dark blue Audi passed them on the way up to the house. 'Voor sprung durk technik,' Alice commented. 'I wonder who that is?'

'Now's our chance to see if Leggo Parsons's gear's working.' Conor leaned over the back seat of the Fiesta and picked up the receiver. 'Jesus. This fucking thing weighs a ton.' He left it where it was and opened the lid, switching it on as Parsons had demonstrated. Nothing. Utter silence. 'It's not working!'

Alice struggled round and knelt on her seat. Then reaching over she twiddled the tuning knob. They were assaulted with harsh white noise for a couple of seconds before they heard Jesse James's unmistakable voice ranting at, presumably, the man who had just arrived in the Audi. 'It's not fucking good enough, Charlie,' they heard him yelling. 'That bastard owes me.'

'But he hasn't got the money, JJ,' Charlie implored. 'You can't get blood out of a stone.'

'The tape. The tape,' Conor hissed. 'Where do we switch on the tape?'

'Get a grip,' Alice muttered and punched the record button.

'That's a matter of opinion,' James barked. 'Tell him I'll take the house in lieu.'

'No good, JJ. He's mortgaged up to the hilt. And what about the kids? He's five young kids.'

'That's not my problem. Go back and tell him the deal stands. He owes me, and however he gets it, I want what's due to me. Got that?'

'Got that, JJ,' Charlie babbled. 'Got that all right.'

'You should never've let it go this far! That's what I pay you for. You should have warned me he was going belly-up. You should've jumped in while he still had something left.'

'I'm sorry, JJ. It won't happen again. I'll tell him all right. I'll tell him.' Charlie sounded close to a heart attack.

'Poor Charlie,' Alice muttered.

'He sounds like he has a king-sized ulcer,' Conor remarked.

They sat outside James's house until after midnight, then went back to the Samovar.

'Where the hell have you two been?' Tony exploded. He looked frazzled. 'We've been run off our feet.'

'Sorry, Tony,' said Alice. 'We've been saving our bacon.'

'Hopefully.' Conor sounded less than confident. 'Though if I may mix a metaphor, our goose will be well and truly cooked if we haven't saved our bacon.' Tony gave them a withering look and went back to what he had been doing.

They realised that they couldn't sit outside the home of Jesse James round the clock. Apart from the fact that they had a business to run, they had to be discreet. In James's kind of neighbourhood any suspicious vehicle consistently parked for long periods of time would result in the neighbourhood watch calling in the cops, and their cover being blown. They decided to vary the times of the stake-out, and just hope for the best that they'd get lucky.

'We could be in for a long haul,' Conor said as Alice was setting off on her first night's surveillance.

'Look on the bright side,' Alice encouraged. 'Tonight could be the night.' She was not especially confident that tonight would be the night, but she thought they were both in need of a dose of optimism.

Tonight was not the night, neither was the next night, or the next, or the one after that. They both found surveillance mind-crushingly boring, Alice most of all, and it usually fell to her to do it, as Conor was needed in the restaurant. Although Tony was turning out to be promising, he didn't have the experience to handle too much pressure with only the assistance of Louis; and there was also the risk of rebellion if they upset him.

One evening, ten days later, Alice was sitting in the car feeling sorry for herself and cursing the fact that the heater didn't work. For mid-April the weather was unseasonably cold. If the depletion of the ozone layer was the cause of global warming, why was the weather so bloody awful? she wondered. Surely if the earth was hurtling towards destruction, the least that could be expected was a couple of good summers. She felt damp, cold and uncomfortable in the extreme, and was beginning to have a bit more respect for the likes of Leggo Parsons. This private-eye business was tedious to say the least.

Just after eleven a black Golf cabriolet stopped at Jesse James's gate and a tall elegant woman got out and spoke into the intercom. She was standing in the shadows so Alice didn't get a good look at her. After a short interval the gates opened and the car disappeared up the drive. James had been on his own all evening and she'd had to endure the sound-track of an erotic video with bland plinky-plonky background music and a script consisting of ooohing and ahhhhing and moaning and thrashing about. She did her best to block from her mind thoughts of what James might be doing, all by himself on the zebra-print sofa. The sound-track ceased abruptly as his visitor arrived. She was unable to discern what the woman said over the intercom but James replied, 'Hello, babe, park round the back out of sight.'

A well-spoken, strangely familiar woman's voice filled the

car a few minutes later. 'You know he'll kill me if he ever finds out about us, don't you, Jesse?'

'He won't find out. Come here, you.'

The oooohing and ahhhhing started again but this time for real. The bedroom mike switched on as they tumbled into the room and Alice almost forgot to switch on the tape. 'Shit!' Her shaking fingers fumbled with the switch.

'Oh, God, Jesse . . . Oh, God . . . Just there, no, lower.' More moaning.

'Come on, Patricia . . . Ooooooh fuck! that's good . . . Do that again.'

Alice sat bolt upright in the seat. 'Good grief! Patricia,' she said aloud. There was more oooohing and ahhhing followed by panting and the slapping and squelching sounds of frenzied sex. Alice was feeling distinctly uncomfortable listening in. It was sleazy enough eavesdropping on a live sex show, but the fact that it was her ex-stepmother made it even more gross. After an energetic fifteen minutes there was silence followed a moment later by the sound of a cigarette lighter.

'Do you have to smoke?' Patricia's voice.

'Somehow a wine gum doesn't hit the spot.' James's voice. The sound of a slap and laughter.

'Idiot!'

A further silence.

'He'll be away next week for three days. He's going up north,' Patricia said.

'I didn't know he still did business with that crowd.'

'Which crowd?'

'The Provos.'

'He'll do business with both sides if the money's right,' she said. 'He's a dangerous man.'

'And you like to live dangerously.'

Patricia laughed. 'Maybe.'

'And is that what all this is about? You living dangerously?'

'Maybe,' she repeated. 'And maybe not. Perhaps it's more than that this time.'

'It better fucking had be with what I'm risking,' James said. 'C'mere.'

Alice, who by this time was sweating profusely, was feeling acutely embarrassed. In fact, she couldn't have felt any more uncomfortable, even if she was listening to Maura and Mick engaging in wild passionate sex (unlikely as the notion might be) instead of the wicked stepmother. Suddenly vivid visions of Maura and Mick having sex came into her mind, and however hard she tried to make them go away, Mick's face, red and sweating, intruded. She was afraid to attempt to blot out the sound effects coming from the receiver in case she inadvertently switched the thing off. Thankfully Jesse James and Patricia reached a further satisfactory conclusion and Alice breathed a sigh of relief.

Patricia left at midnight and Alice went to the Samovar to collect Conor. On the way she got to wondering who *He* was. Surely Patricia wasn't referring to Maurice Broderick. As far as she was aware, he was a pillar of respectability. But then what did she know? Her brief acquaintance with Maurice ended when she was twelve, going on thirteen years old. As soon as Alice walked into the kitchen Conor could see by her face that she'd got a result. They went into the office.

'What happened? What did you get?' he asked eagerly.

'I'm not sure,' Alice hedged.

'How d'you mean?'

Alice took a deep breath. 'At around eleven a car pulled up, and you'll never guess who got out.'

'Who, who?' Conor was in a state of high excitement.

'Patricia, my stepmother.'

'What was she doing there? I didn't think she knew the likes of that James.'

'Oh, she knows him all right,' Alice said. 'And I mean in the biblical sense.'

Conor looked at her blankly for a moment before the penny dropped. 'You mean. . . ?'

Alice nodded. 'And I had to listen to the whole thing in living stereo for half a bloody hour.'

Conor giggled. 'Oh, dear. Was it good for *you*?'

'The thing is,' Alice continued, 'they were talking about Patricia's husband, Maurice Broderick. And by the sound of it, though I find it hard to believe, he's some sort of hard-man drug dealer or something. Patricia was going on about him killing James if he ever found out he was shagging her.'

'Do you believe her? Are you sure she meant it literally?'

'I don't know,' Alice said.

'How about Melanie? Surely she'd know.'

Alice wasn't keen. She was becoming fond of Melanie and didn't want to jeopardise that by saying the wrong thing. For all she knew Melanie might be fond of Maurice Broderick. 'I'm not sure how to broach the subject. I mean I can hardly come right out and say, "Hey, Mel, d'you know if it's true that your stepfather's some sort of psycho drug dealer?", can I?'

She had a point. 'I suppose not.' Then it occurred to him. 'I bet Leggo Parsons would know.'

The black-rooted blonde was on the phone when they walked in. She was spelling out a name into the receiver. 'P-R-O-T-H-E-R-O-E as in er . . . Protheroe. First name Alan. He's Welsh . . . yes.' She was holding the cigarette between her middle and index finger this time and, as she waved them through to Parsons's office, they were showered with the ash worm.

Parsons was sitting at his desk reading some typewritten sheets of paper. He looked up as they came in. 'Did you get a result?' he asked, and the caterpillar jumped an inch and a half up his forehead.

'Maybe,' Alice replied. 'Do you know anything about a man called Maurice Broderick?'

'You mean Boom Boom?'

'What?'

'You never heard of Maurice Boom Boom Broderick?'

'I know Maurice Broderick,' Alice said. 'But I never heard him called Boom Boom. He's married to Patricia, the woman James is shagging.'

A wide grin broke out across Parsons's face. 'Boy, did ye get a result!' He looked smug. 'I told ye yeer best bet was his house.'

'About this Boom Boom,' Conor interjected, steering Parsons back to the subject.

The private eye gestured towards the two client chairs, once again covered in files. Alice moved them back on to the floor before sitting herself down. Conor remained standing. Parsons took a slurp from his coffee mug. 'Is he tired of livin' or what? That fella's a psycho.'

'That's what you said about James,' Conor scoffed.

'Yeah and was I wrong? Was I? Listen.' Parsons was in earnest. 'James is Broderick's enforcer but he's a pussycat compared to Boom Boom.'

'Boom Boom?' Alice muttered. 'Why Boom Boom?'

The ex-cop cocked his head to one side. 'In the early days if anyone crossed him . . .' He pointed his hand at Alice and Conor with his index finger extended and his thumb raised, mimicking a gun. 'Boom boom, they were blown away.' He blew imaginary smoke from the end of his finger and continued. 'He's more subtle these days, of course, gets the likes of James to sort out any little problems, and no doubt James delegates the job further down the pecking order. That's why the cops can't touch him. He's a clever bugger. He has a lot of legit business interests these days too, worth millions, or so I'm told.'

'James said something about paramilitaries?'

'Oh, Broderick's not proud, he'll deal with anyone if the price is right,' Parsons said. 'He *owns* the south side. The protection rackets, prostitution and drugs are all controlled by him. But he leases out the territory now, if ye know what I mean.'

'But he's so different from Jesse James. He's so . . .' Alice struggled for a word. 'Cultured.'

Parsons shrugged. 'He comes from a well-off family. Well educated, college, the lot. Though I can't say the same for James. Now yer woman might be going for her bit've rough there.'

'So how did Maurice Broderick get into crime?' Alice asked.

'I dunno know for sure. Word has it his auld fella died during his second year at Trinity and they discovered that Daddy'd drunk the family fortune, so he had t' finance his way through college. He started with a bit've fraud, yeh know, small stuff, stealin' cheques, though he was never convicted.

We couldn't get enough evidence, or it could've been something to do with his auld fella bein' a big barrister. But he's a violent bastard, that's for sure.'

'Magic!' Conor was ecstatic. 'That'll do us! We can blackmail James.'

Parsons disagreed. 'No, it's not enough. Ye'll need pictures. It'd add a lot of weight to the tape.'

Alice was horrified. 'What? You mean of them having sex?'

His eyes glazed over. 'Well, that'd be good. I've got a tiny video camera I could let ye hire, but ye'd have t' get into the house again to plant it.' Conor's guts did a jig. 'Pictures of her comin' and goin' from yer man's house'd do.'

Conor relaxed and heaved a sigh of relief. So did Alice, but for different reasons. Listening to Patricia and Jesse James was bad enough without having to view it in living colour. 'I'll drop ye round an infra-red stills camera. Ye can't be usin' the flash.'

Conor was grinning like an eejitt again. 'We've got him. We've got the bastard.'

'So what do we do now?' Alice asked, ever the pragmatist. 'We can't just go along and throw the tape and the pictures on his desk. What's to stop him having us killed or something?' That wiped the grin off Conor's face. The practicalities hadn't crossed his mind.

Leggo Parsons, Private Investigator, cleared his throat. 'Now there I might be able to help ye.' He paused in case they might be in any doubt that he meant in a professional capacity. 'For a nominal fee.'

Chapter Twenty-Four

Alice struck lucky two nights later and managed to get a fairly passable photo of Jesse James and Patricia sharing a long goodnight kiss on his doorstep. It was only when she got the prints back, four copies as instructed by Parsons, and she had placed one in the envelope along with a copy of the incriminating tape, that she felt that at last they had got Jesse James off their backs. She sent a set to Parsons. He had advised this course of action as being added security (actually his motives were not strictly kosher here, but he fancied having some dirt on James should an opportunity to exploit it arise). A third set she sent in a sealed envelope to her solicitor, in accordance with Parsons's advice, including a covering letter, in the event that anything of a terminal or violent nature should befall either of them etc., etc. The fourth set she locked in the safe.

Conor was over the moon, not only because they'd got the better of James but also because Mason had just received news that he had landed a supporting role in a movie with Liam Neeson which was due to be shot in Ireland in a couple of months' time. Ironically, he was to play a small-time criminal who is caught in bed with the crime boss's wife. His agent was confident that this could be his big break. Mason was equally high. Now that things were on a more even keel, he harboured hopes that Conor could be persuaded to come out to his parents for once and for all. Conor, however, was not aware of this as he and Alice set off to the Quick Call Finance office, toting Alice's cassette player and very smug expressions.

Jesse James was in a state of shock. He had no idea how long he'd been sitting at his desk with his head in his hands. It was dark outside. Deirdre and Jacinta had gone home long ago. The shoe was on the other foot and he'd experienced varying emotions over the past few hours. The initial anger and shock at the audacity of them, waltzing in and threatening him. Then the dawning of the implications, then the ignominy as she'd made him call Joxer Boxer there and then and instruct him that no further collections were to be made from the Samovar.

It had been a difficult call. Joxer must have thought he was crazy. To his 'Yer not serious, Boss?' he'd babbled something like, 'Just do it, when I tell you,' to which Joxer had replied, 'Do it? But yeh just friggin told me t' stop.'

His stomach rumbled. He hadn't eaten since breakfast. The fag hag and her queen had made their visit just as he was thinking of going to lunch. Then afterwards he wasn't hungry. He was sick to his stomach. If Broderick found out, he was finished, in every sense. But then it struck him. Why should Broderick find out? Why should they blow the whistle on him? It was in their interests to keep Broderick ignorant of his relationship with Patricia. Relationship? Was that what it was? He'd have to end it. He began to question his feelings. Was he in love with her, or did he have other motives? Did he just want her because she was Broderick's? No, he told himself. He wasn't sure if he was in love with her. She was a hard woman, harder and more manipulative than any woman he'd ever known, not his usual type at all, but there was something about her that he was addicted to. That was it. She was an addiction and he didn't want to lose her.

With this in mind he realised there was only one solution. He picked up the phone.

They had to put off the celebrations until the weekend as the bistro was too busy for Tony and Louis to be left to manage on their own. Alice didn't mind, but she was looking forward to letting her hair down. They decided to make a party of it and asked along Declan, Melanie and the usual suspects, who included Hugh, Jojo and Gilda and Claire, her old drinking buddy. Her new boyfriend, a chap called Paul with whom she was quite smitten, and a gang from the Samovar, together with their other halves. Madame Max was unavailable as Sunday was her busiest night, but Celeste was off duty and said she'd be delighted to come. Conor and the lads prepared a buffet and they bought lots to drink. Spike, Conor's DJ pal, had to decline the invitation but he gave them all free passes to go along to TRANSV later.

Alice felt as if a huge weight had been lifted from her shoulders. She could see a future now. In a couple of months they'd be able to think about their plans for the club. On Saturday afternoon between the lunchtime shift and dinner she had her hair done in preparation and on the Sunday she met Melanie for brunch. She'd been meaning to call her for ages but between one thing and another she hadn't gotten around to it, so while inviting her to the party she took the opportunity to arrange a girly get-together at the Expresso bar just off Grafton Street.

Melanie was there ahead of her and her face lit up as Alice approached. She was glad that Alice didn't hold a grudge against her. When she had first bumped into her that night at the Samovar she had sensed that Alice wasn't altogether pleased to see her, but then she had relaxed and thawed out once she realised that they had both been in the same boat. Well, perhaps she didn't realise the extent of it, but she could empathise with her as far as Patricia was concerned.

Alice on the other hand was toying with the idea of pumping her about Maurice Broderick, but again, she wasn't sure how to broach the subject. Melanie, however, afforded her the perfect opportunity when Alice asked her how she and Declan were getting on and if they were an item. Melanie blushed at this and became flustered and evasive. Alice was surprised. A simple yes or no would have done. Then she noticed Melanie swiping away a rogue tear that had escaped from the corner of her eye. She was at once embarrassed. 'I'm sorry. It's okay,' she said. 'It's none of my business anyway. Forget I asked.'

Melanie closed her eyes and shook her head, then reached across the table and grabbed hold of Alice's hand. 'No. I'm sorry . . . It's just he's been so patient. I feel really bad about it, but, well . . .' She left the sentence unfinished. Alice opened her mouth to change the subject but Melanie suddenly said, 'No. I have to talk about it. My therapist said I shouldn't be ashamed to talk about it. It wasn't my fault.' She looked right into Alice's eyes as she spoke.

At the mention of the word 'therapist', Alice remembered Declan's comment about Melanie having problems. With a mother like Patricia it wasn't surprising. 'Only if you want to,' she said.

Melanie nodded. 'I want to.' She rummaged in her handbag and drew out a tissue, then blew her nose and dabbed her eyes. She laughed nervously. 'I must look a fright,' she said. Alice just smiled kindly and squeezed her hand in encouragement. When she had composed herself again, Melanie leaned forward across the table and lowered her voice. 'I . . . I've had a few problems, you see. I find it difficult to . . . well, I'm not able to let a man . . . I can't bear to be touched,' she said. She blushed and averted her eyes, staring down at the table-top. 'You see, when I was young . . . when we went to live in Blackrock, Maurice, my stepfather, well, he used to come to my room at night. He used to . . . to . . .' She cleared her throat and looked up at Alice again. 'He sexually abused me.'

Alice was shocked. 'He abused you?' Melanie nodded. Alice felt as if she'd been punched. It had never crossed her mind that anything of that nature was going on. 'I'd no idea,' she said lamely.

'There's no reason why you should have. Declan's been marvellous. If it wasn't for him I'd never have started the counselling and the therapy. But I don't know how long he'll hang around waiting for me to get over it. I know it's silly, and I really want to be close to him, I really care about him, but as soon as . . .' She shook her head and whispered, 'I just can't.' She started to cry again.

Alice felt terrible. Ashamed that she had felt so badly done by and, if she admitted it, so jealous of Melanie whom she'd always assumed had everything. Tough bond-trader Melanie, who excelled in a man's world with a killer instinct, as Declan had put it. She moved her chair around the table next to her stepsister and put her arms around her. She didn't give a jot for the quizzical glances of the other diners. 'It's okay, Mel. I'm so sorry. I'm so sorry that happened to you. I'd no idea. You poor thing.'

After a little while, Melanie stopped weeping and wiped her eyes. 'Thanks. I feel better now. Every time I talk about it, I get upset, but I feel better afterwards. My therapist said it's like the grieving process.' She gave a nervous laugh. 'Silly, isn't it? I can function perfectly well on every other level, but when it comes to . . . to the most basic human emotion, I'm a mess.'

Alice shook her head. 'Hardly your fault.' The waiter came over with a worried look on his face. 'Is everything all right?' Alice told him they were fine and ordered fresh coffee. When he had gone she said, 'You don't need to worry about Declan, Mel. He'll wait as long as it takes.'

'How do you know? What did he tell you?' She looked wounded, obviously thinking that Declan had betrayed a confidence.

'Nothing,' Alice said, anxious to allay her fears. 'I asked him if you were an item and, well, his words were, "I wish". He just said you had a few problems and he'd hang around for as long as it took. I thought maybe you were involved with someone else, or had just broken up with someone or something like that . . . I think he's in love with you.'

'Really?' Her eyes lit up and at the same time filled with tears again.

Alice nodded. 'Really.'

The fresh coffee arrived and Alice poured. 'Did your mother know?'

'Not at first. There was this whole this-is-our-little-secret thing. He kept telling me that it was our secret and that I was special. But I knew it wasn't right. I didn't want him to do it. I wanted him to stop. Then I told her and she slapped me hard across the face.' She touched her cheek. 'I couldn't believe she'd do that. She called me a filthy liar, then a slut. I was only fourteen, for God's sake.' Anger had replaced the tears now. 'And an innocent fourteen at that, at least innocent about sex. She said I was making it up to get noticed.'

Alice had no difficulty in believing that of Patricia. 'The bitch. So what did you do?'

Melanie smiled a sad smile and gave a little shrug. 'I fitted a bolt to the inside of my bedroom door,' she said, 'and kept out of his way. He didn't like it. I'd hear him tapping on the door but I'd pretend to be asleep. Then he tried to get round me by buying me presents.'

'Did you know he was a criminal? A drug dealer?' Alice asked.

'What?'

'Maurice Broderick's a drug dealer.'

'Don't be silly. He's a pervert, a bastard, but he's a businessman.'

Alice shook her head. 'No, Mel. No. He's a criminal. Don't ask me how I know, it's complicated, but he's some sort of godfather. He controls all sorts of rackets like drugs and prostitution and stuff.'

Melanie looked astounded. 'Does my mother know?' Alice nodded, regretting now that she ever had mentioned it. Melanie had enough on her plate, but her stepsister just sighed and said, 'Why doesn't that surprise me?'

They parted company an hour later. Melanie was brighter, but Alice, for the first time, sensed the deep sadness in her. For her own part, she realised how unscathed a dodgy start in life had left her and thanked her lucky stars.

Folks started arriving at the Samovar at around nine-thirty and, after eating and drinking and generally making merry, they all adjourned to TransV at around midnight. Alice was on top of the world. Getting Jesse James out of the picture was like winning the lottery. Conor was in quite outrageous form. He seemed to have adopted Hector's persona on the dance floor, if not his sense of rhythm, and was flinging himself around in gay abandon. The music was loud, the club was crowded, they were all having a good time.

Later, just before two, Alice was sitting up on the balcony taking a breather. She rested her arms on the balustrade and leaned her head on her hands, watching the dancers below. Melanie was dancing in a group with Declan, Gilda and Jojo.

She looked happy in Declan's company and he in hers. She herself felt content and hopeful. Conor and Mason were nowhere in sight but she could see Hugh and Claire giving it some to a U2 track. Celeste was bopping away more sedately with Paul. She sensed someone behind her and a moment later heard a chair being dragged back. She glanced over her shoulder. Sean Holland was standing behind her staring. 'Oh, hello,' she said, and turned her gaze back to the dance floor.

'What's the story?' he said.

Embarrassed and apprehensive, Alice, without turning around, muttered, 'Sorry?'

She heard Holland give an exasperated sigh. 'The real story with you and Conor Finn?'

The pit of Alice's stomach gave a lurch. She turned to face him. 'How do you mean, the *real* story? You know the real story.' She could feel her face heating up and was glad of the dim lighting.

Holland stared at her for a moment then raised his eyebrows questioningly. 'Do I?'

'We told you. That day in the restaurant. What's your problem?' She was getting both irritated and nervous now. What did he expect her to say?

Holland shrugged, then stood up and moved over to the balustrade beside Alice and stared over to the far side of the club below. 'I just wondered. Especially when I look down there and see your *husband* snogging the Diet Coke man.'

Alice's head snapped round and she searched the floor below, finally picking out the bright yellow of Mason's shirt in the dimness, his arms wrapped around Conor. Unable to think of any plausible explanation she just shrugged. Holland leaned his back against the rail and folded his arms. His interest wasn't in an official capacity. In that sense Alice's complicated private life was no longer his concern, but he didn't like to be made a fool of. Alice on the other hand, maybe because Jesse James was no longer a threat, threw up her hands to it. 'Okay. So we're not a couple.' Holland couldn't stop a snort escaping, to which Alice snapped, 'Well, if you don't want to hear me out . . .'

He lifted his hands, palms out, in a placating gesture. 'Sorry.'

'That day. That day at the Samovar when you came in with the cops . . . Well, you see, how can I put this?' She tried to arrange her thoughts in some semblance of a coherent story. 'The thing is, Conor's parents think I'm married to him. It sort of happened by accident.' She was about to explain how, after he and Hector plighted their troth, Conor had wanted to come out to his parents, but pulled herself up short. The circumstances didn't call for honesty on a suicidal scale. 'I went home with him because he wanted to come out to his parents. It was just after Hector and I got married. Anyway, he sort of lost courage and then Maura and Mick jumped to the conclusion that he and I were married.' Holland's face registered astonishment at this. Alice just said, 'Don't ask.' Then she continued, 'Well, anyway, he sort of went along with it. There was nothing I could do. I could hardly stand up and yell, "No, no, it's not true, he's really gay," could I?'

'I suppose not,' Holland conceded. 'So they really think you and Conor are married?' He shook his head and smiled.

Alice took it as a criticism. 'He's my friend. They're lovely people. What else could I do?'

'And what about Hector?' When it became obvious that Alice wasn't going to comment, he said, 'Look, that business is finished with. It's just curiosity on my part. Personally I got the impression he was gay.'

'So why was he granted a visa then?'

'He made quite an impression on Carmel McGuire. I suppose she swayed the decision. According to Carmel, he's the most heterosexual, sexy, charming man she ever met and obviously madly in love with you.'

Alice guffawed. 'Poor Carmel.'

He grinned. 'She thought he was way too good for you. She's led a very sheltered life, has Carmel. I think Hector's full-on, in-yer-face charm swept her off her feet.'

They were both silent for a while, then Alice asked, 'So what are you going to do?'

'Do? Nothing. I told you, that business is over with. Like I said, I was just curious. You don't strike me as a woman who'd put up with her partner snogging another man, that's all.'

Over his shoulder she saw Conor and Mason approaching. They were deep in conversation and didn't notice Holland until they were right up to the table. When they did, they stopped dead in their tracks and Conor blanched. 'It's okay, Conor. He knows about you and Mason. I explained about your parents.'

'What about Hector?'

'On second thoughts, let's not go into that,' Holland said. 'It could be more information than I need to know. So, would you guys like a drink?'

Chapter Twenty-Five

Maura Finn was running late. She had intended to put a load of washing on before she left to tend her cake stall at the Country Market, but everything was conspiring against her. Mick hadn't woken her when he'd gone out to do the milking and so she'd slept late, only waking when she'd heard him coming in at seven-thirty. Then the ginger cat had gone into labour and was hiding in the back of the hot press and she'd wasted half an hour trying to coax her out into a box she'd prepared for the purpose next to the range in the kitchen. Mick tried to persuade her to leave well alone. 'Sure leave her be. She'll be grand. It's warm and dark in there, she'll be grand.'

Maura had let it be, but it was more because of the time constraint than Mick's persuasion. She wasn't keen on having the cat give birth along with all the clean clothes. After they'd eaten the breakfast, Mick went out to the fields. He said he'd some fences to mend. She was worried about him. He'd been looking peaky lately and had a shortness of breath she hadn't noticed before. She'd spoken to Doctor Flynn about it, at least mentioned it in passing at a fundraiser for the Kosovo refugees the previous week, but he'd made light of it and said that none of them were getting any younger and suggested that Mick lighten up on his work load a bit. As if.

Maura packed the van with her cakes and loaves of soda bread and headed off down the lane towards Tanagh. As she was turning left into the main road she met the green An Post van with Seanie Grady at the wheel. She pulled in and took the mail to save him the journey up the lane, then set off again. Trade was brisk. The usual faces, the chat. By eleven she'd sold out, so went over to the café for a cup of tea and a sandwich to keep her going. There was a stew in the oven for Mick's lunch so she didn't need to hurry home. It was nice to have a half an hour to herself. She chose a table in the corner, ordered a toasted ham and tomato sandwich and a large pot of tea. While she was waiting for the waitress to bring over her snack (she was Mrs Kelly's youngest who had dropped out of school just before the Leaving Cert, and her bursting with brains) she took the post out of her bag and leafed through the envelopes. There was a brown one with a harp addressed to Mick. She held it up to the light. It was thin. Could be a cheque. She put that to one side. The next envelope was a folded gummed airmail form from America. She smiled. She didn't need to turn it over to read the sender's name to know it was from her brother, Father Paddy, in Philadelphia. She put it down. She'd read it later at tea time so Mick could enjoy it too. Paddy's letters were a joy. There was the usual junk mail. A coupon for some new miracle toothpaste, an advert for the sale at McCall's, the local shoe shop, and a supermarket booklet with lots of coupons for this and that. Maura put that on the pile for later. She'd go through it and see if there was money off anything she routinely bought. She didn't hold with buying stuff she'd end up throwing out just because she'd seen an ad or because there was a few pence off.

The handwriting on the last envelope was unfamiliar. Neat, in black ink, probably written with a fountain pen. She held it up to the light. One sheet. Postmark Dublin. She had no notion who it could be from. She picked up her knife, wiped the mayonnaise off it on a paper serviette, and slit the top of the envelope.

Alice heard the phone ringing as she opened the front door of the apartment. She wasn't feeling the best, the afternoon after the night before. They'd stayed in TransV until it closed and she'd even had a bop on the dance floor with Sean Holland. She'd revised her opinion of him. Off duty he bore a startling resemblance to a human being. But now she was looking forward to a long relaxing hot bath and a snooze before the evening shift.

Maura sounded upset. 'We've had a letter,' she started. 'One of those poison-pen things.'

Alarm bells sounded in Alice's head. 'You don't want to take any notice of that sort of thing,' she said nervously. 'Really, Maura. Those things are just full of malicious lies.'

'Don't you want to know what it says?'

'Erm . . . Only if you want to tell me.' Alice cringed. She heard Maura sniff at the other end of the line as if she'd been crying. She cleared her throat. 'I'll read it to you,' she said. 'There's no address, it just starts off, "Dear Mr and Mrs Finn, I think you should know your son is gay. He and I are lovers." *Lovers*,' she repeated. ' "I tell you this for his own good. He cannot go on living a lie. I hope you will understand why I have done this. Have a nice day." And it's signed "Sincerely, Mason Fitzpatrick." That's the young American man who was at the Point with Declan, isn't it?'

'That's right, Maura, but you shouldn't take any notice of him.' Then, 'Eh . . . Has Mick seen the letter?'

'I didn't show it to him yet.'

'Well, I think you should just tear it up and throw it in the fire.' Suddenly Alice's heart was murderous towards Mason.

'And not show it to Mick?' Maura was shocked. 'We've never had any secrets. I have to show it to him.'

Alice didn't know where to go from here. 'But why, Maura? It's lies. That Mason's an unpleasant lying toad.'

'But why would he lie? Why would he say something like that if it wasn't true?' All Alice could think of saying at that point was, 'Got me there, Maura,' but somehow it didn't seem appropriate. 'No,' Maura continued. 'I have to tell Mick. Anyway, if it's true, Declan'll need our support. If that's the way he is, it doesn't matter. He's still our son.'

It took a moment for Maura's last statement to sink in. 'Declan? You said Declan.'

'That's right, dear. But he's still the same person. You mustn't be prejudiced.'

'I'm not, Maura. I've nothing against gay people, but I know it's not true. Declan isn't gay. Mason might be, and maybe that's why he wrote the letter, he obviously fancied Declan, and I suppose Declan must have rejected him, so he's hitting back the only way he can think of. Maybe he thinks that if he writes it down it'll be true . . .' Alice knew what she was saying sounded like balderdash, and rambling balderdash at that. Maura wasn't listening. She was still wittering on at the other end of the line with phrases such as 'live and let live', and 'gays are people too, you know'.

If only Declan hadn't stopped Conor from telling his parents the truth. But then, would the reaction have been the same if it had been Conor? Declan looked so obviously heterosexual, it wouldn't necessarily need to be public knowledge and Mick needn't be embarrassed in front of his friends. Come to that, who would have suspected Mason was gay at first sight? And she'd seen how proud Mick was of Conor when he came home with a wife and scotched the rumours. Yes, it was a whole different ball game with Conor. Mick was a product of his upbringing in a small rural environment of the 1950s, where the church had a huge influence. She couldn't blame him for having certain prejudices. At heart he was a kind man. 'You mean you don't mind?' Alice said, when she finally got the chance to get a word in edgeways.

'Well, I'd prefer it if he got married and settled down. I know Mick'll find it difficult, but at the end of the day, he's still our son.'

'The thing is, Maura,' Alice started, but Maura cut her off.

'Sorry, dear, I have to go. I hear Mick coming in.'

'But, Maura . . .'

'Bye, bye, dear.' And she hung up.

Alice was left standing, staring at the receiver. Her first reaction was to phone Declan to warn him. She replaced the receiver and dialled his mobile. She was put through to his message minder and hung up. Somehow it didn't seem fitting to leave the message, 'Hi, Declan, it's Alice. By the way, your parents think you're gay. Mason wrote them a poison-pen letter and they got the wrong end of the stick. Have a nice day,' though she was sorely tempted.

She had a quick shower, dressed and dried her hair, then tried Maura again. There was no reply. She needed to talk to her. She needed to talk to Conor. She needed to gouge out Mason's heart with a blunt tin spoon, but none of these was an option as Mason was up in the north filming a commercial and Conor was at the wholesalers with his mobile switched off. What was the point of having a bloody mobile if he kept it switched off?

She tried Declan again before she left for work. Thankfully he answered. She quickly, and as coherently as she could manage under the circumstances, filled him in on the afternoon's events, and her concern about the unanswered phone at his parents' home.

'Mason told them I'm gay? Why the hell would he do that?'

'He didn't mention your name, your mother just assumed it was you because Conor introduced Mason as *your* friend. She just put two and two together and got five. I told her it wasn't true, but she was upset. She just kept saying stuff about it being okay, that you were still their son and stuff. Anyway, I was just about to tell her that Mason was referring to Conor, when she had to go because she said your father was coming in.'

'She didn't mind? She was okay about it?'

'Well, I think she was a bit disappointed, but she seemed to be handling it. She was fine. That's why I was going to tell her that it was Conor he was referring to. I thought it was as good a time as any seeing as the damage was already done. She hadn't told Mick then, of course. I don't know what he'll make of it.'

'Did you tell Conor yet?'

'No,' Alice said. 'I can't get hold of him, or that rat Mason.'

'Why d'you think he did it?'

'Oh, come on, Declan, it's been a situation waiting to happen. He's been going on about it ever since he moved in. I thought I'd gotten through to him, but obviously I was mistaken.'

'D'you think Mam told Da?' he asked.

Alice sighed. 'She seemed pretty adamant about telling him. I guess she knows best.'

'That figures. But of course she still thinks it's me.'

'She still thinks Mason was talking about you, yes. Does that make a difference?'

'Suppose not. He'll hit the roof anyway.'

'You don't know that,' Alice said. 'Maybe this is all for the best.' She was trying to reassure him, but deep down she had a bad feeling about it. She asked Declan to keep trying his parents' number while she headed off to work to put Conor in the picture.

Conor was completely stunned. He kept repeating, 'But why would he do that', and 'He promised'. Alice couldn't get much sense out of him.

Suddenly the office door burst open and Declan rushed in. 'It's Da,' he said. 'He's had a heart attack.'

On the drive to the hospital, all they talked about was the letter. Conor was beside himself with guilt. Although Alice tried telling him that it wasn't his fault, that it was all down to Mason sticking his oar in, all he could focus on was his father, and the fact that he could well die. Declan was suffering to a lesser degree with similar pangs. He bitterly regretted the fact that he hadn't seen it coming and warned Mason off, or at least made some effort to talk Conor into taking the same action. He was glad Alice was the one who took the call. Despite the fact that they'd had a shaky start, in the last few months they seemed to be getting on well and he knew he could rely on her to be sensitive about his parents' feelings. In his present mood, Conor might well admit everything causing his mother to keel over too, despite her p.c. pronouncements that 'gays are people too'. He didn't agree with Alice's assertion that now was as good a time as any. Particularly considering the results, i.e. his father's heart attack. He, like Alice, wondered if her understanding was more to do with the fact that she was under the misapprehension that the letter referred to him, and not to Conor.

When they arrived at the hospital just before midnight, they were directed straight up to the coronary care unit, where they found Maura sitting in the corridor outside. She leapt up when she saw them and hugged her sons. Alice stood back and waited.

'How is he?' Declan asked.

Conor was having a hard time keeping back the tears. 'How serious is it? He won't die, will he? He isn't going to die?'

'The doctor said we'll know by the morning. If he gets through the night he's a good chance.' Maura looked exhausted.

'Can we see him?' Conor asked.

'Best not just yet.' Maura patted his shoulder. 'We'll only be in the way. They'll come and get us when we can see him. They're very good.'

Conor and Declan sat down to wait. Alice said, 'I'll just go and look for the ladies loo.'

Maura followed her. 'I'll come with yeh, dear.'

Alice splashed her face with cold water and dried it with a paper towel. Maura came out of the cubicle and held her hands under the running tap. 'Was it the letter?' Alice asked. 'Is that what caused the attack?'

Maura looked confused for a moment. 'Oh, no. I never got to show it to him.' She stuck her hands under the hot-air dryer. 'He just walked in the door and collapsed. He must've been feeling unwell, and that's why he came back to the house. Thank God. I hate to think what would've happened if he'd had the attack in the top field.'

Alice was relieved. At least now Conor could unload the guilt monster that was weighing him down. She considered telling Maura the truth, but then lost courage also, despite Maura's initial reaction to the letter and her talk of gays being people too. She didn't fancy taking responsibility if Maura landed in a dead faint on the lino at her feet. Though on further reflection, if that did happen at least she was in the right place.

They returned to the corridor where Declan was now pacing backwards and forwards and Conor was sitting, his head in his hands. He looked up and jumped to his feet as they approached. Alice was conscious of him drawing in a deep breath. 'About the letter, Mam.'

Declan shot a look of alarm in Alice's direction.

'Let's not talk about that now,' his mother said.

'Well, the thing is, I think we should,' Conor persisted. 'You see . . . well . . . we . . . *I* haven't been quite honest with you.'

'I don't think you need to bother Mam with that now, Con.' Declan cut in with a cross between urgency and blind panic in his tone.

'How d'you mean, not quite honest?'

Alice could see that Conor was struggling to find words which would soften the blow. He gave up and chose the direct approach. 'When Mason said your son was gay, he meant me, not Declan. You just assumed it was Declan because Mason was introduced to you as his friend. In fact, he's *my* friend. My *boy*friend.'

Maura looked utterly confused. 'But you're married. How could you be . . . you know . . . ?' She looked over at Alice for help.

Alice would have been grateful at that moment if God, or whatever higher being, had chosen the moment to atomise her into tiny particles of antimatter. 'Well . . . no . . . em, we're not married. You see . . .'

'Oh, I know you're not *married*, but you're *as good as* husband and wife . . . you told me all about it that day in the restaurant.'

'No, Mam. You don't understand. It was a lie. We just told you that because I was afraid to tell you I'm gay. Alice went along with it because she's my friend.' He reached out and grabbed Alice's hand. 'She wanted me to tell you. She said you'd understand. And, God knows, I tried to that time we first came down to Tanagh, but when it came to it, I chickened out. Then when you jumped to the conclusion that I was married to Alice, I just . . .' He shook his head and averted his eyes.

Maura looked at her eldest son. 'Did you know about this?'

'I'm afraid so. I'm sorry.'

Conor reached out to her and touched her shoulder. 'I'm sorry you had to hear it like this.' His voice was wavering now. He was close to tears. 'And I'm sorry about Da.' At the mention of his father he broke down in tears. Alice put her arms around him to comfort him. Declan looked sheepish and had his hands in his pockets. Alice couldn't read Maura's expression. She wanted her to hug her son and to hear her tell him that was okay, that she didn't mind, but Maura stayed silent, turning the information over in her mind. If she were to be honest, it was a tad more information than she needed, all this talk about *boyfriends*. But Maura was a practical person. She assessed the situation, weighing up the pros and the cons. After a minute or two, she fluffed up her hair with her fingers and straightened her back. 'What's done is done. It's a pity you felt afraid to talk to me, son. I am your mother, after all.'

'He was afraid, because he didn't want to hurt you, Maura,' Alice said. 'He was afraid you'd think less of him.'

Maura sighed. 'I suppose I can see that. We were so pleased when he brought you home.'

'I'm sorry if I let you down.' Alice didn't know what else to say.

'We better get the tea.'

Alice followed her down the corridor. As they got to the machine she said, 'What are you going to do? Are you going to tell Mick?'

'Best not. Not just yet, anyways. I'll choose my time and tell him then. He'll be fine. He'll be fine.' Then she stopped dead in her tracks and slapped her hand to her mouth. 'Oh, my God. I had the two a' ye sharin' a bed!'

Alice grinned. 'I was quite safe under the circumstances.'

Maura smiled. 'I suppose yeh were that all right.'

Declan was leaning against the wall staring at nothing, and Conor was sitting with his head in his hands again when they returned with plastic cups of, approximately, tea. Alice went straight over to Conor and sat down beside him. She put her arm round his shoulder. 'Your father didn't see the letter, Conor. It wasn't the letter that caused the attack.'

Conor snapped up in his seat. 'Are you sure?'

'She's right, son. Yer da didn't see it. I never got to tell him about it. He collapsed as soon as he came in the door.' Conor heaved a sigh of relief and started to weep, once again burying

214

his head in his hands. Maura smiled at Alice then sat on the other side of her son, putting her arms around him, hugging him and rocking him backwards and forwards like a small child. 'Never mind, son. Sure it'll be okay.'

Maybe it wasn't such a surprise after all.

Alice got up and walked over to Declan. 'It's as well that it's out in the open,' she whispered, expecting Declan to mutter something scathing. But he just nodded his head. 'You're right,' he said. 'Better to get it out into the open.'

He put his arm around her and gave her a squeeze. Suddenly she felt bereft. Along with his admission, Conor had effectively revoked her membership of the Finn dynasty. Had anyone asked only a matter of hours before she'd probably have pooh-poohed the idea that she enjoyed being part of the family. But now, despite the fact that she regularly suffered her most embarrassing cringe-making moments whilst in their company, she realised how much she cared about her adopted parents-in-law. She also felt that she had let Maura down in some way. Gained her affection under false pretences.

They sat in the corridor all night. A nurse offered Maura a bed, but she declined, preferring to keep vigil. At five-thirty a doctor come out to them. 'He's responding well. You can go in two at a time. Are you all family?'

Alice hung back, then Maura reached out and grabbed her hand. 'We're all family,' she said.

Alice burst into tears.

Mick was recovering well. The attack had done very little damage to his heart due, in part, to his own action of returning to the house when he felt it coming on, and largely to the prompt response of the new, fully equipped coronary ambulance (for which Maura and Mick had helped to raise the funds). It got Mick to the hospital well within the 'golden hour'.

Declan drove his mother home so that she could get a change of clothes, and Conor and Alice stayed at the hospital. The nurse sent them down to the canteen a short time later to get something to eat. Alice was ravenous. Miserable and ravenous. Stress had that effect on her. Conor sat at a table and Alice brought over two full Irish breakfasts with toast and tea. She tucked in but Conor just moved his around the plate. He had no appetite. He still felt responsible, despite the knowledge that the letter wasn't the cause of his father's attack. It could well have been, had he seen it. He could see why Mason had acted the way he had, but on the other hand, who gave him the right to unilaterally make the decision?

'You need to eat something, Conor,' Alice said, feeling ashamed that she'd cleared her plate in no time flat.

'I was thinking about Mason,' he said. 'It's my fault he sent the letter. If I'd been up front that time I had the chance, none of this would have happened.'

'Mick would still have had his attack.'

'I know, but it'd probably have been easier for Mam if I'd told her the truth under different circumstances. She's enough to deal with at the minute without this.'

As he was talking, over his shoulder Alice caught sight of Mason, standing at the doorway of the cafeteria looking around. He spotted her the next moment and made a beeline for the table. His face was the colour of putty and his eyes bloodshot and puffy. Alice couldn't tell if it was from lack of sleep or if he'd been crying. She immediately jumped up to head him off.

'What the hell are you doing here?' she hissed, blocking his route to Conor.

'I'm so sorry,' he said, staring over her shoulder towards the table where Conor was sitting, so engrossed in his own thoughts that he was still unaware of his lover's arrival.

'Get the hell out of here. Haven't you caused enough trouble?' At that moment Conor looked round. For an instant he froze, then leapt up. Alice was in his way. 'It's okay, Conor. You don't have to speak to him.' Conor made no reply, just flung himself at Mason. Stunned at the suddenness of it, it took Alice a moment to react, but as she stepped forward to come between the two of them, to put a stop to any fisticuffs, Conor threw his arms around Mason and burst into tears. The floodgates opened then. Both Conor and Mason were bawling and, in between sobs, muttering and mumbling to each other. Alice couldn't make out what they were saying, she only caught every other word, but the gist was that Mason had only heard about Conor's da when he'd phoned the Samovar at midnight. He'd dropped everything and driven straight down from County Antrim. He was distraught at the thought that he might have caused the attack. Conor was reassuring him that his da hadn't seen the letter. The cafeteria staff took no notice, accustomed as they were to the tears of the bereaved. Alice left them to it. She didn't trust herself to be so understanding.

Declan stayed on to keep his mother company and Alice drove Mason's hire car back to Dublin. Conor lay across the back seats and slept, Mason dozed in the passenger seat beside her. She was as well pleased. Spaced out and jumpy from the combination of lack of sleep, coupled with emotional overload, it was unlikely that she'd have had the concentration to talk and drive at the same time. They arrived back at the apartment at eleven-thirty. Conor, somewhat refreshed by his sleep and revitalised by his new 'out of the closet' status, had a quick shower and went off to the Samovar. Mason had a couple of mugs of strong coffee and headed back to Antrim in the hire car, and Alice fell into bed and slept like the dead.

Conor woke her with a mug of coffee at five-thirty. 'I phoned Mam and Da's doing fine. The doctor reckons he'll make a full recovery.' He walked over to the window and swished back the curtains. 'Of course he'll have to slow down a bit. Cut back on the work load.'

'And pigs might fly,' Alice commented, knowing that Mick would rather be dead than spend his life like an invalid.

'Mam'll make sure he looks after himself. She'll make him get some help in.'

She closed her eyes again and pulled the duvet over her head. 'Your mother must hate me.'

'You? Why would she hate you?'

Throwing the duvet back she heaved herself up into a sitting position. 'What d'you mean, why? I lied to her. We both lied to her.'

Conor grinned. 'Don't be soft. You're family. She's mad

about you. They both are.' He held out the mug of coffee and Alice took it. 'Anyway,' he added, 'she always said she was sorry she never had a daughter. So I think you're it.'

'She said that?'

'Yeah.' He hiked his shoulders. 'But, um . . . Well . . . if she doesn't tell Da about me, will you hold on to your designated daughter-in-law status? For the moment anyway. Is that okay?'

'Whatever. Now go away. I want another ten minutes before I get up.'

The hot stream of the shower revived both her body and her spirits and after she had dressed for the evening shift and applied her make-up she was in fine form. Conor was out of the closet, well, half-out, Jesse James was off their backs, the spectre of Hector had disappeared. Things were looking up at last.

Chapter Twenty-Six

It was the best sort of evening, early bookings of four or six for the most part, which meant that they'd be able to have an early night and a full till. Alice was standing behind the bar enjoying a caffè latte. It was ten-fifteen and the last diners were on to their desserts. She heard the door open and glanced up, mentally groaning that they'd have to serve whoever, as officially they took orders up until ten-thirty. It was with equal surprise and pleasure that she saw Melanie standing in the doorway, and she hurried over as soon as she spotted Alice. Something about her expression suddenly gave Alice a very bad feeling. Her face was white as a sheet and she had a crumpled, badly folded newspaper in her hand. She was waving at Alice as she approached. 'Did you see the news? Did you see it?'

'Mel, are you okay? You look as if you've seen a ghost.'

Melanie had reached the bar now. She dumped the paper down and unfolded it. 'Did you see? Did you see? He's dead. He's dead.'

Alice spun the paper round. 'Who's dead? What are you talking about?'

'Look! Look! Read it.' Her finger stabbed at the paper in jerky staccato movements. 'Someone shot him.'

Alice stared at the banner headline, almost unable to take it in. 'BUSINESSMAN SLAIN IN CITY GUN HORROR.' She read down the paragraph.

Maurice Broderick, a well-known Dublin businessman, was shot dead in his car as he sat at traffic lights on Dorset Street late this afternoon. Witnesses say that the killers, riding a black

Japanese motor cycle, rode up alongside Mr Broderick's Jaguar and the pillion passenger shot him several times in the head at close range. They made their escape along the North Circular Road. Gardai are seeking witnesses.

It went on to give details of Maurice Broderick's business interests, at least the kosher ones, but Alice couldn't concentrate. Her eyes kept straying back to the lurid headline, 'SLAIN IN CITY GUN HORROR'. Melanie was talking to her but all Alice was aware of was the sound of the blood pumping through her brain. It didn't take Einstein to figure out that there was a pretty even chance that Jesse James was behind this, present circumstances considered. After a moment she pulled herself together in time to hear her stepsister say, '. . . And I'm not sure how I feel about it. I mean I don't know if I'm glad or if I feel cheated that he got away with what he did to me.'

Alice wasn't sure how she felt about it either, but in her case the choice of emotions was limited to dread and fear. She picked up a brandy bottle and a couple of glasses. 'Let's go to the office.'

Melanie didn't seem to notice how disturbed Alice was. She sat down beside the desk and took the proffered drink. 'Do you think I should phone my mother?'

'Why on earth would you do that?' Alice asked, rather more sharply than she intended. 'I thought you two weren't speaking.'

Melanie took a thoughtful sip of her drink. 'I suppose you're right.' She paused for a moment, then smiled. 'I suppose it *is* a sort of justice in a way. I for one won't be crying any tears for him.' She nodded as if she had suddenly come to a decision. 'Yes. I think I'm glad. I think I *am* glad he's dead.'

Alice, who was sitting on the edge of the desk, was less pleased. Okay, Broderick was no loss to mankind, but if it *was* James, and if he was capable of killing Broderick to save his skin, what would he do to them? They'd threatened to send the tape and photos to Broderick, knowing that there was every chance he'd have James killed. 'Um . . . excuse me for a moment, I have to tell Conor.'

Melanie reached over and picked up the brandy bottle. 'May I?' Alice nodded and escaped to the kitchen.

There was a clatter as Conor dropped the stainless steel pan of broccoli spears he had in his hand. It bounced across the tiled floor and finally came to rest after it hit Joe on the back of the legs. Joe yelped and leapt out of the way. Conor's bowels turned to water at the implications. Alice didn't have to spell it out. 'Oh fuck. Fuck. Fuck. Fuck. What the fuck are we going to do?'

'Not panic for one thing,' Alice hissed. 'Keep your bloody voice down.'

Conor, obviously unable to grasp the concept of remaining calm, grabbed her by the shoulders and started to shake her. 'Then what the fuck do you suggest we do? He'll fucking kill us.'

Put like that, panic didn't seem such a bad idea, but it was a luxury they couldn't afford. 'Look. We don't know that it was James. It could have been someone else. I'm sure Broderick wasn't short of enemies.' Conor wasn't listening. Furthermore he was still shaking her violently. Her brain and her teeth were rattling. The shaking response was in danger of becoming a habit with Conor. To avoid permanent injury she attempted to prise his fingers loose but it was impossible. She resorted to her one trusty self-defence move – shooting her two hands up between his arms and flinging them apart – then she clattered him hard across the face. Much as she abhorred violence, her slapping response to his shaking thing was also becoming a habit. It was only then that she realised there was total silence in the kitchen. That the entire staff, including Mandy and Joan, had been standing, gobs agape, watching the whole sorry spectacle. After an embarrassed three seconds, Alice barked, 'What are you lot looking at?' A further millisecond of silence and they all returned to what they had been doing, muttering and mumbling amongst themselves.

Melanie met them at the office door. 'What's the matter? Are you okay?' She looked at the red welt on Conor's cheek.

The impression of Alice's fingers was glowing red and puffy. Conor, looking dazed, gingerly touched it as Alice led him to a chair and made him sit. Melanie thrust a glass of brandy at him. 'What happened? Who attacked him?'

'Eh . . . me,' Alice said. 'He was hysterical.'

'Oh, God. Oh, God. What are we going to do?' Conor wailed.

Melanie stared at him uncomprehendingly. Why was he so upset about a monster like Maurice Broderick? To her knowledge Conor didn't even know her stepfather. 'It's a long story,' Alice muttered lamely.

'But did he know Maurice? Why is he like this?'

'He's not upset about Maurice. It's something else. Something a bit serious. Well, something very serious.'

Reminding Conor of the seriousness of the situation wasn't a good move. 'Oh, God! Oh, fuck! We're finished. He'll fucking kill us.' He took a slug of brandy, then choked as it went down the wrong way.

Conor's hysteria was getting to Melanie now. She jumped up and walloped him on the back. 'Calm down, Conor. It can't be that bad. Maybe I can help. Is it money?'

'In a manner of speaking,' Alice said. 'The guy we think did this . . .' she indicated the headline screaming out from the *Evening Herald* '. . . is a criminal.'

Melanie shrugged. 'Obviously.'

'No, I mean he made us pay him protection money. Anyway, we decided to do something about it and bugged his house . . .'

'You bugged his house!' Melanie cut in, astonished.

Alice nodded 'Yes.' Melanie opened her mouth again, but Alice threw up her hand to forestall her. 'Don't ask. Anyway we found out that this man, this Jesse James, was having an affair with your mother. That's when we discovered that Maurice Broderick was this godfather type of person. Anyway, we sort of blackmailed James. Threatened to send Broderick the tapes and photos if he didn't lay off.'

Melanie gaped at her. 'You bugged his house?' She seemed more taken by that than by the fact that her mother was having an affair with a man who could be capable of murder. 'You actually bugged his house?'

Impatient that her stepsister was dwelling on a detail she said, 'Yes, Melanie, we actually bugged his house. We had to do something to get him off our backs.'

'Did my mother know?'

The question hadn't come up before. 'I don't know. Why?'

'Because if she did, she could well be implicated in Maurice's murder, don't you see?'

Alice shrugged. 'I suppose so.' She didn't see that it made much difference, James would still be out to get his pound of flesh. And if Leggo Parsons was to be believed, there was every possibility that it would be in the literal sense.

Melanie gripped her arm. 'You should go to the Guards. You should tell the cops.'

'Tell them what? That we illegally bugged Jesse James's house and that we were blackmailing him? I don't think so, Melanie.'

'You weren't really blackmailing him. You were just, well . . . you know . . .'

'I'd say blackmailing covers it pretty well.'

Alice spun around to face the door. Jesse James stood there, grinning. He tossed the four tiny micro-transmitters across the room at her. One hit her a glancing blow to the temple as she ducked out of the way. It stung. An inch to the left and it would have taken her eye out. The others bounced off the desk and landed on the floor. 'Who'd you get these off?'

Alice, dumbstruck, rubbed the side of her face. Conor's eyes were the size of saucers and he had his hand over his mouth as a whimper escaped.

Melanie got up and thrust out her hand to James. 'Melanie Broderick. I'm pleased to meet you.' This momentarily threw James. More so when she continued, 'I believe you're screwing my mother.' As introductions go it was a bit of a conversation stopper. James stared, not sure what to make of her. She took his hand and pumped it. 'I want to shake the hand of the man who killed Maurice Broderick. Congratulations for having the guts to do it.'

He could see the likeness to her mother. She was as striking looking, though he wasn't as a rule partial to blondes. His face broke out into a broad grin, which instantly faded as the words registered. He snatched his hand back. 'What are you doing here?'

'I came to bring the good news of my stepfather's demise to my stepsister.'

James shot a quick look in Alice's direction. 'She's Maurice Broderick's *daughter*?' Although he had never met her, he was aware of Melanie's existence, but had never heard of Broderick having a daughter of his own. It didn't make sense.

'No. Alice's father was one of my mother's former husbands.'

Alice still didn't have the use of her vocal chords. Conor had gone an even whiter shade of pale now and his mouth was opening and closing like a goldfish. Still, Melanie seemed to be doing all right. It surprised Alice that her stepsister was so cool while she was frantically fighting the urge to flee. James walked over to the desk and sat on the edge. 'I thought you and your mother didn't get on.'

Melanie smiled at him. 'Not really. In fact, I could go as far as to say that I hate her, but I hated Maurice more, so I guess you did me a favour.'

James grinned at her, and held up his hands, palms outwards. 'Me? I wouldn't have the first idea what you're getting at.' He laughed. Melanie laughed too and gave a girly shrug. 'Well . . . whatever you say.' It was all very cosy. Alice was starting to get a tad uneasy about their palsy-walsy act when James stopped smiling and reached out, grasping her arm. 'You!' he barked. 'You didn't think you'd get away with blackmailing me, did you?'

'It was worth a try,' Alice said. 'Surely you didn't expect me to just pay up without a fight.' She shrugged free.

James glared at her. 'It would've been the cheaper option. The price of your policy just went up to five hundred a week.'

Alice was incensed. 'Five hundred! That's ridiculous. We can't pay you five hundred a week.'

The mention of five hundred stirred Conor back to life. 'You'll finish us. You'll put us out of business.'

Jesse James cast a disdainful glance in Conor's direction. 'Oh, the fairy speaks.'

Alice was flittering with rage at this point. She faced up to James. 'Look here. What's the fucking point of putting us out of business?' In the heat of the moment she'd forgotten that they'd already been through this argument to no avail at an earlier date, but James didn't reiterate, he just gave her a shove in the shoulder and grinned his evil grin. 'As James Stuart said when they asked him how it felt to be seventy, "It's better than the alternative." '

Alice instantly grasped his meaning, but Conor repeated, 'The alternative?'

James reached down and clutched a wodge of his shirt front, almost lifting him from the chair. 'The *alternative*, shit for brains. The alternative. Geddit?'

Conor looked up at him helplessly and shook his head. What could be worse than losing the business? Then his stressed-out, sleep-deprived, almost liquidised into meltdown brain slowly began to compute and he gulped. 'Oh . . . the *alternative*.'

'Are you still seeing my mother?' Melanie asked out of the blue.

The question took James by surprise. 'Yeah. Of course. Why?'

'So I'll probably see you at the funeral, then?'

James nodded. 'Yeah. But if you hated him so much, why are you going?'

Melanie gave another of her little girly shrugs. 'Oh. I just thought I'd pay my respects to the widow.' She paused, then, as if it had just occurred to her, added, 'Oh, and I want to make quite sure he's properly dead so I can do a little dance on his grave.'

'Jesus! You must've really hated the bastard,' James remarked.

Melanie didn't comment further. She stuck out her hand. 'Nice to have met you, Mr James. Give my best to Patricia.'

Bemused by her up-front, in-yer-face manner, James took her hand and shook it. 'I surely will.' Then he turned to Alice and Conor. 'I'll expect the first instalment on Friday. We'll talk again about the arrears.'

Alice cringed. 'Arrears. Great!'

He strode towards the door, then stopped. 'I think I'm being pretty fucking reasonable under the circumstances,' he barked. 'Thank your lucky stars I'm in a good mood today. See you Friday, then.'

Alice was on the verge of calling him a bastard but then remembered his reaction the last time. Instead she just glowered at him as he opened the door and left.

None of them spoke for a good ten seconds then Alice broke the silence. 'Why were you so bloody pally with him?'

Melanie smiled. 'I was just trying to lull him into a false sense of security.'

'What?' Alice and Conor said in unison.

There was a tap on the door and they all froze. The next minute the door opened and Sean Holland stuck his head in. 'Sorry to bother you,' he said. 'But could I have a word?'

'A word? About what?' Alice snapped. 'This isn't a good time.'

Well accustomed to that sort of brush-off when acting in his professional capacity, he pushed the door fully open and walked in to the office. 'We found Hector.'

Alice glanced over at Conor. She wasn't sure if he'd heard what Holland had said. He was sitting with his eyes tight shut and his hands clenched in his lap as if anticipating a loud bang.

'Is he okay?' the civil servant asked, jerking his head in Conor's direction.

'Um . . . we've just had some bad news. He's a bit shocked.'

'So don't you want to know where he is?'

'Who?'

Holland gave her a quizzical look. 'Hector. Hector Hanusiak?'

'Oh . . . yes.' Hector was the least of their worries, but she thought, seeing as it was Holland, she should show an interest.

'He was picked up for drunk driving down in Killkenny. They're deporting him back to the Ukraine tomorrow.'

'I don't suppose he had eight grand in used notes secreted about his person?'

Sean Holland smiled and shook his head. ''Fraid not.' He glanced over at Conor again. 'Are you sure he's okay?'

Alice nodded. 'He'll be fine. I told you, we just had some bad news.'

Melanie said, 'Who's Hector?'

'I was bloody married to him briefly before he stole all our money,' Alice muttered.

Holland glanced over at Melanie then smiled as he recognised her from the evening he'd bumped into them at TransV. She smiled back then gave an exaggerated sigh. 'You haven't had much luck lately, have you, Alice?'

'What the hell are we going to do?' Conor mumbled to no one in particular. 'He'll fucking kill us. He'll fucking kill us all.'

'No. Not at all. There's nothing to worry about. Hector's in custody, anyway, I'd have thought he'd be the one who's afraid of you,' Holland said.

'Not Hector, Jesse James,' Melanie explained helpfully. Alice gave her a hefty kick in the shin to shut her up. She gave a yelp and bent down to rub her ankle.

'Oh, shit. Jesse James is going to kill us,' Conor repeated. 'What'll we do? What'll we do?' He snatched Alice's sleeve and started twisting the fabric. 'Jesse James is going to kill us.'

'Jesse James?' Holland frowned, then, indicating Conor with a twitch of his eyebrow, looked directly at Alice and whispered, 'Is he psychotic or something?'

'He's that all right,' Conor mumbled. 'He's a fucking psycho and he'll fucking kill us if we don't pay up.'

'Shut up, Conor,' Alice barked. He was really losing it now, she thought. The last couple of days had been too much for him between the letter, his father's attack, coming out to his mother, the weeping and gnashing of teeth with Mason and now Jesse James and his understated threats. If the truth be known, Alice was pretty close to the edge too, but she was made of sterner stuff than her partner. 'Shut up, for God's sake.' She prised Conor's fingers away and looked up at Holland. 'He's fine, he's fine. Really.'

Sure.

'Are you a cop?' Melanie asked.

Holland shook his head. 'Department of Foreign Affairs. Why?'

'Shut up, Mel.'

'No, Alice. He might be able to help.'

'How?'

Holland was now utterly confused with the talk of psychotic Wild West outlaws. 'He needs a psychiatrist, not a cop.'

'There's nothing wrong with Conor,' Alice sniped defensively. 'I told you, we've just had some rather bad news.'

'Tell him, Alice. Tell him. He might be able to help.'

They were all mad. Frustrated, Holland threw up his hands. 'Help with what?!'

'Nothing,' Alice muttered stubbornly, glowering at Melanie.

Melanie gave an impatient shrug. 'For heaven's sake. Look, Sean – it is Sean, isn't it?' He nodded. 'These two are being subjected to extortion by a criminal.' She reached over and stabbed her finger at the paper, which was lying on the desk. 'The same criminal who killed this man today.'

Alice was livid. 'Shut the fuck up, Mel. It's none of his business.'

'Oh? And what are *you* going to do about it, eh? Pay up and keep quiet? You won't get another chance to blackmail him. Not this time. He'll be on his guard.'

Alice winced.

'Blackmail? Jesus! Will someone start from the beginning?'

Chapter Twenty-Seven

'You bugged his house?'

Alice gave an impatient sigh. 'Yes, we bloody bugged his house. How many more times do I have to say it? We bugged his house. Okay?'

They were sitting in the office and Alice had just related the events in approximately chronological order, starting with Joxer Boxer's visit and ending with Maurice Broderick's murder.

'So if you think James is definitely implicated in the killing, shouldn't you go to the cops?'

'And say what? Anyway, we don't know he actually did it. We've no evidence.'

Holland didn't know what to make of it all. But between one suspect marriage (the less said about that the better), one completely phoney marriage to a homosexual, protection rackets, blackmail and murder, she certainly led a varied and interesting life. The old Chinese curse came to mind: 'May you live in interesting times'. Alice Little certainly lived in interesting times. He wondered what she'd done in a previous life to deserve such a deal.

She was on her hands and knees now, crawling around on the floor. In Holland's opinion both she and Conor were as mad as hatters. 'You actually bugged his house?' he repeated, still finding it hard to believe. That stuff only happened in spy movies.

Her head bobbed above the desk again. She had a thunderous expression on her face. She dumped three tiny button-like metal discs on the desk top and disappeared from view again for a moment before standing up and tossing a fourth on the desk. It bounced across the polished surface and Holland caught it before it hit the floor. He opened his hand and examined it.

'That's one of the bugs . . . Oh, did I mention we bugged his house?'

'Okay, okay, I get the point,' Holland said, stung by her sarcasm. 'How does it work?'

Alice picked up one of the three lying on the desk and held it between her thumb and index finger. 'It's battery powered. We went to his house on the pretext of a meeting to talk about a loan and planted them. Then we sat outside and picked up the signal on a receiver with a recording facility.'

'But where did you get them? It's not the sort of equipment you can routinely pick up at Marks & Spencer's . . . is it?'

'Humph,' Alice snorted. 'I'd have thought your department was well into bugs and dirty tricks.'

That got up Holland's nose. 'If we were, you'd probably be in jail,' he sniped.

'Please,' Melanie cut in, 'bickering will get us nowhere. We need a plan. Can't you think of anything?' She looked directly at the civil servant. 'Surely there's something they can do to get this James character off their backs.'

'Absolutely. They should go to the Guards.' He glanced over at Alice. 'You should report the extortion to the cops.'

'And they'd arrest him and his expensive lawyer'd have him bailed before the ink dried on the arrest warrant. No thank you very much. That solution doesn't appeal. Anyway, we've no proof. It would only be our word against his. That means we'd have to give evidence in court, and I wouldn't fancy our chances between now and the trial . . .' She paused. 'If it ever came to trial.'

'How do you mean, *if* it ever came to trial?'

Alice gave him a wry look. 'You can't have a trial without witnesses.'

She had a point.

'Then you'll have to *get* evidence,' Holland said. 'Where did you say you got these yokies?' He held up the bug.

Alice sighed and sat down in her chair behind the desk. 'From a private eye, Leggo Parsons. He's an ex-cop.'

'Can't you go to him again? Ask him to get the evidence?'

Alice guffawed. 'Again? When he heard who we wanted investigated the last time, he wouldn't do it. *More'n my life's worth* sort of attitude. We had to plant the things ourselves.'

'Hmmm. Well, there's no chance of you getting back into his house now, that's for sure.' Holland stating the obvious.

'We don't need to.'

All eyes were on Conor. It was the first time he'd offered anything to the discussion other than near-hysterical ravings about Jesse James killing them. 'We don't need to. The adapter's still in there. At least I bet it is. If he'd found it he'd have chucked that at us too.'

Holland looked helplessly at Alice. 'What's he talking about?'

A broad grin spread across her face. 'Conor. You're a genius!' Holland and Melanie still hadn't a clue what they were on about. 'Parsons gave us this other transmitter. It was concealed inside a three-way adapter.' She picked up one of the mini-transmitters again. 'These yokes are useless in any case now because the batteries are probably dead, but the other one, the one still in the house, is plugged into the mains. It's still transmitting. All we need is to hire the receiver from Parsons and we're in business.'

'But how?' Melanie asked. 'Surely an illegally bugged conversation, assuming James admits all to someone or other, can't be used as evidence?' She caught Holland's eye. 'Isn't that a civil liberties issue? Anyway, what's to stop him denying everything? People make confessions in police custody all the time then retract them.'

'So, even if he admitted riding up on the motorbike himself and pumping however many rounds into Maurice Broderick's head, it wouldn't be evidence?'

Alice addressed the question to Melanie, but Holland replied. 'Not in my understanding. The cops are obliged to caution prisoners before they question them, advising them . . . well, you know the form, you've seen it enough times on the

TV, so I guess any halfway competent lawyer could get an illegally obtained tape thrown out, no problem.'

Conor sagged in his seat again. 'So where does that leave us?'

Alice wasn't listening, she was turning over her own thoughts in her mind. 'Okay, so what if we heard something on the tapes that led us somewhere else?'

Melanie frowned, uncomprehending. 'How do you mean?'

'I mean what if we heard something, maybe about a crime he was going to commit, like a bank job or something, a plan. Couldn't we go to the cops with that?'

'Is he into bank jobs? I mean does he do stuff like that?' Melanie asked.

Alice shook her head. 'I don't know.'

'That could just do it, Alice,' Holland said. 'But in a slightly different way.'

'How?'

'Okay. Even if you went to the cops and James was arrested and charged with obtaining money with menaces, as you pointed out, that isn't going to solve your problems for the aforementioned reasons.' Alice nodded. 'So what if you could put him out of circulation by removing all his assets. His power stems from his money these days. He pays people to do his dirty work, principally this Joxer character, right?'

The two women nodded but Conor wasn't convinced. 'Maybe. We don't know that, but what are you getting at?'

'You've heard of the CAB, The Criminal Assets Bureau?' Another collective nod. 'Well, they have quite extraordinary powers. If we could get any evidence of, say, tax evasion, monies earned through illegal means, properties purchased with ill-gotten gains, that kind of thing, and I mean real hard evidence, like ledgers, bank statements and the like, we could toss it into their lap. They'd do the rest. They've the power to confiscate all suspect assets. James wouldn't even have the first idea where the information came from.'

'It's a great idea, but we've about as much chance of getting that sort of information as we have of getting him to go down to the Bridewell and put his hands up to Broderick's murder,' Conor whined.

Alice wasn't so certain that the plan was a non-runner. 'Conor, do you remember that day we were in the Quick Call office?'

'Vividly.' He flinched at the memory.

'D'you remember that book he took out, you know the one, when he was threatening us about . . .' She faltered for a moment, conscious of the company, then continued, '. . . about Hector.' Conor shot a quick look in Holland's direction, searching for a reaction, then nodded. 'Well, he obviously had stuff in there about us, so who's to say that the stuff doesn't include our payments?'

Holland rubbed his chin as he mulled Alice's last remarks over in his mind. 'Quick Call? What's that?'

'Quick Call Finance. James calls it a finance house, but it's really a loan-sharking operation.' Conor explained. 'It's on Mercer Street.'

'You know, that could be how he launders his money,' Melanie piped up. 'He probably has a list of mythical clients with outstanding loans making payments . . . At least, if I were him, that's how I'd do it. It'd be a quick and easy way of laundering the regular protection payments.'

'So you mean he could be paying tax on the extortion money?' Conor couldn't disguise the fact that his ghast was well and truly flabbered by the notion.

Melanie shrugged. 'Guess so, though I doubt he declares it all.'

'But if he doesn't declare it all and we could get hold of that book, or any papers showing a discrepancy, that would be enough to go to the CAB with?'

'As far as I know,' Holland said. 'Look, leave it with me. I've a few contacts in the CAB. I'll see what the criteria are.' He stood up and stretched his back. 'In the meantime, why don't you get this receiver from your private eye friend. It can't do any harm to eavesdrop on him. You never know what you'll find out. From what you've said he strikes me as a cocky bastard.'

'He's that all right,' Conor muttered.

Holland headed for the door. 'I'll give you a call when I've spoken to my contact at the Bureau.'

Alice got up to see him out. 'It's good of you to take the trouble,' she said, 'but, out of curiosity, why are you bothering?'

They were standing in the restaurant now and, with all the diners gone, Mandy and Joan were setting up the tables for the following day. Holland paused by the bar. He was trying to figure it out himself. After a moment he shook his head and grinned. 'I was born on the feast of Saint Jude. Maybe I've a weakness for hopeless cases.'

'Alice Little? Good God, the last I heard of her she was a shop assistant.'

'So is she your stepdaughter then?'

Patricia shrugged her elegant shoulders. 'I was married to her father once.' She sneered at his memory. 'Before he went and killed himself leaving me with horrendous debts.' She didn't acknowledge that these debts were incurred keeping her in the manner to which she had rapidly grown accustomed. Patricia hadn't thought of Alice in years, in fact not since the day she had written her last cheque for the nuns. She was surprised that the girl had actually managed to make something of herself. With a father like Roland she was at the disadvantage of coming from a rather inadequate gene pool. 'And you say Melanie was there too?'

James nodded. 'Bold as brass. She introduced herself and insisted on shaking my hand.' He gave a sly grin. 'She seems to have jumped to the conclusion that I had Maurice killed.'

Patricia frowned. 'I don't like this. Where would she get that idea?'

James smiled. 'Relax. There's no proof. I've seen to that. No one can lay it at our door.'

'Well, I hope not.'

He smiled reassuringly. 'Don't worry, it's taken care of. She won't pull one over on me again in a hurry.'

'Alice pulled one over on you?'

James bit his tongue. He had omitted to mention the blackmail or indeed that anyone was aware of their affair, afraid that Patricia would call it off, finish it. 'They tried. Nothing serious, but you can't let that kind of thing go, can you?'

'I suppose not,' Patricia said.

Jesse James was in his element and ready, with Patricia's help, to take over Maurice Broderick's business interests. It was all going according to plan. The more he appeared to be legitimate, the less danger there was of the cops getting anything on him. Things were changing. Since a well-known crime reporter had been shot by a North-Side drugs gang, the Department of Justice had been throwing money at the cops to clean up the city. He was only lucky that he'd been out of the country at the time. In one way it had been all for luck. In one fell swoop the cops had wiped out most of the opposition. He'd been smart enough to keep his head down for a while. He wasn't into the drug trade even though that's where the big money was. That was in Broderick's control and Broderick was untouchable, had friends in high places. A nod and a wink and the word to lay off, in return for some hefty brown envelopes long ago distributed to a few significant up-and-coming politicians in the early seventies. It had paid off. Even that custom was coming to an end now, what with the press and the public baying for those same politicians to explain their lavish lifestyles. 'Political contributions'. 'Election expenses', the same politicians had bleated in their defence when grilled by the various tribunals' senior council. It was a sad day when it was impossible to buy a bit of immunity. The country was really going to the dogs. Of course, only Broderick's foot soldiers had felt the full force of the law, and he (James) was one step above the foot soldiers. He was Broderick's lieutenant. His enforcer. Broderick was his role model. And it had been he who had encouraged James to delegate as much as possible these days, particularly as he had no criminal convictions, paid his taxes and although the cops were well aware of him, he knew he was smarter than any of them. Smart, because he was careful, no convictions. Smart because he'd built up a reputation amongst his peers, Mr ten per cent. No direct involvement, apart from the insurance business, and there was no danger that any of his clients would go to the cops, too afraid of the consequences. But in the new climate he was anxious to put all that behind him. He wanted to be completely legitimate, and getting rid of Broderick was the answer. It occurred to him then that he should be grateful to Alice and the queer. If they hadn't tried to blackmail him he'd never have thought of getting rid of Broderick. Now all that he had to do was get Patricia to marry him and he'd have it all. He chuckled to himself. Even though, if all went well, he'd be letting go of the insurance business (at a price) he'd enjoyed the look on their faces when he'd waltzed in there and told them that the premiums had gone up to five hundred a week.

'What's funny?' Patricia asked.

He reached out for her and wrapped her in his arms. 'Nothing, sweetie. I'm just happy. How about you?'

Happy? She was glad to be shot of Maurice. But now that he was dead and it was no longer dangerous, the gloss had gone off her relationship with Jesse James. She'd learned a lot from Maurice, picked up a good deal of savvy on the way. Times were changing. It was time to get out. Time to liquidate all his assets and move abroad. She smiled up at her (soon to be former) lover and kissed him on the lips. 'I'm very happy.'

Chapter Twenty-Eight

It was on the drive home that the idea had first occurred to Melanie. Immediately she did a U-turn on the Clontarf Road and drove back into town. Alice was still up, too hyper to sleep, but she had packed Conor off to bed with a warm milky drink and a couple of Valium she had purloined from Madame Maxine. He was out for the count now, snoring gently.

Melanie came straight to the point. 'I got to thinking on the way home. If Sean Holland's right and the CAB can confiscate all of Jesse James's assets, surely the same thing applies to Maurice Broderick, or more accurately, to his widow?'

'I guess so.'

'You see, I was thinking,' Melanie continued, 'if James is shagging my mother, and he really did get Maurice blown away, ten to one he's got his beady eyes on Maurice's turf. It makes sense, don't you see?'

Alice nodded. 'I can see where you're coming from, but whatever about James, how can we get evidence against Maurice? As Parsons said, he's untouchable.'

'*Was* untouchable. He's dead, remember?'

'True, but doesn't that make it harder to get stuff on him?'

Melanie opened her bag and rummaged inside, eventually pulling out a bunch of keys. 'I still have house keys for Blackrock. And I know where he keeps his spare set of keys for the safe, for his filing cabinets, and I also know the password he uses to unlock his computer files.'

'Good grief! how do you know all that?'

Melanie grinned. Her eyes were alight and she was bubbling with excitement. 'When we first moved into his house in Blackrock, before he started to abuse me, I suppose while he

237

was trying to soften me up, so to speak, he used to let me play with his computer. Under supervision, of course. He had games on it. I was going on twelve, but he'd sit me on his knee and we'd play the games together.' Alice noticed her give an involuntary shudder. 'I didn't see anything sinister in him sitting me on his knee like that at the time, I suppose I thought it was nice to have a father figure, you know. Anyway, unless he's changed the password, and I can't see any reason why he would have, we could go in and have a look through his files. There's bound to be something a bit iffy in them. And think of it, if Maurice's assets are confiscated, James can't make use of them, can he?'

Alice could see where Melanie was really coming from. 'Or Patricia,' she added.

Melanie shrugged. 'Or Patricia,' she confirmed. 'What do you think?'

'It sounds too easy and very dangerous. What if she, or worse, James, caught us?'

'Why would they? We know they're going to the funeral. We could go in then. The house would be empty.'

Alice could feel the excitement rising. 'When's the funeral?'

'Day after tomorrow. One o'clock.'

They stood in silence, both grinning like Cheshire cats. Alice held up her hand and they both slapped a high five.

'Yessss!'

Sensitive of Conor's fragile mental state, she didn't enlighten him regarding Melanie's plan. Time enough when they got a result, although he was a lot better the following morning, particularly after a call from Mason and another from Declan reporting Mick's continued recovery. He'd been hoping to speak to his mother, to try and judge by her attitude how she felt about him now that he'd come out to her. Despite her calming and comforting words and declarations that he was still her son, he felt vulnerable where she was concerned, glad though he was that he had told the truth at long last. Declan had said that she was sleeping, but he wasn't convinced that that was true or if she was just avoiding him. Sensing this,

Declan reassured his brother that Maura really was asleep, and advised him to call her after ten that night when she'd be home after her evening visit with Mick. Madame Maxine's pharmaceuticals had calmed him down now and he felt a tad embarrassed by his hysteria of the previous night. What a spa. He tentatively broached the subject over breakfast with Alice. 'I lost it last night, didn't I?'

'A bit, but I wasn't exactly Miss Calm and Collected either. To tell you the truth, when I saw James walk through the door I thought I'd pass out.'

'Really?' He'd thought she was pretty calm throughout it all. How did she do that? More to the point, why was it he was incapable of hiding his emotions? He'd learned long ago never to play poker. His face gave his hand away every time.

'Of course. I was terrified.' She took a sip of coffee. 'But that's all the more reason to go and see Parsons and get the receiver again. I'm fed up with James putting the fear of God into us. Every time we seem to be getting somewhere something happens, and I for one am not going to put up with it any more. It's time we made our own luck, Conor. If we can only get rid of James.'

'You make it sound so easy.'

'Face it, Conor, if we can get James off our back, for once and for all, the rest's a doddle.'

Parsons's sister was having a particularly bad-hair day. It looked self-inflicted as the formerly dark roots glowed a sort of coppery orange colour, and the ends pale yellow and frizzy as the result of a home perm. It gave her all the appearance of having been wired up to the mains. She, however, was oblivious of both the effect of her scary hair and of Alice, engrossed as she was in this week's *Hello!* magazine, left eye squinting against the smoke of her Benson & Hedges.

Alice coughed in an effort to attract her attention. 'Um, excuse me.' Ms Parsons's right eye wandered unwillingly from the colour double page spread of some unrecognisable minor European royal and his current blonde TV-presenter girlfriend, taking a short break in the Maldives. Alice indicated the closed glass door of the inner office. 'Mr Parsons, your brother, he's expecting me.'

Ms Parsons nodded, showering the golden couple with grey ash, then flung her arm towards the closed office door. 'G'wan in.'

Leggo Parsons was more industriously occupied. He was crouched over his desk, his finger tracing down the column of a volume of the London telephone directory. He looked up as Alice entered. He'd been expecting her ever since the news about Broderick had broken. 'How'ya,' he said, then his eyes returned to the column of phone numbers. 'Take a seat. I'll be with you in a minute.'

Alice chose the seat furthest away from the haze of cigarette smoke that hung like a cloud in the vicinity of the desk. After a moment Parsons gave a grunt, reached for a biro and scribbled down a number and an address. 'Case solved,' he said, looking up. 'Missing person.'

'You found them in the phone book?'

The detective grinned. 'People rarely look in the obvious places. I solve fifty per cent of me missing person cases by lookin' them up in the phone book.'

That explained all the phone directories in his room. Alice couldn't hide her astonishment. 'Are you serious?'

Parsons nodded. 'Yeah, either in the phone book or the electoral role.'

'Good grief.'

'I was expecting you,' he said, flipping the heavy volume shut and dropping it to the floor with a thud. 'Bit of a bummer, yer man gettin' shot.'

That was one way of putting it. 'Bit of a bummer, all right.'

'I suppose he was back to see ye.'

'Before Broderick was cold,' Alice said. 'The thing is, we need to hire a receiver from you again. We want to try and get something else on him.'

Parsons guffawed. 'Pwah. No chance. He'll be on his guard after the last time.'

Alice dug her hand into the pocket and drew out the four

bugs, then placed them on Parsons's desk. 'He threw these back at me last night . . .'

'There you are, then.' The private eye was leaning back in his chair now with his hands folded in his lap, at least as much of his lap as was visible beneath his big belly.

'But he didn't find the other one. The one in the adapter. It's still there. More than likely still transmitting.'

The caterpillar took a hike up his forehead. 'Are you serious?' The violence of the muscular spasm resulted in a long waxy blue-black strand detaching itself from Parsons's skull and it was now standing out from his head like a question mark. Alice found it hard to drag her eyes away from it.

'Um . . . so could we hire the . . . um,' she glanced over her shoulder at the bookshelves, 'the receiver again?'

Leggo Parsons pursed his lips. 'No can do, I'm afraid.'

Her heart sank. 'But why not? We need it, Mr Parsons. We really need it.'

He pushed back his chair and heaved himself out of it, then lumbered over to filing cabinet. 'Sorry, no can do,' he repeated. 'I hired it out to someone else only yesterday, but . . .' He slid open the top drawer and lifted out a slim briefcase. 'Seein' as it's ye, and ye're old and valued clients, I'll let ye use me own personal receiver for a few bob above the normal rate.' He placed the briefcase on the desk and popped the locks. It was certainly an improvement on the previous model. 'Taking into account that ye've returned these wee buggers undamaged.' He picked up the bugs and popped them in his pocket. Alice fervently hoped that they were undamaged after bouncing around her office the previous night.

The detective sat down in his chair again. The faux leather padded seat farted under his weight. 'So was he mad, was he?'

'That's one way of putting it.' Alice winced at the memory. 'He's upped the ante to five hundred a week, so you see we're desperate. We have to do something.'

'I suppose that's what yer man thought. That's why he did Broderick in.'

'You think it was him too?'

Parsons shrugged. 'More likely that Joxer fella, but James'll be behind it. Stands to reason, so ye be careful, yeh hear?' Alice smiled and nodded, touched that he showed concern. As she stood up to leave, Parsons cleared his throat. 'But, um, in case the worst comes to the worst, I'll be needin' a deposit on the . . .' He jerked his head in the direction of the briefcase. '. . . on the doings, just in case yer man catches ye and, well . . .' He shrugged leaving the rest to her imagination. It was comforting to see he had so much confidence in their mission.

Chapter Twenty-Nine

'You bugged his house!'

'Yes, Declan, we bugged his house.'

'You *bugged* his house!'

Déjà vu.

Declan had turned up just as they were closing up for the night in response to Melanie's phone call. Unaware that he hadn't been party to any of the Jesse James business, that he'd no idea that they'd been paying large amounts of money to him under duress, she'd mentioned their plans in passing when he'd phoned. Worried about her safety after he had failed to dissuade her, he'd driven straight up from Tanagh and stormed into the office demanding to be put fully in the picture. Though irritated by his attitude, Alice had filled him in. 'What the hell else could we do, Declan? He was bleeding us dry.'

'I don't suppose going to the cops crossed your mind?' he sniped.

Alice threw her eyes up to the ceiling. 'Conor, explain to your thicko brother why we didn't go to the cops, will you?' She slumped down on to the sofa. She couldn't be bothered to go through it all again. Melanie cast an apologetic glance in her direction. Conor, who was in a far calmer state of mind now after a friendly and positive phone conversation with his mother, reiterated the reasons, but it was obvious that his brother wasn't convinced.

'Couldn't the cops give you protection? This man has to be stopped. It's a matter of principle.'

All right for him. His life, income and the result of many months of hard work weren't on the line. 'Get real, Declan.'

Melanie intervened. 'She's right, Declan. Going to the cops

at this stage is not an option. There isn't enough evidence. It's only Alice's and Conor's word against theirs. We need evidence. We need hard evidence.'

Declan was anxious by her use of the collective noun. 'We? What's this *we*? Why are you getting involved?'

That got up Melanie's nose. 'Excuse me? I think that's my business. How dare you tell me what to do?'

Realising that there was no dissuading them, he threw up his hands. 'Okay. Okay, I'm sorry. I didn't mean it that way. I'm just concerned about you.' His eyes travelled around the room. 'About all of you. This guy sounds dangerous. Are you sure there's no other way?'

There was a firm, collective 'No'.

Declan was still very agitated. 'So what d'you think you'll find out if you do bug him? And how are you going to get the bugs back inside his house?'

Conor explained about the bug that was still *in situ*, then continued, 'So all we have to do is sit outside his house and hope that he blabs about something seriously dodgy.'

'Like what?'

Exasperated, Alice stood up. 'We've no idea, Declan. We're clutching at straws here. Hopefully Melanie and I will have an easier time in Maurice Broderick's house.'

'You bugged his house too?'

Alice's eyes shot skywards.

Declan gave up trying to talk them out of their clandestine activities after it became clear that there was no point. Either that or he got fed up with talking round in circles. However, and to Conor's relief, he insisted on being allowed to accompany Alice the following evening when she planned to try out the receiver and check whether the transmitter was still doing its designated task. When Alice balked, he pointed out that James would recognise her car and that his Merc would be practically invisible in the neighbourhood compared to the rather battered and elderly Escort. She gave in, not very gracefully, in the end. Secretly, she was glad of the moral support, but after the show of bravado she had put up while he was trying to talk her out of it, she'd have stuck her hand into boiling lard rather than admit it.

Melanie called at the restaurant for Alice at twelve-fifteen the following day. She was as hyper as Alice at the prospect of poking around Maurice Broderick's files, though each had differing motivations. They were both quiet during the drive out to Blackrock. As they drove through Monkstown on the coast road, Alice realised that the last time she had been along that road, albeit driving in the opposite direction, was the day Patricia had driven her into town and deposited her with the nuns. It was a damp and dismal day. Just the day for a funeral, she thought. It had belted down with rain at Roland's funeral too. She couldn't remember her mother's, or even if she'd been allowed to attend.

The traffic was moderately light and fifteen minutes later Melanie drew the car into the kerb a few yards from the gate of the house. It was clearly visible up the drive. A small Edwardian villa. The garden was as well tended as she remembered but somehow the house looked smaller, the drive shorter. 'D'you think it's safe to go in?' she asked. 'Do you think they've gone yet?'

Melanie glanced at her watch. 'They should have, it's five past. The funeral's at one.' She slipped the car into gear. 'Here goes.'

The car purred up the drive and Melanie parked around the back next to the garage. She was nervous as hell. Alice shared her anxiety. After Melanie had cut the engine they sat stock still for a good half minute before Alice took a deep breath and then exhaled. 'Okay. Let's do it.'

They both got out and Alice followed her stepsister as she made her way round to the front door. The key slipped into the lock and in no time at all they were inside, the door firmly closed behind them. They stood in the silence, listening. There was no sound, bar their breathing, no sound at all.

'Come on,' Melanie whispered, then led the way up the stairs to her stepfather's study. The house looked much as Alice remembered it, though it had a fresher, newly painted feel. Patricia had kept all the period details intact, much to her credit. It was certainly a desirable residence. She felt strange about being back there. She had never considered the house to be her home, but it was part of her past nonetheless.

She nudged Melanie. 'How long ago did you move out?'

Melanie pushed open the study door and they sidled in. 'Four years ago. As soon as I left college and got a job . . . Jesus Christ! What has he done to this place?'

The décor of the study was in total contrast to the rest of the house. Broderick's taste was as far removed from the traditional as it was possible to get. Minimalist to say the least. Textured raw silk, in subtly varying shades of beige and cream, covered broad floor-to-ceiling panels around the walls. The walls were completely flush, all the cornices and mouldings had been removed. The desk was a huge sheet of glass standing on chrome trestles in front of the bay window which was dressed with a white opaque Japanese influenced blind. There was a chrome and black leather Philippe Stark chair behind the desk. The floor was of polished beech and had a charcoal and cream rug of an abstract design, about eight feet square, in the centre. A horrifyingly uncomfortable-looking, high-backed lime green sofa sat about four feet out from the wall, and that was it apart from subtle lighting and a Zen flower arrangement of a twig, a couple of fat grey pebbles and a lone lilly sitting on a grey, unpolished granite plinth near the window. The only sign that the space might be an office was a state-of-the-art slimline phone and fax sitting on the desk top, its cord snaking incongruously off the glass and across the floor to a phone point near the window. Grudgingly Alice had to admit the effect was stunning, though the words *anal* and *retentive* did come to mind. However cutting edge the room might have been in style, it presented them with one minor problem: there was no sign of any computer, let alone anything as philistine in design terms as a filing cabinet.

Melanie was stunned silent. She'd been half-dreading entering the room again with all its past associations. Her enthusiasm had been mere bravado, whistling in the dark.

'Where's the computer? Where are the files?' Alice strode

into the middle of the room, turning this way and that. 'What's he done with the bloody files?'

'He always kept the spare set of keys in the top right hand drawer of the desk.' Melanie said, hurrying over and placing her hands on the huge sheet of laminated glass. 'He always kept them in the . . .'

'Evidently not any more, Mel.' Alice kicked herself for believing that anything could fall into their laps so easily.

Melanie lifted her hands from the cold glass and stared at the misty imprint. Then suddenly she spun around and darted over to the wall on the left of the sofa. 'Hold on a minute. There used to be a dressing room here. He used to keep his stationery supplies in a huge walk-in cupboard here.' Unwelcome memories tried to insinuate themselves into her mind's eye, but she forced them away and started tapping the panels. 'There was a room, there was a room.' Tap, tap, tap.

'Calm down, Mel. It's okay. It's okay.'

Tap, tap. tap. 'No. I know it's here. I know it's here.'

'Calm down, Mel.'

Tap, tap, tap. 'I know it's here. I know it.' Desperate. Then there was a subtle click, the spring-loaded catch released and the panel swung open revealing a large space. The lights flickered on, illuminating a row of ordinary metal filing cabinets along one wall, and industrial shelving on the other stacked with office supplies.

'The keys, the keys,' Alice babbled. 'Where are the bloody keys?' She heaved at the heavy metal drawers one at a time but they were all locked. Melanie was meanwhile examining the contents of the shelving.

'I don't know, but I've found his laptop.' She lifted the soft black case down from the second to top shelf and set it down at a more comfortable level. She looked over at Alice. 'Cross every extremity that you have and pray that he hasn't changed the password.'

Alice stood holding her breath, as if that would help. Melanie unzipped the case, lifted the laptop out, then booted it up. The hard drive burbled and clicked, then the message 'enter password' appeared on the screen. Melanie exhaled, cast a quick glance in Alice's direction, and typed in DEMELZA. She waited a beat, bit her lip, took a deep breath, then punched the 'enter' key. After a split second the computer buzzed, the screen went black for a nano-second before displaying the message 'loading windows 98'. They both exhaled.

'Demelza?'

Melanie nodded, keeping her eyes on the screen. 'It was his pet name for me. Another of *our little secrets*.'

'Oh.'

Melanie's practised eye was scanning the files now. 'Hunt around and see if you can find those keys,' she said. Alice did as she was told, running her hand along the shelves, looking in any likely hiding place, but came up with nothing. Melanie meanwhile was opening files at random and scanning the contents. 'There's far too much material here to go through. It'll take too long.' She turned to Alice. 'See if you can find any disks. I'll have to copy all the files and look at them later.'

'What, all of them?'

'All of them. It shouldn't take too long. I'll use file compression.'

'Okay,' Alice said, without an ounce of comprehension, 'whatever you say.' She handed her stepsister an unopened box of computer disks.

While Melanie was feeding the A drive, copying the files, Alice sauntered back into the office and over to the window. If it had been her office she'd have placed the chair on the other side so she'd have the breathtaking view out over Dublin Bay. But then if it had been her office she would have decorated it more functionally, more personally. There were no photos, no personal effects of any kind. She shuddered at the thought of what had gone on in the room so many years before. Poor Mel. What was going through her mind right now? She glanced at her watch. One-twenty. No panic. Plenty of time. She sat in the high-backed chair and stared out at the sea.

Melanie meanwhile was cursing the laptop for its slowness. It seemed to be taking an age to copy the files. Mechanically she fed the disks into the drive when directed, numbering the full ones as she ejected them. There had been a small chaise in the space now occupied by the filing cabinets. She felt the sinews in her neck tighten as she remembered. It was covered in threadbare tapestry. Patricia had banished it to Maurice's office as she had said the sight of it offended her. Unconsciously Melanie rubbed her elbow, recalling how the rough fabric had chafed her soft skin.

'Mel, Mel! There's a car. They're back!' Alice, standing in the doorway in a panic. 'It's only half-past and they're back. Hurry!'

Jerked back to the present, Melanie stared at her. 'Back? They can't be.'

'They are. They are.'

'But there's still half a dozen more files left to copy.'

'We've no time. We have to get out of here.'

The sound of Patricia's shrill voice echoed up from the hall and they heard the front door bang. Footsteps across the parquet towards the drawing room. 'Quickly!' Alice whispered, as she gathered the full disks together and shoved them in her bag. Melanie ejected the remaining disk and snapped off the computer.

Together they crept across the room. Alice eased the door open and peeked out. The hall below was empty but the drawing room door was open and they could clearly hear the sound of ice cubes dropping into a glass. 'No lemon.' Patricia's voice. 'You know I can't bear lemon.'

'Sorry. Forgot.' Jesse James's voice.

'What'll we do?' Alice hissed. 'How are they back so soon?'

Melanie shrugged. 'Maybe I got the time wrong. Come on.' She pushed past Alice and stepped out on to the landing. 'Let's go and pay our respects to the widow.'

Alice grabbed her arm. 'Are you mad? Are you out of your mind?'

Melanie shook her arm free. 'If we're up front she'll never suspect. If they catch us sneaking out they'll smell a rat. Come on.' Melanie strode towards the stairs, leaving Alice no option but to follow.

'What's that? Did you hear something?' Patricia's footsteps across the carpet. Melanie was halfway down the stairs, with

Alice a couple of paces behind, as she stepped into the hall. 'What the hell are you doing here? How did you get in?' James was behind her, staring up at them, a look of utter amazement on his face.

'Good to see you too, Mother.'

They were all standing in the hall now, James between them and the door. Patricia looked as elegant as ever in a simple black suit. 'I said, what the hell are you doing here?'

'We came to pay our respects,' Melanie said calmly. 'Didn't we, Alice? You remember Alice, don't you Mother, the waif you threw out into the snow?'

Patricia's pallid complexion reddened from the neck up. 'I did no such thing. How dare you? I made good provision for . . .' Realising that her daughter had successfully changed the subject, she pursed her lips and narrowed her eyes. 'What are you really doing here?'

Melanie shrugged. 'Told you. We came to pay our respects.'

'I'm sorry for your trouble,' Alice said lamely, casting a longing glance at the front door and escape. She had to hand it to Mel, she was cool as a cucumber. The high-stress quotient involved in trading bonds or equities or whatever she did was obviously standing her in good stead.

Melanie dug her hands deep into her pockets and made a show of looking around. 'You've decorated. It looks nice. I was showing Alice the house. I like the colour you've chosen for the hall – what is it?'

'Nutmeg,' Patricia said, bemused. 'It's called nutmeg.'

'How did you get in here?' James asked. His voice was polite but with an edge to it. He was conscious that this was not yet his turf. He cast a furtive glance in Alice's direction.

Melanie smiled at him and held up her key. 'I found this in the bottom of my bag. Hope you don't mind, Mother, but we didn't want to wait outside and we weren't expecting you back so soon.' She caught Alice's eye. 'Maurice was certainly despatched with indecent haste, eh, Alice?' She giggled. 'Don't you think?'

Now visibly seething, Patricia snapped the key out of her

daughter's hand. 'You won't be needing this. Wait until you're invited before you call in future.'

'I won't hold my breath,' Melanie muttered.

Alice made a move towards the door. 'Well, I'm sure you're tired and I guess you've things to do. We'll leave you to it.'

'Aren't you going to offer us the traditional refreshments?' Melanie asked with mock surprise, but Alice yanked her towards the door.

'Sorry, can't wait. Have to get back to work. Sorry for your trouble, Patricia.' She heaved the hall door open, dragging her protesting stepsister after her.

'But we didn't make a toast to the dear departed.'

'Shut up. Come on.' Alice bundled Melanie ahead of her and stuffed her into the car. 'Are you out of your tiny mind?' she hissed. 'They knew we were up to something. What was that all about, toasting the dear departed?'

Melanie giggled and slotted the key into the ignition. 'You're no fun.' As they drove down towards the gates Alice turned around and saw Patricia and James watching them from the drawing room window. 'Anyway,' Melanie continued, 'surely you wouldn't begrudge me the opportunity to wind my darling mother up?'

Alice sighed with relief as they turned into the main road and sped back towards the city. 'I'd sooner you chose a less dodgy moment.'

'Relax. We got away with it, didn't we?'

'What was that all about?' Jesse James poured himself a stiff Bushmills.

Patricia was standing with her back to the fire. 'Stupid girl,' she muttered. 'Stupid, spiteful girl.'

'Did you believe her?'

The widow ignored the question. 'You do your best for them,' she murmured, 'best schools, best college, best of everything I gave her. Sacrificed my youth and how does the little madam repay me?' Although she didn't say it aloud she was remembering the way Maurice had doted on the girl and how she made sheep's eyes at him, trying to steal him away.

That hurt. It was a betrayal. Then claiming that he'd . . . never mind. It didn't bear thinking about. As if Maurice would do such a thing. As if he'd want that child instead of her. All her life Patricia had been aware that her most precious assets were her good looks and the ability to make men fall in love with her. The concept that a slip of a girl could be any kind of competition was something she wouldn't acknowledge. She was staring at nothing, talking to herself now. 'And as for that other bitch. I looked after her when that spineless bastard left me with nothing but debts. Cared for her.' She shook her head. 'I didn't have to do it. I could have put her into a children's home. It isn't as if she was flesh and blood.'

'Don't let it get to you.' James moved towards her, wrapped his arms around her and kissed her hair. He'd never seen her like this. Vulnerable, hurt. It made him feel good. It made him feel that she needed him. 'Don't worry about it. She's a nothing. She's not worth it. It's time to look to the future. Time to leave the past behind.'

The past. Yes, it was certainly time to leave the past behind. What James was not aware of was the fact that Patricia had booked herself a first-class ticket on the mid-afternoon flight to Mexico the following day. That she had placed her affairs in the hands of her solicitors with instructions to liquidate all her assets. That would take time, she knew, but in the meantime she had plenty in the off-shore account to keep her in the manner appropriate for the widow of a man of Maurice Broderick's stature. She sighed, then looked up into his eyes and gave a heroic smile. 'You're right. Time to look to the future.'

Chapter Thirty

Melanie stopped off at her apartment to pick up her own laptop then they drove back to the Samovar to report their progress to Conor. He was madly impressed by Melanie's somewhat embellished version of the encounter. Alice, glad to have got away with it, let her tell it her way. Then, after she had fixed them up with a late lunch, Melanie retired to the office to examine Maurice Broderick's files.

Declan arrived at about five to take Alice over to James' house in Sutton in the hope of getting something on James. Melanie took a break and, egged on by Conor, retold her story. There was much hilarity, but Alice suspected that the up-beat atmosphere was more to do with nerves than with the quality of the anecdote. By the time they left half an hour later, however, Melanie still hadn't come up with anything iffy in Broderick's computer files, but was still anxiously looking.

It was dark by the time they made it out to Sutton. Declan parked behind a big silver Audi about thirty yards from the house. The porch light was on, and there was light filtering through the drapes to the left of the front door which, if Alice remembered rightly, was the long sitting room with the awful stripy carpet. It appeared that they were in luck and James was home. She desperately hoped, considering who was sitting beside her, that Patricia wasn't with him. Listening to her former stepmother cavorting with her younger psychotic lover would have been far too embarrassing to bear. She snapped the locks of the briefcase receiver and opened the lid. Declan got very interested then. 'How does it work?' he wanted to know. She switched it on as Parsons had instructed. The car was filled with a blast of white noise so Alice reduced the volume and started to fiddle with the tuning knob. Declan was leaning over watching her, anxious to have a go. When there was no sound of any conversation he tried to yank it from her hands. 'Here, let me do it. You're not doing it right.'

She swatted his hand away. 'Piss off, Declan. I know what I'm doing.' She slowly twisted the knob first in one direction then the other. Nothing.

'Maybe it's not working,' Declan offered, sounding sulky that he hadn't been allowed to play.

'There's no reason why it shouldn't be.' He was irritating the hell out of her now. She gently eased the tuner again and heard the sound of a door slamming. It was definitely coming from the speaker. 'There! That's it. Did you hear it?'

They sat in silence, straining their ears. A little while later a phone rang. The ringing had a muffled quality to it, as if it was in another room. This puzzled Alice as, to her recollection, James had an extension in the long sitting room. The ringing stopped but there was no sound of talk; in fact, there was no further sound for at least an hour until the phone rang again. By nine they were both bored out of their brains and feeling dispirited. Conversations had petered out after the first half hour and time hung heavily. Alice glanced at the dashboard clock every couple of minutes, willing the time to pass more quickly, and she was having difficulty keeping her eyes open due to the oppressively stifling atmosphere caused by the car's de-mister. Declan too was in danger of nodding off. Suddenly he snapped awake at the sound of footsteps. He gave Alice, whose head was lolling on her chest, a sharp nudge in the ribs. Somewhat disoriented, she leapt up in her seat, a serious case of whiplash only prevented by the headrest. 'What?'

Declan held up his hand indicating she should listen. A door closes. Louder footsteps. A car door opens, slams. The sound of an engine turning over, then purring softly. Alice couldn't figure it out. Was it the TV? Was James watching some TV programme? A moment later they both ducked down below the dash as a set of headlamps glided down James's drive towards the electric gates. Then she had it. 'Shit! He's got it in the garage. He must have moved the adapter into the bloody garage.'

When James had driven past they both sat up again. 'Well, that was a very productive evening,' Declan said testily, circling his head to ease the stiffness in his neck. 'I told you it was a waste of time.'

Alice, whose back was equally stiff, was tired, thirsty, and grumpy with disappointment, but had no intention of giving in to Declan's despondency. 'Early days yet. You didn't expect we'd get lucky the first time, did you?'

Actually he had, and the realisation that they might have to spend many more such evenings cooped up in the front seat of his car on the off chance that this James character would oblige them by incriminating himself in the privacy of his own garage was unappealing to say the least. The gloss had gone off the private eye game all of a sudden, so when Alice said, 'Let's call it a night,' he didn't argue.

They trudged dispiritedly into the Samovar and Alice went straight to the office, hoping that Melanie had come up with something on Broderick. Hopefully something particularly serious that would also implicate James. Conor, unable to concentrate and having abandoned the kitchen to Tony and Louis, was sitting on the sofa, Melanie sat behind the desk with the laptop switched off. Both wore miserable expressions and were nursing hefty glasses of strong drink. Alice slumped down on the sofa next to Conor. 'You didn't get lucky, then?'

Melanie took a gulp from her glass. 'How about you?'

In an effort to impress the object of his affections, Declan was suddenly upbeat again. 'Hey, cheer up. It's early days yet.' He walked over and sat on the corner of the desk near Melanie, sliding his arm around her shoulder and giving her an encouraging squeeze.

'Was the thing not working then?' Conor asked.

Alice took the glass from his hands and took a sip. 'It was working all right, but it's in the wrong place now. It looks as if he moved it to the garage.'

'Bummer.'

'If only we had that book of his. The one he had in his office that day. I'll bet there's enough in that alone to hang him.'

Conor retrieved his glass and took a drink. 'We should be so lucky.'

Declan stood up and stretched. 'Well, I'm off home. How about you, Mel?'

All right for him.

Melanie nodded. The stress of the day, and now the disappointment, had left her exhausted. She had found nothing whatsoever of an iffy nature. No reference to anything other than his legitimate companies. Nothing that the CAB would be remotely interested in. She zipped her computer safely back in its carrying case. 'What are you two going to do now? Are you going to pay up?'

Anger at the thought of meekly paying James suddenly boiled up in Alice. She jumped up from the sofa and dragged Conor to his feet. 'No, we're bloody not. Are we, Conor?'

'Aren't we?'

'No. We're going to get the better of that bastard if it's the last thing we do.'

Melanie smiled. 'That's the spirit.'

'So you're going to the cops now?' Declan asked, hoping that Alice was at last going to do the sensible thing.

'Don't be so fucking wet,' she sneered at her erstwhile brother-in-law. 'We're going to get that book. We're going to go to his office and get the book.'

Conor was horrified. 'How?'

'How do you think? We'll break in. How hard can it be? People do it all the time.'

'*Criminals* do it all the time,' Declan snorted. 'You'd never be able to. Look at you, for God's sake. You're ordinary people, not criminals. A chef and a waitress.'

Ignoring Declan, Alice took a hold of Conor's upper arms and said earnestly, 'We have to do this, Conor. It's our only hope.' As the words tripped off her tongue she thought it sounded a bit melodramatic, but Declan's subsequent guffaw firmed up her resolve. 'Are you with me?'

Declan thought she had finally flipped and was waiting for

his brother to talk her out of it, but there was something about the way he was taking the thing so lightly, something about the way he was dismissing them as a couple of losers, that got up Conor's nose too. He'd been on an emotional roller-coaster over the past couple of weeks and now he felt the stronger for it. Instead of even attempting to talk his partner, his best friend, out of it, he nodded vigorously. 'I'm with you.' Then added, 'Let's do it.'

Chapter Thirty-One

They found a parking space five doors up from the Quick Call Finance office into which Alice manoeuvred the car with some difficulty. 'Shouldn't one of us stay here with the engine running?' Conor asked hopefully.

'That's for bank jobs.'

'Oh . . .' Disappointed. 'So what do we do now?'

Alice hadn't a notion. The idea of breaking into James's office and stealing the book had seemed so simple less than fifteen minutes before. Now here they were sitting outside like a couple of eejitts without a clue. Carried away by their anger and enthusiasm, they hadn't even brought as much as a screwdriver with them. Alice could just imagine Declan's reaction when they returned to the Samovar empty-handed.

'I forgot there was no back way in,' she commented. Actually the thought of a back entrance hadn't crossed her mind but she was feeling foolish and had the need to appear as if she had thought of a plan.

'He mightn't even keep it in the office.' Conor was thinking aloud. 'I mean, he'd be mad to keep the thing in the office. If I were him I'd keep it with me all the time. I wouldn't risk keeping it in the office.'

'Shut up, Conor. You're not helping.'

'Sorry.'

But he did have a point. In the heat of the moment, spurred on by Declan's off-hand, dismissive attitude, logic hadn't entered the equation. James probably kept the damn thing at home, but there was no chance of them getting in there again. Alice leaned her head on the steering-wheel and gave a heavy sigh. Was this it? Were they fated to pay the likes of James for the rest of their lives or until he bled them dry? What was the alternative? Risk life and limb by going to the cops? Why was it that just as things seemed to be going their way, someone always pulled the rug out from under their feet? She lifted her head and looked up at the sky through the grubby windscreen.

'Now look here, God. Enough is enough. If you're an anyway decent God at all, give us a break. One little miracle. That's not too much to ask, is it? One little teeny tiny miracle.'

There was no clap of thunder. No flash of lightning.

'Shit!' Conor dived down under the dashboard, whacking his head on the glove box. 'Isn't that him? Isn't that James?'

Confused, Alice dragged herself back to reality and peered across the street. The brake lights of a large top-of-the-range Beemer flashed on then off. A moment later Jesse James got out and, fumbling with his keys, walked across the road. Alice ducked down out of view, but not before her eyes registered the fact that he was carrying a briefcase. When they looked up again he was nowhere in sight, but a chink of light filtered out through a crack in the office door.

'Stay here. Keep the engine running.'

Assuming that she had finally taken leave of her senses, Conor quipped, 'I thought that was only for bank jobs.' Convinced that she was joking, hoping to God she was joking.

'No. I mean stay here and keep the engine running. I'm going in.'

Before he had a chance to try and stop her, Alice leapt from the car and hurried up the street.

'Should I call the cops?'

'No, Declan! Don't be stupid, you can't do that. Technically they're the ones committing the crime.'

'But what if . . . ?'

Melanie was as worried as Declan but she couldn't see that calling the cops would help anyone. At least not yet. 'Anyway,' she cut in, trying to take the harm out of it, 'they probably won't manage it. I don't think any of those shops on Mercer Street have back access.'

It was small comfort. Declan felt ashamed that he hadn't

made more of an effort to stop them, or at least offered to go along to watch their backs. But right up until they walked out of the door he didn't believe that they were serious. The situation was surreal, all this talk of gangsters and protection money and bugs and breaking into offices.

There was a tap on the door, then Sean Holland stuck his head in. 'Where's Alice?'

Melanie sighed. 'Don't ask.'

The light was on in the hall. Alice peeked in, then crept towards the stairs. She could hear the low mumble of James's voice. A one-sided conversation. Obviously on the phone. She edged her way silently up the stairs, not sure what she was doing there at all. Somewhere in the back of her mind she had half a plan. Hide somewhere until he had gone then have a poke around his office. She could easily break the glass in the door. No one to hear or see. She had reached the top of the stairs now, ahead of her a short coridor and another flight of stairs set at a right angle. The office door was ajar. She heard James replace the receiver and froze for a beat before scurrying along the landing, making for the second flight of stairs. Her heart was pounding as she hoisted herself up with the aid of the banister, then slumped down out of sight to get her breath. Silence. She strained her ears. Rustling. James moving around the office. The rasp of metal on metal as a filing drawer was pulled open. A moment later the same sound followed by a clunk as he slammed it shut. Her heart had slowed to a moderate gallop now. She eased herself into a standing position and peeked around the corner. James was at the door of the office, his briefcase at his feet, fumbling with the keys. She dodged back out of view. Then the phone rang. She heard James curse under his breath. The rattle of the keys again and the door opening. She peered around the corner again. James was nowhere in sight. She could hear him talking on the phone. Then her eyes homed in on the briefcase sitting outside the office door, inviting her to take it.

Without further thought she flew down the stairs, grabbed the leather briefcase and thundered down the next flight towards the front door. She wasn't aware of James behind her, too intent on escape. As she cleared the door and hit the street she thanked God for teeny tiny miracles.

'They did what?'

'They'll be back soon. It was a knee-jerk thing,' Melanie said. 'But after Maurice Broderick's files came up blank I think they were disappointed.' It sounded lame, but it was all she could come up with.

Holland was astounded. 'Disappointed? So they decide to break into that psycho's office. Are they mad?' He shot an accusing look at Declan. 'Didn't you try to stop them?'

They were all sitting in the restaurant now. The last of the punters had gone, apart from Madame Maxine who had come down for a late supper and to collect a parcel the postman had left for her. She made much ceremony of opening it there and then and had oohed and ahed about the quality of the workmanship as she lovingly stroked the shiny leather of her brand new executive bull whip. Holland found himself rather intimidated by her, especially after she snorted when he made the remark about Declan attempting to stop Conor and Alice. 'What? Stop yer woman when she's hell-bent on doin' somethin'? Get real.' But Declan was grateful for the support. It assuaged his steadily growing feelings of guilt. She had the whip in her hand and was gently flicking it as she spoke. 'Anyways, as Melanie says, they'll be back any minute. Quit worryin'.' She coiled her new acquisition and, returning to her table, looped it over her shoulder and sat down to finish her supper.

Although this was the first time he had laid an eye on Madame Maxine, Holland, although intimidated, was heartened by her confidence. She looked as if she'd been around the block a few times and what Melanie said made sense. What hope would they have of actually managing to break in anywhere? They weren't criminals. 'Maybe we should drive over there,' he suggested, catching Declan's eye. 'What do you think?'

Declan nodded. 'Mightn't be a bad idea.' He needed to do

something. As Holland pushed his chair back to stand, the door burst open and Alice and Conor bundled in. They were both breathless and hyper. Alice was clutching a briefcase and a hardback A4 book in her arms. 'It's all in here,' she babbled. 'The lot, it's all in here.' Her eyes were bright and she wasn't making sense. 'He wrote the bloody lot down in here. It's all in here.'

'But are you sure he didn't see you?' Melanie asked after Alice had calmed down sufficiently to tell the story. 'Surely he saw you.'

'I don't think so,' Conor said. 'We were out of there like bats out of hell.'

Holland was leafing through the notebook, every now and then giving a gasp or muttering, 'Good grief.'

Madame Max was highly impressed. 'Fair play t' ye.' She stood up from the table and lifted her plate. 'Mind if I help meself to dessert?' she asked.

Conor waved her towards the kitchen. 'There's your favourite in the fridge,' he said.

Holland flipped the book closed. 'There's enough here to put James away and the CAB lads'll have a field day.'

'Is there any reference to Maurice Broderick?' Melanie asked hopefully.

'There are a couple of references but nothing much, I'm afraid.'

Alice couldn't believe their luck. It occurred to her that maybe she should go to Mass after the timely intervention of the Almighty. It was the least she could do.

That was the moment when the rug was once more yanked from beneath them. The door smashed open and James was standing there wild-eyed, waving a gun around. 'Give it back, you fucking bitch. Gimme the fucking case.'

Chapter Thirty-Two

Everyone froze. 'I said gimme back the fucking case, you slag.'
He grabbed Alice roughly by the arm. 'Where is it?'

'I don't know what you're talking about.' Alice yelped as his
fingers dug into her flesh.

'Don't give me that, you bitch. I saw you. I saw the both of
you.' He was incandescent with rage, shaking and trembling.
He twisted her arm up behind her back and she screamed. She
could feel the coldness of the steel as he pressed the barrel of
the gun against her temple. He glared at Conor. 'Give it up or
she gets it.'

Holland slipped the book under a leather menu cover and
nudged the briefcase forward with the toe of his shoe. 'Here.
Leave her alone.'

James was twitchy with nerves. He darted a look at the case
then his eyes jerked around the room. He waved the gun in the
direction of the bar. 'Over there, all of you.' No one moved
until he let out a roar, then they all shuffled over and bunched
together with the exception of Alice, whom he was still holding
fast. 'Now stick your hands on your heads where I can see
them,' he barked. It was like a scene from an old Bogart movie.
Without warning James gave Alice a vicious shove in the back
and she stumbled, landing on her knees. Holland leapt forward
and helped her up. 'You okay?'

Alice nodded. She was white as a sheet. He put his arm
around her and led her over to the bar with the others. James
had picked up the case now. He was obviously wondering
what to do next. Keeping the gun on them he placed the case
on a table and snapped the locks. Holland's heart sank.

Things happened like lightning after that, although in

everyone's memory everything seemed to happen in slow motion. Later Alice put it down to something she had seen on television about adrenaline speeding up the brain's reactions thus making events appear to happen slowly. As James looked up and opened his mouth to let out another roar, behind him Alice caught sight of Madame Maxine flinging her arm back. Then the loud crack. The leather snake of the whip wrapping itself around James's wrist as it was expertly wielded by the dominatrix. It was an Indiana Jones moment. The look of shock on James's face and the gun dropping to the floor and skidding across the tiles. Alice and Holland made a dive for it. Alice got there first, grabbed it and with shaking hands pointed it at James. He made a lunge and the gun went off. James stopped ashen-faced as chunks of plaster rained from the ceiling.

Epilogue

James was carted off by the cops. Because of the use of a firearm he was denied bail, much to the relief of all. Spurred on by that fact, Alice and Conor told the cops about the protection racket which was borne out by the details in James's little black book along with the details of many other victims.

Melanie was somewhat disappointed that Patricia would be left with most of Maurice Broderick's fortune intact. Though her mother only learned this after a phone call received from her solicitor as she lay on a Mexican beach. The same couldn't be said for James. The CAB, after an indecently short high court action, confiscated all his assets.

The Samovar went from strength to strength, and six months later they opened the basement club which also proved to be a winner. Alice's life had at last taken a more normal turn. Mason and Conor got a place together, and Maura eventually told Mick that his younger son was gay. He took it pretty well, his only stipulation being that it was a private matter and it was okay as long as Conor didn't come down wearing funny cloths and the like. He was, however, disappointed that Alice was no longer his daughter-in-law, having grown very fond of her, until Maura pointed out, sure wasn't she better than a daughter-in-law? Wasn't she like a *real* daughter? This, when Maura related the story, pleased Alice no end.

The following spring, the usual suspects plus Sean Holland (he and Alice now being an item) and Mason, in the guise of being a friend of the family, made the trip to Tanagh where they all celebrated the marriage of Declan to Melanie Broderick in the local parish church.

That summer Jesse James and Joxer Boxer were sentenced to fifteen years each at the state's pleasure in Mountjoy prison. Nothing was ever heard of Patricia again.